Thomas Kehoe

TIME SHIFT

TMK Books, New York, NY

DISCLAIMER

The views and opinions expressed in this book are entirely those of the author, and do not necessarily correspond with those of any corporation, military service, or government organization of any country. The characters are either fictional or based upon historical figures.

This book is an original publication of the TMK Publishing Group.

TIME SHIFT

A TMK book / published by arrangement with LULU

CONTENTS

"THOSE WHO CANNOT REMEMBER THE PAST ARE CONDEMNED TO REPEAT IT."

George Santiana

...Or go back and try again.

PROLOGUE

July 7th, 2001, 9:14 AM Central Standard Time
DFW Airport, Dallas, Texas

He pushed up the thatched cover where he had been entombed for the past twenty hours. The rush of fresh air into his hand dug tomb tasted good. The sudden assault of Texas sunlight caused his retina's to shrink painfully. Mirza Hoseyn Ali Nuri welcomed each sensation. His life expectancy was now being measured in minutes.

This was Jihad, he would be with Allah before this day was out. He rejoiced when he had been chosen for this most important of missions. Mirza Hoseyn Ali Nuri's Islamic faith had given him the strength and courage to accept it. It would be his fanatical adherence to his faith that would have him sitting with the prophets after the bullets of the non-belivers took the only gift worthy of Allah.

Mirza Hoseyn Ali Nuri, who had been named, ironically, after the disciple of Mirzh Ali Muhammad of Shiraz, the founder of the pacifist Babis sect, was two hundred meters south of Runway 5A. He stood up and hoisted a Stinger ground to air missile launcher to his shoulder. The weapon was close to twenty years old. It had traveled from the United States to Afghanistan in the 80's as part of Reagan's convoluted arms for hostages deal. It had worked it's way to Srpska where it was stored for seven years. Now, it was back in the US, where, as a single use weapon, it would finally spit its destructive package before casually being tossed aside.

He heard the pilot spool up the three massive engines of Air Force One. It was the only plane that would be taking off for the next few minutes at this very busy airport. These Americans, Mirza thought, are quite punctual. He knew his chances of killing the president of this Godless country were exactly fifty percent, assuming his Stinger worked properly. The president always traveled with two identical planes to thwart attacks such as the one that was about to occur.

Mirza Hoseyn Ali Nuri decided to unleash his missile on the first plane for no other reason than he was anxious to get it over with. He flipped open the safety cover and toggled on the power. There was an audible humming and an array of small diodes that told him the Stinger was operative. He was suddenly aware of how dry his mouth was. His hands were shaking too. Fortunately, the weapon would be addressing the more delicate aiming chores for him.

He sighted the Stinger on the now moving Boeing 747-200B as it started to roll down the runway. It took less than two seconds for the internal guidance system to acquire the tremendous heat signature the aircraft was giving off.

Captain Gerald Larson heard the distinctive beeps generated by the missile warning system built into Air Force One. The last time he had heard those warnings was while jockeying his F/A-18E Hornet over Baghdad during the Gulf War. It got his attention then and it got his attention now. Even back in Saudi, however, he never had a missile lock during take off!

His first thought was that there was a malfunction. How the hell could he be painted while on a runway in Dallas? Captain Larson had been in the drivers seat of Air Force One for eighteen months and in the copilot chair for two years prior and had never had anything malfunction. He was flying the best maintained aircraft in the world.

Even as he was developing a protocol, his copilot, Captain Shiffman, was running a diagnostic on the cockpit diodes.

"I'm not seeing any problem here," he reported.

"Abort takeoff."

Engines were thrown into reverse, wheel brakes were applied and the nose of the plane, which was already light, dove to the tarmac. The eight hundred thousand pound craft shuddered to a stop.

Mirza was confused. Even from his obscured vantage point he could tell it was a dramatic shut down. Having no idea his guidance system had set off a warning in the cockpit he suspected, buy some unfortunate turn of events, that he had been compromised. He cursed his impatience and steeled himself against the volley of bullets that would certainly arrive momentarily, dooming his personal Jihad to failure.

But nothing happened. He looked around. There was no movement. The only noise was the chirp from the target acquisition signal of the Stinger. Mirza Hoseyn Ali Nuri pulled the trigger and unleashed the fury of Allah.

The missile sprang from its sheath and charged towards the waiting plane. Captain Larson knew immediately what that bright flash meant. This was not the first ground to air missile to be shot at him. He knew, short of a major and quick malfunction of the weapons guidance system, that it was going to hit his plane and there was nothing he could do about it. Captain Gerald Larson felt very uncomfortable.

He watched in the same detached perspective one views a developing accident from across a street. Captain Larson had a similar experience on only the second sortie he had flown over Iraq a decade before. A surface to air missile had locked on to his plane, making him, he recalled, very uncomfortable then, too. The difference was, while in the air, he could do something about it.

The missile had acquired the port side engine. Captain Larson admired the true path it was taking. By the time it passed under his cockpit window it seemed to be flying in slow motion, mere yards off the ground. In the superheated speed his mind was operating in, it felt as if it took an extraordinarily long time for the missile to meet the engine.

But it did.

The initial explosion blew the engine into thousands of pieces of metal that impregnated the side of the plane, dissecting those in rows twenty eight through thirty five. In an effort to maximize valuable space aboard the craft, engineers thought to store fuel in the wings. The second explosion Mirza Hoseyn Ali Nuri heard was the twenty two thousand pounds of fuel in the port side wing erupting. With barely enough time to give thanks to Allah for this wondrous victory, the fuel in the starboard wing exploded. Mirza Hoseyn Ali did not hear that third explosion, however, because of the bullet, exactingly delivered by a Secret Service sharp shooter, that had opened his head on his port side.

Within minutes, runway 5A held the smoldering carcass of Air Force One. Engulfed in the carnage was the charred body of the forty third president of the United States, George W. Bush.

CHAPTER 1
Pre- Apocalypse

July 7, 2001, 10:26 EST
Bathesda Naval Hospital, Maryland

Lieutenant General Michael V. Hayden was finally going to have his fourth incisor removed. It had been causing him pain for some weeks now, but every time he made plans to have it addressed, something came up. Today, the world seemed to be in relative peace, so he scheduled the procedure with his oral surgeon for late morning.

It was no simple matter making the arrangements. Michael Hayden was a spook. Not just a spook, Mr. Hayden was the head spook. As director of the National Security Agency, he knew things that could cause the country some embarrassment, if not an outright war, were any of it were to slip out while he was under anesthesia. While he would be getting the best sleep he'd had in the four years since he'd taken over the NSA, there would have to be two agents, both with the same security clearance as he, watching over the proceedings. As Director Hayden's classification was Above Top Secret, this necessitated recruiting some very high placed personnel to sit in on his induced nap.

There was a knock on his changing room door.

"What is it," he barked with some annoyance as he pulled on a hospital gown. Michael grumpily queried a stern looking nurse earlier as to why he needed to put on a hospital gown for a tooth extraction. "Men in your shape are prone to cardiac arrest; we want quick access to your vitals." He wished he had asked her nicer.

"Mike, let me in, there's been a development."

Hayden recognized William Black's voice. Bill was the Deputy Director. He was one of the two agents assigned to sit in on the procedure.

Michael pulled his gown on quickly and opened the door. The words "There's been a development" never suggested good news.

"What the hell is it, Bill." He was cranky and feeling foolish standing there with his bare ass hanging out.

"Air Force One exploded, the president is presumed dead."

Christ, Hayden thought. He steadied himself against the door jam and took a breath. President Bush and he had played golf together three weeks ago.

"Do we know what happened yet?"

"Preliminary reports are that his plane was struck with a stinger missile while on the tarmac in Dallas. A terrorist was dropped by a Secret Service sharp shooter moments after he lit the stinger off. The body is in a hangar at the airport. The Secret Service guys are searching it, I'll have a report in a few minutes." Black took off to arrange for a staff car back to headquarters.

Michael was already pulling off his hospital gown before the door shut.

As he was tying his shoes, Agent Black banged on the door again.

"Come on in, I'll be ready in a moment. What do the Service guys know about the shooter?"

"They haven't gotten back yet, however, there has been another development." Bill Black was looking real white. He had to be prompted to give up what he knew.

"Prime Minister Chretien has been attacked, there are no details yet, this just happened about three minutes ago."

Canada has never had a Prime Minister assassinated, who the hell cares enough about Canada to do something like that? One world leader assassinated could be the work of a lone nut, two world leaders assassinated sounded like a sophisticated plot to destabilize the Western World. Lieutenant General Michael V. Hayden knew that he was going to be living with a painful tooth for the near future.

During the drive back to NSA headquarters in Fort Meade, Maryland, Director Hayden learned that Prime Minister Chretien was dead, King Charles had been unsuccessfully attacked while in Belfast and that the leaders of half a dozen countries from the former Soviet Union had been assassinated.

Commissioned in 1917 by an act of congress, Fort Meade was one of sixteen cantonments built for troops drafted to fight in the war to end all wars. Major General Gordon Meade's defensive strategy at the Battle of Gettysburg was the turning point for the North a little over half a century before, earning him this high honor. From World War One, to Korea, to the Gulf War, over four and a half million men have been trained there.

Five years after being established by a top secret presidential directive issued by President Truman on November 4th, 1952, the NSA consolidated its headquarters at Fort Meade. An amalgam of earlier intelligence organizations, the National Security Agency was responsible for military and nonmilitary intelligence interests, both domestic and abroad.

Hayden looked at the marble sign post erected for the visit of President Bush senior in '91. It was intended to create a "dignified and professional look." He thought it did just that. His car screamed down Canine Road, siren blaring, making it difficult to hear what Black was saying. Within moments, they were pulling up to the headquarters complex. Made up of two high-rise buildings, it was completed and dedicated by President Reagan in 1986. The complex houses logistical and support activities as well as a technical library.

Michael Haden gazed out of the large, bullet proof plate glass window across from his desk. He was tired and in pain. The reflection bouncing back at him from the glass was not that of the man who took over the NSA four years ago. His hair never even had a chance to go gray, it just went. While most men his age celebrated losing weight, Michael couldn't keep it on. He'd had most of his pants taken in twice in a year. His formerly round, cherub like face was now gaunt and his eye glasses were almost coke bottle thick now. Michael Hayden looked and felt considerably older than the fifty nine years his birth certificate reported.

Two squirrels were playing tag on the lawn. Surely there were any numbers of children not far from the NSA compound doing the same, oblivious to the drama developing on the world stage. Twelve thousand miles away, there was a group of men with an agenda that would darken their young lives.

His contemplative moment was abruptly broken by a parade of specialists filing into his office, each with thick folders held tightly to their chests. He knew they had little in the way of hard reconnaissance. In a fast moving crisis such as this, CNN was usually the best place to gather information. Since recent government cut backs, they now had the best assets in the business. He hated that. Michael muted the bank of televisions on the wall and joined his agents at the conference table.

"What do we know so far?"

Agent Janice Morrow was the first to answer. Her specialty was international terrorism and it was clear that the transpiring situation was right up her alley.

Thirty two years as a spook and a two pack a day habit caused her to hit the wall somewhat prematurely. Her stunning looks had been a great asset to her while she was in the field. Beneath the years of stress and self abuse were the remnants of that beauty.

She stubbed out a cigarette and opened her files.

"It seems that we have a highly affective terrorist attack going on as we speak. The body at DFW belonged to one Mirza Hoseyn Ali Nuri. He had entered the country legally with a student visa. He was twenty seven years old, lists his residents in Brooklyn, New York and, other than his drivers license, sixty two dollars in cash, a library card and two credit cards, he had a single piece of paper in his pocket with the word Jihad written on it. We seem to be in a holy war."

"Do we have a record on this guy?" The pain in his mouth was no more noticeable now than the beating of his heart. During his stint as Director, Hayden had overseen any number of possible crisis scenarios, war games, really. The one that caused the most difficulty was painfully similar to the one that was playing out right now.

"We'll have something shortly." Morrow had twenty eight agents working this. Within the hour she'd know not only where he was from, but when he had his last bowel movement.

"Terry, bring me up to date on the carnage."

Terry Myers had two hundred and three agents reporting directly to him and was embarrassed that everything he was about to tell Director Hayden came right from television reports.

"There have been attacks on twenty eight world leaders." He looked down at the papers he had compiled in front of him. "Lets see, we are acutely aware of the loss of President Bush. King Charles has superficial wounds, but his son, William is dead. Chretien up in Canada is dead. Prime Minister Vajpayee of India is in a comma, not expected to live. The Prime Minister of the Republic of Ireland, John Bruton, is no more..."

He shuffled through his pile of unbound papers, each containing information about a dead or dying head of state. "The Honorable John Howard of Australia survived a failed attack. Simitis of Greece also survived an attack, there is no word on his condition. Chancellor Gerhard Schroeder of Germany is dead. His counter part in Austria may not have faired any better, reports are sketchy, but Heir Chancellor Klima will not be waltzing any time soon, if ever. That's it for the majors, so far." This was a crisis in progress. Every head of state not dead or in a hospital by now was in a bunker somewhere fearing for his or her life.

"Every country in the former Soviet Union, except for Srpska, has had some sort of an attack. We're not even positive who is running a number of those countries. Even CNN is unclear as to what's going on out there. And, this late breaking news," he was looking at one of the muted televisions on the wall, "if President Luzkhov of Russia was in that car, he's dead too."

When faced with such a staggering amount of information, Hayden's investigative instincts kicked in and he quickly looked for anything that stood out. "What the hell is going on in Srpska, how did they dodge this?"

"You'll recall that there was a coup there almost two months ago, very bloody," Agent Myers volunteered. "The Muslim party lost almost all of its seats in the elections held last spring. There was overwhelming evidence of fraud by the majority Croatian Democratic Alliance. The aggrieved Muslims slaughtered the Serbs. Of course, a few years ago, the Muslims were the object of an ethnic cleansing, curtesy of the Serbs. The Muslims publicly executed the president, Radovan Karadzic, and formed a majority Muslim government. The acting president, Adel Taner An Sari, is the suspected leader of what had been considered a small terrorist organization named Gamat Islamya." The instability in Srpska had been an area of major concern for Terry and his group all spring.

"The Squad of Terror," Morrow added. "It started out as a small group working in the Middle East. They seem to be a resurrection of the fanatical Kharijites, dating from the seventh century. Headed by a thug named Mou Stafa Hamza in the early nineties, they were mostly responsible for suicide bombings in Israeli marketplaces. Particularly brutal in that they seemed to target civilians. An Sari took over after Mossad blew Hamza's head off with an exploding cell phone. Neat little trick, they successfully altered the brain patterns of two big name terrorists that way," Janice admired the ingenuity demonstrated time and again by her counterparts in Israel.

"An Sari lived in Bosnia-Hercegovina as a child, emigrated to Syria after his parents were killed. He's a charismatic leader, very young to be in a position of power." She looked in a file before her, "Twenty eight or nine. He's secretive, as to be expected, we have very little information on him. Under his leadership, Gamat Islamya grew exponentially. Three years ago, he moved back to his home town of Visegrad, where he was able to take a beaten Muslim population and whip them into a powerful political organization. They are quite fanatical. An Sari is a fundamentalist of the Ayatollah Kulmani sort, has a strong hatred for the West and, of course, America in particular. Most fledgling governments welcome diplomatic contact with the US. He wouldn't let Ambassador Carter across the boarder, just a minute," the phone in front of Agent Morrow rang. She listened for a moment. "Keep me up to date." As she hung up the phone, she looked over to Hayden, "There's a connection between Mirza Hoseyn Ali Nuri and Gamat Islamya, I'll have more shortly."

"This just in sir." Steve Law, Hayden's secretary, charged through the door and handed Hayden a piece of paper.

He impatiently grabbed it from his hand, he knew it was not good news. "NORAD is reporting a ballistic missile launch outside of Kharkiv, Ukraine."

CHAPTER 2
It Begins

July 7, 1:37 PM
23 kilometers East of Kharkiv, Ukraine

Two Russian made Lada military trucks charged over the crumbling road toward missile silo sight M7-r342. The trucks were exchanged for a small amount of cash and a large amount of Vodka from an enterprising procurement officer in the Russian Army. The drivers made no pretense at stealth as they pulled up to the first gates in the early afternoon.

A soldier jumped out of the back of the first truck, hauled a TOW antitank missile to his shoulder and fired point blank at the guard house. The concussion from the blast killed the offending soldier and ripped a whole in the gate big enough to drive two trucks through.

By the time the small convoy reached the second gate, there was already some activity by the guards. The second man to unleash his antitank missile learned from his friend and stood back considerably from his target. The fiery explosion resulted in an open invitation to the concrete bunker that housed their objective.

A third missile unveiled most of the upper structure of the silo. Twenty seven men poured from the trucks and charged the exposed stairway. The first wave of defenders disappeared into the hallways of the structure, clearly not inclined to give their lives for the Motherland.

Ashraf Sallmawy smiled as he watched the Russian soldiers flee. Fifteen years ago his attacking band would have been cut to pieces before they even arrived at the first gate. The Soviet Union was strong back then. Now, in its misguided chase of capitalism, Russia has become weak. Rubles spent on the military were now being spent courting

Western business or were siphoned into the pockets of corrupt politicians. The army had been without effective leadership for over a decade. The soldiers were unmotivated, poorly equipped and often, unpaid. Adel Taner An Sari was right, these infidels would run when confronted with the might of Allah.

The fighting grew fierce as they got closer to the control room. A jamming device on the second truck would keep the Russian's plea for backup from being broadcast. Ashraf could hear the high powered weapons God had blessed his men with hammering closer to their objective.

The thunderous volley of automatic weapons fire stopped abruptly. Ashraf made his way down towards the control room, stepping over twenty two Russian bodies to three of his men. Herded at the back of the main computer area were the officers who had the keys and the codes to launch the deadly missiles.

"You will give me the launch codes," he said to a low ranking officer in broken Russian.

The Russian hesitated. Ashraf pulled out an Italian built 9 millimeter Beretta and shot him in the head. The officer collapsed to his knees, leaving an unsightly crimson stain on the wall behind him. Ashraf did not have time to waste getting cooperation from the officers who had what he needed. It was his plan to execute the lowest ranking officer left after the conflict to loosen up the others. Banking on the low moral of even the highest ranking officers, he knew that an aggressive show of force would be enough to persuade these cowards to give up their terrible information.

Before the first officer's body was fully prone, he turned to the next man and made the same request, "You will give me the launch codes."

Even as he was reaching into his pocket to get the key to the safe that held the codes, Ashraf placed a bullet in his forehead. The next officer in line didn't bother to wipe the bits of brain from his face, he just quickly handed Ashraf the keys to the safe that held today's codes.

His men had already relieved the ranking officers of their launch keys. A group of men, who had been trained by a Russian nuclear scientist for a small amount of cash and a large amount of vodka, were already at their posts preparing for the first live launch of a nuclear missile, with intent, in history.

Ashraf pulled a cellular phone from his pocket.

"Adel, it is I, Ashraf. By the generosity of Allah, it is done. The fury of our cause will reek terror in the land of the non-believers."

Adel Taner An Sari hung up the phone. The Mussine was calling the chosen to evening prayer. An Sari looked out the small window of his bunker and smiled as he listened to the high singsong voice echo down the alley ways of Banja Luka, the new capitol of Sprska. It was not long ago that the call for prayer would have been answered with a bullet.

August 7th, 1992
Visegrad, Sprska

"**Adel, you must** come with me, move quickly. We will stay to the side streets, look no one in the face, come now." Adel Taner An Sari had never seen his father in such a state. Although it was a warm afternoon, his mother had shoved a kerchief over his head and one of her dark jackets around his shoulders. She handed him a heavy back pack as he ran out the door. A thirteen year old Adel sensed that his world, already defined by violence, was going to get worse.

Visegrad is an ancient city. It was populated by the Turks until the end of World War II. Split by the Drina

River, it does not look demonstrably different now than it did five hundred years before. There are many low stone buildings scattered about the city, most of the streets are cobblestone. Prosperity departed Visegrad when commerce along the Drina dried up two centuries earlier and faced further deterioration under Soviet rule. The city is united by a massive stone bridge build in 1510 during the days of the Ottoman Empire.

The city was a shell now. Every third building was in rubble. Adel and his friends used to rummage through them looking for valuables. One day, a building collapsed, killing two of his classmates. Suddenly, the war became terribly real.

Adel knew enough not to query his father, Ibrahim, as they walked through the streets. Ibrahim was trying to keep their demeanor casual, but Adel could feel the tension in his father as he struggled not to break into a trot. It was difficult for Adel to heed his fathers warning about making eye contact. There was much activity in the streets. Even looking down he could recognize the boots warn by the new Serb military.

They kept to the side of the road, taking care not to draw attention to themselves. His father was clearly worried, he had taken Adel's hand, something he had not done since Adel was little, and finally began to run.

As they turned the corner to the main street running through town, his father grabbed Adel by his mothers jacket and pulled him back. There was a large gathering at the end of the block. In the seconds he could see what was happening, he recognized a number of his Muslim neighbors being herded by a group of Serb soldiers.

"We are out of time," his father bent over, his face pale despite the physical exertion of their quickened pace. "I was hoping to get you out of town, that's going to be impossible now. The Serbs are rounding up the Muslims, I fear for the worst. Follow me."

He dragged Adel across the street and with a swift and concentrated move, kicked open the side door to the elementary school that stood on the corner. The shouts of the soldiers and the muffled cries of their captures filled Adel's father with immediacy.

"You must hide in the school. When it gets dark, leave the building and head for the border. I am going to go back for your mother. There are many refugees over there, look for the camps. We will catch up to you by tomorrow." His father held Adel's face in his hands, he felt them trembling. "I love you."

Ibrahim bent to hug his only child but turned instead as two Serb soldiers drew near. He shoved Adel back through the broken doorway and began walking toward the soldiers. Adel quickly moved deeper into the building. He knew that this was going to be the last time he'd ever see his father.

Adel worked his way to the forth floor of the old wooden building. Before the war he had gone to school there. Now, only the Serb children went to school, the Muslim children made do with home studies, when possible.

He made his way to the roof. There he found a drain hole in the knee wall on the perimeter where he could look out without being seen. Below him lay the Northern sector of the town. He could see all the way to the big stone bridge where he and his friends used to drop rocks into the Drina River after school, pretending to be pilots flying bombing missions.

Adel pulled off the back pack his mother had thrown on him during his hurried departure. He suddenly realized how heavy it was. He also realized how tired he had become. As he rummaged through the pack he found food, water, a change of clothes and his dads binoculars. It was the binoculars that held his interest presently.

It was turning dusk. The sky was changing from lavender to indigo. The wishing star was newly arrived. Adel had never seen a sunset from such a panoramic perspective. At ground level, the hilly terrain generally obscured the view. By the time one was aware of the sunset, it was over.

There was an almost carnival like atmosphere below. The sun was making its farewell by painting the tops of the highest trees in hues of gold. The streets were filled with people, every light in the town was on. There were bonfires scattered about and the air was heavy with noise.

Things turn quickly for a thirteen year old. The drama of the past hour was evaporated by the heady excitement of being alone on his roof top perch. Comforted by the height, Adel got up on his knees to provide himself a better view. The strong smell of burning wood filled his nostrils. The activity below was at a frantic pace.

A screen of black finally descended, replacing the beautiful pink sky that had so pleased Adel moments before. The new evening began to take on a sinister atmosphere. The voices that had sounded merry while the sun still shone now sounded angry. Now he could hear the protestations of his Muslim brethren.

The distinctive squeaky sound of a light tank caught his attention as it made its way down the main street, heading for the bridge. Adel realized that the sounds of firecrackers exploding were more than likely gunfire. His youthful excitement was gone. The fresh image of his fathers troubled face filled his mind.

Adel had been aware that the Serbs had taken some Muslims away, but his father assured him that fate would never befall the family of Ibrahim Taner An Sari. Ibrahim was a computer programmer. He was the only man in the entire town of Visegrad, and maybe in the entire country, who could comfortably program in C++. It now seemed to young Adel that any friends his father had made in the newly formed government were of no help.

Adel's attention was drawn to the bridge where the tank had just arrived. He drew the binoculars to his eyes in an effort to ascertain what was going on.

The huge bridge was crowded with people. A massive klieg light had been set up to illuminate the center portion. Soldiers with guns had corralled hundreds of men, Muslims judging from their distinctive dress, near the middle of the bridge. There were a handful of people standing on a twenty foot square, low, wooden platform that hung a foot or two out over the water. Adel recognized one man, Milan Lukic.

Milan Lukic was a butcher. He worked in a shop blocks from where Adel lived. Each Wednesday afternoon Adel's mother would take him there to purchase meat for the week. That was in a happier time. He recalled Milan often offering him lollipops, red was his favorite. Milan was tall, with an athletic build. He had played soccer for one of the local teams. Always with a smile, Adel was initially pleased to see that Milan Lukic seemed to be in charge.

Through his binoculars, Adel spied Milan turning toward him and bringing a megaphone up to his mouth.

"Rise up, Serb brothers. Kill the Muslims."

Adel was confused. Why would the man who smiled at his mother and gave him red lollipops want to kill Muslims, or anyone else? Surely this was some kind of play. Yes, there he was on a stage, surrounded by people, he must be putting on some kind of performance.

Milan Lukic kept chanting the words, "Kill the Muslims," over and over until a man, with his hands bound behind his back, was dragged up on stage. His back was to Adel, he was prostrated before Milan.

He could clearly see Milan, standing before his kneeling prisoner, laughing maniacally. The kindly face of the butcher was now contorted and baleful. The overhead klieg light was casting a menacing glow on this twisted play.

Adel could see Milan holding something over his head. There were two wooden handles, one in each hand, and they seemed to be attached. The occasional glint of light suggested they were connected by a wire. The crowd was frenzied. Milan lowered the handles and wrapped the wire around the kneeling mans neck.

Milan began to pull on the handles. He was bare chested, sweat shimmered off him. His muscles danced under his skin as he pulled his hands further apart. Although Adel could not hear from his position, he could see that Milan was laughing. Each time the prisoner twitched, Milan Lukic would laugh harder. He was possessed, clearly in the presence of the devil.

The wire worked its way under the mans skin, his head dropped suddenly on one shoulder as his neck muscles were severed. A spray of blood washed over Milan. He howled like a wild animal and strained in an apparent effort to sever the head with his home made garrote. Fatigue prevented this final ignominy. Milan let go, the body slump to the floor.

Adel watched in horror as the near headless body began twitching. The blood pooling up at Milan's feet was almost black. One of the soldiers grabbed the dead man by the feet and dragged him to the edge of the platform. Milan took the man by the hands and the two of them heaved the body forty feet down into the Drina.

Adel Taner An Sari lost what was left of his childhood at that moment.

The crowd roared as another man was pulled from a cordoned area adjacent to the stage. He too had his arms bound behind him. Twice the man dropped to his knees during his short walk to the center of the stage, clearly aware that his life would be coming to a painful end. Two soldiers each grabbed an arm and dragged him to a waiting Milan Lukic.

The same horrible show was replayed for Adel. This time, Milan was successful in severing the head. He seized it by the hair and held it up for the amusement of the crowd, blood dripping out the exposed neck and down Milan's arm. The body was unceremoniously tossed into the Drina, the head was stuck on a pole tied to the front of the stage.

Adel scanned the prisoners with his binoculars. He couldn't tell if there were a hundred or five hundred men, it was impossible to count. They were all moving around behind the wooden barricades that had been erected. They reminded him of the tigers he had seen in a zoo when he was little, appearing uncomfortable to be where they were. Surrounding the prisoners were soldiers with automatic weapons.

After a few minutes, he found what he hoped he would not. Initially he got just a quick glance, but several seconds later he was sure. His father was amongst the group of men who were being executed one at a time.

Adel Taner An Sari was petrified. A thousand thoughts charged through his head as to how he could save his father. From sneaking through the soldiers and snatching him, to turning into a super hero and flying down to save them all, he knew he had not the wisdom nor the weaponry to realize his objective. Though mature for his years, Adel recognized that he was thirteen, old enough to comprehend the horror that was playing out before but still young enough to dream of morphing into a super hero. Despite all he had been through during the past four years, he suddenly felt like the little boy that he was.

Adel watched this frightful drama for hours. When Milan Lukic grew weary, he dispatched prisoners with a bullet to the head. The Drina was still. The hundreds of bodies that had been tossed into her floated around the bridge pilings and obscured the water for thirty meters. Around the perimeter of the bodies the water was a muddy red. Each new body pushed this frightening flotsam further out. The severed head that Milan had put on a stake ages ago viewed the tragedy through blank eyes. His ghastly face seeming to sag deeper with each execution.

Adel was panicked. It was late, later than he had ever stayed up. There couldn't have been much more than fifty men left in the pen. His father was one of them. Maybe, just maybe, he pleaded to Allah, this Milan Lukic would get tired and stop for the night, please yes, please do not kill my father.

The sonic crack of a bullet awoke him. Adel had fallen asleep, his head resting on the rough brick wall that had hidden him this evening. He woke with a start. His initial thought was that he'd just had a very bad dream. As Adel's mind eased him back to the present, he grabbed the binoculars that had fallen to his lap and quickly began looking for his father.

The holding area was empty. Milan was gone. The soldiers were taking down the barricades. The stage was awash in blood, the harsh artificial light giving it a bizarre iridescent glow. Adel rapidly moved his gaze from man to man, hoping to glimpse his father walking home, all the while knowing he was part of that terrible congregation floating on the water.

Adel Taner An Sari sat down and cried. His mother had probably been killed during the evening. The glow he saw to the south suggested that his whole neighborhood was ablaze. Young Adel now had only one thing to live for.

Revenge.

Adel Taner An Sari knelt down on his prayer matte and closed his eyes. As always, for the past decade, the vision of the severed head on the bridge filled his mind. As always, Adel began his evening prayers with his request for revenge on the infidels. This night, however, he ended with thanks.

By the grace of Allah, his Army of God had meet with wild success. Twenty eight world leaders were either dead or dying. He was now in control of nineteen Soviet missile sights. He wielded the sword of rightness that would enable him to do God's work, to rid the planet of its Godless inhabitants, allow Allah to start again, to rebuild a world where a young boy would not learn to hate before he became a man.

Already there was a gift on its way to America, homeland of the devil himself. The city of New York would be rubble shortly. The rest of the world, however, must be warned. As the Koran had taught him, those who are to be executed must be given time to repent, to make peace with Allah. They must die with Allah in their thoughts in order to enter His kingdom, where food was plentyful, wine flowed freely and seventy virgins awaited.

Adel rose from his prayer matte and walked into the next room. There was a full crew from CNN equipped, as per his request, with a live satellite feed. Within moments, Adel Taner An Sari would speak to the world.

It didn't take much to get the crew there. As the world was coming apart and fingers started to point to Gamat Islamya, a call from the most powerful terrorist in the world was answered promptly.

"**As we told** you earlier in the evening, we now have the head of the terrorist organization Gamat Islamya, Adel Taner An Sari, on a live satellite feed from Visegrad, Srpska. Mr. An Sari has claimed responsibility for the multitude of assassinations today and the nuclear missile heading towards New York." Wolf Blitzer was at the anchor desk in Washington.

"We now go live to Visegrad."

Adel waited for the red light on the camera to come on, as he was instructed, before beginning to speak. His faced filled almost every television screen in the civilized world. He appeared too young and smooth of face to seemingly be in control of the fate of the planet.

"My name is Adel Taner An Sari." He spoke in English, a language he had mastered as a child. "I am responsible for the many acts of retribution performed today by the Army of God. It is the will of Allah that this planet be cleansed of the sinners who have corrupted His gift to man. It is my desire to give all of you the opportunity to repent for your disrespectful ways and ask forgiveness so that you may enter the Kingdom of Heaven this day."

Adel was speaking without notes. He did not have much to say. "I will be instructing my followers to unleash all of the nuclear weapons we control. It is my understanding that forty five percent of the worlds population will die immediately, many will be dead within two weeks, the rest, within four months. May Allah be with you."

With the red light still glowing on the top of the camera, Adel turned and walked back into his sparse room. He heard the sharp crack of bullets as his guards killed the camera crew. Adel made eighteen phone calls, then lay down in his bed and prepared to meet Allah.

The apocalypse had begun.

CHAPTER 3
Developing a protocol

July 7, 11:48 PM EST
Washington, DC

The President had called a high level cabinet meeting. Had he not, Director Hayden would have. As his car charged through the darkened and empty streets of Washington DC, Michael's mind wandered back to November 9, 1989. He was the Director for Defense Policy and Arms control in Washington at the time. He recalled being huddled around a television in the secretary's area with a dozen other people.

The fall of the Soviet Union came as an embarrassing shock to the US intelligent community. Again, there was CNN breaking the biggest story of the century. Both the NSA and the CIA had egg on their collective faces. Their very survival was questioned when neither of them could predict the fall of the Evil Empire.

As his colleagues and most of the world rejoiced, Michael returned to his desk and quietly began to worry. The Soviet Union had ceased to be a real threat under President Reagen. His aggressive military build up in the eighties buried an already near terminal economy. Gorbachev had to decide who to feed, his people or his military machine. In their weakened state, Russia could do nothing more than defend itself, which suited the US just fine. We had no desire to take over and rule the mess that was the Soviet Union.

While watching young men and women dismantle The Wall with sledge hammers and spoons, Michael shuddered as he considered the myriad of smaller and larger disconnected pieces of what would now forever be referred to as the former Soviet Union. From the key stone country of Poland, to Ukraine and Belarus, Luthuania, Latvia, Estonia, Georgia, Moldova, Azerbaijan, Turkmemistan, Uzbekistan, each had the potential to become a wild cannon. Now there was not just one country to deal with, but dozens of lesser, and potentially more dangerous and unstable players.

As Boris Yeltsin struggled to reinvent the government, a fiscal crisis gripped the region. The oil rich countries to the south were hoarding their money, the fertile countries to the west fed their own. The industrial countries produced goods only to find there was no market for their poorly built wares.

Of primary concern were the thousands of nuclear weapons that were scattered all over the new Commonwealth of Independent States. When Michael started hearing that the military was not being paid, he knew it was only a matter of time before the black market would be choked with sophisticated weapons. Sixty Minutes did a piece on pounds of weapons grade plutonium that had disappeared from a number of sights. That report helped convince the US to turn over billions in aid to help ease the former Soviet Union into Democracy.

As each state broke away from Russia, the military became fragmented. Once a powerful and a comfortably predictable adversary, the US was now faced with renegade generals controlling hundreds of thousands of troops, sophisticated aircraft and armored vehicles… And ballistic missiles.

When Boris Yeltsin died of a massive heart attack while in the midst of firing his entire cabinet, the former Soviet Union imploded. No fewer than three generals claimed to be in charge of Russia. An already fragmented military solidified into three separate armies, twice engaging in limited skirmishes amongst themselves.

The initial fear of a recreant general actually using the nukes quickly turned to fear of the generals loosing control of their terrible charges to fringe terrorist organizations. Computer simulations were run for months, strategies were formed and reformed, but there was no way to predict that which had no cadence. Gamat Islamya became Mrs. O'learies cow and it wasn't only Chicago that was going to burn.

July 7, 10:58 PM EST
Norfolk, Virginia

Rachel Ben-Gurion had gotten the boys out of bed and placed them between herself and her husband, Allen, on the sofa. They were all glued to the television, along with the rest of the civilized world, watching the developing situation. Dov and Yehuda were only two and four. They had quickly fallen back to sleep, but both Rachel and Allen felt the need to have their children close at hand. Had they still been living in Brooklyn, surely they would be over at Rabbi Ben-Gurion's house with his extended family.

"I cannot believe this is happening," Rachel had moaned again. "Why would that man want to destroy everything?" It was the question on the lips of the entire world and the very question Dan Rather was attempting to answer. He had retired exactly one week prior. CBS reactivated him in an effort to bring the comfort of familiarity to the unfolding drama.

The events in Sprska of a decade ago were being revisited. Dan remembered reporting on the ethnic cleansing during the early nineties. He also remembered reporting those horrors without much fanfare. No one protested in the streets for an end to the holocaust befalling Muslims on the other side of the world. Acquiescence to evil can cause it to propagate. It seems that mankind is slated to pay large for its ignoble lack of courage.

Rachel finally broached the question that had been on both of their minds for the past few hours and neither wanted to address.

"I suppose they will be calling you back?" There was much timidity in her voice.

Allen Ben-Gurion was a naval aviator currently assigned to the aircraft carrier *USS John C. Stennis*. He had returned from a three month tour four days ago.

"I'm sure they will. We will probably go straight to THREATCON DELTA. The country hasn't been there since the World Trade Center mess." He was looking out the window, starring at a street lamp across the alley, trying to avoid looking into the pool of tears he knew were forming in Rachel's eyes.

He felt guilty every time he left her. She really shouldn't be in this situation. She was suppose to marry a Rabbi and live in the relative stability of Crown Heights, Brooklyn. He was supposed to be a Rabbi. By now he'd have finished his formal studies and he'd be teaching at his fathers Yeshiva, being groomed to be the Rosh Hayeshiva.

But there was warrior in his blood. His father understood Allen's calling even as he threatened to remove his name from the family Talmud. Rabbi Yehuda Ben-Gurion was the son of David Ben-Gurion, one of the founders of Israel. Ben-Gurion fought along side Menachem Begen with the underground during Word War II. His brilliant tactics literally saved Israel during the Six Day War.

Allen grew up hearing stories of courage and daring do that swelled his chest with pride to be part of the lineage of Ben-Gurion. Brilliance and sheer will were necessary to get an appointment to Annapolis. He graduated seventh in his class and was quickly sent to aviation training in Mera Mar. He excelled there. He also dutifully came home and married Rachel Finkle. Now with two houses against him, he took her to his first assignment in Maryland.

It was hard on both of them. With no Hasidic community for support, Rachel struggled to keep a proper home. Allen often worked on the Sabbath. So many of the ancient laws were broken. She had a heavy heart. But Allen was driven to be a warrior. The only way out of this was to endure the ultimate disgrace, divorce. She loved him to much for that.

When the children came, it was somewhat easier. Rachel busied herself providing them with an exceptional Hasidic preschool environment. Allen was a tremendous help when he was around. He helped her keep the house kosher, though she knew it was impossible for him to keep kosher while he was away from her.

Rachel hated the whole convoluted arrangement most when Allen was away on tour. He'd be gone for three to six months. When he was home, by the time they had become reacquainted, it'd be time to start another tour or to go off to some far away place for additional training.

Allen knew what Rachel was thinking. He didn't have the words now to comfort her. He never did. He'd make his good-bye's as quick and surgically as possible to make it easy for all of them. It never did.

With little new information coming in, Dan Rather was beginning to repeat himself. Then the phone rang. Although she knew the call would be coming, Rachel was still startled.

"It's not fair, you just got home. Couldn't they call someone else?" She knew they couldn't. This departure was more poignant than any of the others. This time he was going to war.

July 8, 12:17 AM EST
The White House

Hayden was the last one to walk into the Oval Office. The Presidents staff and the military were all accounted for. There were pockets of informal discussions raging about the room.

"Mr. President." Director Hayden extended his hand.

Richard Cheney did not look well. It had not been a very good presidency for him thus far and he was still hours away from his first full day in office. He had been sworn in less than ninety minutes after President Bush's death. Since then, conditions had deteriorated at an exponential pace.

Less than forty eight hours ago, Vice President Cheney's life was consumed with the ethical question of genetic engineering. A bill in the house outlawing any further experimentation with designer genes was deadlocked. As VP, it was his duty to cast the deciding vote.

It all came to a head two months before when the flamboyant Dr. Valentine, at Harvard Medical School, produced the first genetically altered clone birth of a male child. The fact that the genetic material came from Elvis Presiley both shocked and thrilled the Nation. Figuring the populaces interest would be peaked with the recreation of a cultural icon, hence assuring his funding, Dr. Valentine initially chose John Lennon as his first genetic progeny. After Yoko Ono refused to turn over any genetic material, he approached the family of Princess Diana. While her brother showed interest, the Royal Family objected strenuously. The strategic purchase of a comb at Sothbeys Elvis Presiley auction resulted in a wealth of material from

Time Shift/34

which to work. Thirteen months later, the King was reborn.

That all seemed a life time ago. Richard Cheney was now faced with the most volatile situation facing the world since the Cuban Missile crisis almost forty years earlier. A military counter measure was contra indicated here. As a five time Congressmen from Wyoming, he had little need for military protocol until 1989, when he was appointed as the Secretary of Defense. His five year tenure was dramatic and active as he oversaw the two largest military campaigns in recent US history, Operation Just Cause in Panama and Operation Desert Storm. Those campaigns were relatively easy, invade a defined country and kick the presiding dictators ass. This current crisis was far more complicated.

"Gentlemen, let's begin. Dr. Roche, congratulations on shooting down that missile heading for New York." Dr. James G. Roche was the Secretary of the Air Force, one of his F22's splashed the nuclear missile twelve nautical miles off the coast of Manhattan.

"Thank you Mr. President, however, there is the nuclear fallout to deal with. If the prevailing winds stay constant, a cloud of nuclear material will hit land in about thirty minutes at the New York, Canada boarder. My people tell me we are looking at one to two hundred thousand deaths depending on exactly where it lands and how far inland it blows. Evacuations have begun, but frankly, I don't know where the hell these people can go."

Dick Cheney closed his eyes. He could not fathom two hundred thousand deaths. He had to remind himself that eight million lives had been spared.

"We still have a much bigger problem on our hands" Dr. Roche continued. "Seventy percent of what the Russians had in the way of nuclear weapons are now in the hands of Gamat whoever, and they plan to light them off. There is no way we can tag them all."

"Even if you could, it would only slow down the inevitable." Kelly Powelll was the Presidents Science Advisor. She had jet black hair, cut tight to her face, and stunning green eyes. At twenty nine, she was way too young and pretty to be in her current position. She was also way to brilliant not to be.

"If approximately fifty of these megaton warheads explode, that cloud heading towards Canada will look like a summer breeze." Kelly had stopped smoking four years ago. She started again two hours ago and she needed to continue right now. "Let's disregard the point of impact deaths for a moment. We have two fatal conditions that we will have no control over. The first, and most obvious, is the nuclear fallout. This stuff will get into the upper atmosphere and encompass the globe within days. Poison will drip out of the sky for months."

Kelly couldn't concentrate. She put the cigarette she had been fondling under the table between her lips and fired it up before anyone could tell her to stop. When no one said anything, half the people in the room lit up.

"The second problem will be debris. On impact, millions of yards of dirt will be thrown into the atmosphere. This stuff will be dense enough to block out up to seventy, eighty percent of the sun light." Kelly took a deep drag on her smoke. How could I have given these things up, she wondered? "The debris will have the secondary effect of solidifying the nuclear material, making it fall in a much more concentrated, hence deadly, form.

"The bottom line, Mr. President, is nuclear winter. This debris will remain in the atmosphere for twenty four to as long as fifty months. In a much shorter period of time, we will loose all of our plant life. That, as you will remember from High School Biology, is the beginning of the food chain. As people are dying from radiation poisoning, they will also be starving to death. Complex life on this planet will cease to exist within two years."

"Give me a military solution, gentlemen," President Cheney looked to the Generals and Admirals under his command.

"We are at THREATCON DELTA, our highest military alert." General Henry Shelton headed the Joint Chiefs of Staff. "It doesn't make sense to throw our nuclear stuff at, well, who. Attacking the Commonwealth of Independent States is pointless. Our intercontinental ballistic missiles were deconstructed under Clinton. The only ICBM'S we have available are on our nuclear sub fleet. It will take hours to get them in position to make a strike, and even then, it wouldn't exactly be surgical. We also don't know which silo's are in terrorist hands."

General Sheldon felt emasculated. He was in charge of the most potent war machine in history but could do little with it.

"I'm not sure we want to be adding more nuclear material to the atmosphere in any case. I recommend we send our planes in. We have been in touch with what is left of the governments we need to be and have been granted clear access over every country in the affected areas. Unfortunately, it is going to take time to get our units armed and over there.

"Our allies are planning pretty much the same thing. However, most of the governments are a mess. This whole plot was brilliantly thought out. An Sari created total confusion with one hand and then exploited the appalling conditions in the former Soviet Union to grab their nukes, which, by the way, were supposed to have been dismantled with ours under the Start Two Treaty."

An aide handed a paper to President Cheney. He read it to himself.

"This is from NORAD, they have detected three more missiles heading for Great Britain, France and the US. Ours appears to be targeting the West."

Michael Hayden's tooth began to throb. He puffed on the cigar General Shelton had given him. How could I have given these things up, he wondered.

"President Cheney, I have a solution. I must ask, however, that the room be cleared of anyone who does not have top secret clearance." Technically, it should have been anyone without above top secret clearance, but that would have left him sitting alone in the office.

"In light of what's going on, Mr. Hayden, is that really necessary?" Cheney didn't have the time nor the temperament right now for spook bullshit.

"That's your call." Just as well, Hayden thought, anyone here could broadcast our most vital national secrets now, it wouldn't matter. Life was going to change in a most dramatic way within a few hours.

"The NSA's blackest project is called Time Shift. We possess the practical application to manipulate time."

"You aren't talking about time travel?" Dick Cheney was indignant. Was this man going to tell her that the government had a way back machine?

Surprisingly, Hayden was not prepared for his attitude. He had been steeped in this project for years and now, for the first time, he realized how crazy it sounded.

"Well, ah, yes, for almost fifty years now we have had the technology to travel back in time." He realized he was going to have to convince the President and his staff that we were capable of this science fiction feat. Michael sat back and collected his thoughts.

"Let me start from the beginning." The astonished faces around the room distracted him. He focused on President Cheney.

"This project had its gestation during the forties, coinciding with the advent of the atomic bomb. The Manhattan Project brought together the finest physicists in the world. The United States was the beneficiary of fascism in Europe that caused many of these men to

emigrate here though out the late thirties and early forties."
Hayden took a long drag on his cigar. He felt overwhelmed
by the task at hand. He had to educate his audience in a
number of highly complex theories and further convince
them that they were beyond the theoretical.

"Time travel was addressed by Einstein way back in
1905 when he developed his special Theory of Relativity.
This simple theory, addressing the relation between mass
and energy, changed the way the world was perceived from
a physical perspective."

Kelly Powell was intrigued. She had gotten one of
her Doctorates from Yale in Physics. She had engaged in
more than a few energetic discussions with fellow
physicists about the potential of time travel. The quantum
physicists in the group often threw up theoretical road
blocks when it came time to explain how the speed of light
could be reached when the object in motion undergoes a
large increase in mass at a relatively low energy.

"How do you suggest the problem of mass increase
was resolved?" Kelly couldn't help herself. She stubbed
out her cigarette and sat up in her chair. This was
fascinating.

"In 1945, Edwin McMillian deduced that as the
particles gain mass, the frequency could be lowered to keep
them in sync by increasing the speed in steps. This
research lead to the Betatron cyclic accelerator after
scientist hit the wall at 15 MeV with the Cyclotron. His
research became crucial later in the project."

Kelly glanced over to a perplexed President. "15
MeV refers to 15 million electron volts and is a unit to
measure extreme speed. The Betatron and the Cyclotron
are particle accelerators. These things are used by
physicists to accelerate charged elementary particles to
high energies. Accelerators are used to explore atomic
nuclei. This allows nuclear scientists to identify new
elements and to explain phenomena that affect the entire

nucleus. Speeds up to 50 GeV, or 50 billion electronic volts, have been achieved at Stanford University with their Linac."

"Substantially higher speeds have been achieved at Brookhaven; however, I am getting ahead of myself here." Hayden continued, "The work of Wilhelm Reich was of particular interest to Einstein. Though later discredited, Reich's work on antigravity equations helped Einstein over some difficult spots. As work on the A Bomb continued, Einstein and Oppenheimer would toy with some of the more advanced applications of the theory of relativity." Michael could actually hear eyes glazing over as he droned on. He was not much of a speaker and his tooth still hurt. This was necessary information and by God, they were going to hear it all.

"Eventually Dr. John von Neumann, who was also working on the Manhattan Project, was introduced into this informal discussion group. Von Neumann brought to the table a theory called Hilbert Space. In 1926, von Neumann met a mathematician named David Hilbert. Hilbert had developed several different methods of new math. Von Neumann's gift was the ability to take abstract theoretical concepts in math and apply them to physical situations. The pieces began coming together.

"Electromagnetic energy was the physical key to altering the time continuum. The government was aware of the theoretical discussions taking place and wondered if there was a practical application there to hide battleships from the newly developed radar. The theoretical work was done quickly and by July of 1943, a ship, the *USS Eldridge*, was fitted for a formal experiment.

"Two huge generators had been fitted to the fore and aft of the ship to generate the needed electricity to perform the test. On August 12th, at the Philadelphia Navy Yard, the experiment was run. The switch was thrown, the generators took a few minutes to get up to speed and the

USS Eldridge disappeared from radar. It also disappeared from view.

"For seven minutes, the *Eldridge* was gone. During the time it was suppose to be in Philadelphia, it appeared in Norfolk, Virginia. It appeared there seven minutes back in time."

"Wasn't that called the Philadelphia Experiment?" President Cheney had read his share of government cover up books and was an closet fan of the X-Files.

"Well, it was known as the Rainbow Project to those working on it. When bits of information leaked out, it was coined the Philadelphia Experiment for obvious reasons."

"Weren't there a number of deaths and injuries as a result of that experiment?"

"You did see the movie, Mr. President. No, there were no personnel on board the *Eldridge*. I am afraid there was much misinformation disseminated about the project after word leaked out. Remember, we were at war.

"Well, as you can imagine, there was much confusion as well as excitement when all the results were analyzed. The theoretical theses worked out by Einstein and his fellow scientist turned out to be practical. There was still an incredible amount of work to be done. They were still unsure if living tissue could be time shifted."

Hayden had run this all through in his mind a number of times before the meeting, hoping he could tell this complex story in a cogent way.

"At this point, the government realized the immense implications the manipulation of time represented. They tightened up security, dramatically paired down the number of peripheral people involved and reclassified Rainbow as a black project. They renamed it Project Time Shift. Time Shift was this countries first black project and the second to be classified as above top secret. The first, of course, being the Manhattan Project."

Kelly Powell gripped the arms of her chair. There were a hundred theoretical possibilities she had considered during her career as a scientist, but time travel was the last one she expected to become a reality during her lifetime. She wasn't sure if her lightheadedness came from this startling news or the fact that she had just smoked a pack of cigarettes during the past two hours.

"It wasn't until June of 1947 that Project Time Shift was ready for the first formal attempt at time travel. The research had been moved to the Roswell Army Air Field in late '45."

"The 509th Bombardment group was stationed there. That was our nuclear bomber group." General Shelton added.

"Yes, General, we had all of our nuclear bombs there and it was one of the most secure bases in the country at the time. The plan was..."

"Oh my God," the President blurted, "the Roswell Incident!"

"Well, that became the cover story after the experiment went bad. As I was saying, the plan was to send four men two days into the past on July 5th. They were dressed in high altitude suits and placed in a disc approximately thirty feet in diameter. The thing was loaded with high out put generators and the large magnets necessary to produce the electromagnetic energy needed to push time."

This accident was every bit as bad as the Apollo tragedy, thought Hayden, however, these four men will never be memorialized.

"The disc disappeared, but did not reappear where it was expected. For hours, they didn't have clue as to where it, or the men, were. On July 3rd, a civil engineer named Grady Barnett stumbled upon the disc while working in the Plains of St. Agustin, some 180 miles west of Roswell.

It took Barnett two days to get back to Socorro, where he lived, and make a report. What he claimed to have found was a crashed flying saucer with four dead aliens in it. He described the bodies as small, with large heads and silver suits. The craft, he had measured, was thirty feet in diameter. Of course, the Socorro Sheriff's Department immediately contacted General Ramey at the air base. A crew was sent out to collect the disc and the horribly distorted bodies."

"So," concluded Kelly, "the problem of increased mass at terminal speeds was not solved. Why did the bodies shrink instead of enlarge?"

"My understanding is that living tissue has to be protected from the incredible amounts of electromagnetic energy being produced. Remember, Dr. Powell, I am not a scientist, some of this stuff is quite beyond me." Hayden did not have time to be going into irrelevant details now.

"In order to cover up what was really going on, General Ramey came up with a brilliant solution. He first had debris from one of the advanced, and top secret, weather balloons the US was experimenting with at the time, dropped on a sheep ranch about 75 miles northwest of Roswell. The farmer, Mac Brazel, found the stuff and reported it to a Sheriff Wilcox.

"He, of course, reported it to the base, at which point, Ramey called the Roswell Daily Record and reported that he was in possession of a captured disc. The story was quickly retracted and a legend was created that has kept a generation of theorists busy investigating UFO's. And, no, if I may anticipate your next question, Madame President, we have no captured alien space craft, we are not in contact with any advanced alien cultures and to the best of our knowledge, Earth is the only inhabited planet in existence."

Cheney was a little let down. He had a life long fascination with UFO's. After arriving in Washington in 1969 to serve with the Nixon Administration, he cornered the Director of the CIA at a reception in the White House and queried him as to our Countries involvement with UFO's. An embarrassed Richard Cheney was dismissed with a gruff laugh.

"Although this first experiment ended in disaster, the Time Shift scientists gleaned a wealth of information. It was Dr. Oppenheimer who took the lead at this point and attacked the problems still facing time manipulation with stunning determination. He turned time travel into a personnel quest. It seems that he had a great deal of remorse for his work in developing the atom bomb. Unfortunately, he wanted to go back in time and destroy all knowledge that would lead to the splitting of the atom. By 1954, he was removed from both the Time Shift Project and from the Atomic Energy Commission. He was the appointed chairman of the General Advisory Committee.

"By the mid forties, when the theoretical inched towards the probable, it was decided a committee needed to be formed to deal with the moral, ethical and practical applications of time travel. Twelve men were chosen. They were called Majestic-12, or MJ 12. The original members were made up of military, scientific and political men." Hayden flipped through a binder in front of him. "Here it is, the list is an impressive one for the time, Admiral Hillenkoetter, Dr. Bush, Secretary Forrestal, he died in '49 and was replaced by General Walter Smith. Then you have Generals Twining, Montague and Vandenberg, Doctors Bronk, Hunsaker, Mensel and Berkner. And finally, Mr. Souera and Mr. Gordon Gray. If we had time, I would give you a brief bio on each man. Take my word however; these were heavy hitters in the late forties."

"Dr. Bush invented the differential analyzer while at MIT" Kelly added. Looking over to President Cheney, she added "It was a device used to rapidly and automatically solve complex mathematical problems. It was the forerunner of the modern computer."

"That is correct, Dr. Powell, his work was instrumental in the final stages of Time Shift. Both he and Dr. Bronk were the only members to be actively involved in the project."

President Cheney was aware of MJ 12, but his knowledge of them came from UFO conspirators who had these prestigious men bartering humans for alien technology.

"It was their responsibility" Hayden continued, " to decide how and when this new technology should be used. They quickly realized that the United States would shortly be in a position to change the history of man kind. There was obviously no precedence here. These men recognized that they possessed Pandora's box.

"Their first decision was to keep knowledge of the Time Shift Project from the public at all costs. The name was changed to the Babylonian Project, a nod of the head to the civilization that devised the first accurate calendar. It was also decided not to let elected officials, including the President, know about it either. Work on the project was broken down into smaller projects so that few of the participants would be aware of the larger picture. It was possible to have a physicist work on pertinent equations without him or her knowing ultimately what was going to be done with their work. The technicians often thought they were working with NASA on space related hardware. Within a decade, there were only a handful of individuals who knew what Babylonian was all about.

The largest debates were about what to do with the ability to manipulate time. Ideas ranged from the noble, helping to write the original constitution to ban slavery, thereby avoiding the Civil War, to the foolish, funding government spending by gambling on horse races where the outcome was known. They were sober and passionate discussions with consideration given to long term results that would be deemed as consequential changes to history."

"Were religious considerations given. I see there were no clerics on MJ 12," President Cheney asked.

"Yes. However, not directly. Leaders of the main religions were questioned, of course, dealing in theory, by Mr. Gray, who reported back to the group. There was a semiserious proposal to go back and meet Jesus.

"After six plus months of debate, it was realized that time travel could be extremely dangerous and that there was no immediate justification to do it. By this time, Babylonian was eating up two thirds of the black project money taken from Congress and a decision was made to moth ball the project.

"Then, the Soviet Union detonated an atomic bomb. The Cold War was on and for the first time in history, two countries had the capacity to kill every living thing on the planet.

"Mutually assured destruction was the buzz word that brought MJ 12 back together. Technology was progressing rapidly. The atom bomb gave way to the hydrogen bomb and all indications were that weapon systems would only get more powerful. It was unanimously agreed that there was one scenario that warranted a trip back in time, the prevention of a nuclear war.

"Project Babylonian took on a new urgency. Efforts were increased. In 1951, another experiment was tried. After the initial disaster, the plan was to send an unmanned craft back two days into the past. The craft went back in time, but only seven hours. We did not possess the ability to measure time accurately enough to manipulate it precisely. It wasn't until 1955 when the first atomic clock was developed within the Project that precise time calculations were resolved."

Again, Dr. Powell jumped in, "That would have been the Cesium Beam Atomic Clock." She was dumbfounded that the first atomic clock was an offshoot of a time travel experiment. Turning to the President, she added "That atomic clock related the number of spectral lines caused by the cesium-133 atom alternating between an excited and a grounded state."

The President didn't have a clue as to what that meant but appreciated Dr. Powell's efforts in keeping her informed.

"Were they using ephemeris time?"

"Yes, Dr. Powell." Beating her to the punch, he turned to the President, "Due to the fact that the rotation of the earth is not regular, it varies between one and two seconds a year, a new time measurement was needed that combined both sidereal time and solar time." Fortunately the President didn't slow him down by questioning him as to what sidereal time was.

"Another experiment in late '55 put an unmanned capsule exactly two days back in time. Now all efforts were centered on how to transport living tissue.

"It was discerned that the different vibration frequencies between living tissue and inanimate objects was the problem. It took twelve fried monkeys to work that out.

"Dr. Bush devised a frequency modulator, based upon the pioneering work of McMillian ten years earlier, that synchronized all the natural frequencies within, what had now been coined, the time cocoon. By March of 1956 they had successfully sent a man back two days in time.

"The project was now moved to a base in New Mexico called Area 51. And again, no Mr. President, we never had alien crafts there that were being back engineered," he knew he was thinking it. "We do have, and have had since the fifties, our black projects operating there. Most recently, the Aurora Project, our super high speed reconnaissance aircraft." Although still technically classified, there was so much good information on the street about it Hayden was hardly concerned about a security breech. He was also trying to further his credibility.

"By '58, we could successfully send a small, manned craft back to any point of time in history. However, for reasons I will share with you in a moment, MJ 12 needed the ability to send a large craft through time. The answer came, surprisingly, from the work of Nikola Tesla."

Kelly interjected, "Wasn't he discredited?"

Christ, I'm never going to get through this, Hayden thought. He did feel that he had an ally in Dr. Powell and didn't want to alienate her. Figuring he may as well bring the rest of the room up to speed, he gave a brief bio on Nikola Tesla.

"Tesla, born in the late 1800's in Yugoslavia, was known as the father of radio. It seems Marconi may have borrowed some of his research and ended up receiving most of the credit. Well, by any accounts, Tesla was brilliant. He spoke several languages and he worked his way across Europe working as an inventor and an electronics engineer. While in Paris, his work was noticed by Thomas Edison. Edison hired him and brought Tesla back to the US.

"They had a large falling out when Tesla tried to convince Edison that alternating current was better that the direct current Edison was backing. Westinghouse recognized Tesla's genius and financed his idea to harness alternating current from Niagara Falls. From there, Tesla had a number of impressive experiments.

"However, as Dr. Powell pointed out, at the end of his career, he was indeed discredited. He claimed to be clairvoyant and to possess a number of paranormal abilities. He had convinced the financier J. P. Morgan that he could build a huge tower on Long Island that would provide free electrical power. Morgan eventually realized that what he was proposing was impossible and pulled the financing."

"Where does he fit into the story?" General Shelton was getting bored with these little side trips Dr. Powell was creating. He wanted the facts.

"His contribution to Project Babylonian," Hayden continued, "was, what was called, the Delta Time coil structure. The Delta T coils enabled the scientists to shield a greater area than the earlier technology had. The time cocoon was now substantially enlarged."

"Why was it so important to be able to send some immense structure back in time?" the President asked.

"Yes," added the General, "how big an object are we talking about here?"

"I'll tie this all together shortly, allow me to continue," Hayden raised his hands to deflect anymore questions. "After years of debate and discussion, as noted before, MJ 12 decided that the only reason to manipulate time was to stave off a nuclear war. The question then was how to do that. They considered Oppenheimer's idea of going back and interrupting research on nuclear fission, but they decided that man would inevitably split the atom and there would be no stopping that. They also recognized that the technology would be necessary in the future.

"They then thought about trying to limit the spread of the technology. One thought was to prevent Thedore Hall from leaking the implosion principal to the Soviets back in 1944. It was decided that their scientist would have figured it out eventually and those efforts were abandoned. Finally, they decided that the only way to prevent nuclear war was to prevent any other country from having nuclear technology outright."

"Why should the US be the only ones with such destructive force, isn't that dangerous?" President Cheney felt an uncharacteristic liberal bent emerging.

"I'm not prepared to address the moral implications that question begs, Mr. President. I'll ask you, however, if only one country could possess nuclear weapons, which country would you want that to be?"

"Well," Shelton demanded, "what the hell was, is, the solution?" He'd lost his patience. The General was not one hundred percent sure what he was hearing was possible, and if it was, he was damn well sure, as the top military man in the country, he should have been made privy to this information earlier.

"It was decided that our most powerful ordinance, a nuclear powered aircraft carrier, would be sent back to 1941 to dismantle the Soviet Union."

There was a stunned silence in the room. General Shelton was the only one at the table nodding his head in agreement.

"Why 1941?" Admiral Vern Clark, Chief of Naval Operations, entered the discussion.

"The objective here is to keep another government, in this case the only government who has the nuclear tonnage to create trouble, from developing a nuclear capability. There is precedence here. In October, 1964, at the urging of McGeorge Bundy, his National Securities Advisor, President Johnson seriously considered a preemptive strike on China to preclude them from developing a nuclear capability. Obviously he didn't go through with it, but he was serious enough to have developed a protocol for an attack.

"From our vantage point, it may have made sense to slip back to the middle 1800's and attack Czar Nicholus, who would be indefensible, and split up Russia as we see fit."

General Shelton was not only nodding his head again, but smiling. There was an irresistible urge, to a military man, to go to war against a foe that could not only be vanquished, but toyed with in the process.

"There are a number of problems there. The first, and most difficult to justify, is why would a pre-world power America go to war with a friendly nation? World opinion would not be with us. It may also prove a tad difficult to convince a pre civil war Lincoln, and his cabinet, that we need to attack a sovereign nation because we need to stop them from splitting something they could barely imagine exists."

They were all nodding, Hayden was making his point.

"Additionally, it will be tough enough to explain our current technology to a 1940's America. Consider discussing mach 2 capable aircraft with people who may not be prepared to accept the concept of air travel. It would be quite a challenge getting them to accept time travel.

"MJ 12 thought this through, and they thought it through well. They recognized that the only time in past history when the United States could justify war against the Soviet Union was during World War Two. As Stalin was carving up Europe, we were in a fairly good position to demand he cease. This posture would quickly lead to armed conflict, that we, with the help of a fully outfitted aircraft carrier fitted with tactical nuclear weapons, could win decisively.

"MJ 12, which, by the way, is now MJ 9, two members have died and a third developed Alzheimer's, put together a detailed plan of action. The hull design of our Nimitz class carriers had been designed to accommodate the equipment necessary to time shift. All of the computers and navigational equipment have been shielded to protect against the tremendous amounts of electromagnetic energy needed to send a thousand plus foot long object back in time. Admiral Clark will confirm that we always have at least one Nimitz Class carrier in port at all times. That edict was instituted right after the Cuban Missile Crisis when, to the horror of MJ 12, we had no carrier in port ready to shift. The Missile Crisis was the first and last time Project Babylonian was close to being activated. John Kennedy was the first president since Roosevelt to be made privy to the project. Unfortunately, he became obsessed with the incredible power of Babylonian and tried to wrest control of it away from MJ 12." That, Hayden did not mention, was a fatal mistake.

"The *USS John C. Stennis* is in port right now, just days back from a port visit to Jebel Ali," the Admiral volunteered.

"As we speak, she is being specially equipped for this mission. MJ 12 does not have the power to activate Project Babylonian, that decision is reserved for the sitting president, but they do have the authority to order the preparation of which ever carrier is in either the Norfolk or the San Diego base."

"What special preparation does she need?"

"Admiral, your ship is being loaded with the most modern weapons in our arsenal, some of which are still experimental. As I alluded to previously, MJ 12 fully thought this out. They had built a series of warehouses near the docks where the carriers are based. They are innocuous looking, Admiral Clark, you have driven by them most likely dozens of times. This is where all of the equipment has been stored for Babylonian. They are all off limits to base personnel and are run by the NSA."

The Admiral shook his head. There were thirty huge warehouses on the base. The amount of material needed to keep an air craft carrier operational, with a full compliment of six thousand crew, is enormous.

"The *John Stennis* is being loaded not only with it's normal stores, but with additional weapons, computers and the spare parts that would be difficult to find or manufacture in the past. There won't be a square foot on her deck that will be empty. Before she goes operational, it will be necessary to off load the extra material on shore."

"When did the NSA take control of Babylonian?" General Shelton was still miffed that he had been out of that loop.

Hayden was annoyed by the constant interruptions. "In 1971, in an effort to strengthen the influence of the Director of the National Security Agency over other intelligence activities, the SCAs were confederated under a Central Security Service with the Director of the NSA as its chief. The newly reorganized NSA now possessed centralized coordination, direction and control of the Government's Signals Intelligence and Communications Security activities.

"Two years later, MJ 12 turned over operational control of Babylonian. The NSA staffed the supply warehouses, programmed the software necessary for a time shift and oversaw the maintenance of the equipment on board the carriers."

Dr. Powell was doing complicated mathematical calculations in her head. The military aspect of Project Babylonian did not hold the cache for her that the scientific news did. She was becoming mentally overloaded until one thought snapped her back, 'what is going to happen to me at the moment of time shift?' The present will cease to exist, the present will be sixty plus years ago. *I will cease to exist!*

"Dr. Powell, are you OK?" Kelly had turned white and was rocking back and forth in her chair.

"Oh, yes," back to reality where it was considerably more comfortable. "Well, there are some issues we haven't discussed."

"Yes, Dr. Powell, there are loads of issues we haven't addressed yet," Hayden finally had enough and for the first time raised his voice, "and probably will not. Our best estimate is that there are roughly eighty five ballistic missiles pointed at us and will be arriving within hours. With all due respect, we haven't got the time to stray off point." Hayden was sorry he had snapped at Dr. Powell. She sat in her chair, staring down at the table looking like a school girl who was just chided by the principal.

Without looking up, she softly asked "What is going to happen to us?"

Hayden took a breath. Kelly was by far the youngest person in the room. Softly he answered her, "We will either die in a nuclear holocaust or cease to exist as the carrier shifts back in time. The odds of being born by the same parents are astronomically small. As to the disposition of our souls, well, we just don't have time to crawl into the more esoteric questions of time travel."

The room was silent. In the drama of this new information they all were receiving, Kelly seemed to be the only one who had thought this past the immediate. Each person sitting at the table fully realized that one way or the other, they were not going to be around to greet the new day.

President Cheney broke the quiet. "Director Hayden, when do you intend to send the *John Stennis* back to and what will it do once there?" Dick was sure that last statement was not grammatically correct. Discussing time travel was creating havoc with his tenses.

It was after one in the morning, Michael Hayden was bone tired and his tooth was acting up again. He hadn't eaten in hours and it was pretty much a given that he was going to miss breakfast. It was time to finish this up and send the *John Stennis* back while there was still time to do so.

"MJ 12 decided to sent a carrier back to December 15, 1941."

"Why not just a week earlier and prevent the attack on Pearl?" General Shelton asked.

"The Japanese attacked on the seventh. Four days later, Germany and Italy declared war on the US. We need to be in the war in order to destroy and dissect the Soviet Union. If we repel Japan with the incredible force available on the *Stennis* we risk the chance of scaring away the Axis."

"From there, we will quickly force Japan into a conditional surrender. Remember, Japan will become an important alley in the future; we want to do as little damage to them as possible. The next step is controversial, but has been shown, through computer scenarios run on the Cray's at Meade, to be the best way to go.

"We are going to support, in a very covert way, Hitler."

"Jesus Christ," Admiral Clark slammed his fist on the table. He was a silver haired fire plug with an uneven temperament. "What the hell are you talking about?"

"Admiral, here are the facts. Even with the fire power on the *Stennis*, it will be very difficult to bring the Soviet Union to its knees. Remember, we need to get them not only to surrender but to put ourselves in a position to dismantle them. We would like to do that without nuking the shit out of them, although that will certainly be a fall back position." Michael was sorry he had used profanity in front of the President. He was brought up well in the fine Southern tradition that did not have a man using untoward language in mixed company, much less before the President of the United States.

"We intend to let Germany do a maximum amount of damage to Russia. The intention is to do that in two ways. First, we will get the Allies to ease back on to Western front. Second, we will provide covert help to them in a number of decisive battles in Russia that will allow them to keep going, prolonging their engagement. We will make sure they get through the winter of '42 and will be operational throughout the summer of '43, if the war goes on that long. Once Germany defeats Russia, a fresh and very fortified United States will then dispatch Germany."

"That certainly makes sense," agreed Shelton.

"The specific battle plan is being loaded into the computers on board the *John Stennis* as we speak, as well as the specific orders and the full background for this operation, now officially dubbed Operation Floating Thunder."

Richard Cheney was feeling very uncomfortable. He knew what was coming next. If he had heard correctly, the president was the only one who could authorize the use of Babylonian. He would not only be ending his own existence, but that of every living thing on the planet. But what were his options?

He was aware of the underground base in Utah built to protect the government from the devastation of a nuclear war. He would also be able to save his own family. What kind of world, however, would be left for the few thousand survivors to live in? With the majority of the current government well past the age of procreation, there was not much hope for the proliferation of man kind. And who would really want to live in a society derived from politicians and lawyers? The ratio of women to men in both the House and Senate was still only one to twenty despite the gains made by women during the past decade.

This, however, was not about him. President Richard Cheney was poised to make a decision that would affect the fate of man. He was being called upon to sacrifice the lives, no, the existence, of not only himself and his family, but of every person on the planet. There was also some question about affecting the existence of all those now dead but born after December 15th, 1941.

All eyes had migrated to him, as each person in the room realized that President Cheney was the one to make this terrible decision. The room was again silent. Dick closed his eyes. He imagined the many difficult decisions that past presidents had to make in this very room. Lincoln and the Emancipation Proclamation, Truman and the Atomic Bomb, Kennedy and his civil rights directives, all hard calls. Each President had made the tough decision, and the right one. The country and man kind in general, benefited from the courage of their resolve. In each case, the ethical and moral questions were staggering. No more so than now.

"Mr. President," Hayden could see the pain he was in, he spoke softly, "we must move now. My people are projecting that the terrorists will have the majority of the missiles operational within hours. If one of them goes off within ten miles of the carrier, we will loose her electronics, leaving us impotent."

President Richard Cheney turned to his secretary, "Get my girls and grandchildren here as fast as possible, use Air Force One if necessary, just get them here."

He turned to Director Hayden. "I authorize Operation Floating Thunder, may God forgive me." President Cheney buried his face in his hands and wept.

July 8, 3:32 AM EST
Norfolk, Va.

Allen Ben-Gurion was driving the family Caravan north east on route 564, heading for the naval base. The boys were fast asleep in their car seats, Rachel was staring out the window, so full of emotion she wasn't registering anything her eyes were seeing. It had started to rain, a light drizzle, just enough to mix with the grease on the road to make things slippery. Allen was concentrating on his driving, mostly to keep his mind off his family.

He hated these good-byes. After who knows how many of them he'd done, he figured he'd have gotten used to them, but he hadn't. Allen felt a deep burning love for

Rachel every time he left her. The prospect of separation always sharpened his feelings, making departures all the more difficult.

He turned around and looked at his sleeping sons. They looked so precious when they slept. It bothered him as he thought of how much of their lives he had missed and would miss as he traveled the world, protecting a people who didn't really seemed to appreciate the sacrifices offered up by a handful of men and women to protect their freedom.

Dov's first steps he viewed on video tape. He wasn't there for his son's first birthday party. He also wasn't there when Dov got sick and there was a scare that he had meningitis. By the time Allen had found out about it, the scare was over. Rachel spent a torturous eighteen hours all by herself wondering if her youngest child was going to see the next day.

Little Yehuda seemed to double in size by the time Allen would return from a tour. He was always so shy of his father for days after Allen's return. A neighbor across the hall had taught him to catch a ball. It wasn't long before he'd be learning to ride a bike. Allen wondered if he'd be home to teach him.

It was difficult to be away from Rachel for months, to deny his carnal needs. Women were so often taken with Naval Aviators. His fellow pilots would return to the ship with stories of debauchery. His faith begged him to not even listen. The love of his family begged him not to partake. It was the latter that made it easier to resist.

As he pulled into the base, Allen had made a very big decision.

"Rachel," he put his hand on her knee, "this will be my last tour. I will resign my commission upon return. We will never be apart again."

Rachel had no more tears left in her. She grabbed Allen's hand, squeezed it, and brought it up to her face.

She had two conflicting emotions, each diametrically opposed to the other, overwhelming her. The deep sadness of Allen's departure was squeezed by his unexpected but joyous news. "Oh God, bring him home to me," she prayed silently.

Their sensitive moment was broken by the guards request to see Allen's identification. Allen and Ensign Fallon had played racket ball two days ago, the usual wave in fell victim to THREATCON DELTA.

Allen had never seen the base so busy. There was always much activity the day a carrier left port. With over six thousand men and women based on the ship and many of their family members in attendance to see them off, the base generally had the feel of a stadium right before a championship game. Early this morning, however, everything felt very differently.

There were far fewer family members congregating near the dock to send off their warriors. Even from a quater of a mile off, Allen could see that equipment was being loaded on to the *Stennis* at a furious pace. A marine Lance Corporal waved Allen's van over a hundred yards before it reached the parking lot reserved for the fly boys.

"You gotta get out here, sir. Sorry, those are my orders, THREATCON and all."

Allen dreaded this moment. Rachel found some more tears to shed. She leaned over and hugged him hard. He gently touched the faces of each child, being careful not to wake them.

Her last words rung in his head as he walked toward the carrier, "I love you Allen Ben-Gurion, please come home to me."

"I will do that," he vowed, knowing he did not have the right to make that pledge as he headed off to war.

As he drew closer to the aircraft carrier, the intensity of the activity increased dramatically. The rain had stopped, small puddles reflected the artificial light that embraced the area. The deck of the *Stennis* was completely covered. He had never seen so many stores being stuffed into her. From his vantage point, he thought he saw the tail of a Stealth F-117 Nighthawk hanging off the deck. "Those are not carrier based planes, what are they doing there," he wondered out loud.

"Must be the new F-117 Seahawk, I didn't think they were operational yet," returned a sailor to his right. "This is real weird."

"Neither did I. What are those things around the bulkhead of the ship?" Allen was pointing to the Delta T coils that had been attached every sixty feet around the deck of the *Stennis*.

"Thought you'd know, Lieutenant."

The coils were even now being powered up. They cast a blue glow giving a bizarre look to everything on the deck. All of the Babylonian hard and software had been installed. The NSA technicians were going through final checks before debarking the ship.

It was an almost chaotic scene. A typical boarding took hours. The crush of sailors and aviators trying to get on the *Stennis* was reminiscent of attempts to board Space Mountain shortly after lunch. "This is going to take a while," Ben-Gurion told Seamen First Class Timothy Irwin.

Director Michael Hayden's helicopter landed in a parking lot a hundred yards from the *USS John C. Stennis*. Commissioned on December 9th, 1995, she was the third newest carrier in the fleet, three years behind the *Truman* and five behind the *USS Ronald Reagen*. She operated under the motto "Unwavering advocate of peace through strength." Many of her crew felt that was a little high brow, so it was informally changed to "Be good or we will kick your ass, because we can." Her claim to fame to date was the first landing of a Super Hornet on a carrier deck. That got a nice article in *Aviation News*.

It took Hayden and Black twenty minutes to work their way through the sea of sailors. The Shore Patrol did their best to clear a corridor for them, but it was still slow going. It was after four in the morning by the time they were sitting down in the Captains ward room.

"Captain, please clear the room of everyone but you and your XO." Hayden was still working under a top secret classification. He was also aware that the fewer people who knew what was going on the better, at least until they were safely back in 1941.

"My Executive Officer is in Bremerton visiting the *Nimitz*, he'll fly out tomorrow."

"Get your Command Master Chief in here, he'll be your new XO."

"That's she, Hayden, Captain Kelly O'Brien. This is her first tour, I'd much prefer to keep Captain Aninowsky, he's been with me for three years."

"There's no time, Harsh, here are your orders." Hayden and Captain Harsh Yoder were neighbors a lifetime ago when they were both stationed in Newport. They hadn't stayed in touch, but did run into each other now and again at various functions.

"Get O'Brien in here," Yoder hollered out his door.

"What the hell are those poles your people are attaching to my ship? Michael, I recognize that we are at THREATCON DELTA, but there's some mighty bizarre shit going on here. Your guys are crawling around some very sensitive places, would you bring me into the loop here." Captain Yoder did not like people screwing around with his ship.

Captain O'Brien arrived and took a seat next to Yoder. Introductions were curt.

"Harsh, most of what you need to know has been down loaded into your computers under Operation Floating

Thunder. Your immediate orders are in here." Hayden handed Captain Yoder a sealed envelope.

"They have to be something if the Director of the NSA is here delivering them personally."

"I am here to remind you that you have sworn an allegiance to the United States of America and, in accepting your commission, have agreed to obey orders without question." Hayden was a little formal.

Captain Yoder was taken aback by Blake's tone. "What have I ever done that would have you questioning my loyalty to the country that I have served for thirty five years?"

"It's not what you've done, Harsh, it's what we are asking you to do now."

July 8, 6:12 AM EST
Newport News Channel, Va.

Captain Yoder had driven the *USS John C. Stennis* on a heading of N36*58.11'W76*21.79', right into the middle of Newport News Channel, approximately two miles off shore. His mind still had not come to terms with what Hayden had told him. There was no time to ponder the reality of what he had just learned. Another seventeen missiles had been fired, four of those were heading for the United States. Project Floating Thunder needed to get underway.

It had started raining again. It was a hard, wind driven rain. Director Michael Hayden stood alone on the dock, looking out into the bay. He was soaked. Visibility was about a hundred feet. He couldn't see the *Stennis*, but he could see the blue light given off by the Delta T coils positioned around the ship. It was an eire sight.

Hayden's tooth throbbed, his stomach was so empty it hurt and the driving rain felt like needles pricking his face. The dense, low clouds prevented him from seeing his last sunrise. The blue lights became more intense. They started to oscillate. There was a searing flash...

CHAPTER 4
1941

December 15th, 1941 6:18 AM EST
Newport News Channel, Va.

"My God," **moaned** Captain Yoder. He was gripping the arms of his chair. He felt sick, hangover sick, and woozy. It felt as if his bones had liquefied and were just now hardening. Harsh Yoder turned to his left and hurled what little there was left in his stomach.

His crew was at battle stations, that was his last order before leaving the twenty first century. Scanning the bridge, he noticed anyone who wasn't sitting was now on his or her knees depositing their last meal on the floor. Captain O'Brien was seated to his left, puke all over her shirt, trying to get up. Looks like she had a big dinner, Yoder guessed.

"Status report," he yelled. His throat was dry.

People were struggling to their feet, doing their best to ignore the mess and smell that enveloped the area, and began trying to communicate with the rest of the ship. Yoder leaned forward to survey the deck. From the Captain's chair, four stories up, he could survey the entire deck, where everything still had a blue glow to it. There were sporadic sparks coming from the Delta T coils.

Yoder glanced at his chronometer; the digital readouts were all at 0. His watch had stopped at 6:14, the moment of time shift. There was a thick fog surrounding the ship. The electronic equipment on the bridge seemed to be working. He could see sailors moving about on the deck below.

The radar looked to be working. "Give me a fix Ensign."

"Sir, we are at N36*58.11'.W76*21.79'."

'Exactly where we started out.'

He turned to the Comms Officer, "See if you can raise the base." Yoder needed to know *when* he was.

"I'm getting nothing, sir."

Reports were coming back, there seemed to be no damage to the ship.

Without any visual or radio contact, there was no way of knowing where the hell, when the hell, he was.

"Sir, all satellite contact is down. Comm links are off line. We have no communications."

Either all the communications equipment has malfunctioned, or we are indeed sitting in Newport News Channel one week after the Japanese attacked Pearl Harbor. Yoder felt his head start to throb.

He walked across the hall and stepped out on to the Vultures Nest. It was a narrow balcony that allowed full survey of both ends of the deck. It was cold and damp. A lot colder than it should be in July. Kind of like winter in Virginia.

"Shit, we're back in 1941."

"Excuse me Sir?" It was O'Brien. She had followed him out on to the nest.

"Captain O'Brien, call a staff meeting, pronto. You might want to change your shirt. Keep us on battle alert."

"Holy shit, what the hell was that?" Tommy's eyes were burned; the pain caused him to close them tight. His retina's had the last thing he saw etched onto them. He steadied himself by gripping the table he was standing next to.

The guard booth Tommy Moretti stood in was over a hundred yards from the water. He fumbled around the table and found the field phone. Tommy cranked the handle a few times.

"Yes sir, I know it's early, but there's something going on down here." His voice was full of anxiety.

"Yes sir, but I can't see. There was a giant blue flash out in the water..."

"No, there was to much fog to see much past the water's edge. I was just looking out the front of my guard booth and then there was a flash.

"No, well, I did hear a humming sound, wait, it's still there, but it's getting fainter."

Admiral Bellinger was already getting dressed. He called for his secretary to get him an MP and a jeep.

"This is Captain Yoder; please give me your undivided attention."

Tim Irwin leaned his mop against the stainless steel counter and looked up at the monitor hung in the corner of the cooking area. He was cleaning up the partially digested remains of a not very memorable meal, though oddly, it was not as bad coming up as it was going down.

This was Tim's first assignment since leaving boot camp two weeks earlier. He had spent a few days visiting his parents in Babylon, NY, then headed down to Norfolk. He wasn't even assigned to the *Stennis*. Upon arrival, his orders were changed and he was told to 'get his ass on the aircraft carrier.'

When battle stations were called, he didn't know where to go, so he went to the galley. Hell, he was a cook, maybe they'd need him to make some donuts when the fighting started. Wouldn't he feel like a dick kneading dough while his shipmates were on deck throwing bullets at the bad guys. Timmy was still a cheesed at being told, after a battery of tests, that he was best suited to being a cook. He'd never done much more in a kitchen than heat up a can of Spaghetti-O's, now the Navy recognized his apparently hidden talents in the culinary arts.

Captain Yoder could be seen on any of the two hundred plus television monitors spread about the ship and could be heard on one of the speakers that was placed in every compartment.

"First of all, I want to assure every member of my ship that we have not been attacked. What I have to tell you is going to be difficult to believe, I'm not even sure how to go about this." Harsh hadn't enough time to prepare a speech but was anxious to let his crew know what was going on. His executive staff was still sitting in the ward room, silently staring at each other. He thought he heard someone crying as he left.

"This is right out of science fiction. Well, the short of it is that we have, what is called, time shifted. The current date is December 15th, 1941." Yoder paused, if the meeting fifteen minutes ago was any indication, he was talking to six thousand plus people who were trying to decide if they had heard wrong or if the Captain had lost his mind.

"You did not hear wrong, the current date is December 15, 1941. As you all know, our world was facing total destruction a few hours back," or was it sixty years in the future, "and there was nothing we could do about that. Even if we were able to neutralize all of the incoming ballistic missiles heading for the US, which is doubtful, the detonations in other parts of the world would throw enough debris into the upper atmosphere to cause a nuclear winter. It would last long enough to kill all the plant life on this planet. That would pretty much be the ball game."

Tim Irwin, Seamen First Class, gripped the metal counter he was standing next to. A thousand thoughts charged through his head, "This can't happen, the captain is nuts, will I be born again in 1974, where is my family? When will we go back?"

Captain Yoder continued, "The first question my staff asked me is when will we go back. It seems, unfortunately, that this was a one way ticket." Harsh had taken a cursory look at the Operation Floating Thunder files. "Backwards time travel is possible, forwards time travel either is not possible or the egg heads who figured this out haven't figured that out. The bottom line is that we are here for the duration. There are going to be many questions concerning the implications implied by time travel, I am not prepared to discuss them just now.

"The second question the staff had was what is our mission plan. I cannot give you those details, but we have direct orders from the President of the United States," would that be Cheney or Roosevelt? "I can tell you, however, that we will be fighting in the Second World War."

The largest fighting ship in the world was silent. The only audible noise was the mechanical heart beat of the *Stennis*. As Captain Yoder sat staring at the red light on top of the camera before him wondering what to say next, he heard a roar. Quiet at first, it progressively grew in intensity until, like a wave rushing to shore, it hit him.

Six thousand fighting men and women, with fists in the air, turned their confusion and fear into a focused energy that would help carry them through this difficult time. They were, after all, warriors. Now, not only were they going to war, but they were poised, by virtue of their vastly superior weapons, to be an "unwavering advocate of peace through strength." Axis ass was going to be kicked in a most aggressive way. The crew of the *USS John C. Stennis* was ready for a fight. The crew of the *USS John C. Stennis* needed a fight.

"We're getting into a shooting war and I'm a fucking cook!" Tim was angry. He was also scared and confused, just like the rest of the crew. Only his release would not be splashing Tojo's Zero's over the Pacific, his release would be cooking poor quality beef byproducts and listening to fly boy's tell stories about their latest victories. "This sucks on so many levels."

Captain Yoder felt a flush of pride to hear the reaction of his crew. He was hoping for a quick engagement to keep the moral up. When they finally sat down and thought about what has happened, the morale officer was going to have her work cut out for her.

"Our first priority will be to make contact with our counterparts on shore. For now, stand down. Remember, we are all in this together. There are going to be some acute emotional reactions over the next few hours and days. We must stay focused, we have a war to win." Yoder nodded to the camera man to shut down.

Harsh leaned back in his chair and closed his eyes. "Holy shit."

The gallery staff started to wander in. Tim hadn't met anybody. Most of them had just finished the last tour together and had already formed that subtle bond men typically develop when they live and work in close quarters. They were either full of bravado over the impending war or white faced over the news that they technically had not been born yet.

"Hey, I'm Parnes Williams, from Toledo, Ohio." Tim was constantly amused that every time he met someone in the service they felt compelled to announce where they were from. Parnes was a tall, lanky black man with a loose stride and enormous hands.

"Ain't this some shit," Parnes extended a giant hand.

"Tim Irwin, nice to meet you, and yes, this is some shit." He considered whether to add, Babylon, New York, but decided against it.

"Where you from?"

Jesus, "Long Island, New York." At some point, Tim wondered, the question may be *when* you from!

"Man, we gonna kick some ass." Parnes was dancing around the kitchen, shooting an imaginary gun.

"No, my brother, you and I are going to cook some ass. Take a look around, this is our battlefield and here's your weapon," he tossed his fellow kitchen warrior a pot.

I gotta get out of here, Seaman First Class Irwin decided.

"All right, how do we go about contacting our friends on shore? We need to do something before this fog lifts." Captain Yoder was back in his ward room with the executive staff.

Ensign Robert Caulfield was head of the communications department, "With a little back engineering we should be able to communicate by radio. I'll need, however, some frequencies. We don't want to just start broadcasting randomly."

It would have been nice of MJ 12 to have provided us with them, thought Yoder. His initial glance at the Operation Floating Thunder file before the meeting reveled nothing that would seem to be of help as to how and who to contact on shore.

"We need to talk to the Base Commander, maybe our data base has something on who that might be. Bobby, would you boot up your terminal and look into that. You should find loads of history on our server, the NSA guys added a huge amount of memory to the main frame and filled it with some very specific information about World War Two and the 1940's in general."

Ensign Caulfield started a search while the Captain kept talking.

"We will try to keep as low profile as possible while sitting exposed in the middle of Newport News Channel. The recommendation is to have the Base Commander..."

"That'd be one Admiral Bellinger. These new files are huge, there's a couple of terabits of information in here."

"Thanks Bob, we'll need to have Admiral Bellinger secure the base. We will have to put into dock to clear some of that stuff off our deck."

"Sir," Captain O'Brien joined in, "I wonder if we just want to sit here and let them come to us?"

"I'd hate to spook them, Captain. I know if I were Base Commander and woke up to find an aircraft carrier that was not registered to the US Navy sitting two miles off my base, I'd be some what uncomfortable. It's barely a week after Pearl; they are probably a little jumpy. I sure as shit don't want to take any incoming fire."

"Found them, Captain, I have the frequencies of every radio on the base. I could also tell you how many toilets the place has. This data is incredibly complete," Bob Caulfield was glued to his monitor.

"Excellent, Bob, print them out. Captain O'Brien, come with me to the radio room and let's introduce ourselves to Admiral Bellinger. The rest of you, work out a protocol for proving to him that we are on his side and that this is not some enemy trick."

Seaman First Class Tommy Moretti was being attended to by a pharmacist mate as Admiral Bellinger arrived. His eyes were bandaged and he was sitting on a stool, drinking a cup of coffee. Lieutenant Avallone had already questioned him. Frank Avallone was the head of base security. He had been working with Admiral Bellinger on tightening security for the past week. Two nights ago he was yanked out of bed because, what had been ascertained later, a squirrel had dropped nuts on one of his younger guards. Everyone was pretty edgy since Roosevelt declared war.

"What happened Frank, we don't have another rogue squirrel here do we?" Bellinger was tired. Every American military installation in the world was on heightened status. He'd had meeting after meeting making sure everything and everybody was tight. The constant rains of the past week had not helped any. It had been a cold, wet winter in Virginia. Not nearly as bad as the winters of his youth in Massachusetts, but nasty just the same.

"Moretti here says he saw blue flash out on the water. It must have been pretty intense, he is temporarily blinded."

"He going to be all right?" Moretti couldn't have been days older than eighteen. He looked like he should be heading for the high school prom, not a war.

"Won't know for a while, I'll send him to the hospital when you're done with him."

Bellinger walked over to the young Seamen, "Moretti, how you feeling, it's Admiral Bellinger."

Tommy Moretti sat up right and saluted, spilling coffee all over his lap.

"Sir, I'm sorry I bothered you, I thought we might be under attack, like at Pearl." His voice was high and very tense, he spoke rapidly.

"Calm down, son. I just want to know what you saw." Bellinger was hoping that what ever it was would not be the last thing this young man would ever see.

"Sir, it was just a brilliant flash of blue light. I recall there was a loud crack, kinda like thunder when it hits real close. I thought I saw the silhouette of a ship, a real big ship, which I found odd as the fog was so thick I could barely see down to the dock. There was a humming sound, like I said before, but it seems to have gone away."

"Frank, why don't you get a boat out there, look around the harbor. This fog should be lifting soon, it's almost seven."

It was a three minute drive back to his office. As Admiral Bellinger was walking in the door, his secretary was holding up the phone. "It's for you, sir, a Captain Yoder, he says it is urgent."

Bellinger repeated the name as he walked over to his desk, he didn't recognize it.

"Admiral Bellinger, this is Captain Yoder of the *USS John C. Stennis*."

"Captain, I'm not familiar with the *Stennis*, where is she based."

"Norfolk, Virginia, Sir."

Bellinger was getting agitated. "This some kind of a joke. I've never heard of the *Stennis* and I sure as hell would have if she were parked on my base!"

"Admiral Bellinger, I apologize for sounding somewhat cryptic, but the *Stennis* is an aircraft carrier and she is sitting two miles out in Newport News Channel. The fog has lifted somewhat, you should be able to get a visual on us."

"Just a minute." Bellinger put the phone down, grabbed a pair of binoculars off his desk and walked to his window. He had a spectacular view of the docks and the harbor.

"Oh my God." She was sitting port side in to the shore. Admiral Bellinger needed to move his binoculars stem to stern, on tight focus he couldn't get all of her into view. And there, in large white letters, was *USS John C. Stennis*, whoever the hell that was. She had to be all of one thousand feet. Her deck was loaded with boxes and crates. And the damn strangest airplanes he'd ever seen.

Lieutenant Avallone came crashing into his office and stopped abruptly when he saw Admiral Bellinger staring out the window.

"What the hell is that?" he barked.

"That, Lieutenant Avallone, is the *John C. Stennis*."

He turned, walked back to his desk and picked up the phone.

"I'm sorry, Captain, Yoder was it? That is one large ship you have there. What's it doing here?"

"That, I'm afraid, is a long complicated story. May I invite you aboard for breakfast Captain, we have the best galley in the Navy."

"Oh my God!" He was speaking to his Boss. Father Anthony Salvatore was the ships chaplain. This was his second tour on board the *Stennis*. There was a line outside his door. He knew what they wanted, but he didn't think he could give it to them. He'd had his face buried in the Bible for the past ninety minutes. Not surprisingly, there was nothing that addressed time travel.

They would be questioning him about where they stood in this new universe. They would want to know if they hadn't been 'born yet,' were they still baptized. Would the good works they had done during their lives still 'count for them?' Would the bad things they had done during their lives still 'count against them?' They would want to know what has happened to their families.

These were overwhelmingly complicated religious and personal issues and Tony Salvatore did not have a clue as to how to address them. Every one of the six thousand men and women on the ship was facing the loss of every loved one in their lives. On a typical cruise, he'd be called upon to comfort two dozen people who had lost a parent to death or a spouse to divorce. The last cruise provided him with the horror of telling a mother that her little boy had drowned. It took him days to come to terms with that. Now, the entire crew was facing a similar reality.

He knew it would take some days and even weeks to allow the emotions of such devastating losses to seep to the surface. Father Salvatore would be called upon constantly to provide comfort and healing. But who healed the healer. Who was going to help him deal with his own tragic losses.

Anthony had just turned thirty on December seventh, 'a day that will live in infamy.' He got more than a little ribbing about that at the Immaculate Conception Seminary in Lloyd Harbor, New York, where he spent four years learning the priest game. On each of the four birthdays he'd spent there, his friends would through the now famous "Infamy Day Party." They would throw back a beer or two and spend the rest of the evening misquoting various passages from the bible. The one who could come up with the most "Infamous" quote would win. They were hard pressed to credit their favorite quote, "Let's take a little nip and get bombed," to any book of the Bible, but they were rebel enough to break their own rules.

Such hi-jinks were about as wild as he could remember. He knew he wanted to become a priest after coming home from the Marist Missionary Camp he attended one summer when he was ten. He had the calling, as his Parish Priest had dubbed it. Tony dedicated his young life to good works and service to God. His life was insulated for eight years by the Nuns at Saint Pat's Elementary School in Huntington, by the Brothers for four years at Chaminade High School in Mineola, another four years with the Jesuits at Fordham, and, of course, another four years at the seminary in Lloyd Harbor. By the time he was ordained, he needed to get away from New York. He also needed to get away from Jane Graves.

Throughout his formative High School years, Anthony didn't have any girl trouble. Not that he didn't break any hearts. He was a nice looking young man with a wonderful personality and a sweet disposition. His mom even told him so. All right, maybe his mom was the only one who told him so. It never took much more than a quick glance in the mirror to recognize that his nose was a little too 'Roman.' And maybe he was on the short side. It would have been nice had his parents gotten him braces like his sister. "You're going to marry God, he doesn't care if your teeth are straight," was the answer he got when he questioned his mother about the unfortunate migration of his incisors.

But it was during his first assignment at Saint Patrick's Church where he met Jane. She was five years his junior. Light brown hair with large round eyes and a nose that mocked his own in its perfection, she made him wonder, for the first time, if he had made a mistake becoming a priest. They bonded hard and were frequent companions. As the years progressed, their forbidden passion was palpable between them. There were dark nights alone in the chapel when Father Anthony would beg God to unburden him of the lust that grew in his heart.

The answer came innocuously enough, as answers to his prayers had always come, with a letter to his Parish from the Navy looking for chaplains. Join the Navy, see the world, save some souls. It seemed like the perfect answer for his need to get away... To run away.

Now, here he was, eight hundred miles and sixty one years away from home, preparing to explain to every man and woman who walked through his door that their families were nothing more than memories. "I need your help," he was looking up at the ceiling, "if you're still there."

"Well, Captain Yoder, I believe you are right about your galley," he turned to O'Brien, "can you get me another one of those, what are they again?"

"Pop tarts, Sir."

Admiral Bellinger was overwhelmed. There was no other way to put it. For the past three hours, Captain Yoder and his staff had ferried him about the *Stennis* introducing him to twenty first century fighting technology. Nuclear power, mach two fighter planes, smart bombs, it was all more than he could comprehend. While having the wonders of computers explained to him, he actually became dizzy. What a wonderful place the twenty first century must be, he thought. Why, however, have they come back?

All of his professional questions were answered. Few of his personal questions were. During moments when his mind wasn't racing to comprehend what he was seeing, he was contemplating questions about how the war they had just entered would turn out, though looking around made that pretty much rhetorical. These men know much. There computers seemed to know even more. They probably know when and how he was going to die!

"The question that must be uppermost in your mind, Admiral Bellinger, is the one I cannot answer. Our mission here is classified. As you know, you are our first contact. What we need now is to meet with President Roosevelt. I would appreciate your helping arrange that."

"Of course, I'll put in a call to Secretary Knox. He'll arrange a meeting with Roosevelt." How the hell was he going to explain this over the phone? "In the interim, I'll assign a dock to you and get some equipment to help you clear your deck. I don't know where exactly, but I'll find a place to store that material."

"I'd need everything that goes on from here on in to remain classified," Yoder added.

"Right now, Captain, that's going to be impossible, you're sitting right in the middle of Newport News Channel. There's probably half a hundred people on shore as we speak with some serious questions, not to mention all the men on the base. I'll assure you of this, however, we will tighten up security like never before.

"Captain Yoder, I am glad you are on our side. Let me get out of here, there's much to do."

It was early evening before the *Stennis* was docked. Bellinger provided a security detail on Yoder' request to keep unauthorized personnel off the ship. And to keep his personnel on it. Most of the crew had been on at least one tour with him. They were an unremarkable group from a disciplinary perspective, however, he would take no chances. There was real danger having one of his crew running rampant in a 1941 America.

By nine o'clock Yoder had turned over his ship to Captain O'Brien. From what he had seen of her so far, he liked. She was sharp and professional. She had to have something on the ball to become one of the first female Captains in this man's Navy. He was glad to see a deeper integration of woman into the services. After Congress finally passed HR-345.002, opening up combat units to women, they began taking their military careers more seriously. The men began taking the women more seriously also.

Harsh Yoder sat at the small desk in his tiny state room. Ranking officers in the other branches of the service would never put up with accommodations this cramped. Another perk from the Navy.

He hadn't slept for over thirty hours, he was stupid tired. There was now time to reflect on what had transpired this day. If felt more like a week since he left the year 2002. It was a stunning transformation. Harsh wasn't scheduled to join the world for another thirteen years. What then, would he be born again? How the hell would that work? He was to tired to think analytically now.

Harsh picked up the only photograph on his desk. It was taken in '91. His wife was holding their little boy, he was only four. He rarely let this picture trigger his emotions, but tonight, he was to tired to keep them at bay. Tears encroached on the corners of his eyes.

His little boy. He so loved that little guy. It was because of him that Harsh almost put in for a desk job. Now he sat crying over someone who has never existed. If he never was, maybe the pain Jeb felt never was. Maybe those last hours, when the leukemia tortured his little body, had never happened.

Harsh prayed to a God he hoped had traveled back in time with him that it hadn't happened. But he would never be able to erase from his mind the look of fear on Jeb's face during those last hours as the reaper stood over him. At the end, he simply said "Daddy," and went limp. Jeb died in Harsh's arms.

Harsh wept. He let it flow, it was the only way. It was a necessary purging, something that had to be done every so often. These were emotions that could not be put off to long for fear that they would consume him.

The marriage broke up months later. Neither could look at the other without seeing Jeb. Harsh put his damaged heart into the Navy while Linda went back to school to get her law degree. They were still friends.

Harsh crawled into bed and passed out.

Allen Ben-Gurion woke up with a start. He had slept deeply. It took two steps to cross his tiny room and arrive at his desk. Like he did every morning when he was on tour, he grabbed a piece of stationary and a pen and began to write, "Dear Rachel..."

Oh my God, he realized, she's gone. Yehuda and Dov, his parents, all gone. *Israel* is gone! Allen held his head in his hands, he was overwhelmed. His last promise to Rachel would not be kept, he would not be coming home to her.

Throughout the ship, men and women were waking up to the cold reality that their memories were now merely fantasies. Everything and everyone left behind did not exist for them and never did exit. There was a malaise creeping from deck to deck like a fog. There was no joy on the *Stennis* this morning.

"**Captain, it's Admiral** Bellinger on the line." Yoder took the receiver from Ensign Grant.

"Good morning Captain Yoder, how are things on the *Stennis*?"

"I wouldn't say we're in bristol fashion just yet. Operationally, we seem to be sound, but emotionally, I believe it will take a few days to get back up to speed. Have you arranged my meeting?"

"Yes, President Roosevelt and his cabinet will see you at 0200. I'll have a staff car ready for you at noon." Bellinger spent twenty minutes on the phone with Secretary Knox trying to convince him that he wasn't out of his mind.

"Great, however, I think Captain O'Brien and I will chopper over, it'll take barely twenty minutes by air. Maybe you could prepare the White House for our somewhat unorthodox arrival; we'll land on the South Lawn."

Admiral Bellinger recalled being shown the helicopters below deck. Vertical take off and landing capabilities, their 'unorthodox arrival' will certainly help Web's credibility and Yoder's, for that matter. He still was a little unsure if Knox really believed what he had been told.

"Why don't you fly over with us?"

President Franklin Delano Roosevelt sat in the Oval Office. He had wheeled himself around his desk to face Frank Knox.

"Frank, what's this all about? Henry will be here shortly."

With that, Henry L. Stimson walked in.

"Mr. President, Frank, why the urgency, have we been attacked again?" Henry Stimson was the Secretary of

War to a country that was at war. He was a very busy man at the moment and didn't suffer interruptions gladly.

"Frank, the floor is yours."

"Henry, Mr. President, I received a call from Admiral Bellinger last night."

"Bellinger is the Commander of the Navel Base at Norfolk," Henry volunteered.

"Continue," Roosevelt requested.

"I have yet to personally confirm what he told me, but it is of a most fantastic nature. Apparently, yesterday morning at around six or so, an aircraft carrier suddenly appeared in the middle of Newport News Channel."

"Is it one of ours?" Roosevelt was alarmed, shouldn't he have been informed earlier?

"Well, sort of. What I mean, Mr. President," Frank was wondering if he would be relieved from his Cabinet position after he completed the next sentence, "is that it is commissioned to the United States Navy. However, its origin is the year 2002." He got just the look he expected from Franklin Roosevelt. The President cocked his head slightly and squinted.

"Are you suggesting, Mr. Knox, that there is a ship sitting off the coast of Virginia from the future?" Roosevelt was incredulous, what sort of poppycock was this?

"Yes Sir, remarkably, that is exactly what I am saying." Frank was looking down at the Presidential Seal on the carpet. He suddenly didn't want to be there.

"Frank, are you feeling all right?" Stimson was out of sorts.

"Gentlemen, I understand your reaction. I had Admiral Bellinger on the phone for quite some time. I've known him for fifteen years, he's an officer and a gentleman. He's a Harvard man, for Christ sakes, class of '21." Knox hoped that would add some credibility, Roosevelt was a Harvard man himself, class of '03.

"This is all quite remarkable, Frank. If they are indeed from the future, why then are they here?" Roosevelt questioned.

"You can be damn well sure it has something to do with this war you've gotten us into, Franklin." Stimson had been an isolationist before his Cabinet appointment thirteen months prior.

"From what Admiral Bellinger told me, the weapons technology aboard that ship is astounding. They have planes capable of traveling three times the speed of sound. There are some type of unmanned bombs that can fly hundreds of miles and level an entire city. Apparently the power plant doesn't even run on fossil fuels, it uses some sort of nuclear reaction, I don't understand, but it is quite astonishing!

"The Captain of the ship, it's called the *USS John C. Stennis*, by the way, will be here in ninety minutes, I thought it prudent to have you meet with him as quickly as possible. He will, what did Bellinger say, chopper in, I think. They have some sort of plane that can take off and land vertically. Captain Yoder, Harsh Yoder, asked that the South Lawn be cleared."

"Harsh Yoder, that's an odd name. Do you know anything about him," asked the President?

"Nothing more than he's the Captain of an aircraft carrier from the future," replied Frank Knox.

"This is outrageous," added Stimson. "Let's be sure to have a security detail out on the South Lawn."

Captains Yoder, O'Brien and Admiral Bellinger had taken off from the recently cleared deck of the *Stennis* less that twenty minutes before in a Sikoursky Sea King helicopter. Arnold Bellinger was excited enough to loose the cool, dispassionate professionalism a Captain was expected to wear on his sleeve. He had flown only a handful of times before this, infrequently enough to make each flight a thrill. His sailor days were spent at fifteen knots, maybe twenty if his ship was in a real hurry. Now, here he was, clipping the trees at, what did the pilot tell him, a hundred and fifty miles an hour.

Admiral Bellinger had been given a helmet with a head set built into it. Although the helicopter was fairly noisy, he could hear what everyone was saying quite clearly. The pilot, Lieutenant Gary Smolinsky, spent much of the short flight showing off his chopper. He seemed genuinely pleased to be explaining next century technology to his last century passenger. Captain Yoder just sat back and enjoyed the ride. There was definitely some fun to be had telling the guy who was still riding a horse what your new Ferrari was capable of.

As Yoder looked out the window, he was surprised at how different the landscape looked. He made this flight fairly often back, well, in the future, and always enjoyed the relatively leisure pace of a helicopter. It gave him time to do just what he was doing now, enjoy the view.

His initial reaction embarrassed him. Everything was in color! Harsh's perception of the 1940's was formed mostly from old film clips and movies, all shot in black and white. The sepia world his mind had told him to expect just wasn't there. While it was true, most of the cars seemed to be black, he was tracking a stunningly shiny red Hudson traveling along a main road.

The land was surly less crowded. The chopper hadn't yet reached the city. The suburbs of Virginia they were currently flying over were bucolic and peaceful. The houses were small, wood framed buildings, each with a laundry line full of clothes strung out across the back yard. Many of the chimneys betrayed the fire that was burning in the hearth with white plumes of smoke on this cool winter afternoon. He could almost smell the pies cooling on the window sills. Harsh guessed that most of the houses were occupied right this moment with, what would sadly become a rarity in the coming years, stay at home mom's. Some of whom were outside, each of whom looked up as this most bizarre looking flying machine flew over them, the rotors snapping their distinctive, if not strange, whooping sound. A few waved, most were to stunned to do anything but stare.

The big difference between then and now was the wonderful lack of mini malls and fast food restaurants. No happy clowns or giant hamburgers trying to entice every passerby to partake in some unfortunately unhealthy meal. There didn't seem to be a lick of neon within ten years of here. There also seemed to be a few highways missing. Aside from the presence of color, it was all just as he was expecting it to be.

The view of Washington, DC, startled him. The majority of the large buildings that gave 2002 Washington its distinctive look were simply not there, yet! The absence of the infamous Watergate, the Hilton, the garish Trump Palace, left a void that caused his eyes to settle on the Capitol Building. The City looked more stately, more like the Capitol of the United States rather than just another major metropolis.

Lieutenant Smolinsky banked the chopper over the White House, faced it into the wind and started his decent. Yoder scanned the area, he saw that there were at least fifty soldiers, each holding an M1 rifle to his chest, surrounding the spot that the helicopter was heading for. He was amused to see them wearing the old steel pot helmets and leggings.

"Some greeting they have for us." Captain O'Brien had noticed their welcoming committee also.

"Let's play it cool. Put yourself in their position, this has to be even more disturbing to them."

"I'm sure it's just a precaution. I spoke with Frank Knox myself to set up this meeting." Admiral Bellinger was embarrassed by such an obvious and unwarranted show of force.

Smolinsky parked the three ton chopper with the grace of a ballet dancer. The soldiers moved back as the rotor wash charged the air. The door dropped open and Captain Yoder stepped down onto the lawn. He was overcome with the urge to say "Take me to your leader."

As a Captain, and the Captain of an air craft carrier at that, he was used to having a ranking officer duck a little and run over to greet him as he exited the craft. Everyone before him seemed to be in fear of loosing their heads and opted to let Yoder come forward, unescorted.

Captain Yoder looked for the man in charge. His experience told him that if there are a bunch of civilians around, the guy in the uniform is the one you want to see, if the inverse is the case, it is probably the guy in the suite who reigns supreme.

"I'm Captain Yoder."

"Captain Yoder, I'm Secretary of the Navy Frank Knox," he extended a hand.

"Nice to meet you sir," he had to speak loudly to be heard over the noise of the helicopter, "this is my Executive Officer, Captain Kelly O'Brien, and I believe you know Admiral Bellinger."

"Nice to meet you too, please, come with me, President Roosevelt is waiting."

Franklin Delano Roosevelt had struggled to his feet. He stood behind his great mahogany desk, leaning on his finger tips to keep his balance. If this man he was about to meet was indeed from the future, then he would certainly know that Franklin suffered from poliomyelitis. If not, he was not about to show weakness. He did not become President by showing weakness.

Captain Yoder was surprised by how little the White House had changed, or not changed, since his last visit. He, Captain O'Brien and Frank Knox were being escorted through the halls by four armed guards, two leading, two behind. Admiral Bellinger stayed in the outer office. Yoder, O'Brien and Bellinger were ushered into the Oval Office. Two of the guards left, the other two positioned themselves towards the back of the room.

"Captain Yoder, I presume." Roosevelt offered a hand.

Captain Yoder felt a tingle go up his spine. This was a figure from history, a legend. Although Harsh did not agree with President Roosevelt's New Deal, his taking the Nation off the gold standard or allowing deficits in the budget, he was prepared to recognize the strength and courage Franklin Roosevelt showed during one of the more difficult periods in American history. Within two months of his first term there were thirteen million unemployed Americans and almost every bank in the country was closed. By year three of his Presidency, the Nation had achieved some measure of recovery. He did all that while battling the ravages of polio.

"It is an honor to meet you, Mr. President. May I present my Executive Officer, Captain Kelly O'Brien." Yoder felt like a kid sneaking up behind his favorite sports hero and touching his jacket.

Roosevelt was wearing a dark suit with a white handkerchief sharply folded in his breast pocket. His hair was gray but full. He was strikingly handsome. Yoder was surprised at the strength of Roosevelt's handshake and even more surprised at the rich timber of his voice. The old kinescopes he had heard of Roosevelt addressing the nation on the eve of World War Two did not do him justice.

"Captain Yoder, please have a seat. You've already met Frank Knox, Secretary of the Navy, and this is Henry Stimson, my Secretary of War."

Captain Yoder had read a brief bio on each man from the data base on the *Stennis*. Stimson was a tall wiry man who would guide the Country through the war and return to his law practice in 1945, shortly after Roosevelt's death. This was his second stint as Secretary of War, serving in the post between 1911 through 1913 under President Taft.

Knox was a quiet, thoughtful man who was wise enough to know that he did not know as much about naval warfare as his Admirals and would give them the freedom they needed to win the war.

They all sat, Knox and Stimson flanking Yoder and O'Brien. Roosevelt could see how uncomfortable Captain Yoder was, and as the consummate politician, took the pressure off him by speaking first.

"Frank here tells me you are from the future, the year 2002, I believe."

What a conversation this is going to be, thought Harsh. He had with him a copy of a file entitled, "How to broach President Roosevelt on Operation Floating Thunder." It printed out to one hundred and forty eight pages. MJ 12 had spent considerable time pondering how to approach this delicate and awkward subject. It had made sense to Yoder three hours ago when he read it, but now, sitting face to face with the man, it seemed a little formal.

Yoder liked Roosevelt immediately. The President made direct eye contact when he spoke and sported a comforting smile as he did so. It was easy to see how the country put their trust in him during the depression and had returned him to office twice after his first term. Yoder felt very much at ease with the man.

"Yes Sir, July 8th, 2002."

"Can you appreciate that I find that difficult to believe?"

"Not a lot more difficult to believe than I do, Mr. President. Less than forty eight hours ago, I had no idea that we, the United States, had the capability to travel in time. From what I have been told, this is the first time this technology has been used. Once you, or one of your emissaries, are able to visit the *USS Stennis*, I believe you will no longer have any doubts about the veracity of my claim."

"All right, Captain Yoder, lets, for the moment, assume that you have indeed traveled sixty one years back in time. Why are you here?"

There's the big question, Yoder knew. He thought they might spar a little more over Harsh's outrageous claim. Roosevelt was a man of action. He needed the facts, not unlike he himself when he faced Michael Hayden over Floating Thunder for the first time.

"The short story is that the world of 2002 was facing annihilation from terrorist wielding nuclear weapons. A nuclear weapon is, essentially, a bomb, about the size of your desk, with enough power to easily level Washington. The United States alone had as many as forty five of these weapons on their way as we shifted out of that time continuum." Yoder paused to let this information sink in.

Stimson had a thousand questions. He was up on the edge of his seat, biting his lower lip, trying to keep them from erupting out of his mouth. Less than two weeks ago, Stimson was appointed to the Top Policy Group and was made privy to the ongoing research on the atomic bomb. Harsh was aware that the President was not in that loop yet and made it a point not to betray Stimson's position.

Stimson recognized that Roosevelt would address everything in his own methodical, thoughtful way. The two men were very different. Stimson sat back and accepted that he was along for the ride.

"We'll get back to exactly what a nuclear weapon is in a moment, I think Henry will be quite anxious to hear more, but who is threatening America," asked Roosevelt?

My God, thought Yoder, how am I going to explain the geopolitics of sixty years into the future? He closed the note book that was on his lap and placed it on the President's desk. Yoder took a deep breath and began, what he hoped, would be a cogent explanation of the expansion of Russia, the fall of Communism, and the key role terrorism will play in this twisted story.

"At the end of World War Two, which, by the way, we win, Russia will embark on an expansionist policy. They will have lost over twenty million men repelling Germany from its boarders. It was an appalling loss of humanity. To be sure that never happens again, Stalin will decide to buffer Russia with what will be called Satellite States. He will consume Poland, Yugoslavia, Ukraine, Romania, Belarus, Latvia, Luthuania, Estonia, Bulgaria, half of Germany, well, suffice to say, Stalin will be taking over every country that he now shares a boarder with except for China."

"Churchill is very concerned that Uncle Joe, as he likes to refer to Stalin, is prepared to assume an expansionist posture." Roosevelt was not surprised at Churchill's insight, "It looks like he is correct."

"He certainly was, or is. Under this tyrannical and terrible reign of terror, Stalin will build Russia, or the Soviet Union, into a world power, second only to the United States. By the way, Stalin will kill an estimated six million of his own people to purge the country of everyone who is foolish enough to oppose him openly.

"Russia will also develop a nuclear capability months after we develop ours. Prior to July 8th, 2002, the United States will have been the first and only country to use nuclear weapons. We will drop two nuclear bombs in 1945, one on Hiroshima and one on Nagasaki, forcing Japan to sue for peace.

"At war's end, Russia will refuse to leave the countries it occupied during the war. They will try to take all of Germany. The Allies will contest their occupation leading to a dramatic and huge air lift operation. Russia will eventually back down, but not until it has control over roughly half of Germany."

Roosevelt was keen to know exactly how he was going to win this just born war, how many casualties he could expect, but he realized, if this fantastic story Captain Yoder was telling was true, then a history that has yet to be written will be rewritten.

"This will mark the beginning of, what will be dubbed, the cold war. Throughout the decades, the Soviet Union will export communism throughout the world, from Indonesia to South America and right near our boarders in Cuba. In 1962 we will come dangerously close to World War Three when the leader of Russia, Mr. Krushchev, will attempt to place nuclear weapons on Cuban soil. There was a tense standoff between he and our own President Kennedy, Joe Kennedy's son, that will see Krushchev backing down."

Roosevelt had just received a series of calls from Joe Kennedy. He was in England and wanted to know how he could help with our war effort. Roosevelt didn't trust Kennedy, he wasn't planning to return his calls. He was sure this bit of news would please that opinionated bastard.

"Around this time, the term 'mutually assured destruction' was coined. Both the United States and the Soviet Union possessed enough nuclear weapons to destroy each other seven or eight times over. We had somewhat of a Faustian bargain. There will be a constant escalation of arms during the next thirty five years. In 1981, Ronald Reagen will enter office. He will adopt a hard line policy towards the Soviet Union. The United States will see a dramatic increase in defense spending. We will surge ahead of the Russians in terms of weapons technology. Between the clear failure of communism and their failure to keep up with us in terms of the arms race, their empire imploded.

"For the next seven or so years, the West attempted to prop up their economy, sending billions of dollars in way of hard currency and aid. Each of the satellite countries broke from the Soviet Union, further fragmenting their economy. The tragic result of all this turmoil was that the Soviet Army began to fall apart. Soldiers were not being paid, equipment was not being replaced. Most of their Navy sat rusting in port.

"As I already mentioned, they had developed a huge nuclear capability. They had hundreds of missile silos spread all over their vast territories that they were ill prepared to defend. Ultimately, and I am simplifying this, a Middle eastern terrorist organization called Gamat Islamya took control of these silos and, for perverted religious reasons, decided that the world needed to be destroyed in order to be cleansed."

"It doesn't sound like we are going to leave our children much of a world to live in." Roosevelt had always hoped to leave a legacy of peace and prosperity. He had been developing the concept of a world organization that would settle international difficulties, thus avoiding wars. It sounds as if his hope for uniting nations may have been stillborn.

"That's not necessarily true. Your New Deal will have evolved into strong and important social programs that will assure virtually every American at least a subsistence standard of living." While Harsh was not exactly a fan of the proliferation of social programs Roosevelt's national policies had spawned, he felt empathy for a man who may have felt, from this incomplete snap shot of the future, that he had not made a lasting contribution. "Please take heart in the fact that I graduated from Franklin Delano Roosevelt High School. As a matter of fact, close to ten percent of all public High Schools in the country will be named FDR High." He had made up that number, but he couldn't have been that far off.

"It is indeed rare for a man to hear of his posthumous rewards, Captain Yoder, I thank you for that."

FDR was certainly quite gracious, "Your welcome, Sir."

"I presume you are here to prevent that nuclear attack, Captain."

"Yes Sir, we are indeed."

"Why come all the way back to 1941, could you not have traveled back to days or weeks before the attack and prevented it then?"

"No Mr. President, we could not have." Harsh was feeling another long explanation coming. "The problems in the Soviet Union are systemic, we could probably have stopped the current attack, however, that would not end the potential and probability of it happening again. The Soviet Union, in it's 2002 configuration, is an overt threat to humanity.

"A little more background would be helpful. These nuclear bombs, first of all, are exponentially more powerful than the bombs dropped on Japan in 1945. I referred to those bombs before as nuclear, but they were in fact hydrogen bombs. Hydrogen bombs were the first of several generations of weapon that evolved to the high tonnage nuclear devices that will proliferate. Their delivery system is via a highly sophisticated missile, an unmanned plane, not unlike the V2 rockets being used by the Germans. Now, however, they travel faster than the speed of sound." Stimson looked like he was ready to jump out of his chair again. Yoder figured he would be having quite the meeting with both he and the Joint Chiefs of Staff in the coming days explaining the weaponry he was hinting at now.

"There are two primary problems here. First, while we can shoot down a handful of these missiles as they come in, we could not destroy them in the numbers necessary. Second, if even a dozen of these warheads detonated, and remember, the United States was not the only country targeted, the resultant explosions would throw enough nuclear waste into the atmosphere to kill most of the population of the countries targeted.

"The second problem is something called nuclear winter. Each detonation would throw millions of yards of debris, dirt really, into the atmosphere. This debris would stay in the atmosphere for two to five years. During that time, it would choke off upwards of eighty percent of the suns light. Plant life would die off world wide within months, the rest of the worlds populations would starve within a year or so."

"It sounds like no country should possess such apocalyptic power."

"Well," continued Harsh, "that is why we are here. The ultimate goal is to keep Russia from developing that power."

"This sounds like it is going to start getting complicated," there was polite laughter from each of Roosevelt's guests, "why don't we continue this over dinner."

"What the fuck are you doing?"

Sean Cooney sat at the computer terminal just outside his sleeping quarters.

"I'm making a million bucks, dick head, a million 1941 bucks. That's real money," he replied to his bunkmate, Walter Swenson.

Sean Cooney was the toughest man on the *Stennis* and more than likely, the entire navy. Just ask him, he'd tell ya. A click over six feet tall, he sported a regulation short, flat top hair cut. His angular cut chin, intense blue eyes, red hair and freckles screamed Irish. He fashioned himself a Celtic warrior in the wrong century. His buddies back home were not nearly as surprised as they should have been when Sean showed up to a fight he had picked earlier in the evening with a bouncer, naked and painted blue. The bouncer ran, Sean got arrested for indecent exposure and a local legend was born. You didn't utter the name Blue Balls in Hoboken, New Jersey without generating some kind of violent response. When he left for the Navy two years ago, there was both joy and sadness in Frank Sinatra's home town. The *Stennis* picked up one hell of an addition to its fire suppression team.

"What's all this crap?" Walt was holding half a dozen pages that Sean had printed out.

"Scores, my man, baseball scores." Walt wasn't the sharpest tool in the shed, earning him a nick name of The Professor. Sean answered the question that was already formulating in Walt's size six brain, "We're gonna bet on baseball games that we already know the scores to. Somebody updated the main frame with all kinds of shit from the forties, we're gonna make a friggin fortune."

Dinner was served in the South Dinning Room.

"Harsh Yoder, that's an interesting name, would you hail from the Pennsylvania Dutch Country?" asked Franklin Roosevelt?

"Quite perceptive of you, Mr. President. My father was a lapsed Mennonite. The day he turned eighteen, he walked off the farm, put his thumb in the air and didn't stop until he reached New York City, where he joined the army. Seems he was fascinated with machinery, alcohol and easy women. He spent the War years working on trucks at Fort Hamilton in Brooklyn.

"After the War, he became a mechanic. Old Jebadia Yoder worked on Milton Berle's cars, eventually became friends with him and became a writer on his television show. I was brought up in an eclectic atmosphere of self restraint and wild excess. My mother was a Rockette. He fell in love with her while watching the Christmas Show at Radio City. He met her back stage and they were married three weeks later. Jeb Yoder was a wild ride. He spent the first eighteen years of his life without an identity, so he named me Harsh, just to make sure I'd have one. It worked. He died in 1980."

"That's forty years from now," interjected Henry Stimson.

"It is hard to accept that he is alive. I suppose he's still on the farm in Pennsylvania. The dynamics of this time travel thing are painful. I could meet my father before I was born. Of course, the paradox here is what would happen to me if I killed him before he met my mother?"

"You'd probable get the chair, maybe life if you had a good lawyer," Frank Knox added.

"I don't think that's what Captain Yoder was wondering, Frank," Roosevelt was smiling. "Why don't we retire to the study for some brandy and Harsh can let us know how we are to prevent Russia from developing this nuclear capability."

Sequestered in red leather chairs, the five of them were each handed a snifter of Courvousier brandy. Stimson and Knox seemed somewhat uncomfortable having Captain O'Brien invade their traditionally male lair. Kelly could sense that and realized she was indeed in 1941 America where woman were not Captains and they did not take war meetings with the President. It angered her as she thought how hard she had to fight to make her way to the top at the end of the century, now she was almost back to ground zero.

"Well, Captain Yoder, tell us what your plan is." Henry Stimson was not yet a believer. He was born only two years after the Civil War ended, his mind would not let him accept the fact that time travel was possible. The Manhattan Project was very theoretical as he had just recently learned and there were no guarantees that it would go past that.

"Secretary Stimson, MJ 12, Majestic 12, they were the architects of this plan of operation, devised a three pronged attack."

"Who were, or will be, the Majestic 12?' Roosevelt was quite methodical and wanted all of the pieces before him.

Now we are getting into some choppy waters, thought Yoder. It was clear in the approach papers MJ 12 had written up that he was acting as their emissary but what he divulged to Roosevelt about the future was at his discretion.

"In 1946, less than a year after America dropped a pair of atom bombs, President Eisenhower commissioned a secret society of thirty two prominent men known as The Jason Society."

Roosevelt felt a chill charge up his spine. Already he was planning to run for an unprecedented fourth term. Could he be ousted from office by a General? Or will he be around in '44 to defend his office? These glimpses into the future were becoming disconcerting.

Even as he said the words, Yoder knew that, at some point, he'd have to address the question of Roosevelt's mortality. He continued, "The Society was initially formed to concern itself with the ethical and practical questions of what to do with this remarkably destructive new technology. Research into time travel began early in the Manhattan Project," he hoped Roosevelt wouldn't query him on the Manhattan Project, figuring Stimson would address that with him later, "and ran concurrently. As the research evolved, twelve of those men were splintered off to from Majestic 12. They would now deal specifically with time travel.

"Again I ask, who sat on the Majestic 12 panel."

Harsh picked up the binder on the table next to his chair. He pulled out a pair of reading glasses and thumbed through the pages. "Admiral Hillenkoetter, Dr. Bush, Mr. Forrestal, General Twining, General Montague, General Vandenberg, Doctor Bronk, Doctor Haunsaker, Doctor Mensel, Doctor Berknew, Mr. Souera and a Mr. Gray. These were the initial members." Yoder didn't mention that Forrestal will have died in '49 or that he would be Franklin's Secretary of the Navy.

"That's quite a list, I know most of those men, some personally."

"For what it is worth, Mr. President, they, and those who sat on MJ 12 after them, acted with forethought and restraint with this potential Pandora's Box. After years of debate, it was decided that the only use of Project Babylonian, as this project was dubbed, would be if the world was facing nuclear destruction."

"Well then," Stimson took on a demanding tone, "what is their plan to muzzle Russia?" Even though Stalin and Hitler had signed a non aggression pact, there was a real concern as to what Russia's real motives were.

"MJ 12 developed a three pronged attack. First, we intend to dispatch the Japanese. We estimate that within seven days we will have them suing, no, begging for peace."

"Our own estimates are that it will take three years and up to half a million causalities to bring the Japanese Empire to its knees, how dare you suggest that your ship can do it in a week! Next you will be telling us that you can re-create the world in that same period." Stimson was incensed.

"I am not claiming that we have the power of God, Mr. Stimson, however, I stand by what I say, and, we will not take any causalities."

Stimson jumped from his chair.

"Please, Henry, let's listen to Captain Yoder." Roosevelt saw that he was going to have to keep his Secretary of War calmed.

"I will look forward to having you aboard the *Stennis* shortly, Mr. Stimson, I think you will agree that Japan will pose little challenge after your tour. The next step in Operation Floating Thunder may sound a little disturbing at first, but it will enable us to achieve our goal most economically and with the least amount of casualties. The *Stennis* will covertly support Germany's war efforts against Russia."

"My God, what are you suggesting?" Now it was Frank Knox getting hot under the collar.

"Please, let me finish. By allowing Germany to vanquish Russia, we will then have only one enemy to fight and prevent the Red Army from occupying the buffer countries. As impressive as the fighting technology on the *Stennis* is, we have a limited amount of planes and armaments, most of which cannot be replicated with 1940's technology. When the *Stennis* strikes, we need to be sure and surgical. After defeating Russia, a German Army spread out across Europe and Asia will not be terribly difficult to destroy. Once you see how the War went historically, you will have a better understanding of what I am proposing."

Stimson was all for Russia's demise. Stalin was a dangerous and unpredictable foe. He lacked integrity and could not be trusted. A world without Stalin would be a safer place.

"I will be looking forward to meeting with your generals and presenting our war strategy."

"Assuming," added President Roosevelt, "that you can verify everything you have told us. How do you propose to do that?"

"You will need to come aboard the *Stennis*, Mr. President, I believe I will be able to alley your doubts there."

"One last question, Captain Yoder," it was after eleven and Stimson had more work to do, "under whose authority do you operate?"

"The President of the United States, Sir." Yoder was not anxious for this potentially volatile discussion.

"Can I assume you are referring to President Roosevelt?" questioned Stimson.

"No Sir, I am operating under the direct orders of President Richard Cheney."

"You are part of the United States Navy, you will defer to the acting President of the United States."

"No Sir," Captain Yoder was quite forceful, "my orders come directly from my Commander and Chief. My orders are to save the human race. Those orders will supersede all others."

Both men were on their feet, nose to nose. Stimson was not going to be pushed around by a punk four striper who technically hasn't even been born yet. Yoder was not going to be pushed around by an old man who clearly had not gotten the big picture.

"Gentlemen," Roosevelt commanded, "that may not be of issue once we visit the *Stennis*. Let's plan to do that tomorrow afternoon."

"How did it go?" Admiral Bellinger asked Yoder as they climbed into the helicopter.

"Hard to tell. Kelly, what did you think?"

She waited for the chopper engines to settle in before responding. "Certainly the most interesting evening of my life. Roosevelt seems quite open and willing to accept what you'd told him. Knox seemed somewhat ambivalent. Stimson is a crotchety old man who will need to see before believing."

"They'll be taking a tour tomorrow afternoon," Harsh shared with Admiral Bellinger.

"That should have quite an impact on old Henry," added Bellinger.

Yoder turned to his XO, "This is going to be important, let's have a staff meeting at 0600."

December 18th, 1941, 7:23 AM
USS Stennis, Atlantic Ocean

"Roger, Dancer, your deck is clear, I've got you on visual, come on in, watch your altitude and check your lineup. The wind is gusting at 10 knots due south, you've got an easy one." Viga Hall was the Landing Signal Officer, it was his job to bring the jets home.

The *Stennis* was three miles out in the Atlantic. Captain Yoder had called for a number of exercises to make sure everything was squared away for President Roosevelt's visit later that afternoon.

"Roger that, Tower... eight miles out." Kaitlyn Savage was easing back on the throttle of her F/A-18E Super Hornet to 180 knots, on her way down to a landing velocity of 160. The next forty seconds would be the busiest moments any pilot will ever face. Each landing on an aircraft carrier was a controlled crash.

She would need to line up her jet on a moving one thousand foot long runway that was pitching and rolling. Any subtle deviation in altitude, speed, pitch or yaw would result in a fiery death and the loss of a painfully expensive air craft.

Lieutenant Hall stood on the exposed port side of the carrier. His binoculars were tightly focused on Dancer. All LSO's are fighter pilots themselves. He knew the difficulties of keeping a twenty ton craft on a glide path two degrees above the horizontal. When the swells were up the carrier would pitch through as many as three degrees, a degree and a half either side of the horizontal. That translates to a sixty foot rise between the stern and the bow every half a minute, a scenario that will tighten the sphincter of all but a few fighter jocks.

Even in the calm seas Dancer had today, putting down on a carrier was still highly challenging. She wouldn't glide her jet in and flare out right before touchdown as a commercial jet pilot would. Lieutenant Savage would fly her jet right to the deck, slamming her Hornet down and hoping that the small hook hanging from the belly of her air craft would grab one of four arresting wires and bring her to a safe, if not violent, stop. If not, she'd have to immediately shove the throttle to its stops and take off the stern of the carrier. This was a black and white maneuver, either you were successful or you weren't.

Viga instinctively edged towards the pit, a padded basket hanging off the deck. If a jet lost control, there is no place for the LSO to hide, they just jump over the side, hopefully into the pit. "Conn Captain, two degrees left rudder... steer two two zero, give me twenty knots over the deck." Lieutenant Hall was also in contact with the Conn, ordering minuet changes in the speed and direction of the carrier to make the pilot's job as easy as possible.

Less than thirty seconds out, the scream of the Hornets engines made their audible presence. The hydraulics operator, on the deck below, was being kept informed of Dancer's progress. He was responsible for setting the amount of tension necessary on the arresting wires to bring the fifty thousand pounds of force the Hornet would exert to a stop from 160 knots in less than two seconds.

"Lookin good, Dancer, keep steady, pull up your nose a little."

This was Dancer's thirteenth carrier landing. She wasn't superstitious, but the riding her fellow pilots of the Pukin' Dogs Squadron gave her did not make this any easier. She was feeling real tight where the sun don't shine, her palms felt sweaty through her nomex gloves and she was loving every second of it. Dancer's life was paved with challenges. There was not one she had not faced and conquered.

"Your one hundred feet...ninety... sixty," Viga was calling out the altitude.

She had the meatball right where it needed to be and she was lined up square. Dancer had one hand on the stick, the other on the throttle in the event she got a wave off.

Through her headphones she could hear the LSO counting her altitude down, forty, thirty, twenty. Above the scream of the engines Dancer listened for the distinctive sound of the metal hook sliding along the deck. The hook caught the arresting wire unleashing powerful hydraulic pumps that dragged the F/18 to a stop.

"Nice job Dancer," Lieutenant Hall knew that any carrier landing that didn't kill you was a good one, "did you hear it?"

"Not this time, Viga, did you coat my hook with rubber?" Viga couldn't believe that Kaitlyn thought she would be able to hear the metal to metal contact when the hook caught the wire above the incredible screech of the engines.

Lieutenant Savage crawled out of the cockpit of her Hornet. She stood on the deck and waved to her LSO. Lieutenant Hall saluted her. Even from over a hundred feet away she was something to look at. No one in this man's Navy filled out a flight suite like her. She stood five seven, had a taught, muscular body and a great set of... "What a good looking woman," he said to no one in particular.

"Wow, who the hell is she?" Larry Douglas shouted to his partner as they choked the wheels of Savages jet.

"Dancer, she was a nugget last cruise, I met her a few times. Very hot. I may need to give her a shot of

Danny tonight," Danny Holden grabbed his crotch to underscore his statement.

"She wouldn't piss on you if you were on fire. How'd she get the call name Dancer?"

"Word is she danced her way through college, exotic shit, man. Can you imagine that naked?"

CHAPTER 5
Introductions

December 18th, 1941, 12:45 PM EST
The White House, Washington, DC

Lieutenant Smolinsky had parked his Sea King on the South Lawn, this time he was not ringed by armed soldiers. As the rotors settled down, two marines, in full dress uniform, exited the chopper and stood at attention on each side of the door. Captain O'Brien walked fifty feet to where the President Roosevelt was waiting.

She delivered a textbook salute.

Roosevelt was balancing on two mahogany canes. "Captain, allow me to introduce General Marshal, Admiral Nimitz and General Eisenhower. Frank and Henry will be joining us also." Eisenhower was there at Captain Yoder's request. President Roosevelt had no way of knowing that Prime Minister Churchill would be lobbying to have General Eisenhower take charge of the Allied forces. It was assumed, at this point, that Marshall would be getting the fifth star.

O'Brien felt another rush, similar to the one she got when meeting Roosevelt the day before. Nimitz was close to mythical figure to her. While other girls in her Advanced Senior English class were writing papers on women's rights or sexual harassment in the work place, Kelly O'Brien put together a thirty two page treatise on *Admiral Chester A. Nimitz's, a man of courage, a plan of courage and how he won the naval war, 1941-45.* It was a dry piece, but it got her an A+ and a wonderful letter of recommendation from Dr. Gordon that helped get her into Annapolis.

She turned and delivered another round of salutes. "Gentlemen, it is an honor to meet each of you. Your contributions to the War efforts will be legend."

Nimitz, Eisenhower and Marshall all looked at one another. They had been bought up to speed less than an hour before. They were still arguing with Stimson when the helicopter touched down. Now here was a relatively young woman, wearing a Captain's rank, telling them they would be historical figures. If she had not arrived in that utterly fantastic machine, they'd surely not given her any quarter.

Kelly noticed General Marshall staring at the chopper. "It's a Sikoursky Sea King, they're called helicopters, Sir. They have vertical take off and landing capability." She turned to the rest of her distinguished party, "Why don't we go ahead and board, Captain Yoder is anxious to show you all the *Stennis*."

"A grand idea," replied Roosevelt. Frank Knox and Dwight Eisenhower flanked the President and guided him across the lawn to the waiting chopper. All were seated, buckled in and given helmets which were rigged with headphones and microphones.

"Welcome to my craft, I am Lieutenant Smolinsky, your pilot for this short flight to the *USS John C. Stennis*. Our flying time will be approximately twenty seven minutes," he knew it was going to be exactly twenty seven minutes, but aviators love to sound nonchalant when it came to facts. He had heard another pilot, during the Gulf War, after destroying a column of eight tanks, report, "The target has been acquired and terminally slowed down." Finely crafted understatement, he thought at the time.

Smolinsky built up the power, released the clutch and the Sikoursky leaped into the sky.

"As soon as we arrive, Captain Yoder plans to demonstrate some of the air wing capabilities aboard the *Stennis* before it gets dark, then he'll give you a tour of the ship." Captain O'Brien was acting as the official guide until they arrived back on the *Stennis*. At that point, the heads of each department will take over.

"Does this craft have an offensive capacity, Lieutenant," Eisenhower directed his question to the pilot. He was already formulating a protocol for this new tool of war.

"Sir, you don't have to yell." Most people figure that because it is so noisy in the chopper they have to holler to be heard, not realizing that the ICS is quite sensitive. "This helicopter is primarily used for rescue ops, but we can hang a mini gun out the door if the need arises. There are a number of attack choppers in the fleet, however, we don't have any on board the *Stennis*."

For most of the flight, the five men stared out the windows and tried to come to terms with what was happening. Roosevelt, Stimson and Knox at least had almost a day to contemplate and digest this remarkable turn of events. Marshall, Eisenhower and Nimitz were not even into their second hour of awareness and were struggling to accept time travel, as well as dealing with weapons of war more than half a century into the future.

As they broke the coast, the *Stennis* was a small dot out in the Atlantic, barely visible. It was severe clear, a perfect day to show off the most awesome concentration of mobile power ever assembled.

Those in the back had no forward view. As Smolinsky approached the *Stennis*, he banked starboard and started to circle the ship.

"My God, she's huge. Must be a good hundred feet longer than the *Yorktown*," the *Yorktown* was commissioned in 1937 and was the first of the new Yorktown Class carriers in the fleet and fortunately, not docked at Pearl a week and a half earlier. Chester Nimitz was smiling.

"She is the second newest of our Nimitz Class carriers" Captain O'Brien just let that hang in the air.

"Did I hear you right, Captain?"

"Yes, Admiral," Kelly wanted to be the one to deliver that bit of information, "this is a Nimitz Class carrier. You made quite an impact on modern naval war fare."

Chester Nimitz was a little disturbed at being referred to in the past tense, but he was still smiling.

"What are all those men looking for." There were over a hundred men sweeping along the deck, all staring down, the President was stumped as to what they were doing.

"They are doing a FOD walk down. FOD stands for foreign object damage. The gas turbine engines on the jets are susceptible to small pieces of debris. A quarter inch washer could cause seventy five thousand dollars of damage to an engine."

Smolinsky put the Sikoursky into a circling pattern as Captain O'Brien continued her introduction to the *Stennis*.

"She is one thousand and ninety two feet long. The flight deck is two hundred and fifty seven feet wide and covers four and a half acres. The height keel to mast is equal to twenty four stories. She weighs in at ninety seven tons. There's more than sixty thousand tons of structural steel down there and more than nine hundred miles of cable and wiring running through her."

Kelly would not be delivering any of the really sexy information during the tour so she tried to add a little wow to some of the more pedestrian facts she was allowed to disperse. "There are two thousand telephones on board and over thirty thousand light fixtures." She knew she may be getting a little obscure, but Kelly had spent the better part of last night doing research and she wasn't about to let it all go to waste.

"You certainly seem to be intimate with facts about the *Stennis*, Captain," the Secretary of the Navy said into his helmet mic.

"Sir, I could put your feet to sleep with the inane facts I have at my disposal. For example, if you stacked all of the required technical manuals up, they would be as high as the Washington Monument. Want to know how many sheets we have on the ship? Twenty eight thousand," she didn't give Knox a chance to answer. "If you, for some odd reason, decided to line up all the bed mattresses end to end, they would stretch for more than nine miles. And while I am on the subject, there are fourteen thousand pillow cases available to our sleepy crew. Your feet getting numb yet? The *Stennis* cost three and a half billion 1998 dollars. That does include the twenty eight thousand sheets, however."

"That's all very interesting, Captain O'Brien, but could you tell me about her propulsion system?" Admiral Nimitz didn't much seem to care about the linen situation aboard the *Stennis*.

"No Sir, Captain Yoder will bring you up to speed on her power plant and armaments. I'm sure you all are somewhat curious about the aircraft on her deck," O'Brien answered.

"I've never seen anything like them," Secretary Knox replied, "they look like they are right out of an H. G. Wells novel."

"Wells could not have imagined the technology we have sitting down there. Lieutenant, why don't you bring us in."

As Roosevelt carefully exited the helicopter, the military band was banging out "Hail to the Chief." Yoder and his Executive Staff were there to meet him, sailors and marines, in their dress uniforms, lined the deck. Attack aircraft were strategically positioned to impress these dignified visitors. It was a dramatic scene.

Everyone on deck snapped to attention as President Roosevelt stepped on to the *Stennis*. The sound of starched cotton slapping against starched cotton was powerful. There was a twelve knot wind coming out of the east adding structure to the flags flying two hundred and fifty feet in the air.

A Yeoman piped the President's party aboard.

"President Roosevelt, welcome to the *USS Stennis*." Captain Yoder was never more proud of his ship.

Introductions were made and they all departed the deck for the tower. It was a tight fit to get everyone into Primary Flight Control, a glass office twenty four stories above the flight deck. President Roosevelt was seated in one of the two leather chairs that gave a panoramic view of the deck.

"Gentlemen, this is Commander Ed Patrick, he's the Air Boss. Commander, why don't you tell our guests what you do." Captain Yoder had decided to let the officers take center stage while visiting their operation.

Ed Patrick, who by the very nature of his job had to be cool headed, came dangerously close to saying "Holy shit." He had been told that they were back in 1941. The shore line around Newport, Virginia did look different, but meeting President Roosevelt was the first tangible evidence that they were indeed sixty years back in time. He had no idea what Nimitz or Marshall looked like, but seeing Roosevelt and Ike in the flesh was both exciting and disconcerting.

"My responsibilities are to oversee the take off and recovery of the aircraft and the action of planes within five mile radius of the ship. I have six hundred people working for me. With these phones, I am in contact with the bridge and the flight deck.   "During flight opts, I will have communication with the Landing Signal Officers, air traffic control and the planes. The hangar deck, fuel systems, flight deck, arresting gear and catapult all fall into my cog. Let me explain and demonstrate how this all works." Nimitz marveled at how much more complex this all was compared to flight operations on the *Yorktown*. He already decided there was going to be a major reevaluation of how things were done when he got back to his office.

"Let's start with the flight deck. That plane over there," he was pointing to catapult number two, "is an F/A-18E Super Hornet."

"I can't help noticing that there's not a propeller to be seen, can you tell me how you keep those machines in the air," General Marshall wondered?

"If I'm not mistaken, General, you are aware of the work the Army Air Corps is doing with the X59. As you are already finding out, the P39 Air Cobra is an unstable platform for a jet engine. The Germans, with their Comet Program, will have beaten us into the sky with a workable jet propelled air craft, but it will have been to late to have made any impact. I believe that their A6178 has been operational since 1939." Ed quietly thanked the History Channel for much of the background information he was disseminating. "These jet propulsion engines will evolve into some pretty dramatic hardware. We'll get a pilot to give you the very impressive flight envelope and fighting capabilities of these machines later. I'm not necessarily interested in all that anyway, I just need to get them in the air and get em home."

My God, thought Marshall, how the hell could he know about the X59. The US was chasing Germany in an effort to be the first to successfully harness jet power. These people must indeed be from the future or they are extremely well connected.

"Before a plane gets to the catapult," Patrick continued, "there are a half a dozen people responsible to make sure it is air worthy. During preflight, the pilot does a walk around. It is ultimately his responsibility to make sure his craft is ready to go. Then the Plane Captain takes over. He will arm the ejection seat. Again, you'll get a full briefing on the actual systems aboard the jets later so I won't waste time right now explaining some of this stuff. He'll check the air ducts, buckle the pilot in and then begin a series of hand signals with the pilot to check the operational readiness of the craft.

"For example, he'll signal the pilot to start up the APU, then engine two. After verification that engine two is on line, engine one is started. The hydraulic system is checked next, then the Plane Captain will initiate flight control sequencing. The control surfaces, flaps and such will be activated and visually inspected; the horizontal stabilizers are opened and closed. Next up is what's called three down. The tail hook, the speed brakes and the in-flight refueling system are all activated. There is a final walk around and the Plane Captain will check the computer code. If there is anything wrong with any major system, the computer will tell him what it is. There is a Trouble Shooter who will also give his OK. The Plane Captain will then pass control of the craft to a Yellow Shirt who will remove the chains and the chocks. The Yellow Shirt will guide the jet to the one of four catapults.

"The Director will now hook up the plane to the catapult shoe, it's that twenty five foot long groove in the deck right in front of the plane," Ed was pointing to the Hornet that was sitting at catapult number two, ready to launch. "The Shooter now has control of the jet. He checks the CSV to make sure the catapult operator has dialed in the proper weight of the plane being readied for launch. The jet blast deflector behind the jet is risen from the deck to protect people from the jet wash. The pilot will go to full throttle. The Shooter takes one final look, salutes the pilot, who signals that he is ready for launch by saluting back. The Shooter kneels, when his knee hits the deck, the plane is released. Within two seconds, the craft will be going over two hundred knots. Let me demonstrate. We have Dancer down there in that F/A-18E."

Commander Patrick picked up one of the phones in front of him, "Shooter, fire off catapult two."

Within seconds, they could hear the violent sound of Dancer going to full throttle, the steel deflector shot up behind the plane, the shooter dropped to a knee and a fifty thousand pound jet was hurled off the back of the *Stennis*.

"Quite dramatic," Roosevelt stated, "how do you get them back down?"

"Thank-you for asking, Mr. President, that is also, as I mentioned before, my responsibility. It all starts with the LSO, or the Landing Signal Officer. He will radio instructions to the pilots from his perch on the stern of the ship. Using vocal communications and a large illuminated circle called a meatball, he will make sure the aircraft maintains the proper speed, altitude and attitude to put down safely. Carrier landings are the most difficult thing a pilot can do. A goodly part of the two million dollars spent to train a pilot goes into carrier landings. I say landings, but the pilots describe them as controlled crashes.

"They need to bring these planes down onto a moving landing area with their tail hooks extended. The tail hook is an eight foot long bar with a hook at the end that must pick up one of those four arresting wires on the deck. The Green Shirts down there are responsible for the arresting wires.

"The weight of each individual plane must be set on a battery of four arresting cable engines down below deck. The Arresting Gear Officer makes sure the engines are ready, the weight is set properly, the area is clear and that the correct weight is set. There are two thousand feet of cable connected to a massive hydraulic piston that will absorb fifty thousand pounds of controlled collision. If the cables are set wrong, people die.

"I have a plane coming in shortly. If you gentlemen would look to the stern, that officer over there is the LSO on duty. That round disk is the meatball. The LSO is in communication with his pilot, who is about three miles out and very much into his descant. He will need to slow to one hundred and sixty knots."

"That seems fairly fast for a plane coming in for a landing, even for one of those things your people are flying." Nimitz was not an aviator, but as he had not much more than aircraft carriers left in his fleet, thanks to the Japanese, he was becoming quite schooled in most aspects of carrier operation.

"We are facing the same problem that your *Yorktown* faces. If a plane misses one of the arresting wires, it needs to get back in the air in a big hurry or it's going in the water. We get a half a dozen bolters during a busy air operation."

Allen Ben-Gurion, call name Warrior, was driving his plane toward the deck. The weather was good. This was his two hundred and seventh carrier landing and he was one of the best in the business. He got so cocky that he once considered feigning a problem with his radio to see how well he could park his jet without the help of an LSO. Good sense and the fact that it would take him eight hundred years to pay the government back for the loss of a thirty million dollar aircraft belayed that experiment. Knowing that he had a celebrated audience today pushed him to bring his Hornet in perfectly.

"Here he comes," Commander Patrick was pointing to the stern of the ship. Within moments, Warrior's F/A-18E was dropping to the deck. It caught wire number three and went from 160 knots to zero in the blink of an eye. It was a text book landing.

"That's stunning," said General Marshall, "I'm anxious to see one of those planes close up."

"Then let's make that so. I'll take you down to the main deck where the pilot who just landed will give you a briefing on the F/A-18E Super Hornet." Captain Yoder directed his party towards the elevator.

"The Main Deck is where we park the ninety plus air craft assigned to the *Stennis*. We also do our maintenance on both the planes and the jet engines down here." Yoder was working it every bit as good as a cruise ship skipper trying to impress the female cast of *Baywatch*.

They had all been loaded on two electric carts used to ferry large parts around the huge deck. A few bench seats had been bolted to the back, mostly to accommodate Roosevelt.

"This is God damn incredible," Eisenhower and Marshall sat together in the trailing vehicle. "How the hell do they know about the X59, shit Dwight, we've lost two pilots trying to keep that thing in the air?"

"What they seem to know about our operations might be disconcerting, but what about this technology? For Christ sake, we've just entered what will likely be the biggest war in history and we have ourselves one hell of an ace in the hole. I don't care if they're from the future or Mars, just imagine what we can do with those nuclear bombs Stimson was rambling on about. Shove one into the belly of one of these crazy looking planes and we'll have Hitler and Hiroheto doing a God damn jig in Washington without putting a troop in Europe or a ship in the Pacific."

They came to a stop between a Super Hornet and a sinister looking F-117 Seahawk. Marshall and Ike got out and walked towards the Seahawk while Roosevelt, Stimson and Knox stayed seated. Yoder had walked over to Lieutenant Ben-Gurion. He returned his salute and then introduced Allen to the dignitaries.

"This is Lieutenant Allen Ben-Gurion, he just graced us with that ten point landing a few minutes ago.

Made it look easy. Lieutenant Ben-Gurion joined us on our last tour and has been driving fighter jets for, what, four years now?"

"Five years in January, Sir."

"He'll be telling us about the finest air craft available in the twenty first century, Lieutenant," Captain Yoder handed him the floor.

Ben-Gurion had given talks such as he was about to deliver a dozen times. His audiences ranged from Senators and Congressmen to Boy Scouts. This was the first time he felt nervous. It was stunning to see such esteemed figures in history. Allen did what any number of people had done already, he closed his eyes, took a deep breath and prayed that he would not keel over.

"Gentlemen, these are two of the most advanced tactical jet fighters ever created. To your left, we have the F/A-18E Super Hornet, over there, the somewhat odd looking F-117 Seahawk." He walked over to the Hornet.

"The Hornet is an all-weather, day and night, multi-mission strike fighter. It is equally capable fighting in the air, performing a bombing run or supporting troops on the ground. McDonnell Douglas won the contract for engineering and manufacturing in 1992 and became operational by the late nineties."

The fact that McDonnell and Douglas merged was one of many surprises to Frank Knox. He had a personal relationship with Jim McDonnell. Frank had been the one to suggest that McDonnell Aircraft Corporation begin manufacturing airplane parts until the XP-67 bomber destroyer was completed.

"The E model here is a one seater craft, the F series, right over there," Allen pointed to a F/A-18F twenty yards away, "is a two seater, supporting a pilot and a weapons systems officer. The Hornet is configured to carry every tactical air to air and air to ground weapon in the Navy's inventory. With the AMRAAM missile, enhanced radar, and advanced onboard sensor fusion capability, there's not a threat fighter in the twenty first century that the Super Hornet cannot decisively defeat and totally dominate in combat. There shouldn't be anything in 1941 that will offer it much of a challenge, either.

"Let me give you some basic specifications. The unit cost is thirty five million dollars. She is propelled by two F414-GE-400 turbofan engines, each capable of twenty two thousands pounds of static thrust. The Hornet measure sixty feet long, forty five feet tip to tip and is sixteen feet tall. Take off gross weight is sixty six thousand pounds. The ceiling is fifty thousand feet and with a full tank of fuel, she has a range of two thousand miles. Top speed is Mach two, that's twice the speed of sound."

"We didn't believe that it is was possible to break the sound barrier," General Marshall was astonished.

"There is no sonic wall, Sir. The barrier was first broken in 1947 by a test pilot named Chuck Yeager in the Bell X-15. We currently have a reconnaissance ship called the Aurora that can do close to mach seven! It has a flight ceiling of over one hundred thousand feet."

"Christ," Eisenhower barked, "wouldn't that be entering space?"

"Just about, Sir, however we have other craft for that."

"Let's stay on track here, Lieutenant," Yoder wasn't sure just how much of the future needed to be addressed right now.

"Yes Sir."

Ben-Gurion walked over to the port side wing of the Hornet. "The only reason for these planes to exist is to deliver ordinance." He put his hand on a missile hanging under the wing. "These missiles are broken into two categories, air to air and ground to air. This is what is referred to as an AMRAAM, an acronym for Advanced Medium Range Air to Air Missile. It is a medium range missile that uses programmable microprocessors, or computers, with active radar homing. It has its own radar transmitter, allowing the pilot to fire and forget.

"Have you gentlemen been briefed on computers yet?"

"No, Lieutenant, they haven't, why don't you bring them up to speed," Yoder volunteered.

Allen paused. Computers were such an everyday part of life that it took a minute for him to bring himself mentally back to the manual labor days of typewriters and slide rulers.

"A computer, in the latter part of the twentieth century, is considered an electronic device that can receive a set of instructions and then carry out the instructions by performing calculations on numerical data or compiling and correlating other forms of information.

"Although there is work being done on primitive computers now in the forties, it wasn't until, or it won't be until 1945 when the first stored program computer will be created. Mr. Kilburn and Mr. Williams will have built Baby, the prototype of the Mark 1. Although it could do nothing but subtract, it was a major advancement in that actual programs, or assigned sets of instructions, could be acted on.

"The first general purpose all electronic computer was developed at the University of Pennsylvania. It had somewhere around eighteen thousand tubes in it and was as bigger than one of these planes. The first computers were purchased by the Government and were used by the Census Department. By the late fifties, the vacuum tubes gave way to the transistor, which did the same thing tubes did but were dramatically smaller, more reliable and cheaper to build."

Yoder was beginning to wonder if this history lesson was necessary as his eyes started to glaze.

"Ten years later, the integrated circuit was introduced, allowing many transistors to be fabricated on to one silicon chip. At this point, computer technology began to take off. By the seventies, the microprocessor became a reality. The microprocessor allowed many thousands of interconnected transistors to be etched into a single tiny silicon chip. Now computers that were capable of performing five or ten million discrete operations per second were doing billions of calculations per second.

"By the early nineties, computers became a part of every day life. There are computer chips in the clock radios that wake us up in the morning. Computers are responsible for allowing automobiles to achieve fifty miles a gallon. Most every business man carries a computer the size of a deck of cards that will contain all of his contacts, schedules and propriety information. Computers will be link every household in the country by the phone lines to a data base called the Internet. The Internet is like a library where someone can access several billion pages of information about anything imaginable.

"It is highly sophisticated computers that allow a jet such as that F-117 to fly. The F-117 is inherently an unstable craft. Without external help, it is unable to fly. The computers deep in her belly interpret what the pilot wants to do and then performs the necessary actions to make it happen. It is also the microcomputers in this missile that help it seek out a target on its own and destroy it."

The military minds gathered together were racing. The concept of shoot and run was as old as the spear. Why wait around for retaliation when you could deliver punishment from afar.

"This jet was configured to show you a full range of weapons available. The first missile under the Hornets wing is the AIM-9M Sidewinder. It's an air to air weapon, the oldest one here. Its inception dates to the forties. It uses infrared technology that looks for the heat generated from the exhaust of another jet and locks on to it. It will follow every move the targeted pilot makes until it rides up his tail pipe and ruins his day. The Sidewinder has a range of eight miles and carries an eleven kilogram high explosive blast fragmentation war head. It'll accelerate to twice the speed of sound in two seconds."

"The pilot doesn't have to be much of a shot to score with one of those."

"No General Marshall, all of these are pretty much shoot and forget. The pilot's skills are needed to drive these planes around."

"This missile," Allen pointed to the missile adjacent to the Sidewinder, "is called the AIM-132 ASRAAM. As mentioned before, that stands for Advanced Short Range Air to Air Missile. The range for this unit is up to fifteen miles. The ASRAAM is guided by an advanced imaging infrared seeker utilizing image processing systems in order to recognize its target. That gives it all aspect capability. ASRAAM differs from the Sidewinder in that it offers high off boresight targeting via a helmet mounted sight. This missile can be launched over the shoulder simply by looking at what the pilot wants to destroy and pulling a trigger. With thrust vectoring, it is capable of fantastic turns of more than thirty G's. The speeds at which it travels is Mach four. It is the weapon of choice during a furball."

Marshall was fascinated, "Lieutenant, what is thrust vectoring?"

"Simply put, the missile has small jets built into the aft section that, when ignited, enable the missile to turn at an incredible rate."

"This missile is called the AIM-120 AMRAAM. This is similar to the 132 only it is a medium range missile, effective to a range of thirty miles."

"Next we have the S-225 LRAAM. Of course, that would be our Long Range Air to Air Missile. The range is now up to sixty miles."

"Excuse me Lieutenant," Marshall interrupted again, "how can the pilot even know there is a threat sixty miles away?"

"I'll address that in a moment, General, let me finish up with weapons. As well as an increased range, the S-225 carries a larger warhead, thirty kilograms.

Ben-Gurion walked to the front of the plane. "In here is a BK-27mm cannon. They used to be called machine guns, but when it spits out seventeen hundred high explosive rounds a minute, we consider it more of a cannon. It uses gas drive for the gun feed and electrical power of the firing mechanism.

"Under the belly of the plane is a drop tank. We can fit three of them on to the Hornet, giving it a range of four hundred miles. For air to ground operations, we have twenty two different ordinances. Allow me to tell you about a few of them.

"Let's start out with conventional bombs. Computers have taken over from the pilot or bombardier and have made direct hits much more likely. They have the processing power necessary to perform complex mathematical models for ballistics and aerodynamics, which are used to predict the fall line of unguided bombs. These computers calculate the effect of wind, airspeed, air pressure, g-loading, bank angle, altitude, and rate of decent in determining precisely where the bombs will fall. These Mk-81 bombs," there were three piled on the deck next to the plane, "are not much different than what you have in your arsenal right now. It's the delivery system that has changed.

"This GBU PAVEWAY 11 bomb is an excellent example. Although basically a free fall ordinance, it does have an onboard generator that will drive the control surfaces for just about a minute. It is used in conjunction with the TIALD, or Thermal Imaging and Laser Designation system. Again, computer driven, the TIALD feeds the pilot with all the data needed to make the correct attack run, illuminates the target and calculates the correct release point for the weapon. Once released, the generator kicks in and will follow a beam of light, a laser, that the pilot has locked, or illuminated, the target with. If the pilot can hold the plane steady, the bomb is going to hit. The accuracy of this system is measured in inches. I could place a PAVEWAY in the passenger seat of Hitler's Mercedes from five miles out."

"We very well may be calling on you to do just that, Lieutenant," Eisenhower added.

"That would be very much my pleasure," Allen Ben-Gurion responded. Rather sooner than later, he thought.

"Stacked over here we have the CRV-7 rocket, a particularly nasty bit of ordinance. A rocket attack is as terrifying as it is deadly. It has a diameter of seventy millimeters and can accept a number of warheads. We can arm them with high explosives, armor piercing, incendiary, penetrator, flechette or anti-tank warheads. They can be released accurately from four miles. The CRV has an impact speed of thirty seven hundred feet per second. This makes the CRV-7 a kinetic energy weapon, when armed, for example, with the flechette anti-tank warheads. Flechettes are sharp darts make out of a tungsten alloy, which makes them extremely hard. When the rocked is launched, five flechettes break free from the housing and disperse slightly before hitting the target. The energy of the impact, coupled with the hardness of the flechette driving the warhead straight through the armor, creates a devastating explosion inside the target."

"I know the Germans have quite an advantage in mechanized weapons currently, these rockets could be a great equalizer." Eisenhower had been concerned with the devastatingly effective way the Germans wielded their tanks during the blitzkrieg in Poland.

"An even more effective weapon is this AGM-65 Maverick. The Maverick is a guided missile and enables the attack aircraft the capability to put ordnance on the target without having to make dangerous bomb runs over the target. These are particularly effective at destroying tanks, ships and bridges. The electro-optical, or TV missiles are aimed by the pilot with the aid of a television camera in the missile's nose. The image from the camera is transmitted back to a TV in the cockpit. The pilot can then remotely guide the missile to the target. The accuracy is exceptional and has a range of twenty five miles.

"The Durandal anti-runway bomb is quite clever. The delivery system is most unique. The missile is dropped in a low pass over the runway, then slowed by a parachute to the correct delivery angle, at which point, the rocket motor ignites. The acceleration is enough to drive the specially shaped penetrating head though up to four hundred millimeters of reinforced concrete. After a pre-programmed delay, the missile explodes, causing the paving slabs nearby to be disturbed.

"The nature of the weapon means that repair work will be hampered by the unexploded Durandal's. There is just no way to know when they will detonate. The damage is extensive, requiring more that just earth moving equipment to fill the holes. The objective here is to make the runway unusable for considerable lengths of time.

Ben-Gurion walked around the Hornet, followed by Marshall and Eisenhower. Yoder had the cart holding the President, Stimson and Knox pull around to afford them a better view. "The BL-755 Cluster Bomb is an effective anti-personal weapon. Once the bomb reaches a preset altitude, it releases hundreds of sub-munitions, each scattering deadly red hot shrapnel. One bomb will cover an area the size of a football field.

"Lastly, we have the Sea Eagle Anti-Ship Missile. The Sea Eagle uses an active radar seeker and an altimeter to give it long distance sea skimming ability. It approaches the target a a few feet above the waves to avoid detection. It can be launched from seventy miles out."

"I'm no warrior, Gentlemen," FDR spoke up for the first time, "but it appears that we may not have to face our adversaries on the battlefield to vanquish them."

"You are correct, Mr. President. Due to advanced avionics, we can see the enemy and destroy them from miles away. The amount of information the driver of one of these jets needs is astounding. Through use of computers, this information is presented in a fairly simple and logical way.

"Within the cockpit, the pilot is presented with three, well, television screens," Allen had been measuring his words to suit the technological ignorance he was facing. "Each screen will give specific information. For example, one will be dedicated to radar. The ECR-90 radar system in the Super Hornet gives us the ability to engage in the 'Beyond Visible Range' warfare I have been addressing. The radar systems we have on board the Hornet are dramatically more sophisticated than the technology that the English are using on the south and east coasts of England currently. By the middle of the war, two physicists, Boot and Randall, will have invented an electron tube called the resonant-cavity magnetron, which permitted the development of the microwave radar. Obviously, we are well beyond that. The ECR-90 allows the pilot to scan and track multiple targets, returning data on speed, closing speed, altitude, aspect, rang and bearing. By analyzing the radar echoes and comparing them with a database of signals, the radar is capable of distinguishing aircraft types and prioritizing the threats at a range of over two hundred miles.

"The second screen is called the Joint Tactical Information Distribution System. The JTIDS is a tactical display system that provides all combatants with an up to date picture of enemy and friendly positions in the entire theater. A specially equipped plane, called AWACS, or Airborne Warning and Control System, will fly high above the battle arena and transmit the position all the players to both the pilots and commanders offering a major advantage."

Eisenhower climbed up the ladder next to the Hornet and looked into the open cockpit. "Looks pretty complicated up here, Lieutenant."

"That's why it takes years of training before the government will let us drive these planes. The third screen you see up there, on the right, is the Defensive Aids Sub-system, also called DASS. When the pilots most need to operate their defensive system they are probably under the most stress. When you have a bogy crawling up your tail, there is a lot going on. DASS will orchestrate counter measures and defensive systems, such as integration of advanced radar warning receiver, an Infrared warning receiver, a laser warning system, a towed decoy, automatic identification of friend or foe, the ability to select and jam threats and an automatic release mechanism for chaff and flare. DASS offers a complete suite of defensive measures. This plane is tough to shoot down.

"Lastly, the cockpit is equipped with a Heads Up Display System. The HUD will display what ever information the pilot needs on a glass panel in front of him. This enables the pilot to have necessary information available to him at an instant without taking his eyes off the road."

Eisenhower was still on the ladder, "What's this tube here?"

"That is the in-flight refueling probe. The probe allows the jet to take on a full load of fuel while on way to its destination, considerably extending the range of missions.

"As you may have figured, this is a devesting war machine. This one jet can inflict the same damage as a squadron of your current planes."

"This is indeed remarkable technology, Lieutenant," the President was speaking for his staff, "there is no question that these jets will make our impending task considerably less difficult."

"Can we assume that your MJ 12 has a mission plan as to how to use these weapons to achieve the objective you had laid out yesterday, Captain Yoder?" Stimson was now fully convinced that these visitors were indeed from sometime other than 1941.

"What mission plan are you talking about," Marshall and Eisenhower had not been brought fully up to speed as to why the *Stennis* had been time shifted.

"I assume you're here to kick some Axis ass?" Eisenhower asked.

"Things are much more complicated than they currently appear, General, we will have a briefing later on. Lieutenant, why don't you wrap this up with a short walk around of this F-117." Yoder sensed some uneasiness between Eisenhower and the President.

"Yes Sir. The F-117 Seahawk was conceived in a time when radar was so sophisticated that any fly over in an area that was being swept would ultimately be terminal. The plane was designed to be invisible to that radar. The radar cross section of this plane is the size of a seagull. This remarkable accomplishment has been achieved in two fundamental ways.

"First of all, the faceted construction deflects most radar in multiple directions. Secondly, the black covering on the jet actually absorbs any radar energy that is not deflected. This coating is called RAM, Radar Absorbent Material. The plane is all but invisible to the most sophisticated radar equipment ever used. In order to maintain its stealth capabilities, the ordinance is stored internally. The bomb doors open for a moment when the war load is released.

"The F-117 is categorized as a strike fighter. Its mission is to get access to a heavily defended area, deliver ordinance and depart the area virtually unseen and hence, untouched. The Seahawk is not the fastest craft in our arsenal, but because it is pretty much invisible, it doesn't have to be. Maximum speed is Mach one. It has a combat range of seven hundred and fifty miles."

"Thank you, Lieutenant Ben-Gurion. Gentlemen, why don't we retire to the officers mess and have some dinner?"

It was time to make the move he had been contemplating since he had learned of his current assignment. This would be the last time that he would be face to face with someone who could stop the holocaust.

"Mr. President."

Roosevelt was startled. The lieutenant spoke with great force, he commanded attention.

"The Nazi's are killing thousands of Jews each day in extermination camps set up in Poland and elsewhere. Men, women and children are being put to death for no other reason than because they are Jews." His voice was getting louder, probably in response to Captain Yoder's request, then order, for him to stand down.

Tears of anguish filled his eyes as two Lance Corporals rushed towards him. "Six million people will die if you fail to do something. Remember the *St. Louis,* PLEASE, *don't let this genocide continue.*" Ben-Gurion fought to keep some semblance of dignity, he did not want to appear to be insane.

"Take him to the brig. Mr. President, I am very sorry for that outburst, I assure you he will be disciplined." Captain Yoder was red faced and mad as hell.

"It appears that there is more that I need to know, Captain Yoder." Franklin began to realize that this all was going to be dramatically more complicated than he initially suspected.

"I think, Captain, that you may not have been completely forthcoming. Before we accept your mission, the President will need additional briefings." Stimson was shook by the Lieutenant's outburst. Everyone was quite aware of Hitler's distaste for the Jews. Roosevelt had turned back the *St. Louis*, a boat full of Jewish refugees, three years ago. The Jews were a difficult problem. They carried no political muscle, they were misunderstood and frankly, they just weren't very popular.

"What was that young man referring to, Captain?" The carts had arrived at the elevator, Stimson and Knox were helping FDR out.

"Hitler has devised a plan he refers to as the Final Solution. It's diabolical goal is to exterminate Jews."

"Did we allow this to happen?" Roosevelt was horrified.

This was not an area Yoder was planning to engage just now. That God damn Lieutenant was going to be lucky if he ever saw the inside of a jet again.

"It was not a proud moment for the Allies. Hitler was successful in killing an estimated six million Jews, Gypsies, Catholics and handicapped people. It wasn't until late in the war that the US had a hint as to what was going on. In '45, while taking Poland, our troops will come upon concentration camps abandoned by the fleeing Germans. The conditions that these people lived and died in was appalling."

"We must do something, we can't just stand by and let that happen." Politics be dammed, Roosevelt was a compassionate man.

"It will be a complicated issue, Mr. President. I urge caution here."

"How can I be cautious when women and children are being lead off to their slaughter, Sir?"

I may have to keelhaul that Lieutenant, thought Yoder.

"OK, man, but you owe me big time. I'm thinkin I may not be seeing shit duty until ten, twelve years after the war?" Parnes Williams didn't know why he had an advantage, but he wasn't going to trade it away cheaply.

"You fucking dick, you don't even want this duty." Parnes and six others had been picked to serve dinner to President Roosevelt and his party in the Captain's mess.

"Why you even want to wait on the Man, you kissin some brass ass?" Parnes howled at his poetic touch.

"You even know who Roosevelt is, you dumb shit?" Parnes Williams had been Tim's only friend so far, they were bunkmates. He was not uncomfortable talking to him in this jocular bent.

"He some guy they named schools after, probably some general or some shit like that."

"Yeah, he's a general. Did you even *go* to history class?"

"No, man, I was busy with the ladies. I didn't need to know that history shit. Parnes don't look backwards, man, that's where the ugly chicks are."

"OK Einstein, we'll work it out later, just give me the white jacket." He couldn't believe it, Tim Irwin in the same room as Franklin Delano Roosevelt. His father would freak.

Tim was a history buff in a major way. When other kids were playing army with cheap plastic guns, he was clearing the living room to make way for full size maps of various military campaigns. They got so big, he eventually needed an old pool cue with a popsical stick glued on to the end of it to maneuver his troops about. The opportunity to meet FDR in the flesh was not to be missed, even if it meant serving him dinner and pouring his wine.

What other issues have you seen fit to keep from us, Captain." Stimson was getting bitchy. FDR and Knox were looking concerned. Marshall and Eisenhower didn't seem to care much about the politics of war right now, they were in deep conversation as to how to press the incredible advantage that had just drifted into their arsenal.

"Secretary Stimson, World War 11 was, will be, the biggest conflagration in history. There have been volumes written on it and I'm not sure, sixty years later, the scope of it is fully understood. It'll take hours, days, to give you even a cursory understanding of what went on. Remember, I have a mission plan that must be achieved in order to secure the survival of the human race. This is bigger than either of us."

The two men locked horns.

Serve to the left, clear from the right. That was all Tim had been told. The last time he'd seen a white coated waiter, he was celebrating his Dad's seventh birthday at *Peter Lugers* in Brooklyn.

"Pour the wine, and don't spill any." It was delivered pretty much an order from Commander Bosco as he exited the kitchen.

"Yes, Sir."

He heard him before he walked through the door. His voice was distinct if not lower than he expected. Then, there he was, living history. Timmy floated over to Franklin Delano Roosevelt.

"Some wine, Mr. President?"

Time Shift/129

The bottle clattered against the glass as Tim poured.

"You seem a little nervous, son, have you never served a dead President before."

"Yes Sir, no Sir. I'm a huge fan of yours." It just spurted out of his mouth. He tried to actually suck the words back in before they hit the Presidents ears.

"Fan is not what is typically used in conjunction with a politician, is it Henry?"

Roosevelt's good-natured laughter only heightened Tim's embarrassment, causing his face to pass from red to crimson with alarming speed.

"I think you can stop now," Stimson brought Timmy's attention to the fact that the President's glass was now ten percent more than full.

"Oh my God, Let me clean that." In a scene right out of any number of *I Love Lucy* episodes, the painfully full glass of red wine tumbled onto the Presidents lap.

It took a moment before Tim realized that he was rubbing Franklin Delano Roosevelt's crotch.

"What are you in for?" The cell was quite cramped.

Still a little shaken, Tim said, "I rubbed FDR's lap. What about you?"

"I suggested that he needed to stop the holocaust." Allen recognized Tim from the night they both boarded the *Stennis*.

"I'd love to trade you reasons for being in the brig." Tim's head was in his hands.

Ben-Gurion put his head against the wall and closed his eyes. He saw the haunting image of Ruth Karliner in his mind.

When Allen was nine, he had crept unseen into the basement meeting room of his father's Yeshiva where there was a gathering attended by men from all over the community. Sequestered under a table, he listened as

Walter Karliner recounted the terrible story of how, when he was twelve, his family had escaped Germany in May of 1939 aboard an ocean liner, the *St. Louis*.

There was a picture that was projected onto a wall of Walter and his younger sister looking out of two windows as the ship was leaving Hamburg harbor on May 13th. Walter's face, being closer to the camera, was somewhat out of focus, his sister, Ruth, in the background, was clear and sharp. Excitement was etched on their young faces as they began their grand adventure.

The ship arrived in Havana, only to be turned away. Pleas to Congress and the Roosevelt administration for asylum failed and the *St. Louis* returned to Germany. Allen could still see the beautiful face of Ruth, who never saw her tenth birthday. She was exterminated, along with her older sister and her parents. Walter and his brother were the only ones in the family to escape with their lives.

Allen remembered the sense of rage he felt as the Holocaust was made personal for him that evening. Walter Karliner pleaded with the congregation to never forget. Allen Ben-Gurion vowed he never would.

"I think Dwight and I need to hear about your plan, Captain Yoder." The hour Ike and MacArthur had spent with Roosevelt, Stimson and Knox had mostly been spent talking about the absurdity of men traveling back in time.

"General, the reason we are here is to prevent the total annihilation of the human race."

"Are you suggesting that this war will end with the complete destruction of the world?"

"No Sir, but technological developments brought about in the next four years will come to haunt us in the year 2002. The Russians will develop a nuclear capability and will loose control of it to terrorists. Our ultimate goal is to prevent the Soviet Union from ever gaining that capability." Yoder wondered how many more times he was going to have to explain world history sixty years removed.

It wasn't until the President was safely off the *Stennis* that Ben-Gurion and Irwin were released from the brig. They were both ordered to their perspective quarters pending further inquiry.

"We can kick any body's ass from 1942, shit, that's our parent's generation. You don't think you can kick your old man's ass?" Math was not one of Sean Cooney's strong suits. It was closer to his grandparent's generation.

Sean and his rough neck buddies had just finished a grueling workout in the ships gym. Sean was the ringleader, pushing everybody to go further and harder.

As they entered the birding area, Sean scanned the bunks for any that had their heavy blue curtains drawn. A closed curtain at this early evening hour meant one of two things was going on, someone was asleep, or... well, either way, he had an obnoxiously intrusive way to fuck up the moment.

"Come here," he whispered to his muscle headed friends.

He quietly guided them over to the bunk with the name Irwin, T. stenciled on it. He grabbed the curtain and whipped it open. Although he had always hoped to see exactly what he was seeing, after doing this fifty times plus with no success, he had all but given up hope. But lady luck was with him this afternoon. There was that little asshole who thought he was just a little better than everybody else with his Government Issued dungarees around his knees and a fist full of dollars.

Timmy's date with Debbie Gibson came to an premature end. For what seemed like an awfully long time, he laid there with a hand full of himself, wondering if his life could get any worse.

The deafening roar of six squids barking like dogs snapped him into action. He pulled up his trousers, jumped from his bunk and raced out of the area with the mocking sounds of his protagonist chasing him.

He didn't stop running until he found himself at the fan tail. His first thought was to just keep running. The main deck was empty, Tim was alone with his embarrassment.

"My life sucks," he told the Atlantic Ocean.

Things didn't always blow this badly. He fondly recalled his days at the School of Visual Arts in Manhattan. He was a cocky bastard who knew exactly where he was going, Madison Avenue. Tim was going to get into the Ad game. He was one of only two graduates heavily recruited right out of college. He could write his own ticket, and he did. The advertising agency of *Young and Rubicam* considered themselves lucky to have him.

Within three months he created the "Where's the beef" campaign that increased revenue for *Burger King* by twenty eight percent and won him the first of seven CLEO'S and one OBE. By the time he was twenty five he was earning a six figure salary and spending it just as quickly as the checks could be cashed.

Every two years he was off to another agency. By the time he hit *Campbell-Mithun & Esty,* he was thirty and severely burned out. The dishonesty, back stabbing and theft of ideas left him disillusioned and angry.

And then there was the big day. It was a defining day that he could look back on as the single day that changed his life. It started with the numbers 6, 9, 12, 17, 36 and supplemental number 9. As he did every Friday morning, he dropped his lottery ticket on his secretary's desk and asked her to check the numbers. Tim had just taken off his jacket and sat down behind the big mahogany desk that befitted a man of his stature when he heard Janet screech.

A few months before he had won fifteen hundred dollars and that brought a sound considerably less siren like than this.

"You won," she screamed.

He had just gotten to his office door. "No shit, how much?"

"All of it, you won all of it." She was so excited you'd have thought she had won herself.

"How the fuck much is all of it." He was as tense as an addicted gambler during overtime. The answer she gave could change his life.

"Seventeen million dollars!"

Oh yeah, that would do it.

Tim walked back into his office, put on his jacket, grabbed the ticket from a still shaking Janet and headed down the hall.

"Hey Rubin." Rubin Jackowitz was the Creative Director and Tim's boss. A bigger asshole could not be found in New York City. Rubin had recently taken credit for Tim's "Stay Soft" campaign. Sitting on his desk was the spectacular orchid presented to Rubin at a luncheon by Bill Gates himself.

Rubin was sitting behind the even bigger mahogany desk that befitted a man of his stature. "What do you want, Irwin, can't you see I'm busy. And what's all the racquet out there?"

"Tell ya what, Jackoff, here's what I think of you." Even as he was speaking, Tim was unzipping his fly and removing his favorite body part.

Rubin Jackowitz saw what Tim was doing, but his actions were so far out of normal protocol that he was at a loss to develop a response.

Tim Irwin proceeded to urinate into Mr. Jackowitz's prized orchid. The only sound was the dull splash of liquid hitting the petals. With an incredible demonstration of control and marksmanship, Tim filled the orchid flower with his golden stream.

When he was done, he shook it three times, stuffed it back into his pants and left. As he got to the door, the weight of Tim's still warm waste caused Rubin's spectacular flower to bend over, dumping its vile contents onto the impressive mahogany desk.

"This can't be, this can't fucking be!" Tim was frantic. The lottery agent was trying to show him that he had purchased his ticket at 8:03, which meant that his numbers had been entered in the current lottery, not the one just ended.

"For three minutes you're gonna stiff me for seventeen million fucking dollars!" He was beginning to get a little loud.

By nine that night, he had paid his bail ticket, left the city and the career that had betrayed him and wandered back to Long Island.

Life was pretty much down hill from there. He purchased a karate studio with the remnants of his advertising dollars, but that failed after three years. There was an aborted effort to start his own ad agency. The final ignominy was when his wife of four months let him know that she had been screwing one of the partners at the law firm she worked at and that their shiny new marriage was over. The word 'loser' was surgically attached to his psyche.

The next day, Tim joined the Navy to see the world and to masturbate in front of his bunkmates.

"Lieutenant, do you know what keelhauling is?"

This was the first time Allen Ben-Gurion had ever been dressed down by a superior officer and the first time he had met Captain Yoder in person. He did not expect it to be a pleasant meeting.

"Yes Sir, I do." He was standing at rigid attention, eyes fixed at a spot a few inches over Yoder's head. The Captain was a good five inches shorter than Allen, who stood six feet tall. Yoder had a large moon shaped head and a hair line that ran parallel with his ears. He had lazy eyelids that made him appear sleepy. Until he was enraged. Each time he ended a sentence, his eyelids would raise back, making his eyeballs look like a science experiment. The impression it gave was that they were straining to escape from his face. Allen began to mentally work out their trajectory should they indeed pop out of their sockets. He decided that there would be insufficient pressure to shoot them much past the middle of the desk.

"Can you give me a good reason why I shouldn't have you keelhauled?"

How do you respond to a question like that, Allen pondered? Are we in Junior High here? He decided to leave it as the rhetorical question it probable was.

"Don't you ever open your mouth on my ship unless you have my permission, is that clear!"

Where there should have been hair, one large, blue vein appeared and began to throb. If those eyeballs were going to blow, it was going to be now.

"Sir, may I speak freely?" It was a risky question, but the stakes warranted it.

"NO!" Yoder had spent the past two hours trying to figure out how he was going to deal with the mess this fly boy had created. His credibility had been compromised and he was going to have to give up much more information than he was planning on.

Captain Yoder took a deep breath. He didn't like to loose control like this. The last time he barked this loudly was when Captain Rudolf 'which way do I go' Norris crossed his bow during a training exercise.

"Lieutenant, I do appreciate your position. I am painfully aware of the plight of the Jews. I would like nothing more than to prevent the holocaust from going any further, but I have orders..."

"So did Himmler and Goring."

"You are dangerously close to a court marshal, Lieutenant. There is a much bigger picture here than you are aware of. World War 11 will be considerably shorter this time around and at the earliest opportunity, the concentration camps will be liberated."

"But Captain..."

"You are dismissed, Lieutenant."

Lieutenant Allen Ben-Gurion delivered a salute, not out of respect, but out of self preservation. I will not rest until my people are delivered, he committed.

December 19th, 8:12 AM
Norfolk Naval Base

The Stennis was back in port at the Norfolk Naval Base. Admiral Bellinger had made good on his promise to tighten base security. There was not much that could be done when the *Stennis* left port, but once back in, she was fairly well protected. Even the air space over the base had been restricted.

Harsh sat in his office reading over the files left by MJ 12.

"What now?" asked Captain Kelly O'Brien?

"Well, MJ 12 left contingency plans for any number of difficulties. Listen to this, 'In the event there are problems concerning credibility, we recommend showing President Roosevelt and his staff the DVD program titled *History, 1941-2000.*' It appears to be basically a multimedia presentation highlighting major events in history. I'm sure it's geared towards political events that will back up our claims."

"Do you really want to be giving FDR that information?" Kelly questioned, "I'm not necessarily concerned about events in the distant future, but what will happen in the next few years may not be in the countries best interest for him to know. For God's sakes, he's bound to find out the date of his death, do we really want him knowing that? Not to mention the ascendance of Truman to the presidency and Eisenhower's ultimate win in the following election."

Yoder thought for a moment. "I didn't really want to have to disseminate this much information. Just from a humanitarian perspective, I'm not at all comfortable letting FDR know that he has barely four years to live. I am also worried that he'll be making political decisions based on what he will find out from us. That God damned Lieutenant has put me in a very awkward situation. Check the regs, can we keelhaul him?"

Captain O'Brien laughed. "I believe keelhauling went out around the time of the HMS Bounty. However, in his defense, he is one hell of an aviator and an excellent Squadron Leader."

"I'm not unsympathetic to his concern. But we can't just selectively stop the holocaust without shutting Hitler down completely, and that is not in the game plan just yet. When it comes time to hit Germany, I'll make every effort to see if we can't make shutting down the concentration camps a priority." Harsh felt like he was standing at the confluence of good and evil with relation to the holocaust. On the one hand, it was the cruelest example of mass murder in modern history, on the other, the fate of mankind was at stake. It was a painful decision, but for now, he had to turn his back on the plight of the Jews.

"Let's take a look at this presentation. Get this, it was produced by *Buena Vista*."

"Isn't that *Disney*?"

"Gentlemen, thank-you for coming." Captain Yoder had set up the presentation in the ships theater. He had the technicians triple check every component. The NSA guys had upgraded the equipment in the hours before their departure into the past with the most up to date video hardware available. MJ 12 was obviously sensitive for the need to show off twenty first century technology.

The theater going audience consisted of Roosevelt, Stimson, Knox, Generals Marshall and Eisenhower and, having just been brought into the loop, Vice President Harry S. Truman. There had been enough questions addressed by Henry Stimson the previous evening that Harsh knew he was making the right, and only decision, by showing the multimedia history lesson.

"You are going to take a trip shortly that is unprecedented in history. You will be the first individuals to ever receive a look at the unaltered future. I am comfortable with the personal integrity of each of you in this room not to worry that propriety information gleaned from this presentation will be used inappropriately.

"From the discussions we have had over the past twelve hours, I feel that it is necessary to give you a better understanding as to how we, in the year 2002, arrived at the precariously threatening position we, aboard the *Stennis* and the country, were facing.

"What we have prepared for you is called a multimedia presentation. Incorporated in this, film," there was no reason to get involved in a discussion of DVD disks and multi-channel stereo, "will be some narrative and historic clips of events during the years leading up to the year 2000 that have shaped the world of our time." As Harsh left center stage, the lights went down and the show began.

December 7th, 1941, Japan attacks the United States... December 14th, 1941, the United States declares war on the Axis Powers...

The theater was silent. It was a dramatic presentation with so much information it was impossible to comprehend the magnitude of it. FDR seemed the most shaken, his was the only death prophesied.

"Captain, could we have a moment." Henry Stimson recognized the turmoil the President was in and felt it would be best to give him a breather before continuing discussions with Yoder. He pulled Franklin aside.

"My God, Henry, how could it all get so out of hand?" The images of nuclear explosions were etched into his mind.

"Mr. President, are you all right?"

"Oh, don't think I missed the untimely report of my death. It seems I won't be around to see this war through."

For what may have been the first time in his life, Henry Stimson did not know what to say. Even with the diagnosis of a fatal disease there was always the opportunity to refute the physicians expertise.

"Franklin," Henry placed a hand on his shoulder, "we have much to do." He was speaking quietly. "I believe that there are some serious difficulties sixty years from now, however, we need to have more control over this situation."

"How do you think it went?" Captain Yoder was anxious. He did not expect to have to sell the situation to Roosevelt and Stimson. *That old son of a bitch is behind this. Stimson has been difficult since their first meeting.*

"Roosevelt looked disturbed." Captain O'Brien sat with Yoder in a small office off the ships theater. "He had good reason to. Eisenhower and Marshall looked like two kids in a candy store. Every time new weapons technology was introduced I half expected them stand up and applaud. Frank Knox is tough to read and Truman doesn't look like he has fully grasped what's going on yet."

"Well shit, they better get the hell off the pot," Yoder felt himself turning red. He was mad. He was mad that some fucking towel head decided that the world needed to be cleansed, he was mad that he was thrust back sixty plus years into the past, he was mad that the people he came to save didn't seem to give a rats ass, and he was just feeling damn cranky.

"Is there a protocol to achieve our goal without their help?"

"Yes, there is." Harsh shuddered even as he spoke. "It will be fast and hard, and when the fat lady sings, there will be an estimated one hundred million dead Russians and the country will have a half life of about a thousand years."

"Nuclear weapons." Kelly punctuated his thought.

They sat quietly for a moment. "You know, you are the most powerful man in the world right now. It probably frightens them."

Oh my God, thought Harsh, she's right. It had not occurred to him before. He had the power to obliterate countries. There is no one, no country, that could stand in his way. "This is an unprecedented position to be in, and not a very comfortable one either. Nevertheless, I have my orders and *by God* they will be carried out."

"**Captain, the President** would like to see you," Frank Knox had poked his head though the half open door.

"Come on, this is going to be God damn settled right now." Captain O'Brien hadn't known Harsh Yoder but for a couple of days and had yet to see him unwound. She was glad she was not going to be on his ugly side just now.

"Captain Yoder, we have some issues..."

"You know what, Henry, I don't give a shit about your issues." Henry Stimson was taken aback. In the rarefied world of diplomacy he operated in, emotions were always held in check. Differences were dealt with in a civilized manner.

"I have orders and I will carry them out, with or without your help."

"Who do you think you are speaking to."

"The guy who's in my way. That's not a good place to be."

"Gentlemen," Roosevelt realized it was time to act decisively, "Let us sit and discuss this. Captain Yoder, Henry is concerned by the seemingly unchecked power you wield with this incredible weapon called the *Stennis*. I appreciate his view and will report that I am somewhat in accord.

"Please understand, we are, certainly I am, overwhelmed by what you have just shown us. My God, son, questions yet to be asked have been answered. The United States is destined to become the keeper of the gate. It seems that we will drive the world in every important area; socially, economically and politically. We apparently will be somewhat of a driving force in the entertainment field too, that *Disney World* looks like a wonderful place!

"The fact that I know the date of my worldly departure is more than a little disconcerting, although Truman seems to be not terrible perturbed. Just kidding, Harry." Franklin was working hard to ease the tension, he feared for his old friend Henry should it come to fisticuffs with the much younger and clearly more agitated Harsh Yoder.

"I now have a better understanding as to what must be done and why. I think what needs to be discussed is how this goal is to be accomplished, who needs to know and what time frame do we need to work within."

"Mr. President, there is still the question as to where Captain Yoder's allegiance lay, with a president who has not been born yet, or with the duly elected commander and chief."

"Henry, I am not going to make the good Captain make that decision, our goals are aligned. They are not demonstrably different now than they were two days ago. The execution of those goals will certainly be modified. I believe Marshall and Eisenhower will be quite anxious to visit with Captain Yoder and his people to develop a strategy."

About God damn time thought Yoder. "Yes Sir, time is of the essence, there's much ass to kick."

CHAPTER 6
Engage

December 31st, 6:00 AM, 1941
800 miles West of Hawaii

A battle group had formed around the *Stennis* comprised of the *USS Texas,* the *Missouri*, the *North Carolina*, and the heavy cruiser *Minneapolis.* It did not provide the impenetrable wall of protection that twenty first century carriers enjoyed, however, the soon to be nonexistent 1941 Japanese Navy was not the threat the 1980's Russian fleet had been.

"Captain, I've got a reading at 225 mark 44 coming our way at sixty knots."

Yoder was in the con tower, stations were at maximum alert. The *Stennis* was at war and in hostile waters.

"Probably a Zero, how long before it acquires a visual on us?"

"That'd be two Zero's Sir, estimated nineteen minutes before visual."

"Commander," Yoder had picked up the handset patched into the Air Boss, "get me a pair of 18's in the air now."

Within fifty seconds, Lieutenant Yuri Kovalenko, call name Comrade, was at nine hundred feet and climbing.

"Captain," Commander Patrick had bad news, "we've got a malfunction on catapult four, it'll take six minutes to get another ship in the air."

"Shit, by then the engagement will be over. Get it ready in case we need it." This is exactly why we drill the hell out of them, Yoder thought, to have a cluster fuck when it's go time.

"Comrade, transition to 225 mark 44, three thousand feet. You should have two targets acquired on your ECR. They are both to be splashed, repeat, they are to be splashed."

"That's a roger." Lieutenant Kovalenko could see two small blips on his Multi-Function Display. He felt a chill run up his spine. Kovalenko had over fifteen hundred hours in the seat of fighter jets but had yet to fire a weapon in earnest.

The planes he was to down were only moments away, he got off his afterburner, things were going to go fast enough at this point.

"Comrade, this is Captain Yoder, take them down with the cannon." Yoder recognized the fact that the munitions he had were finite, there was no reason to blow off a pair of ASRAAM missiles on such a simple target.

"Roger that." At 1700 rounds per minute, it wouldn't take but a single burst to rip these ancient planes from the sky. Yuri slowed his Super Hornet to three hundred knots and switched from air to air missiles to cannons.

This is the real deal, he reminded himself. The years of training came down to right now. He may have felt a little better about his present task had the Zero's any chance to fight back. By the time they knew they were under attack, it'll be all over for them. There certainly wasn't going to be much of a challenge here.

Tsutomu Yoshimoto and Mariko Nakamura were flying a recon mission. Although the United States Navy had been reduced to shambles by the might of the Rising Sun, Admiral Yamamoto was not going to grow complacent. He would remain diligent and be prepared to fight the round eye in his home waters if necessary. Japan would not be caught sleeping like the Great Giant.

Already, only twenty four days into the war, Japan had achieved unimaginable success. Britain's newest battleship, the *HMS Prince of Whales* and her sister ship, the *HMS Repulse* lay on the bottom of the sea off the coast of Malaya. The Emperor's troops had stormed the shores of Apparri, Gonzaga and Vigan to take the Philippines. The US Navy base at Cavite, near Manila, was now nothing more than rubble. The Sing Mun Redoubt, centerpiece of the defense line in Hong Kong, was taken in five hours, humbling the mighty British Empire. Days later, the British were again humbled in Malaya as they were forced to retreat back to the Jitra Line.

A half hearted attack on the destroyer, *Jintsu,* off the Philippine coast, was hurled back with disastrous consequences to the arrogant Americans. Only days ago, five hundred Japanese troops attacked the quivering British at the Jitra Line, taking more than three thousand prisoners. The Japanese war machine has advanced from victory to victory, proving to the world that they are the rightful rulers of Asia.

Tsutomu and Mariko were proud of their fellow pilots for their remarkable success at Pearl Harbor. They were both disappointed to have not been chosen for that historic mission. Both were anxious to fly their far superior Zero's against the American and British. They too would bring honor to the Emperor.

They were beginning a slow banking turn that would bring them back to the Shokaku Class aircraft carrier, the *Zuikaku,* when Tsutomu saw a flash at nine o'clock. He saw an odd shaped plane bearing down on him. Before he could react, Tsutomu Yoshimoto and his Zero disappeared within a ball of flame.

"Splash one." Lieutenant Kovalenko was unable to take both planes out with a single burst as he had planned.

He would have to come around to reacquire the second plane.

Mariko Nakamura was startled by the explosion to his port side. Just as he was trying to figure out what had happened to his friend, his attention was drawn to the screeching sound of an FA-18/E Super Hornet flying low across his bow.

"Holy Shit!" He reverted to his native language. Mariko had graduated from UCLA in 1939 with a degree in aeronautical engineering. He followed his heart when his home land called, desperately in need of young men with his talents.

What sort of machine is this? He saw a small American flag on one of the two vertical stabilizers as it passed him. The cockpit was covered with a clear bubble, the pilot inside disguised with a large helmet and mask. Panic set in. He needed to get out of there, but he recognized that he was dramatically out matched by this devil machine the Americans have unleashed.

Lieutenant Kovalenko got on the throttle and pulled back on his stick to make as short a turnaround as he could. He did not want to loose his prey. He also did not want to prolong the agony his prey had to be feeling. Kovalenko caught a glimpse of the Japanese pilots face as he passed him. It was a frightening expression. This man was suddenly aware that he was in a fight for his life and was virtually helpless to defend himself. Kovalenko was anxious to end this.

As he came around, Yuri had the Zero painted; the cannon automatically tracked the target. The Japanese pilot was doing everything he could to rid himself of his executor, but all his ministrations were fruitless. Kovalenko suspected he knew as much.

Lieutenant Kovalenko squeezed the trigger on his stick and unleashed a one second stream of lead. The Zero evaporated. "Splash two."

"As you all are aware, first blood has been drawn by Lieutenant Kovalenko of the *Pukin Dogs*, take a bow Mr. Kovalenko." Kovalenko would just as well have forgotten the past hour of his career. There certainly wasn't any honor involved in what he had just done.

Captain Craig VanPelt, the Air Wing Commander, was giving the most important briefing of his career. He sat on the other side close to fifteen years ago during Desert Storm. Captain VanPelt felt jealous of his aviators. He'd love one more chance to crawl back into the ring.

"We now begin Operation Hot Wind. During the next forty eight hours we will incapacitate the Japanese Navy. History tells us that their Navy consisted of, and consists of now, 130 ships. That breaks down to eight aircraft carriers, eighty three destroyers, eighteen heavy cruisers and twenty one light cruisers. By dawn Thursday, all but a handful of them will be below sea level. Your squadron leaders will give you your missions. Gentlemen and ladies, good luck."

"**The Pukin Dogs** are going to take out three aircraft carriers, fifteen destroyers and six of the heavy cruisers over the course of nine missions." Allen Ben-Gurion had been appointed squadron leader during the last cruise. The former leader, Lieutenant Hallowman, had left the cruise early to bury his mother.

"We'll be driving the F22's." The F22 was the United States newest carrier based strike fighter. As well as containing the latest in avionics, the 22's were stealth aircraft. The Japanese had developed a reliable radar system, called cats' whiskers. The missions assigned to the Pukin Dogs were going to be near and over the Japanese island, it made sense to use the F22's. There were only seven pilots certified to fly the 22, five of them, Savage,

Kovalenko, Yamamoto Greenspan and Ben-Gurion, were all proud members of the Dogs.

"The first to go will be the most difficult of our missions. The aircraft carrier, *Kaga*, is sitting port in Japan. She is accompanied by the destroyers *Akigumo, Hatsukaze,* and the *Urakaze*. We will be flying mostly daylight raids. The plan is to use as few missiles as possible. In case anyone has forgotten, it's 1941 and we can't order up a few more Maverick's. We'll be getting in close to make sure we score.

"The weather will be fair, a few clouds at ten thousand feet, light breeze blowing southeast. Myself, Kovalenko, Greenspan and Savage will take this first mission. We will refuel twice on our way there and once coming home. Because these ships are at port, we'll forgo the Sea Eagle's and arm ourselves with Mavericks."

"Why not the Eagles, they have a much better range than the Mavericks?" Greenspan was uncomfortable with this mission. Japanese by birth, he was adopted by Amy and Ira Greenspan after an earthquake decimated his village in '72. The Greenspan's did everything they could to keep little Yamamoto in touch with his heritage. His grandfather had fought with the Japanese Navy in the War, could it be possible that he'd be taking out his own blood? The further away from point of impact he could be, the better.

"Again, we need high probability attacks here, apparently we'll be chewing up close to twenty percent of our stores over the next two days. They just don't want to take any chances of a miss.

"The AWACS will be in the air, although I don't expect we will experience much in the way of fighter resistance. And if we do, we'll send Kovalenko after them." Everybody laughed, except Kovalenko. "They have antiaircraft guns, however, I expect we will be in and out of there before they ever have a chance to lite them up. Let's go over the coordinates and way points." For the next forty minutes Ben-Gurion addressed the finer points of air to ground destruction.

Kaitlyn Savage felt extreme excitement as she sat in her jet, preparing for take off. She had done her walk around and now waited as the Plane Captain scrutinized her steed. Nothing was mentioned, everyone knew that it would be bad luck to do so, but she was about to become the first American woman in combat. It was only right. Congressman Giuliani used Lieutenant Savage as his prototype service woman when he pushed HR-345.002 through committee and then finally as a bill, which allowed woman to fight alongside men. "Why would we leave the best on the sidelines during our most critical moments based upon gender?" he was quoted.

And Kaitlyn Savage was the best new pilot in the service at the turn of the century. She had the extraordinary hand eye coordination and superior intellect necessary to fly fighter jets. But what set her above her male counterparts was an exceptional intuition that often accompanies the shortage of one body part. This physical omission gave her an edge in combat situations. Raw aggression was not necessary if you possessed finesse, and finesse resulted in fewer casualties. Kaitlyn Savage also had the driving determination that pushed her further than most, almost as if she had something to prove.

Kaitlyn Savage did have something to prove. Until she joined the service, her life had been an aimless, hedonistic journey. Born Kaitlyn Clark, she was the daughter of the brilliant bond trader Justin Clark and Caroline Nash, a local news woman who did weekend fluff pieces for FOX. Kaitlyn had a silver spoon shoved in her mouth moments after squeezing out of the birth canal. She lived her first three years in a spectacular Tudor home in the affluent bedroom community of Scarsdale, New York. Both an upstairs and a downstairs maid kept a wonderful home. Daddy was ferried to Wall Street each day by Arthur, the family chauffeur, in a Mercedes Benz limousine. Lucy, her Filipino nanny, saw to her soiled diapers and scrapped knees. Living was easy, until Daddy shot mommy in the head and then put a round behind his ear.

The neighbors were shocked. "He was such a nice man," they were quoted in all the papers, "we can't imagine how he could do such a thing." It took weeks for the Feds to deconstruct Justin's elaborate scheme to defraud Citi Bank out of close to a billion dollars. It was all unraveling, he did what he had to do. The silver spoon was yanked out of Valerie's mouth and she was shipped down to Tampa, Florida, to be raised by Caroline's white trash, trailer living sister.

Gretta Nash couldn't understand why little Kaitlyn suddenly began acting up around the age of seven. Had she asked her common law husband, Bo, maybe he could have told her that it was natural for a child who is being sexually molested by her step father to develop behavioral problems. But she didn't, and Kaitlyn was off to a series of foster homes.

There were two constants in her life, her love of learning and her ejection out of most of the schools she attended. Kaitlyn picked things up quickly, then became bored. Then became unruly. Then became destructive. It was then time for a new school, and frequently, a new family.

She smoked her first cigarette at twelve, got drunk two days before she turned thirteen and had consensual sex for the first time by age fourteen. By the time she had been thrown out of her last school, early in her senior year, Kaitlyn Clark was pretty wordily.

She spent a year visiting the underside of Tampa, doing some of this and lots of that. It was her fondness for education, however, that drew her to the University of

South Florida. She took a GED exam to get her high school diploma, then proceeded to get a four year degree in two and a half years while also learning to use drugs in a responsible manner.

College taught her two things; there were a lot less make work projects in a class if you were having sex with the professor, and that she needed structure in her life. It was her first airplane flight that defined a career for her and allowed her to gain focus for the first time in her life. One of her boyfriends took her up in his Cessena, and at fifteen thousand feet, initiated her into the "Mile high club." The sex was marginal, but the flight was exhilarating. The next day she went to join the Air Force.

A Navy recruiter spotted her heading for the Air Force booth and intercepted her. "The Air Force is full this month, why don't you take a look at the Navy. Sure," he lied, "I can guarantee you flight school." He couldn't, but her aptitude tests placed her squarely where she wanted to go. In a freak of modern military protocol, Kaitlyn was sent exactly where she should have gone.

It was her idea to choose the call name 'Dancer' when she became a pilot. It was, what she thought, a very private joke. When she heard for the first time that there was a rumor going around that she had been a stripper, she became paranoid. How could anyone have found out? It turns out they hadn't. Just the active military rumor mill churning out thousands of unsubstantiated claims per year at every base in the country.

She had enjoyed exposing herself for money. That was around the time she legally changed her name to Savage, feeling very little filial relationship to her birth name, Clark. It spoke to how she felt. She also used it as her stripper name. Kaitlyn's stunning looks and her contentious attitude joined to make her the highest paid dancer on the circuit.

There was never a challenge she hadn't conquered, the woman was fearless. It was now time to do what she had signed on to do, fly airplanes, break things and kill people.

"Eighteen minutes to target." It had been a long flight, they were all anxious to deposit their ordinance and go home. Kovlenko and Greenspan were to destroy the *Kaga* and the *Akiguma*. Files from the *Stennis* and radar reports from the AWACS confirmed that the two ships were docked side by side. The *Hatsukaze* and the *Urakaze* were at anchor eight hundred meters off shore, Ben-Gurion and Savage would liberate them from the surface world.

"Arm your missiles." The jets pulled into standard strike formation, one pair of F 22's four miles behind the other pair. Kovlenko and Greenspan took the lead and broke off at ten miles out to line up for their run on the *Kaga* and the *Akiguma*.

Kovlenko toggled his frequency transmit button, "Let's get an SAR picture." Both pilots slewed their APG-70 dishes around and painted the ships. The Synthetic Aperture Radar mode delivered photo quality images to their MFD's from miles away.

The *Akiguma* was approximately one hundred meters from the *Kaga*. Kovlenko tightened his grip on his joy stick, his index finger gently caressing the trigger. The sky was clear and the afternoon sun was at his back. At a mile out, he released one Maverick and vectored it towards his target.

Yamamoto had the *Kaga* painted, its image filled his center MFD. Another image clouded his mind, that of his grandfather. The only picture that remained of Yamamoto Yamora was a head shot of him proudly wearing his Naval uniform. It was taken in 1943, almost a year from now. He had never met the man, but as in the Japanese tradition he was raised in, he revered his ancestors. Right now, right at this moment in an artificial time, what he was about to do did not seem right. Lieutenant Yamamoto Greenspan released his missile and slewed it four degrees starboard. This subtle misuse of government equipment assured a near miss.

Kovlenko's Maverick hit the *Akiguma* mid stern and split her in half. He was pulling an uncomfortable six G turn when he heard Yamamoto's missile explode. It didn't sound right. Yuri twisted his 22 on its back to get a look at the *Kaga*.

How the hell could he have missed? Kovalenko thought. In his current position, he had less than a second to make a decision. He made the one that fighter pilots are expected to make, he banked to port and lined up his jet on the *Kaga*. His SAR immediately acquired the carrier. Kovalenko squeezed off another Maverick and guided it in. He was so close that the flight time of the missile was estimated in seconds. Kovalenko was not going to take the chance of this shot going wide and decided to ride it in as close as he could without taking damage from the initial blast.

Suddenly, a fairly calm sky erupted with puffs of black smoke. The soldiers manning the antiaircraft guns had no idea that they were under attack until the *Akiguma* erupted before them. Kovalenko held his plane true, the 22 was very well armored and he only needed another two seconds to assure a hit.

It was the first of two unrelated freak occurrences that would give Lieutenant Yuri Kovalenko reason to question his initial decision to take the second missile run. An unfragmented projectile, that typically would have fallen relatively harmlessly into the harbor due to its now excessive weight, collided with Kovalenko's F 22.

The fist size piece of steel, made up of an old Dodge purchased from the US in an unfortunate scrap metal deal months before the war, was swallowed up into the air intake scoop under the main fuselage. It quickly rattled its way to the middle of the plane and tore a hole right below the fuel crossover line.

Kovalenko felt his jet buck and then saw flames wrap around the outside of his cockpit.

"Eject, eject, eject!" It was Yamamoto screaming into his headset. From his position, Yamamoto could see the extensive damage to Kovalenko's jet.

Yuri grabbed the two yellow handles above him, yanked them down, and prepared for what he knew was going to be the wildest ride of his life. He heard the sharp crack of the small explosion that blew away the canopy. The intense noise of air rushing around the now exposed cockpit shocked him. He felt the rockets under his ejection seat lighting up. There was a tremendous tug on his limbs as the steel cables attached to his G-suit retracted, keeping arms and legs out of harms way.

It was two days before Christmas when this particular unit was being manufactured in Seattle. Mary McCormick was in a hurry to get to the party. She knew that if she didn't get there quickly, the guys in metal stamping would eat all the shrimp. Mary loved shrimp. She quickly cut her last cable of the day. The cable was six inches to long. This unacceptable breach in workmanship allowed one of Yuri's arm to flail.

"Oh shit." They were the last two undignified words Lieutenant Yuri Kovalenko would ever utter. Due to the violent nature of the ejection, Lieutenant Kovalenko did not notice that his left arm was still in the cockpit of his falling F 22.

"I've got a chute," Yamamoto reported to Ben-Gurion, who was already within eye view of the scene. He banked his jet and moved closer for a better visual.

"Jesus Christ," muttered the Buddhist believing, Jewish raised Yamamoto Greenspan. Kovalenko's left arm was gone. His partially dissected body hung in its harness, gently swaying beneath his canopy.

Moments after his chute deployed, Yuri regained consciousness. It was not the pain that brought his attention to the missing limb, but the red liquid spraying him in the face. He went to wipe his visor off to see what could possible be leaking from a parachute only to find his left arm did not seem to be working. Trauma from the blast, he figured. He made a quick mental check of his other limbs and figured he was still lucky to get out of the inferno flying into the sea with just a broken arm. He used his right hand to clear his visor and then blew his last meal into his still connected mask.

The brachial artery hanging out of his exposed shoulder was spurting brilliant red blood. Now it hurt. Kovalenko looked away and screamed. The thought that he was going to be the first causality from the *Stennis* made him hurl again.

Greenspan and Ben-Gurion circled their friend and felt the anguish that comes from helplessness. The amount of blood filling the air indicated that Yuri would be dead shortly after hitting the water. They could do nothing but turn and head home hoping that Lieutenant Yuri Kovalenko lived long enough to catch a glimpse of the burning *Kaga*.

January 1st, 1942, 10:43 AM
USS John C. Stennis

General Douglas MacArthur sat in Yoder's ward room with his feet up on a desk. He was sucking on a large corncob pipe. He was pissed.

"This is my damn theater, the Pacific is mine. Now I have a Captain, from the by God future no less, running my God damn war." MacArthur was not prone to profanity, as mild as his outburst was, but his pride had taken a hit.

"I appreciate your frustration, Sir." Captain O'Brien had read enough about General Douglas MacArthur to know not to derail his tirade with the facts.

Two days ago, an F-15 was sent to Australia to collect General MacArthur. After a twenty minute briefing, he was stuffed into the WSO seat and expressed mailed to the *Stennis*. "This is one hell of a plane you got here, Lieutenant," he told the pilot. Then he foolishly asked "What can she do?" Two minutes later he neatly tied off his barf bag and dropped it to his feet. "Congratulations Sir," the pilot proudly informed a slightly green General, "you are the first man in history to break the sound barrier." MacArthur didn't think it could get any worse until he experienced his first carrier landing.

"We've worked night and day for weeks on our return plan. Hell, I told those people that I would return. Return as a victor, not as a bystander. And this Captain of yours, Harsh Yoder, what the hell kind of a name is that?" Kelly decided to interpret that as a rhetorical question.

"This guy seems to be taking orders from a group of men who haven't been born yet. This is God damn ridiculous. I know more about this theater of operations than anyone alive."

What a pompous son of a bitch, Kelly thought. A lot of big talk from Dugout Doug. It was less than a month since he had his ass hauled out of Corrigador, leaving his troops to fend for themselves. He just doesn't seem to care how many American lives have been saved. She scrolled through the major Pacific battles that would not take place, Guadelcanal, Siapan, Guam...

She snapped out of her trance when Captain Yoder and Admiral Bill Halsey charged into the room, they were both smiling.

"This is a happy New Year, General, I've got the final numbers on Operation Hot Wind. The Japanese Navy is operationally extinct. We've sunk one hundred and seven of their one hundred and thirty ships. The handful of ships still above the water line are inconsequential. We suffered one causality."

Bull Halsey had been brought aboard the *Stennis* twelve hours earlier. He was overwhelmingly enthusiastic about the stunning destructive power now in American hands.

"I revise my earlier statement, Mac, they won't *even* be speaking Japanese in hell when we're through with those bastards. Their Navy is fucked."

"What about their troops, they have close to a million men running around southeast Asia?" Mac wasn't going to concede to victory in the Pacific just yet. MacArthur was Army, as far as he was concerned, you had no victory until you controlled the ground.

"First of all, General, our goal is not to desiccate their army, we have plans for them," Yoder was beginning to not like this icon of history, "secondly, their ability to move those troops around has just been severely hindered. If need be, we can move around the Pacific waters with impunity, delivering troops or supplies as we see fit. However, although we don't expect the Japanese to run up a white flag just yet, we are prepared to end this part of the war very quickly."

"Whose we, Captain, those gentlemen from the future?" MacArthur took on a sarcastic tone. It was impossible to deny the remarkable technology he had seen, but people from the future? He was having a tough time accepting any of this.

"Shit Mac, uncomfortable with the fact that the Navy bailed your ass out again?" Halsey was not overly fond of MacArthur.

"General, may I speak openly?" Yoder didn't need this inter service rivalry crap right now.

"Certainly, Captain."

"Kelly, could you give us a minute?" Yoder waited until Captain O'Brien left the room, then sat down across from MacArthur.

"General MacArthur," Yoder was struggling to sound calm, "what we are in the process of doing is saving approximately seventy thousand American lives and who knows how many Filipino, French and British lives. I'd like you to imagine going back to 1861 and fighting for the South during the Civil War. Now let's take with you a few fighter planes, a couple of fifty caliber machine guns and a cannon or two. With these weapons at your disposal, your military skills, and with impeccable records of each campaign, do you think you could have done an even better job than General Lee? I suspect that you'd be able to win the war, and win it quickly.

"This strategy has been created by some of the sharpest minds of our time and with the distinct advantage of hindsight. This war is now going to be won more quickly and more economically, both in terms of lives and equipment. Our express goal is to prevent the extinction of the human race, that is the only reason I am here. Believe me, I didn't volunteer for this. As my world was facing total destruction, I received orders to go back in time within hours of finding out that time travel was possible. This has been as strange for me as your first flight in an F 15 was for you."

I doubt that, MacArthur thought as he felt himself getting queasy at the reminder. "I understand you perspective, Captain. This just isn't the way I was taught to fight a war."

"Only because you didn't have the weapons we're carrying available to you." Even in his time, the Navy and the Army were often at odds as to how to fight a campaign.

This was some New Year, thought Yoder. Or was it really a new year for him at all? Although he wasn't around to celebrate it the first time, this is still a past event for him. Harsh made a mental note not to celebrate the New Year until he could emotionally work this all out.

"**You calm him** down some?" Captain O'Brien accompanied Harsh to the main deck, he needed some air.

"Some," Yoder offered, "he is one son of a bitch. History pretty much had him nailed. I'm sure he's a brilliant General, but his people skills stink."

"Halsey seems to be an ally, you should've seen him drool while touring the main deck. I got a guy down there right now with a mop."

The two officers stood ten feet back from the edge of the deck. It was a stunning morning; the water was so blue it blended into the sky at the horizon, an effect Harsh had only seen once before. "You know, history has been changed. From this point on, we may not necessarily be able to count on the information stored in the computers or our heads."

It was a staggering thought. "How many American men who died as we took back the Pacific last go around will not have died. Some of these men will go on to greatness, some might be serial murderers. How many lives will each one of those men change. The whole paradigm has shifted. For better or for worse."

January 1st, 1942, 1:03 PM
White House, Washington, DC

"**If this information** is credible, we have the Japanese on the run." Henry Stimson was ecstatic. Even without the historical records he had received from Captain Yoder, he knew the cost of taking back the Pacific Islands was going to be steep.

"What do you think of our Captain Yoder now, Henry," Roosevelt was equally excited.

"Now I don't care where they're from, it would have taken us two years to accomplish what they did in two days. Let's go ahead and put together a letter to Prime Minister Tojo ."

January 2nd, 1942, 6:45 AM
Tokyo, Japan

"This is outrageous, how could it have happened," Prime Minister Tojo, who had forced Konoye out of office four months previously, was red faced. "How," he slammed his fist on the desk in front of him. In his left hand he held a letter that had just been transcribed from a telex that arrived less than an hour ago.

Prime Minister Tojo,

Recognizing the belligerent status of Japan, and the state of war that exists between us, The United States of America demands your unconditional surrender.
We have sunk 107 of the 130 ships in your now, nonexistent fleet. This took us two days. Mount Nitaka has been retaken.
You have until January 4th to agree to a complete and unconditional surrender OR THERE WILL BE GRAVE CONSEQUENCES.

Franklin Delano Roosevelt, President of the United States of America

There had been confirmations of seventy eight ships being sunk, more were coming in. "How can I fight a war without a Navy, or without an Admiral? Isoroku Yamamoto had performed ritual hari kari several hours ago. Tojo wondered about the condition of his own katana..

"How have they broken our code?" The reference to Mount Nitaka was most disturbing. "Do they know every move we make?" Tojo had questions for which there were no ready answers.

"There have been early reports of fantastic planes that cannot be shot down that are capable of sinking our ships with one bomb." Admiral Chuichi Nagumo had replaced Yamamoto within the hour. The news of Yamamoto's death came as a pleasant surprise to Chuichi. Their dislike for each other was legend. It was to Yamamoto's credit that he chose Admiral Nagumo to lead the strike on Pearl Harbor, despite the fact that Nagumo did not believe in the plan at all. While the attack was widely celebrated, Nagumo was chided by Yamamoto for failing to destroy the American escort vessels, the oil tank farms and the repair facilities, despite the urging of his staff officers to launch a second attack.

"We have no Nihon Kaigon," Hideki Tojo was now purple, "what shall I tell the Emperor, that you have lost his Navy in forty eight hours?"

January 2nd, 11:40 PM
USS John C. Stennis

Do you think we'll hear from them, Harsh?" This was the third time Halsey had asked that question. It was late, the two of them had ditched MacArthur and reconvened in Yoder's ward room for some brandy and cigars. Although smoking was now prohibited in the new Navy, who was going to explain to Bull Halsey that his second hand smoke was giving them lung cancer?

"Bill," they were on a first name basis, "during the first go around, we parked a nuclear bomb in down town Hiroshima, leveled the city. Remember, at this point, Japan had lost the war. We had beaten a path to their door step and were preparing a full scale invasion. Even the Japanese did not expect to be able to keep us out.

"We delivered them an ultimatum. Incredibly, we didn't hear from them for two days. History doesn't record what the hell they were thinking. The smart money suggests that they thought either we didn't have any more bombs or that we didn't have the political will to drop a second one. So, off we go to Nagasaki, level the damn place. The next day they sued for peace. Had the Emperor board the *USS Missouri* right in Tokyo Bay and sign the papers."

"What then?" Halsey was a warrior, there was never any doubt that he was going to run their little yellow asses out of the Pacific, but what do you do with a vanquished foe in the twentieth century?

"The Treaty of Versailles was a valuable historic lesson. Crippling Germany was a big mistake. Years of difficulties after World War 1 opened a window that Hitler climbed through. It was decided to introduce Democracy to Japan and bring them in instead of locking them out. Japan ultimately became our largest trading partner. They put their considerable energies into making money and were wildly successful at it."

"God damn, it'll be one cold day in hell before you found me buying anything made in Japan. I pulled into Pearl hours after their cowardly attack, what a sight," Halsey looked off at nothing as he conjured up in his mind the horror of December seventh, the *Arizona* listing port, pouring black smoke into the sky, bodies of sailors floating in the water. No, he didn't expect to be looking to partner with the Japs any time soon.

"Captain, they have you patched through." Captain O'Brien let Yoder know that the com link set up between the *Stennis* and the White House was on line.

"Come on, lets go to the communications room."

"**Where'd you two** go, I lost track of you in the mess?" MacArthur was already there, suggesting his perceived importance by sitting in the Captains chair right in the middle of the table.

"Hit the head, Doug. See you found yourself a seat." His power play was not lost on Halsey.

There was a speaker phone set up on the table, an innocuous looking device no bigger than a pie plate. A similar piece of equipment sat on Roosevelt's desk in the Oval Office. Due to the lack of satellites, an AWAC had to be put in the air to relay the signal back to a sophisticated high gain antenna on the California coast, then to Washington, where a similar antenna had been erected on the White House, extending close to one hundred feet into the sky.

"Mr. President, can you hear me all right." There was a pause, then a few expletives were uttered by a stunned Frank Knox.

"Sir, just speak out loud as if you were carrying on a conversation in the room, the microphones in the X-344 are extremely sensitive." Yoder recognized the voice of Ensign Gregory, one of the tech guys sent stateside to bring the White House into the twenty first century, communications wise.

"Congratulations, Captain, on your wonderful victory. If I am to understand correctly, the Japanese Navy is out of commission."

"Thank-you, Sir."

"Pretty much lightens your load, Doug." Roosevelt couldn't let the moment pass without firing a small volley at MacArthur.

"I haven't seen a white flag over Tokyo yet, Mr. President." MacArthur was still reeling from this latest technological marvel when he caught the barb.

"You will shortly," Yoder joined in. "For reasons that I had outlined earlier, Sir," he was talking to the

President, "I did not expect Japan to fold with the loss of their Navy. We have only made war more difficult from them, not impossible. As General MacArthur is fond of pointing out, they still have a formidable ground force. Our next strike will be a clear indication to them that we can, and will, pick them apart at our leisure and with impunity."

"I've got your notes right here, Captain," Stimson joined in, "why don't we go over stage two of Operation Hot Wind, I believe we are now referring to it as Operation Deadly Wind."

"Yes Sir, just to make sure we are all on the same page, let me restate our mission plan. As expected, Japan has not surrendered. Operation Deadly Wind will place a nuclear war head on one of their cities. As you know from the reports you have, Secretary Stimson, in 1945, the United States dropped the first nuclear device in history on the city of Hiroshima. A second bomb was forcibly inserted on Nagasaki two days later. Japan sued for peace within hours.

"Hiroshima was chosen in '45 because it was a fairly low density city that was engaged in the manufacture of war material. I believe it was a good choice then. However, this time around, it is my recommendation, based on research done by MJ 12, that we drop a nuke on the city of Sapporo," he could hear maps rustling in the Oval Office.

"It looks to be a few hundred miles east of Tokyo," it was Roosevelt's voice.

"Yes Sir. If those of you right here would look at the map on the monitor, it would be helpful." There was a one hundred inch digital screen hanging on the wall behind Yoder.

"Why the switch from Hiroshima to Sapporo, Captain?" Knox was next to be heard from.

"Secretary Knox, the Japanese are a stubborn people. While we have destroyed their Navy, they still have a formidable army roaming about Asia and are not going to be assuaged easily. Hiroshima is located on the fringe of the country, and although it is a manufacturing city, it holds less strategic importance than Sapporo. Due to its proximity to Tokyo, they will be quite shocked that we could destroy a city so near their capital and with such impunity. It will be made clear to them that should they not heed our ultimatum, Tokyo will be next."

"Well, Captain Yoder, you've answered my next two questions, nicely done. Now, how do you propose that we deliver this implement of catastrophic destruction?"

"Mr. President, do you recall seeing the A/F-117 Seahawk during you tour of the *Stennis*? It was the odd looking black jet."

"Yes Captain, I do. Its main feature was its stealth capability, if I recall."

"That's exactly right and exactly why we will use it. The strike will come at night, at approximately two AM. There is no way they will be able to pick it up on their radar and it is invisible at night."

"Well, I will leave the mission parameters to you. From a humanitarian perspective, I would like to give them twenty four hours to evacuate the city."

"I don't see that as a problem, Mr. President. The fact that we will tell them where we intend to hit them and then do it should add considerably to our resolve."

"Where do you want me to put it, Captain?"
They all were sitting in the briefing room. There were maps lying about.

"From what I've heard about these bombs, just drop the son of a bitch anywhere," Halsey was fascinated with these new war toys.

"Sir, pick a street corner, then tell me on which side of the street you want the nuke, that's how accurate our delivery system is." Lieutenant John Long Bow Wolf was a full blooded Cherokee Indian. He spoke in a slow but deliberate monotone voice. He wore his hair on the long side of regulation and had piercing gray eyes. John Long Bow Wolf looked like a warrior.

"Park it on the corner of Kita-Gojo and Nishi-Jaitchome Avenue's, north side." Yoder appreciated the cool confidence his aviator's projected.

"Not a problem Sir."

"Captain," Kelly O'Brien read from a piece of paper just handed to her. "The 22 you sent up on recon reports no sign of evacuation from Sapporo."

"Those arrogant bastards. Do you know the city's population?"

"Figure about two hundred thousand."

"Get me Roosevelt on the com link."

"Captain, they started it. The more I read from the historical records that you left me, the more inclined I am to not care very much. It doesn't seem that they gave any warning to the people of Nanking.. This Batan death march is something I wish we could have avoided. They have been warned, my hands are clean."

January 5th, 1:56 AM
110 miles east of Sapporo

The city of Sapporo should have been coming into visual range. Even at this hour, there were generally some peripheral lights that would give up a city, but there wasn't a candle burning within a mile of the place. It was going to be tougher than he thought to hit the north corner of Kita-Gojo and Nishi-Jaitchome.

Suddenly, it looked like a fire works display. Hundreds of antiaircraft guns erupted at once. They fired for twenty seconds, then went dark. A minute later, off they went again. They were shooting at something they couldn't see, couldn't paint on radar, nor did they know when to expect it. They had no idea how defenseless they were against his Seahawk. They did the only thing they could, shoot in the dark and hope something hit the invisible apocalypse heading towards them.

Lieutenant Wolf's 117 was the first plane in any history to leave a carrier deck with a live nuke onboard. It was a slightly uncomfortable departure. Although the bomb was not armed, emotionally, the idea of ditching this flying Armageddon in the sea due to a bad launch was disconcerting. Equally disconcerting was the fact that Long Bow was on his way to kill close to two hundred thousand people. Would this make him the largest mass murder in history?

Like most of his fellow aviator's, Lieutenant Wolf had not been in a shooting war. It was easy to drop imagined nuclear weapons on Tehran or Beijing, but this was real. People were going to die, many people, within the next ten minutes. Most of them bearing no culpability in this war that their leaders dragged them into.

He shook his head, there was no time to ponder the morality of his mission, it was time to do his job.

"Tower, this is Long Bow, I'm preparing for my run." His target coordinates had been entered into his attack computer before he launched. Now, he had only to keep his plane driving straight while a laser guided his nuclear tipped missile to the north corner of Kita-Gojo and Nishi-Jaitchome.

"Package away." He kept his eyes on his center MFD showing an illuminated view of the city of Sapporo, curtesy of an AWAC circling nearby. The sky lite up again, more shots in the dark. They were all futile, there was nothing they could do now but prepare to die. He prayed they would die fast.

Lieutenant Wolf was five miles out when the missile detonated, right in the middle of Tanuki-Koji Street, two blocks south of his intended target. Even with the specially built visor covering his eyes, the explosion was brilliant. He had seen old newsreels of atomic and nuclear explosions before, but they hadn't prepared him for the remarkable intensity produced by the fusion of sub microscopic matter.

Within moments, the signature mushroom cloud appeared, quickly reaching ten thousand feet, almost appearing as if the earth was spitting all the evil fouling its surface into the heavens. The cloud was capped by a halo of iridescent orange. The Nighthawk was rocked by three separate shock waves, the first being most severe. At ground level, a visible wave rolled across the city, radiating out from ground zero. Although he could not see from his vantage point, he knew that everything in its path was being obliterated. It seemed to become a living entity, digesting buildings, trees, cars, people. There was nowhere to hide. There would be no way to separate organic material from inorganic material in the morning. The intense heat will have fused flesh and concrete and steel into an indistinguishable composite.

"Come on home, Long Bow."

Father Anthony Salvatore was waiting for him, wondering how he was going to comfort a man who was responsible for the deaths of hundreds of thousands of people.

January 5th, 12:00 PM
USS John C. Stennis

Thank-you for your attention," the last time Yoder was before the ships cameras, he was trying to explain to a shocked crew that they had just traveled sixty one years into the past. "At eleven o'clock this morning, Japan sued for peace. The United States has accepted their unconditional surrender."

Captain Yoder heard a similar roar of bravado reverberating through the ship that he had heard when he told the same crew that they would be fighting in World War 11 not a month ago. "I would like to ask you to take a minute of silence in honor of the two aviators' who gave their lives for their country." Lieutenant Wolf had been found early in the morning with his brains spread over the bulkhead of his small cabin. His death would be officially listed as KIA.

"Oh my God!" Father Anthony seemed to be calling on his boss quite frequently as of late. He sat in the third row of the ships chapel, his head buried in his hands. "Oh my God almighty," he repeated out loud. Less than an hour after he had spoken with him, Lieutenant Wolf had blown his brains out. They talked for barely fifteen minutes. Anthony hadn't a clue as to how to comfort this man who had just killed thousands.

It was odd, Anthony thought, but John Wolf seemed very much at peace. He spoke very little, listened politely to the words Father Anthony was able to summon up. There was very little in the Bible on how to ease the pain of a mass murder. There was very little in the Bible that addressed much of what he had been dealing with during this last very bizarre month. He gave John absolution for his sins, not that he had asked. Maybe it was a little presumptuous to have assumed that he felt what he had just done was a sin, especially as he didn't follow any formal religion.

Now, Lieutenant John Long Bow Wolf was dead, by his own hand, and Anthony didn't even see it coming. This was a big screw up. "Where were you?" He was talking to the boss again. "I asked for the words, you knew that I didn't have the words, *where the hell were you*?"

It was happening, it was not totally unexpected, but there was no denying that it was happening. He was hip deep in a crisis of faith. It happened to Thomas Aquinas, it also happened to Father Kyle Landon. Thomas Aquinas worked it all out and got himself a Sainthood in the end, Father Kyle didn't and wound up marrying a lapsed nun. He had so many questions, the biggest was how God, his Roman Catholic God, could have sent John Wolf off in an airplane to kill two hundred thousand people?

Did He not hear their prayers? Most were vaporized before they even realized they were in need of serious prayer. Did they not think that God would look after them as they slept? Maybe they had taken up with the wrong god? Maybe Buddha was powerless to prevent their annihilation.

Men, women and children, children for Christ sakes, all killed, obliterated, for no reason. Surely there were a handful of evil doers amongst the dead, sodomites, rapists, murders, but even Job could have found ten good men to put off the destruction of Sapporo? What was the point? "Why did you let them all die?"

Father Anthony Salvatore was angry, confused and overwhelmed. Father Anthony Salvatore didn't want to be Father Anthony anymore.

January 5th, 1942, 1:05 PM
Chancellery Building, Berlin, Germany

He was tired. He had spent most of the previous night going over dispatches from the front. Adolph Hitler did not trust his Generals. His push into Russia had consumed him for the past three months. Russia was unorganized and weak. Their only strength was their sheer number of soldiers, which they were throwing at his army recklessly. His troops were superior, as was their equipment. Despite Germany's advantages, Adolph knew that the Russian winter could quickly mitigate his advantage. He had to make his Generals understand the dangerous foe that faced them and get them into Saint Petersburg before the ground froze.

"What is it?" There was a knock at his door, he hated interruptions.

"Fuhrer, Japan has surrendered." Four Generals stood in an adjacent office and argued for thirty minutes over who was going to deliver this piece of particularly unfortunate news. They all knew that any association with information like this could get a man a command on the Eastern Front, thousands of miles away from the wonderful decadence that was Berlin.

Adolph Hitler flew into an immediate and expected rage. General Dorfman was taking a mental inventory of his winter wardrobe as the author of *Mien Kempf* threw expletives around the huge office he occupied in the Chancellery Building. It was a good three minutes before he stopped insulting the Japanese and asked what had happened.

"The Americans bombed the city of Sapporo. The city was obliterated, there are tens of thousands dead."

"How could the Americans muster enough bombers to destroy a city in Japan and then get back to base? This makes no sense." Hitler felt another rage coming. He hated it when things did not make sense.

"My Fuhrer," General Dorfman was speaking almost apologetically now, almost as if it was his fault the fucking Japanese ran like school children at the onslaught of the Americans, "it seems that the city was destroyed by a single bomb, a super bomb."

It was as if General Dorfman had hit him with a sledge hammer. Adolph Hitler stood quietly where moments ago he was ranting. His red face was now white, protruding veins now receded. He said nothing, but he was thinking hard, and what he was thinking was not good for Adolph Hitler or Nazi Germany.

How could they have developed an atomic bomb so quickly? He had scientists in Berlin working on heavy water experiments right now. They had been telling him that they were at least two years away from being able to split an atom, and that the Americans were easily four years behind them.

The paradigm had shifted in an instant. He could now not count on the Japanese to keep the Americans busy in the Pacific, allowing him to concentrate his forces on the Eastern Front. His entire strategy must now be reviewed. Fuck the Americans.

January 8th, 1942, 11:26 AM
The White House

There had been an unexpected snow storm in Washington. Unexpected because the first time January 8th, 1942 happened, the weather was slightly overcast and fifty two degrees. Captain Yoder had plenty of time to ponder just what this meant as he sat in the back seat of the staff car that was ferrying him to the White House for a meeting with the President.

The ancient Dodge, well, in fact it was only two years old at this point, had a set of chains attached to the drive wheel. He had never driven in a car equipped with chains before. It was stunning how many things he took for granted that just weren't available here in 1942.

The chains on the tire kept a rhythmic beat. The snow flakes flew past the window, hypnotizing him. The streets were empty, with the exception of the occasional police car or military truck fighting the weather along with he and his driver.

As they pulled into the White House driveway, a Marine opened the passenger door and delivered a sharp salute, despite the bitter wind that dragged snow across his face.

"Welcome to the White House, Sir." Yoder was quick to return the salute for fear the Marine would freeze permanently where he stood.

Captain Yoder was the last to arrive. The Oval Office was crowded with the most powerful men in America; President Roosevelt, Vice President Truman, Secretary of War Henry Stimson, Secretary of the Navy Frank Knox, Generals Eisenhower and MacArthur, Admiral Halsey. They were all gathered to decide how Japan would pay for its insolent attack on the United States of America.

Despite all the options offered and debated during the past hour, they all knew that it was a lowly Captain who would ultimately give the final direction to the treaty with Japan.

He hadn't been talking for five minutes when the excitable Halsey was on his feet.

"Jesus Christ, son, you're suggesting we leave the Japanese army in tact?"

Yoder wondered if it would have been prudent to have brought Bull Halsey into the loop while he was still aboard the *Stennis*.

"Let's not loose sight of the ultimate goal here, the destruction of Russia. If we can have the Japanese attack Russia from the west while Hitler is attacking on the Eastern Front, Stalin will have to split his forces. With some covert air support during key battles, we should be able to weaken Russia enough to drop her to her knees before the winter sets in.

"The carrot to Japan will be the annexation of the Asian countries east of Russia. This will not only suit their initial goals, but bring stability to that region. I believe you have all read my report on the problems that arose in Vietnam after the War." The DVD show MJ 12 put together had also done a thorough job of covering the Vietnam War. "The French occupied it for a decade before getting their asses kicked at Diem Bien Phu in '54. In order to keep communism in check, as per the Domino Theory that postulated that if one country in South East Asia fell, they would all eventually topple, we sent advisors to Nam to prop up an unfortunately corrupt and inept puppet government. The few hundred advisors escalated to a few hundred thousand troops, ten years of conflict and fifty thousand American deaths. Ultimately, we left the country with our tails between our legs due to the fact that spineless politicians ran the war who didn't have the courage to make the tough decisions. We need to avoid the Vietnam War, gentlemen, it was not only a loosing proposition abroad, but it divided our country at home."

"I agree that it is important not to neuter and humiliate Japan." General Douglas MacArthur was the most knowledgeable man in the room on Japan. He was intimate with their culture and recognized that a weak Japan playing in the same arena as a communist China would not add to world stability. "But is it wise to leave an aggressive country with a large standing army?"

"Japan clearly recognizes the power the United States possesses. Remember, we destroyed one of their cities with a single bomb. Should they begin to act a little to independently, we are in a position to reign them in. We need their participation to minimize our casualties during the coming engagement with Russia."

For the next two days, the treaty with Japan was formulated and fine tuned. In the end, it looked very much like the one MJ 12 had proffered.

January 13th, 9:52 AM
USS John C. Stennis, Atlantic Ocean

"Hey, it's jerk off boy!"

Sean Cooney had been riding Tim ever since his unfortunate masturbation come out party. Tim had just gotten off from breakfast shift and was looking forward to some down time in his bunk. He had developed a protocol of non response. Cooney was not the kind of guy you reasoned with and any retort to Sean's adolescent barbs would only bring a slew of new and equally adolescent barbs.

He was getting tired of it all, though. Tim had requested a transfer to a different birding area, but there didn't seem to be any urgency attached to the paper work as it moved up the chain of command.

"Got another date?" Sean's voice was beginning to haunt him.

"Yeah, with your mother." Tim was sorry he said it before it even left his mouth. The expected barks of disapproval were immediately echoed by the small cadre assembled around Sean. He had no option but to get combative.

"Who you fucking talking to, you little piece of shit." Sean was in Tim's face. It was a comical scene. Timmy was standing there in his underwear and regulation black socks looking like a little kid next to the six foot one Sean Cooney, towering over him, face red and arms flailing about.

"Shut the fuck up or I'm gonna rip your empty fucking head right off your shoulders and shit down your neck."

There was silence. It was the first time in the week since it all started that Tim had responded in such an aggressive manner. In Sean's world, there was nothing else he could do but accept the perceived challenge.

"You and who's fucking army?"

"Jesus Christ, is that the best you can do," what a moron, he thought. Tim was weary of this whole thing. He knew that his initial handling of the situation was just not going to work. When guys like Cooney saw weakness, they just attacked harder. "Your emotional development parallels your mental acuity."

Sean was pretty sure he had just been insulted. The timing was perfect for physical threats. "I'd like to kick the shit out of you, you little cock sucker."

There it was, Tim decided, it was time to end this. Seaman First Class Timothy Irwin was going to do something he hadn't done for three and a half years and vowed that he'd never do again, he was going to crawl back into the ring.

"I think we need to address our differences like gentlemen, Mr. Cooney."

"I think I need to rip your head off right now."

"How eloquent. What I don't want to do after humiliating you right before your chums here is to spend the next month in the brig, Sherlock. Why don't we reconvene this evening below deck," he had just the place in a storage area off the kitchen that would afford them privacy and just enough room to rumble, "and engage in the gentle are of pugilism."

"I'm no fucking homo, man, let's just fight."

Oh Jesus, thought Tim. "I'll be counting the hours."

Tim crawled into his bunk and began to sweat. Not out of fear for what could happen to him, but what might happen to Sean Cooney. He closed his eyes and his mind was immediately filled with mental pictures of his last fight.

Not to long before joining the Navy, Tim was a karate instructor. Although he was only five seven, he was a devastating fighter. Only a handful of men could give him trouble in the ring, and he was so tough that they didn't have a clue that he suffered from anything they threw.

One of his favorite opponents was his best friend, Tom Horgan. Tom was a six foot tall body builder who signed up to take lessons from Tim almost five years ago. Tom was extremely athletic and picked up the finer nuances of fighting quickly. They grew close over the years and enjoyed enthusiastic bouts in the ring every chance they got.

One evening, after hours, Timmy and Tom jumped into the ring. Tim was feeling particularly good. They ramped up the action quickly. Blows were being exchanged that would have dropped anyone else in the school.

They didn't put on the timer, when the terrible T's were in the ring, there were no two or three minute rounds, they kept going until exhaustion precluded anything but standing. It was a good twenty minutes into this endless round when Tim saw an opening. Tom's hands were slightly open, leaving just enough of a gap for Tim to place his right foot into Tom's gut.

Tim chambered his leg, and exploded into a side kick. Tom saw it coming, and proceeded to make the worst decision of his life, he twisted to his right. The toe of Tim's right foot spun Tom around just a little further causing his spine to absorb the tremendous force of the kick.

Tim winced in his bed as he heard, for the millionth time, the hollow crack of Tom's spine snapping. The only solace Tim had from being in the past was that Tom was no longer wasting away in a wheel chair, unable to control much more than his eyelids.

That was the last time Tim was anywhere near a ring. He wondered if he'd be able to reach down and find what he needed to get this Cooney kid off his back.

"Holy shit." Calvert Washington yanked off his earphones. "That was the loudest noise I've ever heard short of an underwater explosion." Calvert was sitting in the back of an SH-2G Seasprite, an ancient helicopter designed in the late sixties to scan the seas around carriers snooping out submarines. It did such an excellent job, there was never any reason to replace it.

"What do you have?" Lieutenant Graco was in the pilots seat.

"Has to be a U-boat. I'll run a sample through the computer, but I can't imagine it being anything else." The Seasprite had a sonar buoy hanging underneath it by a hundred foot cable. The buoy was dipped strategically around the *Stennis*, listening for the tell tale sound of a submarine's engine. Every class of sub had a distinctive sound, making it fairly easy to identify a submerged threat.

"Yep, according to the new data base installed before we left," Washington still couldn't come to terms with the fact that he was now way back in the past and would never see his mother, his seven brothers or his fiancee again, so he just talked about their dramatic departure into the past just as he would the start of a new tour, "that puppy is a German U-boat. I don't think a Russian Salute would be that noisy if they were breaking ten knots and were having a party. This is like shooting fish in a barrel."

"Give me a bearing." Lieutenant Graco needed to report back to the *Stennis*.

"One four mark seven, six hundred meters out, depth, thirty three feet, doing five knots just above the thermocline."

"This is flight niner two, we have a confirmed U-boat twelve miles southeast of your position, request instructions," Graco reported to the *Stennis*.

"Sink it." He recognized the voice of the ships XO, Captain O'Brien.

"Roger that." Lieutenant Graco turned his ship to face the submerged U-boat. He armed a Mk 50 torpedo. "Enter an attack solution into the computer."

"Done." This was sub attack 101. Washington was giddy with anticipation of his first kill.

"Torpedo away." He knew this unsophisticated vessel wouldn't realize they were under attack until the crew was hip deep in sea water. He listened for the pinging generated by the guidance system on board the Mk 50, giving him constant updates as to the position of both the target and the torpedo.

"Five, four, three, two, one." He pulled off his headset so as not to be audibly assaulted by the sound of the impact.

Six football fields directly in front of the chopper there was a plume of water that shot seventy feet high.

"I hope I'm not premature here, but I believe we have a direct hit," exclaimed Washington, in a haughty English accent.

Graco brought the chopper to a hover directly over the point of impact. Within seconds, the water was black with oil and pieces of debris.

"Forgive me Father for I have sinned." Even though he had chosen to receive the sacrament of Confession behind a curtain, Father Anthony Salvatore recognized Pattie Boyl's thick Boston accent. Anthony's mind was already beginning to wander. This was the fourteenth confession he had heard during the past hour and he just wasn't into it. He peaked abound outside the curtain and gave thanks that Pattie was the last sinner of the day.

"Tell me your sins, Patt..." he hoped Pattie hadn't picked up on his name being mistakenly uttered, clearly this big stupid Irishman thought being behind a curtain was going to offer him anonymity. After the past day, Anthony Salvatore was not shocked by the thoughts he was having. He was angry and confused. He wanted desperately to talk to the boss, but the boss wasn't talking. He was never talking. Go read the Bible, his instructors would tell him, the answer you are looking for is in there. Well, he decided this afternoon, it wasn't.

"Father," whimpered Boyle, "forgive me, for I have sinned." You don't know jack about sin, thought Father Salvatore, "It has been two weeks since my last confession."

"Yeah, get to the meat," Anthony said out loud.

Boyle lumbered on, "I had six impure thoughts, used the Lords name in vain twice and took an extra muffin when no one was looking..."

That was it. He felt his face turning red. Father Anthony Salvatore grabbed the curtain separating him from this sinner and tore it down. "You call those fucking sins, do you? You think God's got nothing better to do than to waste time with a shit like you. Go screw a nun, then come back, maybe we'll have something to talk about."

Seamen First Class Pattie Boyle looked like he had just found out there was no Santa Clause.

"There's no such thing as Santa Clause. Or the damn Easter Bunny." Anthony had sensed that and felt the need to inflict as much pain on this pitiful excuse for a man as he could.

Pattie gathered all two hundred and thirty five pounds he brought with him and ran from the chapel.

Anthony was in a rage. "You like that? There's more where that came from. All deep down, buried, repressed. There's evil down there, and it's coming out." His hands were clenched and raised, his head was tilted back. He was talking to the boss now.

"How dare you put me here, all alone. Hand me a heathen who murdered two thousand people and not give me the words. How could you have let that many people die? How can I do your work. How can I care for all these people when I don't even care about myself?" There were no tears, only anger. A life time of repressed rage was escaping and it wasn't good.

"You all right?"

Father Salvatore whipped around to see Lieutenant Savage standing at the entrance to the chapel.

"I, uh, well." The rage had been replaced with embarrassment. And suddenly, for the first time in his adult life, he spoke honestly. "No, I'm not."

Kaitlyn Savage had come down to the chapel to pray. She did that now and again. She had been baptized Catholic, but hadn't attended mass since her parents died. There was still a thin string that loosely bound her to the Church.

Anthony Salvatore stood there, having just opened his heart to someone he didn't even know and wasn't sure what to do next. He decided to unclench his fists.

Kaitlyn recognized the deep pain he was in. She arrived just in time to see Pattie Boyle get the bad news about Santa. She wasn't sure whether to go in or not, but something drew her through the ugly green steel door to confront something. There was something special going on here but she wasn't sure what it was.

Lieutenant Savage walked up to Father Anthony Francis Salvatore and hugged him. Father Salvatore hugged her back and then began to cry.

"You gonna kick that white boys ass." They were words of encouragement from the only friend he had on the ship, Parnes Williams.

"You just make sure we don't get any nosy officers snooping around during the fight, I don't need a month in the brig." Timmy was wrapping his hands, not so much as to protect Cooney, but to protect himself from a broken bone.

They stood in a fairly small storage room that Tim and Parnes had cleared that afternoon. Tim was pleased to have his moral support and Parnes was thrilled at the prospect of Sean Cooney getting the snot kicked out of him. Parnes had been on the ugly side of Sean's simple, if not caustic, wit.

"So, what are the fucking rules, gonna use the Markus of Doonsberry rules?"

"Yes Parnes, we're going to use the rules based on a defunct cartoon character."

There was a thud on the metal door.

"OK, let them in, if things get ugly, see if you can drag me out of here before I get stomped to death." Tim was having second and third thoughts about this fight. He was still haunted by flash backs of his last fight. He was the one who told Tom's little boys that their Daddy would not be able to teach them how to play ball, or how to swim or...

"Jesus, I've got to shake that." He knew Tom would have wanted him to. Tom encouraged him to stay with it, even as he was shitting into a plastic bag attached to his wheel chair. It might have been easier had Tom cursed him and tried to exact a pound or two of flesh, but he hadn't. The man was the epitome of graciousness. Eventually, Tim stopped stopping by to see him, he couldn't handle the pain and guilt. Instead he fed it on his own, let it consume him until he had to run, run as far away from Babylon, New York as he could. Now, here he was three thousand miles and sixty one years away and he still couldn't shake it.

"Ready to die, asshole?"

Cooney paraded in with his entourage of assholes, the Professor leading the pack. He was dancing and throwing punches in the air. Tim caught his antics through the periphery of his eye. Good, he thought, this guy doesn't know how to throw a punch. He seemed to be obsessed with the hook, an amateurish and easily deflected blow. Not wanting to give anything away, Tim just focused on loosening up.

Now the two warriors faced each other. Sean was supremely confidant. Tim was almost half a foot shorter and looked a little soft. He decided that he'd play with Irwin for a while before dispatching him.

"Do you want to fight by the Markus of Doonsberry rules?" offered Tim.

"I heard of them."

Tim laughed quietly to himself. Even in the face of possible personal harm, he couldn't help but afford himself an additional opportunity to allow Sean to make a fool of himself. He also had an ulterior motive for begetting the question.

"Rules are for fucking sissies. You a sissy, Jerk off Boy?"

This was to easy, it was like leading a bull around by the nose.

"Well," Tim replied, trying not to give up his joy at Sean's response, "if that's the way you want it." Cooney had inadvertently added six additional weapons to Tim's arsenal; two knees, two feet and two elbows.

The two bare chested men stood in the middle of the storage room, already sweating.

"Let's do it." Sean was anxious to get started.

Tim sunk into his fighters stance. It felt familiar, even comfortable, like an old pair of jeans he hadn't worn for a while. He rocked back and forth, moving his head side to side like a snake, staring out, keeping Cooney's whole body within sight.

Sean stood like an Oak tree, with his feet planted solidly on the floor. His hands were on guard, but not effectively so. It was clear to Tim that Sean had had no formal training.

Then Tim made his first mistake. He stopped seeing Sean as a whole and focused on his face. For the first time he realized how much like Tom Horgan he looked. Both tall Irishmen, both muscular with that same unfortunate pink hue. His blue eyes and red-blond hair made them a striking match. Now Tim could see the contorted face Tom had made the second his spine splintered. Now he could see the look of horror on Tom's face as he lay on the mat, telling Tim that he couldn't feel his legs. Now he could see Tom's face as he was being lifted into the ambulance, telling Tim that it wasn't his fault.

Now he could feel the fists of Sean Cooney reigning down on him as he stood there, helpless to do anything but cower, his mind unfocused, seeing images that tortured him.

It was probably a badly thrown left uppercut that had put him on his back, his jaw already beginning to swell. He looked up to see a horrified Parnes Williams, urging him to stay down.

Not fucking now, he thought, I've been down long enough. I've been beating my self up, now it's some else's turn. The years of tough luck and mistakes, the lost jobs, the lottery ticket, the unfortunate orchid incident, the equally unfortunate masturbation incident, his wife of mere months, someone is going to pay.

Cooney's going down.

Tim shook off the last blow, he'd been hit harder, and sprang to his feet.

"Givin me another chance to knock your ass on the floor, Dick boy?" Sean wheezed.

Tim slid in under Sean's lead hand and delivered a left jab to the ribs, a right hook to the gut and a left hook to the jaw all with astonishing speed. Cooney was stunned. None of the punches had knockout power, but each stung.

Sean collected himself by moving backwards, a direction he never remembered moving during a fight. Tim closed the distance and then delivered a reverse crescent kick. Again, not a very powerful kick, but simply an invitation to the festival of pain Sean had just been invited to.

There were a series of horribly thrown hooks and jabs, easily deflected or dodged by Tim. Now it was time to start doing damage. He unleashed a low roundhouse kick that landed squarely on the meat of Sean's thigh. Sean took a half step an then pulled the offended leg up to take the pressure off it, the pain was searing.

Like sparing peewees, Tim thought, a phrase he used often in his dojo anytime he fought a lesser opponent. It was all coming back to him. Tim moved like a bantam weight, the additional flesh around his waist not seeming to be of import.

Tim literally pushed Sean's hands out of the way, slid in and delivered a roundhouse elbow squarely to Sean's nose. The sound of the cartilage breaking was sobering. Tim moved out just as quickly, he wasn't ready to finish it just yet.

Sean staggered around the make shift ring. The pain in his thigh became secondary to the throbbing of his shattered nose. Blood flowed freely, dripping onto his chest, making him look like a gunshot victim. This was not the first time he had his nose broken, but he was beginning to feel overwhelmed. None of his blows were landing now, he felt like he was being toyed with. This needed to go to the ground, Sean thought, where his wrestling skills would surely tip the scales his way. Sean had been runner up in the New York State wrestling finals, loosing to a guy who later made the US Olympic team.

He lunged at Tim, got one arm around his neck and dragged him to the floor. When they landed, Sean was shocked to find Tim was on the top, legs spread, head and chest low, perfectly posted.

Excellent, thought Tim. He had spent a year training in the Gracie jujitsu system, Brazilian ground fighting. Tim settled himself, then quickly raised his upper body. Sean did exactly as Tim had planned, he extended his arm in a foolish attempt to grab Tim by the throat.

Tim locked up the arm, threw his left leg over Sean's head and landed on his ass, sitting astride Sean. One leg was over Sean's chest, the other over his face. The offending arm was locked between Tim's legs, the elbow pulled tight against his crotch.

It was over, but Sean didn't know it yet. He violently withered about, desperately trying to extract himself from this unusual position he found himself in. The first indication that he was in deep trouble came when Tim raised his left leg and brought his heel down with alacrity, slamming Sean in the left ear. That might have been the most painful blow he had ever been on the ugly end of. In the space of a second, Tim kicked him twice more.

There was nothing he could do, Sean was completely locked up. Suddenly, he began to feel tremendous pressure on his elbow. Tim was slowly raising his hips, acting as a fulcrum to bend Sean's arm in a direction God's engineers never meant for it to go.

Every time Sean would reach over with his free right arm, Tim would kick him in the ear again. It was an untenable position for Sean Cooney. Now the pressure on his elbow was enough so that if either Tim moved his hips up another inch, or if Sean settled back the same, the elbow was going to snap. Sean held his breath and tried not to move.

"OK, Mr. Cooney," they were the first words spoken by Tim since the fight began less than five minutes ago, "do you have something you want to tell me before I break your arm?"

"Oh shit," Sean's voice had a decided quiver to it, "don't do that."

The room was quiet, Sean's legions were as shocked at the outcome as Parnes Williams, who stood silently in Tim's corner, smiling big.

"Would you care to proffer your deepest apologies for past transgressions?"

"I don't understand what the fuck you mean," Sean was sounding panicky, "you some kind of English professor or somethin?" The pressure on his elbow was growing.

"Say you're sorry, dick head."

"I'm fucking sorry."

"That was heartfelt." Tim was the master of sarcasm.

"I know." Sean was a dim wit.

"If you give me any more shit," he paused and looked up at the still smiling Parnes, "or my man any more shit, you'll look back on this beating fondly."

Tim abruptly let go of Sean's arm, rolled onto his back and then onto his feet. Sean stayed on the floor, nursing his arm.

Timmy's jaw throbbed, but it was, in a bizarre way, a good pain. Physically, he was hurting. Emotionally, he couldn't remember feeling this good. Parnes tossed him his shirt and they left the stock room.

January 19th, 8:52 AM
Norfolk Naval Base, Virginia

"**How was the** cruise back, Captain?"

While Yoder was in Washington, working out the details of Japan's surrender treaty, Kelly O'Brien was driving the *Stennis* back to Norfolk.

"Hit some weather two days ago, pulled through just fine. I believe you had been informed about the U-boat incident?"

"It really wasn't a threat, was it?"

"No, the choppers located it twelve miles out and dispatched it."

"How'd it go in Washington?"

Yoder paused. He had just been part of recreating history. "Politicians in 1942 are not much easier to deal with than in 2002. It was difficult to get some of the military to accept the notion of leaving the Japanese army in tact. I had to go to the computer setup we installed in the White House to convince a General or two that we needed them to achieve our final goal. In the end, they agreed to a treaty that was nearly identical to the one MJ 12 proposed. Stimson and MacArthur are heading for Japan right now to sign up our new allies."

"We lost the *North Carolina* from our battle group, they went to meet up with the *Enterprise*," complained Captain O'Brien, "left us a little light for the trip home."

"I know, we decided we should have some kind of presence in the country we just defeated. Would have been nice if we could have gotten the *Missouri* there instead."

"Would have been poetic justice, to us at least."

"Something happened while I was there that disturbed me. It snowed."

"Well," commiserated O'Brien, "Washington winters can be hinky, I'll bet it was fifty degrees the next day."

"As a matter of fact, it was close to sixty. What concerned me is that the first time around, it didn't snow, the weather was mild with a slight overcast. Why would the weather have changed? I did some research and found that the weather followed the same patterns up until December thirty-first. The following day, the first day of our attack on Japan, the weather patterns started to change."

"So did history."

January 21st, 12 PM
USS Enterprise, Tokyo Bay

General Douglas MacArthur held the zeitgeist of the Japanese people. That, and his excellent record during the American occupation the first time around, convinced Roosevelt that he should accompany Henry Stimson to Tokyo to lay down the terms of the treaty.

The Japanese delegation was looking expectedly somber, trying to stand tall, but looking childlike compared to the color guard of Marines that surrounded them. Emperor Hiraheto was a young man, still in his thirties and looking particularly un-god like in his ill-fitting black tuxedo. The top hat and cane only made him appear as a comical figure. Doug smiled as he thought that this man is worshipped by his countrymen. He wondered if that would change after they got a look at him in this getup.

Konoye was dressed similarly, but without the unfortunate cane. The day after Japan surrendered, Tojo dishonored himself by using a gun to deal with personal failure and Konoye was returned to his former position as Prime Minister. The third politician present was Saburo Kurusu.

The rest of the delegation was represented by the military, with the pronounced lack of presence by the Navy. General Yoshijiro Umezu, Chief of the General Staff of the Imperial Japanese Army and General Soemu Toyoda, both of whom sported stereotypical round glasses, hardly looked like the dangerous warriors they were.

The decks of the *Enterprise* were lined with sailors, forming a human corridor through which the vanquished leaders walked. There were no outward signs of disrespect, but that didn't mitigate the feelings of disgrace felt by these men, who, less than a week previous, had tasted and digested victory.

The *Enterprise* was Bull Halsey's ship. He had made the trip back to the Pacific with Stimson and MacArthur. Bull was sitting next to Mac behind a large desk as the Japanese delegation was escorted into the Captain's wardroom.

The defeated lowered their eyes and bowed. Stimson and Halsey followed MacArthur's lead and returned the bow. The four Japanese sat on United States issue wooden chairs across from the Admiral, General and Secretary of War. Placed before each man in the room was a copy of what was unimaginatively referred to as The Treaty with Japan. It was Halsey's idea not to present the treaty to the Emperor written in Japanese. The word had gotten back about the Batan death march and he was looking for any way possible to give the Japanese a difficult time. It bothered him that within minutes they would become allies of the United States.

"Gentlemen," it was another subtle sign of disrespect to not have singled out the Emperor, "we are here to accept Japan's unconditional surrender and to discuss the terms and conditions of that surrender." Stimson was equally disturbed by the reports still coming in as to the conditions that American soldiers were forced to endure in the Philippines under Japanese capture.

He waited as the American supplied translator finished the arduous task of converting English into Japanese. There seemed to be two Japanese words to his one. Stimson now referred to the treaty before him.

"Japan agrees to the immediate cessation of all hostilities against the United States, Great Britain, Australia, New Zealand and France." As he waited for the translation, he wondered if they would have caught the omission of Russia.

"Japan will begin the immediate repatriation of all American and Allied Prisoners of War..." Secretary of War

Henry Stimson continued for twenty minutes addressing the legalese expected for a document of this weight.

He sat back and passed his copy across the table and asked the Emperor to sign the document. Emperor Heriheto accepted a pen from Douglas MacArthur and signed the last page of the treaty.

Now things are going to get interesting, thought Henry.

"There are additional conditions Japan must agree to that the United States will not put in writing." After the translation, the entire Japanese delegation looked up at Stimson with raised eyebrows. This was highly unexpected and diplomatically unusual.

"I suspect that you must have considered it odd that the United States has not demanded the dissolution of your standing army," and indeed they had. "It is our intention that Japan shall attack Russia."

Stimson waited again for the translator to catch the delegation up and prepared himself for the looks he was bound to get when this new reality settled in.

Their faces gave up nothing, but the tone of their voices did. They requested that the translator ask Stimson to verify what they had just been told. Again, Stimson repeated his last statement, this time slowly, and while staring the Emperor in the eye.

The translator repeated the demand. The delegation sat quietly, not having any idea as to why America would be requesting an attack on their ally.

"You will attack Russia through Manchuria along their western front. This will not be a coordinated attack with Germany. Your position regarding Germany will be a desire to control territory in Asia, expanding the Japanese Empire westward." It was suspected that Japans attack in the west would add urgency to Hitler's attack for fear of loosing out on the oil fields to the south that were necessary to keep his highly mechanized army moving. "It is the intention of the United States to allow Japan to continue a presence in Manchuquo and occupied territories west of Russia upon the successful end to the campaign.

"Japan will recognize the authority of the Supreme Allied Commander, General Eisenhower, in all subsequent military matters. General MacArthur will be stationed in Tokyo to facilitate these measures. If Japan does not agree to this, it is the intention of the United States to dismantle your army and arrest, try, convict and imprison Emperor Hirohito."

MacArthur argued eloquently against the inclusion of that final threat. He expected Japan to respond positively to the opportunity to expand their empire after its humiliating defeat, but Roosevelt wanted to assure compliance. It was, ironically, MacArthur's own words that ensured its addition to the treaty. General MacArthur knew the deep love the Japanese people had for their Emperor, he was, indeed, considered a god. His removal would be unacceptable. They would go to great lengths to keep him enthroned, including, FDR finally decided, attacking Russia.

For the next five hours, items were clarified, incentives were reviewed. Japan enthusiastically agreed with all points, both written and spoken.

CHAPTER 7
EUROPE

January 23rd, 11:43
Oval Office, White House

"**Captain Yoder, this** is not the first time you have shocked me." Franklin Roosevelt was dismayed. This was the most outrageous bit of strategy yet. Coming from the man who brought the Japanese to their knees in a week, he was forced to listen, but he was not at all pleased.

"Mr. President, we need Hitler's attention focused on Russia. If he has to divert troops, mechanized units and his Luftwaffe to fight England, he will never be in a position to bring the necessary force to bear on his Western Front to destroy Russia." Harsh knew this was going to be a difficult sell. FDR and Churchill had already become close friends. It was that relationship that gave birth the Lend Lease Act that was supplying England with the implements of war needed to keep Hitler out of Buckingham Palace."

"You want me to talk Winston into surrendering to Germany. The man who chided Neville Chamberlain not four years ago in the House of Commons for the ill conceived Munich agreement? It wasn't two years previous that he again stood before the House of Commons and gave his impassioned speech, 'We shall fight in the fields, we shall fight in the streets, we shall fight in the hills. *We shall never surrender*." He shook his fist in emphasis.

A bit of unfortunate timing, thought Yoder. "He was also quoted in 1954 as saying 'To jaw-jaw is better than to war-war,' no doubt after a drink or two. The point is, Churchill is a reasonable man who ultimately abhors war. If we can prove to him that his conditional surrender will only keep England on the sidelines for the duration of the German campaign in Russia and that England's causalities will be reduced substantially, I see no reason why he will not ultimately sign on, despite the difficulties he'll face getting the rest of the government to go along.

"There is a precedence here, Franklin." Henry Stimson was uncharacteristically supportive. "Let's recall that there has already been talk of a peace settlement."

"Yes, Henry, but Churchill demanded that the Reichmacht relinquish all territorial gains before Britain would even negotiate," Roosevelt responded.

"There have also been some disturbing historical changes." Keyed by the inconsistencies in the weather Harsh had noticed a few weeks back, he began researching new historical inaccuracies. "Pre time shift, England's air victory over the Luftwaffe during the Battle of Britain stalled and ultimately derailed Operation Sealion. Goering's boast about his Lufwaffe being invincible was clearly wrong, as would have been his suggestion that the invasion of England would take but two or three weeks. During the time Hitler was contemplating the invasion in June of 1940, Goering was pitching his Lufwaffe as a way to destroy the RAF and hence clear the way for the invasion, while Admiral Raeder was pushing for his U-boats to fulfill much the same role. As we know, Goering won. The U-boats were never used effectively against England. At war's end, Churchill stated that his biggest fear was indeed the U-boat.

"Well, apparently due to the arrival of the *Stennis* and the subsequent altering of history vis-a-vis the war with Japan, things are changing. Hitler has been using his U-boats quite successfully and Britain is involved in a siege situation, unable to get supplies and food into the country with any reliability. As conditions worsen, it may not be as difficult as you suspect to get Churchill to agree to our proposal."

Tensions were high. A wrong decision would bring disastrous consequences to the world stage. It was easy to ignore the needs of a time not yet come. Roosevelt had to be concerned with the here and now. If Russia was not defeated, his generation would not be affected by it. There apparently was not much past the next three years that was going to affect him personally, a thought he did not harbor to closely.

Harsh was encouraged by the presence of General George Patton. George despised the Russians, didn't trust them at all. He had even suggested going to war with Stalin. It took very little to convince Patton that the *Stennis* and her crew had been delivered from the future, George believed and was vocal in his belief that he had lived before. Half a century ahead of Shirley Mc'Lean, his brilliance as a general was the only thing that kept him out of the psyche ward after delivering that little nugget to a reporter.

"So, Captain Yoder, you want the British Empire to surrender to Germany..."

"Conditionally surrender, General Marshall," Harsh corrected.

"All right, conditionally surrender to Germany, and to what end, Sir."

Marshall was not exactly on board yet. "If we can allow Hitler to concentrate his war machine on Russia, there will be a considerably greater chance of defeating Stalin and with a much smaller role for us. When it is time to crush him, he will be in a much weaker position. Remember, Stalin will not role over and take it in the shorts without a Herculean struggle." He paused for a moment, waiting for someone to question him as to exactly what taking it in the shorts meant. No one did, he made a mental note to tidy up his vernacular while addressing the President and his staff.

"I like it." Patton's support was not a surprise to anyone. "After the Godless Russians have been defeated, Great Britain can reenter the war with fresh troops and a renewed resolve."

"What makes you think Hitler will agree to a conditional surrender, Captain?" General Marshall was still not convinced England's capitulation was a wise option.

"Hitler's biggest reason for taking the British Isle is to keep the United States from entering the war. Without a foothold in England, he correctly surmises that we will have a terminally difficult time getting troops to Europe. Part of the surrender will state that England will close its doors to America." Again, MJ 12 had this all brilliantly thought out, Harsh realized.

"Let us table for a moment the difficulty of getting Churchill and his government to accept this," FDR spoke, "why would Hitler accept a conditional surrender?"

"There are a number of reasons. He is already finding out that the Western Front is going to be a difficult campaign. He also knows that if he doesn't make substantial progress before next winter sets in, his chance for victory is considerably diminished. Given the opportunity to free up a vast amount of resources now fighting England, he would be foolish not to seize that advantage.

"As per the surrender being conditional, let's recall his dealings with the British four years ago. He sees them as being naive and weak. I do not believe he will have any intention of abiding by the treaty, just as he didn't abide by the Munich Agreement he signed with Chamberlain. This will, however, give him time to dispatch one enemy at a time. After securing Russia, he will, no doubt, turn on

England despite any agreement he will have signed with them.

"To make this ruse more believable, Mr. President, we will have to rescind the Lend Lease Act and develop a policy of isolationism. If Hitler truly believes that we have no intention or ability to enter the war through a secure foothold, he will feel free to pour everything he has into the Western Front."

"Once he defeats Russia, how do we extract England from a very tenuous position?" FDR felt a strong tie to Britain. He could never bring this proposition to his friend Churchill if he could not guarantee that the United States could protect him from a very hostile and potent army.

"Once our number one objective is met, the destruction of Russia, then the gloves come off. Hitler will not have time to hoist a stein in a beer hall to celebrate before the terrible destructive power of the *Stennis* is brought to bear on Germany. It will take days to bottle them up. Remember, even in 1942, it is expected to take weeks to move enough weaponry around to cause any serious threat to a standing army. We now have the technology to stop his army cold within hours. The bulk of his forces will be in Russia, his supply lines will be stretched for thousands of miles. We will cripple them in the east with F 22 attacks and open up the coast of France with our ground support Intruder attack aircraft. He won't know what hit him."

"Who do you suggest should present this proposition to Churchill, Captain Yoder?" The President knew the answer to this question, but hoped that maybe this MJ 12 had come up with a more creative solution.

"The relationship you have developed with him over the past year suggests that you would be the best person to bring this proposal to him. We'll make it a bit easier for you by bringing him onboard the *Stennis* before you two talk and giving him the dog and pony show. He'll get it all, from the multimedia presentation you saw last month to the tour of the ship and all its weapons systems. By the time we turn him over to you, he will be thoroughly convinced that we have the ability to crush Hitler at will."

"It think we need to formalize this plan and then get Churchill over here to, how did you eloquently phrase it, Captain Yoder, take it in the shorts?"

"Well, I was referring to Stalin, but yes, that was pretty much the correct use of that maybe inappropriately jocular phrase, Sir." Yoder was mortified.

Father Anthony felt bad, he felt real bad. What he had just done was wrong and he was going to pay for it. There was no way God was going to let this slide. He stood out on vulture's row, twenty three stories above the quiet Atlantic. The stars were always brighter out at sea where they weren't affected by light pollution. It was a little past midnight. There were a handful of clouds scattered about, blocking groups of stars, making it look as if there were irregular shaped holes in the night sky.

Father Anthony also felt good. This dichotomy was the result of his past hour's activity. He knew what he had just done would be considered wrong, he would probably be defrocked were the Pope to get wind of it. But right now, he didn't care. Anthony decided to table what ever Papal Creed he had just broken and enjoy the moment, the after glow he had heard about but had never experienced.

He had jerked off a couple of times when he was thirteen, but once he decided to turn over his life to God, he stopped. There were a few times back in Huntington when he was sorely tested, but Anthony learned to more appreciate the trials of Job after dismissing the devils temptation of carnal pleasures with his beloved Jane.

But last night, he succumbed. He was glad he had. Father Anthony Salvatore had never felt more alive. He and Lieutenant Savage had been seeing a lot of each other, they had been getting closer each day. There were feelings and emotions evolving, churning, seeping to the surface where they had to be addressed. Both knew it would only be a matter of time before their hearts and bodies would coalesce.

The touch of a woman was the sweetest thing he had ever felt. He was still at a loss as to how the debauchery began. He and Lieutenant Savage were in his office, discussing some fairly sophisticated theological doctrine when the next thing he knew, they were kissing. He was pretty sure she had started it. Yes, it made it easier to blame Eve. He could have stopped that Jezebel, could have walked right out of his own office if need be. But he didn't.

Anthony looked up again at the sky. He used to come up here to feel closer to God. Tonight, he wanted to get as far away from his office, and the chapel that adjoined it, as possible. He was not strong enough to look up at the statue of his Boss just now.

But, oh, how sweet it was. Her lips were so soft. Their breath intermingled, their tongues danced, the intimacy was staggering to him. He touched her through her clothes and felt a passion he could not have imagined two hours before. It was a consuming fire that could only be quenched by the joining of two bodies.

After the two bodies had joined, they laid there, wrapped together, glistening with sweat and sin. He, torn by the intense pleasure and the intense shame. She, by the joy of sexual release, and now unburdened of the absorbing inquiry, "I wonder what it's like to screw a priest?"

The Delta T coils glowed blue around the perimeter of the ship. Harsh viewed them passively from the bridge, he was alone. Suddenly, there was a terrific flash. Captain Yoder felt as if he'd been slammed with a hammer. He felt himself falling backwards, in slow motion, drifting until he hit the deck.

He lay there for an undetermined period of time. His head hurt and his bones were feeling strange, like the first time. He rolled over and threw up. Then he forced himself to his feet and looked out the port side windows. The ship was at dock and the dock was empty, except for a lone figure.

Harsh looked more closely and recognized that the individual was his wife. She wore the white dress he had bought her for the base picnic a few years ago. Linda held something in her arms. He looked closer. It was little Jeb. She looked up at him and waved. She was talking to Jeb, pointing up at him. He couldn't hear her, but he knew she was saying, "Look, it's Daddy." Jeb smiled and waved, kicking his legs in obvious excitement.

Harsh waved and signaled with his hands that he'd come down to meet them. He felt elated. He dashed to the back of the bridge but couldn't find the door. He ran around the room, but the door was gone. Who'd moved the door, he wondered. Better talk to maintenance later.

He ran back to the window to let Linda know he would need a few more minutes. Harsh looked down and saw that Jeb was gone and Linda was now wearing a black dress, the same black dress she had worn to little Jeb's funeral.

He pounded on the window in front of him and wept.

Harsh woke up in a pool of sweat. This was not the first time he'd had this dream. He got out of bed, walked to the sink and splashed cold water on his face. This nightmare had played out in any number of places. He'd chased Linda through malls, office buildings and even a circus. Each time it was the same. He saw her holding Jeb, but by the time he got to her, Jeb was gone and she stood there, dressed in black, empty handed.   This dream, however, was the first time he could not get to her. It was also the first time he'd had the dream since leaving what was now the future

January 25th, 1:13 AM GMT
London, England

The banshee scream of the air raid alarms racked her out of the first decent sleep she'd had in almost two weeks. Audry Leeves forced herself from bed. She threw on a coat over her night clothes and went to the back bedroom to collect Jeffrey, age eight and Emily, three. These certainly have been trying times. The Lufwaffe had been attacking almost nightly. The three of them had been spending their evenings in the cold and smelly underground man made caverns along with the rest of London. Each time a bomb hit it sent shock waves through the walls. With nothing else to do, the men tried to speculate as to where a bomb had landed based on the direction and intensity of the latest wave, each wondering if they would have a home to go back to when these devil birds had disgorged their last bit of evil.

It had been but a fortnight before that Audry had received a visit from the Chaplain, Reverend Bosworth. Her husband, Lieutenant Jonathan Leeves, had been reported missing in action during an engagement over the English Channel. She knew he was even now still strapped into the cockpit of his Spitfire, probably shot to bits, bloated and white. It was a mental picture that tortured her, keeping her from sleep, until tonight, that is. This evening, pure exhaustion had darkened her conscious mind and blessed her with the gift of sleep, giving her a small respite from the hell that her life had become. Audry Leeves learned what true hate was. Each bomb that dropped hardened the absolute loathing she felt for a country that saw fit to steal the father of her children.

Little Emily began to cry. She really didn't understand what was going on. She only knew that she was tired and wanted to lie down in her own bed. Audry leaned down, picked up the child and cradled her on her lap while squatting near the subway gate.

"Madame, may I thank-you for your sacrifice. These are indeed dark times. It is through the courage of your husband and the other brave men in the RAF that will allow us to turn the tide of the war and send Hitler back to the hell he crawled out of."

Audry felt a hand on her shoulder as the stranger spoke softly to her. Without looking up, she thanked him for his kind words. Tears tracked down her cheeks. The hand squeezed her gently. "It has been difficult, what with there not even being a body to morne over. They say he's missing in action, but I know he's dead." Audry now wept.

"There, there Madam, stiff upper lip. We cannot show them weakness now."

Audry put her hand on his and then looked up at him.

"Oh, my, Mr. Churchill, Prime Minister Churchill..."

Winston Churchill surveyed the huge underground train station. There were hundreds of families huddled together, parents trying to comfort their children and each other. The scene caused him great grief and intense anger. His predecessor had all but invited this terror upon Britain because of his unwillingness to take a stand. Now, Prime Minister Churchill was visiting the results of his hard line with Hitler. It was not pretty.

Things were not going well. After the Lufwaffe failed to control the skies, Hitler changed tactics and blockaded the island nation with his deadly U-boats. It was exactly what Churchill himself would have done had he been in the Furor's place. Food was becoming scarce, medical supplies were dangerously low and morale was ebbing. There were whispers of a peace treaty in the House of Commons, an option that Churchill was loathe to entertain. We must preserver, he told his colleagues, Hitler can be beaten. But now, even he was feeling the strain of presenting a strong front.

"What time do we leave for America tomorrow?"

"The plane is scheduled to leave at noon, weather and the Nazis permitting, Sir," replied Andrew Williams, Churchill's personal secretary.

Roosevelt had requested that he fly across the Atlantic, there were some developments that needed to be discussed. He hoped it had something to do with that super bomb just recently used against the Japanese.

CHAPTER 8
The Alliance

January 27th, 11:43 AM
Oval Office, White House

"**Thank-you for** coming, my friend. I trust you had a decent flight?" Roosevelt extended his hand.

"It was quicker than taking a ship, that's about all I can say for air travel, so rushed and uncivilized. Fortunately there was an ample supply of cigars and brandy." Winston Churchill looked over to Henry Stimson and offered a hand. "Henry, good to see you."

"Winston," FDR interrupted, "let me introduce you to Captain Harsh Yoder."

"Harsh, you say," Churchill said with a smile in his voice, "an apt name for such terrible times, wouldn't you say, Franklin."

"I'm not sure Mr. and Mrs. Yoder had any such premonition when they named young Harsh in 1954." Franklin thought it might be amusing to bring Churchill into the loop in a clever manner.

Winston had to remind himself that even though he and Roosevelt had developed a fairly close relationship of late, he was still the Head of State and as such, his position superseded their friendship. Franklin was far to sharp to have made such an obvious mistake as to suggest that this man before him had not been born for another twelve years. After giving quick but thorough consideration, Winston took the offered lead.

"Are you suggesting that the good Captain here was issued a decade plus into the future, Franklin?"

"Please sit," Roosevelt was in his chair, everyone else was standing, "all of you. Winston, we have much to discuss. Before we do, tell me how it goes across the Atlantic."

Churchill's ebullient demeanor evaporated, his face seemed to sag. "Not well. Those goddamn Huns have us bottled up. Supplies, medicine, food, none of it can get in or out. The U-boats seem to have free reign of the channel to the point few are willing to risk sending a ship anywhere near the island.

"The Lufwaffe has turned the tide against the heroic efforts of the RAF last year. Their bombing raids have become a nightly events again and are even more destructive than they were in '41. Moral is low, both amongst the people and in the House. Frankly, there is talk of reopening negotiations with Hitler."

"Winston, there have been some remarkable developments during the past month or so that we need to discuss."

"I hope it has something to do about this supper bomb you used to bring Japan to their knees. My people think you Yanks have been busy splitting atoms." England was in a desperate position and Churchill was looking to America to extract them from the mouth of the Eagle.

Harsh Yoder sat quietly between Secretary of State Henry Stimson and President Franklin Roosevelt. Across from him was Prime Minister Winston Churchill. He was suddenly overwhelmed by the reality of his current situation. Here he was, an arms length from two of histories greatest figures. Each word exchanged was history in the making, and he, the son of a lapsed Mennonite, was part of it.

Churchill sat in a stuffed chair, slumped down, feet splayed out. He was an awkward man, round of build with a large, ruddy face. He puffed on a large Cuban cigar while formulating responses to Roosevelt's statements. Even in this private setting, his voice was authoritative. Churchill had been heavily influenced by the great English writer, Gibbon, from whom he had learned the sonorous rich style of speaking that made him one of the greatest orators of his day.

Yoder had any number of meetings with Roosevelt, his personage had become familiar. But with both he and Churchill in the same room, their combined presence had a synergistic affect, each now larger than their individual selves.

Harsh listened to Franklin's reedy, Hyde Park voice explain that "Captain Yoder here is a visitor from the future." Churchill's expected laughter died quickly as Henry and Harsh corroborated Franklin's fantastic story. Yoder listened as amusement was replaced with outrage at such a foolish fabrication. He witnessed the final emotional swing as Churchill slowly began to accept the fact that there was something remarkable afoot here.

"I find myself uncharacteristically speechless, Franklin, though I reserve the right to maintain a modicum of skepticism."

"I believe we will be able to exorcise that skepticism tomorrow when Captain Yoder entertains you aboard the *USS John C. Stennis*," responded Roosevelt.

Great, thought Yoder, another dog and pony show.

"What happened to Ensign Shah?" Captain Yoder was on the bridge and had just read a report written by Commander Saul Cohen, MD.

"Well, obviously he died," Captain O'Brien replied.

"Is this sarcasm something you are trying out or has it been permanently added to your repertoire?" Kelly was one of the most even tempered officers in his command, if she was feeling the strain, maybe it was time to look into some sort of R & R for the crew.

Kelly laughed. "Sorry, Harsh, I seem to be having one of those days. I've got a jet engine off an Intruder that looks like it'll now be excellent ballast, we have a dead sailor on a table in sick bay and word from my bowels is that this mornings breakfast is pressing for an early departure."

"There is no evidence of foul play, is there?" Having a psycho running loose on his ship would hardly comfort his stressed crew.

"No, preliminary reports suggest natural causes, Saul's doing an autopsy this afternoon."

"Have him call me when he gets the results."

Commander Cohen stood next to the remains of Ensign Ramesh Shah. Four hours ago he was complaining about this morning's breakfast to his friend Ensign Scott while dismantling an engine, then he turned blue, puked and dropped dead.

Saul began the external examination, looking for any mark, lesion or unexplained trauma to the body that might suggest something other than a natural death. He had never seen a body as blue as the recently departed Ensign Shah. There was obvious massive internal bleeding. Shah was twenty eight, six foot two, one hundred and sixty eight pounds and a marathon runner. By all accounts, he was in excellent physical shape, may be the best conditioned man on the ship. Probably some genetic disease took this young man's life, though there was no indication of such in his records, his father and mother were both still alive, well, would have been had they been born!

Dr. Cohen began his internal research by making a Y shaped incision across the chest with a scalpel. There was an unusual amount of blood, confirming his initial suspicion of internal bleeding. He then used an electrical saw to cut through the ribs and remove the breastplate.

There was so much blood Saul needed to suction the entire chest cavity before being able to see the heart and lungs. This was very strange indeed, almost as if an artery had come loose and the heart had been pumping blood directly into the body.

The heart and arteries seemed to be intact, the lungs were blue and healthy. Dr. Cohen lifted the organ tree out of the chest cavity, taking care to keep them intact as they were all linked together. He placed them in a steel sink next to the table Ensign Shah occupied. When he was done with the body, he would begin a careful vivisection of the heart, lungs, liver and other organs that had, until hours ago, kept Ramesh Shah a productive member of the *Stennis* crew.

Commander Cohen grabbed the small electric saw he had used earlier to cut out the breastplate and cut around the circumference of the skull. With a lever like tool, he then popped the cranium open, revealing the gray colored brain. The next phase was something he hated to do. He pulled, from behind his ears, the skin of Shah's scalp and folded it forward across his face. This was necessary in order to remove and weigh the brain. Removing a man's face was about the most undignified thing one could do to a body. Saul quickly weighed the brain and then shoved it back into the empty skull.

He finally collected bodily fluid samples, blood from the heart, urine from the bladder, bile from the liver, so that toxicology tests could be performed later. Had Shah been using drugs these tests would confirm that.

Dr. Cohen made his way back to the sink that contained the organ tree. It was there that he suspected lay the answer to the untimely demise of Ensign Ramesh Shah.

"So, you gonna go and pour some wine on that Churchill dude?" Parnes Williams was mocking Tim.

"Probably. My goal is to pour wine on every major historical leader that boards the *Stennis*."

"Shit," Parnes pronounced the word like it had seven i's, "you gonna get your fat white ass throwed into the brig and I'm gonna have to get me a new best friend."

How did this uneducated, simple black man become my only, if not best, friend, thought Tim. He is amusing, with his stereotypical ethnic humor. The guy was also fiercely loyal. If there was trouble, Parnes Williams would be there. His value in a fight would be questionable, but he would be there swinging. Maybe that's a good definition of a friend, someone who would back you up when your shit was weak.

"You on the serving detail for dinner tonight?"

"Don't even ask me that. Am I gonna need to tie your ass up to your bunk? You one crazy motherfucker."

"Don't worry, I've got no plans to attack Winston Churchill." But he did have plans to meet him, or at least see him. My God, one of the more pivotal players in world history was right this minute taking a tour of the ship, there was no way historian Tim was going to miss this truly remarkable opportunity.

"Probably just turn in early, maybe jerk off." Tim had an endearing self effacing edge to his humor.

Parnes grabbed his formal, short serving coat, answering Tim's earlier query, and took off. It was close to seven, the ship had been a bee hive of activity all day as sailors and aviators showed off their stuff to the Prime Minister of the British Isle. Tim had put in extra hours preparing a lovely crab puff hors d' oeuvre that brought him a small bit of notoriety amongst the handful of gourmet eaters aboard the ship. His skill with pastry dough was becoming legend, surprising himself and surely shocking his mother had she been around to bear witness. Maybe the Navy did know him better than he knew himself!

Tim stretched out in his bunk. He figured he had about an hour before desert, at which point security would be relaxed some and his opportunity to rub metaphorical elbows with arguably one of the greatest Prime Ministers since Margaret Thatcher presented the greatest likelihood for success.

Winston Churchill was astonished. Starting with the flight out to the *Stennis* in the vertical takeoff and landing aircraft and ending with a look at the nuclear powered engines, he was stunned. Add the fact that this ship and its entire crew came from the future, he was again, for the second time in two days, speechless.

"This is some impressive operation," Henry Stimson stated the very obvious.

"Hitler will have his hands full, no question about that." Churchill was anxious to find out when Roosevelt was planning to drop a nuclear weapon on Berlin, but decided to squelch his personal curiosity and maintain his diplomatic composure.

"He won't be the only one cursing the day they laid the keel for this fine fighting ship." Stimson wanted to let Winston know that his dearly hated Stalin was scheduled to feel the ire of the *Stennis* in due course. Unfortunately, Roosevelt would get that honor. Of course, he'd also have to deliver the uncomfortable news about England having to, what was it that Yoder said, take it in the shorts.

"I have so many questions, I don't know where to begin. By the way Captain Yoder, your kitchen is outstanding, what a wonderful dinner."

"May I pour you a glass of Port?" Parnes was trying to figure out who that Churchill guy was. He had it narrowed down to one of the handful of guys wearing suits. Probably the one with the accent.

"Yes, thank-you. Henry, I still believe that ground troops will be necessary to mop up the German army once the Eagle has been de-clawed." Churchill didn't enjoy using euphemisms, he like to speak plainly, but he didn't want to suggest that he was expecting the use of nuclear bombs on Germany.

"We see the *Stennis* in a support role. There will be a massive landing on the Continent and our aviators will make sure there will be a minimum amount of resistance as they wade to shore. Air support will be critical in each major engagement."

"Captain Yoder," Churchill interrupted, "you can count on England's complete support. I'm anxious to sit with General Eisenhower to hear of your tactical plans."

"I think Franklin will want to speak with you before that. After we finish dinner, we'll fly back to the White House to visit with him." Stimson was hoping not be privy to that discussion.

Tim, wearing waiters garb liberated from Parnes' locker, made his way through the kitchen. Dishes were being washed, suggesting that the main course was over and desert was being served. He grabbed a towel and walked casually towards the Captain's mess. There were two marines standing guard, but with the constant flow of personnel in and out, they clearly couldn't keep track of each face.

Tim followed a sailor carrying a tray full of deserts, cream puffs, which he had proudly made the shell for, into the dinning room. The sailor turned left, he banked right and headed for Prime Minister Winston Churchill. His heart was racing, palms were beginning to get moist. Tim had no idea what he was going to do once he arrived at Churchill's chair. Maybe just stand there and stare? Maybe he should have developed a better plan?

Less than ten feet from Churchill, Tim was close enough to hear him speak. He could discern the voice that placated a nation during the blackest of times. He could see the round and ruddy face that so frustrated Hitler. He also could see his opportunity to meet this icon, to brush against greatness.

Churchill had just finished clipping his long, trade mark cigar. Tim spied a brass lighter sitting on the table before him. With the speed of a Jaguar, he moved in and reached for the lighter. Had his middle knuckle been only a millimeter smaller, had he maybe not moved his hand so quickly, had the moon been in the seventh house, maybe that glass of Port would not have begun to wobble. Had he not clumsily reached out to stabilize the glass of Port, it might not have tumbled into Winston Churchill's lap. Destiny, clearly, was not to be denied this night.

"What are you in for this time, Seamen First Class Irwin?"

"You're not gonna believe this, Lieutenant," should he have been surprised to see Ben-Gurion sitting in the small jail cell? "It seems that I poured a glass of wine in Winston Churchill's lap." Tim sat on the bench and buried his face in his hands.

"Do I need to ask you why you're keeping me company?"

"Maybe," answered Allen, "I'm fond of you."

"Yeah, or maybe you had a close encounter with Churchill yourself."

Allen Ben-Gurion leaned his head against the wall and closed his eyes. He smiled at the stunning absurdity of Tim's plight and grew dark at the utter importance of his own mission. Even as he sat in the absolute safety of the brig, Jews were being herded like cattle in transit to their execution. The holocaust must be stopped.

Prime Minister Winston Churchill was ebullient. The darkest days are over. With the devastating fire power now in the hands of the United States, Hitler's reign of terror could surly be measured in weeks. During the flight back to the White House, he had developed a number of possible courses of action that would bring decisive victory to the Allies. They all revolved around a nuclear bomb being shoved up Hitler's ass in Berlin. Since the OSS broke Germany's code with the Enigma Machine, making sure he was in the city when the bomb was dropped should not be a problem. God bless these Yanks, Churchill thought.

"Captain, I see you have delivered Prime Minister Churchill back to me in good working order," knowing he had some very difficult subject matter to broach with Churchill, he wanted to keep things light.

"Would have had him home earlier, but he insisted on playing with all the little buttons on the helicopter. Almost brought us down!"

Seems as though Yoder is reading my mind, Roosevelt thought. He's a good man, sharp and intuitive and loaded with common sense.

"Gentlemen, may Winston and I have a private moment?" It was time. Roosevelt had been rehearsing how he was going to broach this most difficult request all evening. He was still not sure how to do it.

"Is it past midnight? I must be getting back. I'm expecting to hear from MacArthur in a few hours, what with the time difference between Washington and Tokyo, he always calls at the most inconvenient times. Good evening, gentlemen." Henry Stimson was glad to be leaving.

Yoder had been spending so much time in Washington, he had been sequestered in the Lincoln bedroom during his increasingly frequent visits to Washington. Though Lincoln never actually slept there, the room was still steeped in history. The worst of which, being rented out to political contributors, had yet to be written.

A white coated waiter delivered two cognacs to the cloistered heads of state. They sat quietly for a few minutes, Franklin letting time smooth the edges, Winston, allowing Roosevelt the contrived drama of the war ending news he was sure to deliver.

"Quite some day, my friend."

"My mind still reels, Franklin. Imagine, time travel being possible."

"Yes," responded Roosevelt, "it took me a number of days to believe that it was indeed a reality. I put poor Captain Yoder through quite some trouble before accepting his precept that he journeyed back from the tip of the new millennium."

"The technology they have developed is truly astonishing, Franklin, it must be a wonderful place to live. I watched a moving picture show, some sort of a presentation, that demonstrated stunning advancements not only in weapons but in health and entertainment. It seems that your vision of united nations is to be a reality."

"Yes, Winston, however it is that remarkable advancement in weapons technology that is the cause of Captain Yoder's backwards journey. With the splitting of the atom, the world, apparently, was never the same, or will never be the same. My God, this discussion taking place in two time periods is exasperating. The creation of a nuclear weapon has shifted the paradigm of power, allowing even a weak nation to hold the rest of the world hostage.

"Seems they have christened them weapons of mass destruction. With a bomb no bigger than this couch, we decimated Sapporo. The city was leveled. Due to the arrogance of the Japanese, over two hundred thousand souls perished." Roosevelt would never forgive the Emperor for not evacuating the city.

"It clearly is a power that must be kept in the hands of a reasonable nation. A nation with the courage to unleash it only in dire circumstances." England was most assuredly in dire circumstances, Churchill thought. He was trying to orchestrate an opening for Franklin to offer this apocalyptic power to liberate Great Britain from the foul clutches of the hated Hun.

Franklin declined the invitation just proffered, knowing that his friend had no clue as to what was to be asked of him. "I'm sure you gleaned from the feature presentation you were shown on the *Stennis*, Russia eventually developed a nuclear capability and used it to enslave thirty percent of Europe for half a century after this war ended. A strong president in the nineteen nineties pushed the arms race so hard that Russia, the Soviet Union, crumbled under the pressure."

"An American actor, Mr. Reagen, I believe. This truly is a democracy, when a movie actor can become President."

"We're a bit shocked. Frankly, I don't think he's much of an actor. He was, or is slated to be, however, an impressive leader. By the end of, I believe the called it, the Cold War, the Soviet Union was in shambles, their army was unpaid and vulnerable to attack from within as well as from outside." Roosevelt recognized what Yoder must have felt trying to encapsulate this complicated and diverse bit of future history.

"Franklin, what does this have to do with our war?" Churchill was tired, it was almost two in the morning.

"In the year 2002, an organization, they called them terrorists, wrested control of most of the nuclear weapons in Russia. The sole purpose was to unleash them and destroy all of humanity."

"What sort of mad man would want to kill everyone on the planet. Who would he rule? Even Hitler is not quite as mad as that, though, were his back against the wall, he might pull that trigger just out of spite."

"He, apparently, was a religious man," Franklin clarified, "intent on ridding the world of a Godless people.

He assumed that God would begin anew, creating some kind of utopia according to this man's precept."

"I'm assuming," added Winston, "this has something to do with why the *Stennis* is here?"

"Very much so." Here we go, thought Roosevelt. "The *Stennis* was sent back by the United States government to our time to prevent Russia from developing nuclear weapons."

"In order to do that, I'd assume they would have to be soundly trounced in this war."

"Considerably more than trounced, Winston. The plan is to destroy their government, their economy and to demoralize their population. It sounds harsh, but the future of man kind hangs in the balance."

"Are you planning to drop more nuclear bombs on Russia. Is the plan to kill the entire population?" Churchill was not sure he had the stomach for that.

"No. If this is played out properly, there should be very little need, if any at all, for the detonation of any more nuclear weapons."

"I've known you just long enough to know that this plan you speak of is considerably more complicated than I suspect."

"It certainly is." It was time, Roosevelt realized. He was starting to dance around the real issue and it was making him weary. "For better or worse, Winston, here is the plan."

It didn't take but ten minutes. Churchill listened carefully, not interrupting. The idea of covertly aiding Hitler was abstruse. It was Roosevelt's last submission that had Prime Minister Winston Churchill's blood running cold.

"My God, Franklin, you want Great Britain to surrender to Adolph Hitler?"

"**Bless me Father**, for I have sinned." Her voice was muffled and difficult to hear.

Please be the last sinner of the day, Father Anthony silently pleaded. He had very little stomach for hearing confessions lately. His mind, and his heart, were elsewhere.

"Confess you sins to God," he lazily commanded.

"I fucked a priest!"

Oh Jesus! Anthony pulled the screen aside to reveal a not particularly contrite Lieutenant Savage giggling like a school girl.

"What are you doing?" He opened the confessional door to see if there were anymore sinners on line who could have possible heard this most incriminating admission.

She was a wild one, this Kaitlyn Savage, and Anthony had never been happier. This duplicitous life he was now living added a sense of danger and excitement he had never before felt. For the first time in his life, he was living for himself. She drew out of him all the feelings and thoughts that had been buried deep inside of him for decades. It was almost as if he'd been blind since birth and could now see for the first time.

The two of them would sit for hours, hidden in some obscure part of the ship, talking about things he had never considered. "What makes you happy?" she once asked him. A simple enough question that locked his mind tight. He'd never considered allowing himself to probe into his own life to address such, what he formerly considered, frivolous inquiries. What makes God happy, that was the thrust of his life. There had been no consideration for Anthony, his time was spent helping the sick, the destitute, the suffering.

Was this now his reciprocation for a life time of reaching out, of healing, of listening to others spill their soiled lives over his, only to take from him his curative gifts, leaving him nothing in return, save the occasional plate of homemade chocolate chip cookies?

Lieutenant Kaitlyn Savage opened his mind and his heart to the boundless pleasures that were available. She showed him that there was no reason to deny himself anymore. "We are God's children," she reminded him one day, "wouldn't you hope that *your* children would take advantage of all the gifts you had to offer them? Would you want them *denying* themselves just to prove their love to you?" She had an innocent and naive way of taking the most complicated theological issue and dissolving it with crystalline logic. Father Anthony Salvatore speculated that he may be the only man on the ship who was happy residing in 1942.

Kaitlyn Savage reflected that she may be the only woman aboard the *John C Stennis* who was equally pleased to be destined to live sixty years in the past. This goofy looking little man had brought her such joy since their inauspicious first meeting. Back in the future, her stunning looks had precluded her needing to spend time with any but the best looking men around. If they weren't attractive, rich and well educated businessmen, they were beautiful down and out models or actors. She changed men often, always searching for something she couldn't even verbalize. Unable to define it, she was destined to fail in her quest to find it.

And then, along comes a priest. A priest, for God sakes, harboring the gentleness and intellectual honesty that she realized she needed in order to be whole. His vulnerability touched the maternal threads running through her. His simple humor made her laugh and his internal turmoil mirrored her own. Each of them, she realized, could heal the other. A destiny bent on testing Kaitlyn Savage seemed to be taking a break.

"**Saul, I'm sorry** we haven't had a chance to visit, it's been a challenging few weeks." The ship to shore connection was poor, occasional bursts of static had Harsh repeating himself. "Tell me what you know about Ensign Shah."

"Harsh, this is a strange one. By all accounts, he was quite healthy. Exercised regularly, I believe he was a runner and had no overt symptoms of illness, his friends don't recall him having any complaints. The clinical cause of death is massive hemorrhaging. It is difficult to say exactly what brought this about."

"Any history of cardiovascular disease?"

"His paternal grandfather died of a stroke, but the man was eighty two. His parents were both alive when we left and there is no recent history of heart disease. Hell, his heart and lungs were in excellent condition."

"So what killed him?"

There was a pause. It was clear to Harsh that there was not going to be a simple or decisive answer. "The simple answer is that he died of a massive hemorrhage, internal bleeding. Why it happened is the interesting part."

Typical of a Doctor, thought Yoder, to suggest how a man died was interesting.

"It seems that his arteries, and to a certain extent, his veins, have deteriorated. The typical thickness of a healthy artery is four millimeters, Ensign Shah's arteries were less that one millimeter thick. The blood was literally leaching out of his circulatory system. It happened very rapidly, which is why he demonstrated no symptoms prior to death."

"Could this be caused by a viral infection, similar to HIV?" The thought of saving man kind from nuclear annihilation and then destroying it with a new virus suddenly made his head hurt.

"That's the first thing I checked for. The entire crew had been inoculated against AIDS, there is no indication of any virus in his system. Harsh, I'm at a loss as to what caused his circulatory system to crash like that."

"OK, you'll keep me in the loop on this, Saul, report directly to me any new information. You fairly sure whatever he had is not contagious?"

"I don't think there is any need to quarantine the ship. I'm running some additional toxicology tests, I'll let you know what I find. By the way, Harsh, I haven't seen you as a patient for quite some time. The last time I had you on the table, I believe your blood pressure was high, your cholesterol was problematic and you were four pounds from being classified as fat."

"I know, Saul. It's been kinda busy, what with this jump back in time and that pesky Nazi Army running amuck in Europe," Harsh sarcastically replied.

"Fine, I'll save a slab next to Ensign Shah for you."

"Jesus, Doctor," Harsh laughed, "I'll see if I can get down there when I get back to the *Stennis*."

"Come in, Captain Yoder." Harsh was ushered into the Oval Office by a Secret Service Agent. Roosevelt was sitting down, as was Churchill. Stimson stood to greet him.

Churchill did not look well. He couldn't have gotten much more than three hours sleep last night. Harsh suspected, however, he was suffering more from the news he had been given recently than for a lack of rack time.

"Winston is, as you say, in the loop," Roosevelt was amused by Yoder's colloquialisms, "he does have a number of concerns, however."

"That is fully understandable."

"What causes me a tremendous amount of anxiety," Churchill spoke up, "is how you plan to extricate Great Britain from the clutches of Hitler after Russia falls?"

"First of all, let's revisit the basic premise. If structured correctly, Hitler will have moved most of his forces to the Western Front to smash Stalin. There is no way he wants to fight another winter campaign in Russia, he is experiencing the dramatic effects sub zero weather has on a mobile army right now. Once he is comfortable with the fact that England is a non issue, we expect that he will throw everything he has west to assure a fairly quick victory, something of a modified Blitzkrieg.

"Once Russia has been crushed, there is no doubt, despite any treaty he will have signed, that he will pick up where he left off and continue his attack of England."

"I have to go back home and convince the House of Commons and King Edward himself that will not happen!" Churchill pounded the arm of the chair he was sitting in.

"It will happen," Yoder continued, "we all know Hitler to well to believe he will not turn on England. However, the United States is in a position to cut him off before he can even get to the Channel.

"As I have mentioned before, the bulk of his army will be three thousand miles away. His supply lines will be painfully exposed. With the supersonic aircraft on board the *Stennis*, we can cut those lines in two days. Although we will not be able to destroy his army with air power alone, we can make their return to Europe slow and painful. By the time they hit the Caucasus Mountains, England will be prepared to do battle and the United States will have a ground force on France soil. We should be able to engage them closer to their home ground and not have to slug it out in France, as was necessary the first time."

Four and a half hours later, Prime Minister Winston Churchill left the Oval Office prepared to present this shocking proposal to the King and... who else could he tell about time travel, nuclear weapons and airplanes that travel three times the speed of sound? The excitement he felt hours ago when he first sat with his friend had been radically tempered. There was going to be no easy solution, no supper bomb to be dropped on Berlin.

Conditions in England were worsening. Food levels were critical, coal and fuel were heavily rationed. Hitler's U-boats had effectively shut off the island from any but the most daring ship captains. Moral was low in the civilian sector and there was continuing talk in the House about opening talks with Germany. Despite the resolute position Churchill had taken, he too was beginning to question the wisdom of a continued conflict. Did he have the courage to look defeat squarely, even if was to be a temporary condition?

"Come'on Sean, let's go work out."

"Don't feel like it." Ever since the thrashing he received from Tim, Sean had been quiet and sullen. It had been the first true beating he ever had as an adult. It was also a humiliating rout at the hands of a man half a foot smaller than he. His rogue band of warriors had pretty much drifted away. The Professor was the only one who stood by him in defeat and, in his simple way, was trying to pull Sean out of his depression.

Adding to his malaise was the fact that he had lost fifty bucks betting on a basketball game that he knew the score of. It seems that his plan to make millions was all going to hell. The ships computer had New York beating Chicago 71 to 68, the reality was Chicago 65, New York 60. To make things worse, he lost the bet to the Professor, who was in on the scam from the beginning! Then he had to pressure Walter to take the money, Sean was no welcher.

They were on the flight deck, sitting on a rack of ASHRAM missiles. It was a warm but overcast day. Walter was concerned for his friend. He had been with Sean since boot camp. Sean had taken him under his wing and sort of guided him along. He was everything Walter wanted to be, strong, confident and outgoing. Walter recognized the fact that he was not the sharpest tool in the shed and was pleased to have a guy like Sean to look out for him.

He was at a loss, though, as to how to help his friend out. Walter had tried to make Sean laugh, but he also recognized that he was not only obtuse, he wasn't very funny either. He reached back in his mind to try to retrieve some of the more inspirational words that had come his way, but there were few. Walter had grown up keeping to the shadows, reticent to bring any attention to himself. He did recall, however, that he always felt better when he heard of the misfortune of others.

"Wanna hear something I never told you?"

Sean was gazing off at the horizon, giving his loyal friend half an ear.

"Remember that I told you my parents had died in a fire when I was a baby? Well, that wasn't true." Walter didn't really want to go where he was going, but it was the only thing he could think of to bring his buddy around.

"So your folks didn't die in a fire?" Sean's interest shifted from the gray horizon.

"No, you see, my Mom, before she had me, was hit by an ice cream truck."

"Hit by a fucking ice cream truck? Jesus Christ!"

"Yeah," Walter continued, "She was only seventeen. I think she wanted a Creamsicle, ya know, the ones with the orange on the outside and vanilla on the inside?"

"Do I need to know that?"

"Probably not," Walter thoughtfully volunteered.

"I do like those though. Wonder if they invented them yet." Maybe I could make a million bucks inventing them myself? His mood brightened a little.

"Well, before she could order one, bam, the truck hit her. She took it on the head pretty bad. They thought she was gonna die, but she didn't, she's one tough lady. Trouble is, she never woke up."

"She was in a comma?"

"Yeah, that's it." He could never remember that word.

"Wait a minute, this happened before you were born?" Sean was loosing patience.

"Yeah."

"So she recovered from the comma." Sean was used to back engineering Walter's stories.

"No."

"This doesn't make sense." Sean was getting short with Walter, he really didn't want to have to work so hard listening to a story.

"They put her in a special hospital, hooked up to a bunch of machines. They kept her alive even though her head was dead."

"You mean brain dead." This was getting laborious.

"Right. About three years later, they find out she's pregnant."

"Hold it right there." Sean had jumped off the missile rack and put his face in Walter's. "Your comatose mother got pregnant? How the fuck did she get pregnant?"

Walter was quiet. He really didn't want to admit this, especially seeing how irritated the story seemed to have gotten Sean.

"Well, how the fuck did she get pregnant?"

"My father, who was an orderly at the hospital, had sex with her."

"Holy shit." Sean staggered back a few feet and put his hands on his head. This was the worst story he had ever heard. "Why the hell are you telling me this?"

Walter was embarrassed. Clearly his efforts at helping Sean had not only failed, but caused him further discomfort.

Sean sat back down.

"I was trying to make you feel better. I always feel better when I hear bad stuff about other people."

Jesus, Sean thought. It suddenly occurred to him, after the four years they had been together, what a great friend the Professor was.

"Sorry man."

They sat for a few minutes reexamining the horizon.

"What happened to..." did he really want to call the man who raped his comatose mother his father, "your old man."

"He got out of jail after seven years, I never met him."

"That might be a good thing."

"I met my mother though."

Oh Jesus, thought Sean, I don't know if I can handle this.

"I was twelve. My parents, well the people who adopted me, brought me to the hospital one day. They were real religious and pretty strict. It seems that the state decided that my mother had lived long enough and wanted to turn off the machines. My parents were against doing that and went to court to stop it. I had to testify for some reason, that's when I found all this out."

Sean could feel a lump in his throat. Last time he felt like this was when ET waved good-bye to Elliot. He was six.

"They lost their case. The morning they were turning off the machines, they brought me to the hospital to see her."

Sean put a hand on Walter's leg and looked away.

"She looked awful, all shriveled up. I remember that her hair was gray and her fingernails were real long and yellow. I started to cry so they took me home."

Sean wiped a single tear from his cheek and put his arm around his friend. It was the first sensitive gesture he had performed since he was a child.

February 4th, 1942, 11:28 AM
Eagles Nest, Bravarian Mountains

"Is it true, Wilhelm?" Field Marshal Wilhelm Keitel was Chief of the High Command of the Armed Forces and was Hitler's chief of staff. Adolph Hitler stood on the slate patio outside of his mountain retreat. The view touched the artist in him. Mountain peaks soared all about, strong and tall. They were suggestive of the super men that made up his invincible armies.

"Yes, Mine Fuhrer, Great Britain is suing for peace."

The temperature hovered between cold and freezing, even the brilliant sun, seemingly close enough to hurl a rock at, couldn't warm Keitel, who stomped his feet to keep his blood flowing. Hitler stood near a low stone wall, seemingly impervious to the cold that had gripped Eagles Nest.

"It is all coming together." He seemed to be talking to the mountains rather than the Field Marshal standing by his side. He felt a warmth inside of him radiating outwardly. No, what he was feeling was power. He was doing what the great generals of history had failed to do, conquer the continent. Poland, France, Belgium, Austria, already his. Africa, or the oil deposits in Africa, would be his shortly. Now the despised England is crawling to him, begging for mercy. He'll show mercy, right up until Russia is a smoking ruin.

"They are asking for a conditional surrender. We have not received their formal demands yet." Hitler's attention was rudely pulled back to the present.

"We'll give them what they want." He was smiling, Wilhelm did not recall seeing Adolph Hitler in such high spirits. "Just as we gave Neville Chamberlain what he wanted. Are they that naive to think that we will not destroy them when it is convenient for us? Yes, we will give them their terms. Fools."

The day before, America had terminated their Lend Lease Agreement with England. The anti war sentiment his agents had been reporting has clearly been growing. Now, with their doorway to Europe closed, America has ceased to be a threat. Resources can now be reallocated to the Eastern Front. Next year this time, Adolph Hitler would be dinning in Moscow.

CHAPTER 9
The Covert War with Russia

February 7th, 1942, 9:36 AM
Pentagon, Arlington, VA

"Does it look much different?" The car had just turned off Army-Navy Drive, the Pentagon was now in full view.

"The building hasn't changed, the grounds certainly look different." Captain Yoder and General Eisenhower were sharing a ride to what could be described as the most important tactical military meeting in history. The most powerful leaders in the world were convening to plot the extinction of the Soviet Union and the demise of the Third Reich.

"I expect once the landscaping is done, it won't look so imposing."

"Hardly," Harsh countered, "this will become the most feared place on earth. Political debates will rage in public, but once a decision has been made, the deadly consequences will be planned and coordinated here, very much in private."

The prime contract to build the Pentagon had been awarded just seven months earlier. Although it would not be fully completed until January of '43, the building was operational. It was built with the single minded efficiency that is generally reserved for times of war.

In August, the site was nothing more than wasteland, swamps and dumps. Five and a half million cubic yards dirt and forty two thousand concrete piles were used just for the foundation of the building. Four hundred and thirty five thousand cubic yards of concrete were processed out of six hundred and eighty thousand tons of sand and gravel dredged from the nearby Potomac to create the superstructure. This eighty three million dollar temple to war consolidated seventeen buildings of the War Department.

A superb exercise in efficiency, an individual can walk to any two points in the building within seven minutes despite the fact that there are seventeen and a half miles of corridors. Even in 2002, it would still be the largest office building in the world, being three times as large as the Empire State Building and twice the size of the Merchandise Mart in Chicago. Once up to speed, the Pentagon will accommodate twenty three thousand employees in its three million seven hundred thousand square foot interior. They will pace their day with four thousand two hundred clocks, quench their thirst from six hundred and ninety one water fountains and relieve themselves in one of two hundred and eighty four rest rooms.

The car dropped the Captain and the General at the South Entrance where they walked for somewhat less than seven minutes down corridor three to Ring B where the large and still unfinished War Room was located.

Yoder and Eisenhower were the last to arrive. In attendance were President Roosevelt; Secretary of War, Henry Stimson; Secretary of the Navy, Frank Knox; General MacArthur freshly arrived from Tokyo, Prime Minister Winston Churchill, weary after the most difficult debates of his life; General Bradley and the Commandant of the Marine Corps General Vandergrift; Admiral Halsey, and rounding out the English contingent, General Montgomery and Vice Admiral Mountbatten.

Vandergrift, Montgomery and Mountbatten had only been enlightened about future technological advances that had suddenly became current the day before. Vandergrift was excited. He was given a fly by of the *Stennis* late yesterday afternoon. Having had the benefit of first hand knowledge, his enthusiasm was understandable.

Montgomery and Mountbatten had arrived in Washington at three in the morning. They possessed nothing but second hand information from Churchill and they seemed distrustful.

Their skepticism was somewhat understandable. They had heard, just days ago, their formally hawkish prime minister lobbying for Great Britain's surrender. Despite the remarkable information they had recently received, their instinct was to fight. Fight until the last man, that was their legacy, borne from the greatest lineage of fighting men in history. It will take more information than they already had to get them behind this plan of America's.

In the middle of the conference room was a large table that held a detailed map of Europe. On the map were small tanks, soldiers, airplanes and ships, each representing a division or convoy or squadron. The setup looked to be more for puerile amusement than for the deadly serious business that it was.

On the west wall, technicians from the *Stennis* were setting up a large display monitor that, when ready, would supplant the paper map on the table with accurate and up the minute information concerning the position of the various players in this mortal game.

Captain Yoder stood at the head of the table. "Gentlemen, please take a seat." It was time to plot the largest shift of world power in history.

"In order to decide where we need to go, it will be necessary to look back at where we've been." Yoder looked out at the mustered group of leaders and realized that he was about to teach history to those who created it. This was heady stuff. "Some of the following will come as no surprise to most of you, some will not have been discovered until after the war, so bear with me.

"On 18, December, Hitler released Directive 21 that said," Harsh pushed a pair of hated reading glasses on his face and read from page one of a large binder on the table, "The German Armed Forces must be prepared, even before the conclusion of the war against England, to crush Soviet Russia in a rapid campaign. The campaign is code-named Barbarossa and it began on 15, May of last year."

Harsh looked up from the binder and pulled off his glasses. He had spent the past week preparing for this presentation and had most of the important stuff memorized. "The National Socialists in Germany have put a great deal of importance on the conquest of Russia. It is a land of huge resources, iron ore, coal and especially oil, all needed to drive the equally huge German military machine. Additionally, Hitler is looking at the large population as a source of cheap labor. There is also the unfortunate need of the German people to expand, I believe they have a word for it, *Lebensraum*, meaning room to grow, and, I might add, room to exile the enemies of National Socialism. There was speculation that Hitler had been influenced by his visit to the tomb of Napoleon in Paris. He was quoted as saying that he would succeed at what the French Emperor failed to do, conquer Russia.

"Stalin set the stage for the German invasion when he broke one of the secret protocols of the German-Soviet Pact of August, '39," back on went the dreaded reading glasses, "In case of a territorial-political alteration in the region of the Baltic States, the northern border of Lithuania will form the boundary of the spheres of influence between Germany and the USSR." Harsh looked back up to his audience, "He sealed the German-Lithuanian border with motorized forces. This extension of the Soviet power indicated an indirect threat to the Reich by threatening its source of oil in Rumania and its shipping lanes in Scandinavia.

"The key to Operation Barbarossa is movement. The Germans had hoped for quick success before the autumn rains turned the countryside into a sea of mud.

There was also concern that a harsh winter could effectively stop the attack.

"Major General Marcks, Chief of Staff of the 18th Army, was charged with developing the attack on Russia. Marcks designed a plan that would have Germany occupying Russia up to a line on the Lower Don-middle Volga-nothern Duena River. The ultimate goal was the capture of the spiritual center of Russia, Moscow. In what will be recognized as typical of Adolph Hitler, he rejected the Marcks Plan, placing political, economic interests before military needs.

"Major General Paulus was tasked to develop a new plan. In December of 1940, Hitler approved the plan, which was published by the Wehrmacht High Command as Instruction Nr. 21 under the designation "OKW/WFSt/Abt.L (I) Nr. 33408/40, more easily called Operation Barbarossa."

"There is no way the Yanks could have known that," Montgomery whispered to Mountbatten, "we never turned information that specific over to them. Either we have a leak or this man just may be from the future."

"He certainly has my attention," Mountbatten shot back.

Harsh had so much to read he just kept his glasses perched on the end of his nose. "The operational plan for the Central German Army Group is as follows: The objective of Group Army Center is to break through the area around and to the north of Warsaw with their strong tank and motorized formations and destroy the Russian forces located in Belorussia. Conditions must be created for the penetration of strong mobile elements to the north so they can destroy enemy forces fighting in the Baltic Provinces. They will fight in joint cooperation with the Northern Army Group, based in East Prussia. The two armies will work their way towards Leningrad. After achieving the initial directives, the attack will be redirected towards Moscow in order to occupy that important communications and armament center.

"It's nice to have the operational plan of war of your adversaries word for word," Roosevelt's comment was directed at Churchill, sitting to his right.

"I appreciate that some of this is fairly tedious, but I think it is important to have as much background material as possible before we address a plan of action of our own." Yoder hated reading out loud, his monotone voice was even more profound when reciting others words.

"Not at all, Captain. This is all quite fascinating. This is all without precedence, we know what Hitler will do before he does it!"

"To a certain extent, that is true, Mr. President. But let's not forget, since history was changed with the early surrender of Japan, we can't rely on this history one hundred percent. We have already seen examples of that not just to changes in meteorological conditions, but in military tactics, like Hitler's decision to use his U-boats more aggressively against England." From here on out, Harsh realized, they could do little more than speculate.

"In contrast to the Marcks Plan, Operation Barbarossa didn't hold Moscow as the most important objective of the offensive. The force group committed in the center of the front had only the mission of defeating the Soviets in Belorussia and then advancing in the direction of Leningrad. Hitler would not even consider Moscow until the latter part of the campaign.

"In February of '41, the Wehrmacht put Colonel Loebel in charge of the Luftwaffe and also established the first supply bases in Poland. That same month, the Eastern Army, one of three armies involved in Barbarossa, was deployed. Seven infantry and one motorized division rolled to the east on rail. As the same time, the German long range reconnaissance pilots flew deep into Soviet territory, they flew, in case there is any interest, under the leadership of Lieutenant Colonel Rowehl. This group was ordered to photograph Russian territory with four special squadrons to determine the eventual deployment of the Red Army. They were primarily working with the Army Group Center, the second of the three armies involved in the attack. By the way, the planes they are using, the Ju-86-P's, can take pictures from an altitude of thirty six thousand feet. The recon work we'll be doing will have jets operating at twice that altitude with cameras with enough resolution to tell if the guy who squeezed a pile of jakes by the side of the road had corn for dinner." Yet again, Captain Yoder questioned whether he needed to use colloquialisms before world leaders.

"Army Group Center was responsible for attacking Belorussia, taking Smolensk and, with the cooperation of Army Group North, the third of the attacking armies, to occupy Minsk.

"The Soviets had learned much from their unfortunate winter campaign against Finland. In response, they increased the production of heavy weapons from a total of 358 tanks in the summer of 1940 to, let's see here," there was a stunning amount of information available, "to fifteen hundred and three a year later. Aircraft production increased six hundred percent, artillery seven hundred percent and antitank weapons by an astonishing seven thousand percent. By May of '41, the Soviets had one hundred and eighteen rifle divisions, twenty cavalry divisions and forty tank brigades. Stacked in front of Army Group Center, between Bialystock and Brest-Litovsk, there were forty five rifle divisions and fifteen tank brigades. The second largest grouping of sixteen rifle divisions, two cavalry divisions and three motorized brigades was in second echelon between Novogrudek and Baranovichi." It was bad enough reading in front of this group, it was murder trying to read the names of these Russian cities.

"On 22., June of '41, there were one hundred and thirty-nine divisions staged along the boarders of Poland and East Prussia. At 0315 hours, one of the bloodiest battles in history began.

"The Soviets had one hundred and thirty divisions, nearly three million men, poised to engage Germany. They were not, however, well deployed. Despite a two to one numerical superiority in tanks, the Soviets minimized that advantage by dispersing them among infantry units which were now no match for the massed armor of the German Panzer armies. They also enjoyed a three to one advantage in aircraft, but the Lufwaffe destroyed over one thousand planes in the first hours of the attack, many while still sitting on the ground. Air superiority quickly passed to the Germans.

"To make matters more difficult for Russia, Stalin had purged most of the experienced Soviet commanders in the 30's, replacing them with political generals who had limited to no combat experience.

"By the end of the first day of Barbarossa, Germany had advanced forty miles into the Soviet Union. In a week, General Guderian's Second Panzer Group pushed nearly three hundred miles through Russia and had trapped the Soviet Third and Tenth Armies. By 9, July, forty one Red Army divisions are out of action and three hundred thousand Russian soldiers are captured. A highly successful start to say the least.

"In August, Hitler makes, what historians believe, was his first mistake. He orders Guderians's Second Panzer Group to link up with Army Group South. His generals disagreed with the move, but it initially looked like a smart tactic. Within three weeks another six hundred thousand Soviet troops are encircled. This further cemented in Hitler's mind the fact that he knew more than his generals. It will have turned out to have been, however, a terminal mistake as it slowed the march on Moscow, allowing the Soviets to regroup. It also caused the German army to fight through one of the worst Russian winters of the century.

"By late September, the city of Kiev falls. Germany suffers over one hundred thousand casualties, the Soviets loose half a million men. By early October, Army Group South has bottled up and destroyed Soviet units composed of seven hundred thousand men.

"Operation Typhoon, the final drive on Moscow, begins on 2, October. Guderian's forces go north to join the other Panzer groups working toward the Soviet capital. Unfortunately for Germany, the autumn rains begin and the muddy ground all but stops the mechanized drive while the Soviets stiffen their resistance. As most of the diplomats and government officials begin leaving Moscow, Stalin announces that he will remain." While most of this information is now three months old, it occurred to Harsh that it still may be new to many of the men in this room. They were all was years away from his world of instant communication.

"By early November, the ground freezes enough to get the attack on Moscow moving again. Unfortunately, they are experiencing one of the coldest winters on record and the German army has not been equipped with winter gear yet. On the 27th, Germany is within thirty miles of the city. Two days later, Panzer units fight their way across the Moscow-Volga Canal. By 2, December, infantry units reach Moscow's northern suburbs.

"The weather gets worse and Hitler agrees with his commanders and suspends the offensive against Moscow. The next day, Stalin orders a counteroffensive along the five hundred mile front. The objective is to drive a wedge into the Army Group Center, isolate the Germans and then beat them in detail. The German Army is overextended and exhausted, they are vulnerable. Stalin meets with the his first success of the campaign."

"We've heard that there has been a change of command on the Eastern Front."

"You are correct, Prime Minister, Hitler has replaced both Rundstedt and Bock. He also dismissed General von Brauchitsch as Commander in Chief of the German Army and has taken the post himself.

"His first order is to command all units to stand fast and hold their ground. This prevents a route by the Red Army and enables the Germans to fall back to defensive positions that they will hold until this spring. Hitler has now decided that his commanders are worthless and will start to disregard their advice. This will have ultimately been a fatal decision on his part.

"At this point, the losses for both sides are staggering. The Red Army has had five *million* casualties and has had three million more men taken prisoner. They have lost thirty thousand guns and twenty thousand tanks. Germany has not, however, destroyed the Soviets ability to rearm itself, both from within and through the Lend-Lease shipments from the United States."

"I've called back the latest shipment of material. I will be expecting a call from Stalin shortly questioning my motivation. What are we going to tell him, Captain?" Roosevelt was hardly looking forward to that conversation.

"At some point, Stalin is going to realize he is in this alone. I'd like to keep him from that realization for as long as possible, at least until the Japanese begin their attack. The evening before, the Japanese will have pulled their diplomats out of the country and I suggest that we do the same. At that point, Russia will be months from annihilation and Stalin will have a fatally full dance card. I suggest you let him know that with the elimination of the Japanese in the Pacific, American interests have shifted and the populus doesn't have the constitution to engage in a war across the Atlantic that doesn't necessarily involve us."

"That is a little weak, Sir. Henry, let's see if we can work on that. Will we be, at any point, declaring war with Russia?"

"No, Mr. President, our attacks will be covert and with the Pacific secured, we will suggest a position of isolationism. During the next few months, the country will, with help from various politicians, develop a xenophobic posture. Stalin will howl, but there won't be much he can do, other than watch his country fall."

"We have developed a plan of attack and will have the Japanese army in position by 15, March, just as the winter breaks." General Douglas MacArthur had spent the past month in Japan developing an offensive protocol against the Soviet Union.

"I suspect," Captain Yoder, "Stalin will howl considerably louder when he finds that he also has the Japanese army to contend with," added Churchill.

The room was amused. The overall mood of those assembled was similar to that of a professional ball club preparing to contest a match against a lesser opponent, cocky and confident. With the advantages of twenty first century weapons, advanced intelligence and the use of the Japanese army, it did not appear that decimating Russia was going to be a terrible difficult proposition. Nor a very costly task, at least for the allies.

"Gentlemen," Yoder regained control, "I'd like to give you an overview of how Germany's ill fated initial attempt at attacking Russia went."

February 8th, 1942, 3:04 PM
Norfolk Naval Base, Virginia

"I'm glad to see Harsh took my advice." Dr. Saul Cohen was standing on vulture's row with Captain O'Brien, watching sailors disembarking the ship.

"So am I. I think a limited shore leave will help moral. It's hard to keep a ship load of sailors on board while at dock. Even with them being restricted to the base, they should be able to blow some steam. Once we set sail, I don't expect we'll be anywhere close to shore again for some time."

"This feels good." Tim Irwin stomped his feet on the first piece of dirt he could find. There was no hollow sound, just the thud of his boot thumping on solid ground.

"You're not much of a sailor boy. Wait 'till you been out for six months, take you a day to get your land legs back again." This was Parnes Williams' second tour. He enjoyed his role as sea daddy to Tim as per Navy customs.

"Well, six weeks is the longest I've ever been away from land. I'm not really looking forward to an extended tour at sea."

"Why the hell did you join the navy?" Parnes' voice ended the sentence three octaves higher than he began it.

Tim thought for a moment. "Just needed to get away, I suppose."

"You wanted by the law?" His voice entered the area of soprano.

He wasn't in the mood to get into it right now, "Yeah, something like that."

Parnes Williams had a renewed respect for his best friend.

Captain Yoder recognized the need to get his crew some R & R, but also recognized the potential danger of sending six thousand plus individuals from the year 2002 strolling about 1942 America. It was decided, with input from Captain Web, to allow the crew to stroll about the Naval Base. There were a few bars available to them as well as one hundred and seventy seven additional perimeter guards available to dissuade any of the *Stennis* crew from attempting to visit New Port News at large.

"Let's get fucked up, meet us a couple of babes and redefine the term sodomy." Parnes was dancing around again, amusing Timmy a great deal. Tim had not known many black men back in the future. Not as personal friends, anyway. Had conditions been just a little different, he probable would not have gotten to know Parnes. As they walked up a long hill towards the center of the base, Tim figured he could have done worse than winding up with Parnes as a pal.

It was a relatively warm Virginia day. The sun beginning its decent towards the horizon, casting long shadows that you just don't seem to notice while in the confines of a ship, even one as big as the *Stennis*. The trees were bare, but they were comfortable to see, as was the straw colored grass and the battleship gray buildings. Tim missed being on land and wondered if he was doomed to spend his life living on the sea.

What could the government do, after the war, with six thousand people who knew the future? What dramatic changes would occur when the tech guys got snatched up by General Electric, Grumman's and General Motors? Could 1940's society handle the quantum leaps in technology that these men and woman from the next millennium could provide? What about social issues that need a natural evolution to work themselves out? Would it be wise to expose a middle century America to next century institutions such as McDonalds, corporate raiders, MTV, or Howard Stern! If the decision was made that it all would be too much, too soon, what would that mean for the likes of Tim Irwin and Parnes Williams?

"Well, let's at least get fucked up." There were to many large questions on Tim's mind and now just wasn't the time. "Let's party," he accented the r and ended the word with an a, mimicking Parnes' heavily black affectation.

"I'll meet you over there, at the top of the hill near the statue." Father Anthony Salvatore stood on the main deck with Kaitlyn Savage, looking land ward.

"All right, but at some point, we need to stop sneaking around, this is becoming cumbersome."

"We have a lot going against us, Kait, you know that. The least of which is the service fraternization rules. We could face court-martial. That wouldn't help your career and it sure as hell wouldn't help my chances at becoming the next pope." Tony had found his language getting quite a bit saltier during the last few weeks.

"Didn't know you had your guns trained on the top spot."

"Well I don't," Tony shot back, "but I think we need to use a little decorum here."

"Fine. I'll go first. Meet you by the statue, unless I meet someone else first!"

Jesus, she's playful, thought Tony.

"No niggers allowed." He was about nine feet tall, had a face like a pig and a Southern accent right out of central casting.

"You telling me a shit hole like this doesn't allow nigg..., blacks? You gotta be kidding." Racism, worse, institutional racism. Tim was surprised. Early forties in the wonderful South.

Parnes was silent. He had never experienced overt bigotry before. There was still racism sixty years in the future, but it was far more subtle and certainly not tolerated in any public way. He would not have been surprised to find out that this jerks daddy had taken him to a lynching when he was a kid.

Timmy was sure he could drop this fuck with three blows before he even knew he was under attack. Unfortunately, there were probably a dozen more just like him inside. Shit, he'd be fighting all night. A smart fighter knew when the odds didn't warrant engagement.

"I wouldn't drink in a place that allowed a mountain of shit like this in, let's blow."

The Mountain of Shit didn't appreciate Tim's representation of his lineage and stepped aggressively forward.

Tim shot a look squarely into his attackers eyes. The rage he was feeling was communicated in a nonverbal way. It was clear to the Mountain of Shit that this runt of a man before him was a hornets nest he had best not stir. The Mountain of Shit broke eye contact as quickly as if he was staring at Medusa herself. Tim let the stare linger, then turned and walked away. "Let's get the fuck out of here."

There were only five hundred *Stennis* crew members about the base. It was Captain Web who suggested that unleashing a majority of the crew on the base at once might be a security nightmare. Each swarm of crewman would have about fifteen hours of abridged shore leave to do anything they desired within the confines of Norfolk Navy Base. It didn't take Sean Cooney, the Professor and a handful of their cadre to find the underbelly of the base.

"OK, ten bucks each, but for that, you go all the way, right?"

"Sure honey, whatever you want." She was rough looking. Probably had been attractive about three hundred men ago, but the life she had chosen was not conducive to growing old gracefully. Her breath was thick with whisky and cigarettes. She was also just the right age to possible be one of their grandmothers!

It was just getting dark. The door to a tool shed was not locked. Sean was the first in. The others stood outside, trying to look innocuous and to coax a hard on, the latter being the far more difficult task.

"So, you want a dose of Sean," he said as he pulled his dress whites down. She was laying on a sack of grass seed, her skirt hiked up around her waist. She had pulled her breasts out of her blouse, they hung there like a pair of floppy utters.

Sean crawled on top of her and tried to kiss her.

"We'll have none of that. Just get it up, stick it in and be quick about it."

She didn't seem to be particular about protection, so Sean didn't bother with the condom he had cloistered in his wallet. Hell, AIDS hadn't been invented yet, he figured.

"Come on, honey, let's get going."

He had an erection, a nice hard one, not a moment ago. But now it was gone. Maybe they should have gone drinking first. This all was just a little much to deal with sober. Sean dug deep down to where he harbored his most erotic thoughts and sifted through them to his favorite. His eyes were closed, his teeth clenched and his face was turning red. There was just a little bead of sweat forming on his temple.

Shit, even Pamela Lee Anderson couldn't help him out of this one. Once the face of his grandmother appeared on Pam's tight little body, it was all over but for the crying.

"Fuck," Sean whispered quietly.

"Don't worry about it honey, it happens all the time."

Seventy bucks later, she left the tool shed as fresh as she had entered it.

"Couldn't you have gotten rid of him quicker?" Jealousy was a new emotion for Father Anthony. He never really had anything in his life that would wake up the green eyed monster in him.

"What was I going to do, just tell him to fuck off?" By the time Anthony had gotten to the top of the hill, Lieutenant Ben-Gurion had hooked up with Kaitlyn and they spent a good twenty minutes talking. Mostly about how much Allen missed his wife and family. He wondered if he escaped the base and made his way to Brooklyn, maybe he'd find Rachel and the boys in the apartment on Nostrand Avenue? Kait just listened. She knew there was nothing she could say to ease his pain.

"You should talk to him when we get back, Tony, the guy's really having a tough go of it."

"Well, maybe I will. But for now, I don't want to know another person. I want to walk with you, I want to carve our initials in a tree, I'd like to hold your hand, if we dare."

He was so fresh and alive, Kaitlyn thought. It was so endearing. This was something she never experienced, squishy new love. She had lost her cherry at a frightfully young age to a boy five years older than she. From then on in, it has been a long succession of men, with very little emotional involvement to even call it infatuation, much less love.

She grabbed his hand and walked him into the shadows.

It took some investigation and a whole lot of walking, but Timmy and Parnes found a bar that would accept blacks.

"I gotta tell ya, I feel a little out of place here." Tim's shiny white face stood out like a beacon in the night.

"It's always nice to be with the brothers, but I'm a little weirded out myself. These guys seem a little strange, different. Like they just got loose from the master or something."

"You gotta remember," Tim responded, "these guys live with the shit you got before. There are probably still bathrooms they can't use. They'll never be given any more responsibility than cleaning out toilets. Shit, some of these guys may have grandparents that were *slaves*." Tim was never liberal about anything, but he, for the first time, began to understand the horror of racism.

"Let's just get faced, I'll get the first round." Parnes didn't want to start thinking about this new, old, world he was destined to live in.

It was two in the morning, Tim and Parnes had consumed enough adult beverages to have drunk themselves straight. They knew this was a temporary condition and decided to head back to the ship before they simply passed out.

They hadn't staggered more than forty yards from the hole they were drinking in when they heard a familiar voice.

"Takin your nigger back to his cage?"

Stepping out of the shadow was the Mountain of Shit. He was joined by three more mountains of shit.

Parnes was very sober now. Visions of him dancing with a tree limb filled his cleared head.

This ain't good, a newly sobered Timmy thought. I know I could take down one of these guys, probably two, but four is a serious problem. The situation was quickly developing into his personal bete noire. He looked over at Parnes, who was now pale enough that Tim wondered if he could convince these Neanderthals that he was a white guy, just like them.

He would have gone the contrite road if he thought he had any chance, but that presupposed the men he was dealing with were at least marginally bright. Tim figured that if they were both going down, he wasn't going to do it without a little style and a whole ton of misplaced courage.

"Well, if it isn't the Mountain of Shit. And it looks like you got your brothers with you. From the looks of you loads, it appears that your parents are probably related."

As it turned out, the Mountain of Shit was related to the other three mountains of shit and the crack about their parents being related didn't bother them the least. They were related. Was not uncommon in Kentucky.

The Jasper boys said nothing, they just kept walking. Kyle, the baby, was six foot four. The navy had to have his trousers custom made. His CO told him if he didn't get his weight below three hundred pounds, he'd ship his ass right out of the service. Kyle's brothers all had received the same admonition. They were all successful, by about ten pounds, between the four of them. There was close to twelve hundred pounds of bigoted beef looking to uphold the sacred values of the Klu Klux Klan.

Timmy hunkered down into a fighting stance. He quickly developed a protocol. Brother one would take a snap kick to the groin, he'd be effectively out of the fight. Brother number two would be gifted with a stomp kick to the knee. If properly delivered, he'd be sporting a cast for a good six months. That left brother's three and four. He hoped Parnes would join the party being thrown in his defense.

"I'll take the three on the left," he whispered, "you take the guy on the right."

"You shittin, right? You want me to mix it up with King Cong? He gonna rip me in two." There was a decided quiver to Parnes' voice.

"Hey Jerk Off Boy, need some help?"

Sean Cooney and his band of overachievers had been sitting under a tree not a dozen feet from the impending rumble. Not a one of them could figure out how to get back to the ship and had spent the past hour walking in circles. It was the Professor who suggested that they take a break under the very tree they had passed four times.

They were sweet words. Tim looked over to see Sean and his six friends walking towards him.

"I don't know. These guys don't look so tough."

With that, the Jasper boys attacked. Without a word between them, Sean and his crew charged also. It was an ugly melee that found Parnes with his fists on the defensive, feet frozen to the ground, fear preventing him any voluntary movement Tim did indeed take out Brother one with a well placed kick to the meats. Cooney jumped on the back of Brother two, wrestled him to the ground and got him into the very same arm bar Timmy had taught him weeks ago. This time, the entrapped arm was snapped like a twig. Brothers three and four went down in a flurry of fists lead by Walter Swenson.

The avenging nine spent the next hour slapping each other on the back and reliving their reenactment of the Civil War. By the time they arrived at the *Stennis*, their heroic deeds took on *Odessian* proportions. Even Parnes had himself deluded into thinking he was instrumental to the final disposition of the clash.

"Holy Shit!"   **Pete** 'Butter Bean' Peters was looking at the latest photo recon pictures taken of the Western Front.

Pete weighed two hundred and seven pounds, not necessarily enough to have an nick name assigned to him. Unfortunately, Pete was only five foot three. He was Christened Butter Bean in high school, a sobriquet didn't mind, it gave him an identity. His wonderfully positive disposition turned the name from the pejorative it was meant to be during his freshmen year into a moniker of endearment by the time he graduated.

Pete was certainly not a handsome physical specimen, but little Butter Bean was brilliant. He was recruited by all the Ivy league schools during his last year of high school and choose Princeton, mostly for its proximity to his home in the up scale town of Saddle River, New Jersey. He was also heavily recruited by numerous fortune five hundred companies his senior year, but shunned the corporate world because he always wanted to be a secret agent. His physical presence kept him out of the CIA and the FBI. The NSA was thrilled to get him. He had been only working in the underworld for two and a half years when he received a middle of the night call to report to the *USS John C. Stennis* a few months back. He was given a briefing by Ashton Blake himself, it was the first time he had met the Director.

Butter Bean missed his parents, but really didn't leave much back in the future. He was thrilled by the whole prospect of time travel and recognized that he had the opportunity to touch history right where he was.

Pete picked up the phone, "Captain Yoder, this is Agent Peters, there have been some disturbing developments, I think you need to get down here."

Harsh Yoder turned over the *Stennis* to Captain O'Brien and jumped on the helicopter for the short flight to the Pentagon.

The huge screen that hung on the back wall of the War Room was operational. It currently displayed a map of western Russia. Eisenhower, Yoder, Bradley and Halsey were in attendance.

There was a crooked line drawn from Murmansk in northern Finland to Rostov in the south, near the North Caucasus boarder. The Germans were on one side, the Russians were on the other. "This," Pete was using a laser pointer, "is where the 1st Shock, the 20th and the 16th Armies were three days ago." The red beam circled the area around Kalinin, near the center of the jagged line that formed the Western Front, "This morning, they are less than a day's march from Rzhev. Take a look at the 3rd and 4th Shock Armies. Three days ago they were here," Pete was marking an area a few kilometers east of Kholm. "They are now in position to attack Kholm, Velikie Luki, Toropets and Velizh in an apparent attempt to separate Army Group Center from Army Group North."

"Can you tell from your recon pictures what condition the two German Armies are in?" Eisenhower had been receiving spotty intelligence during the past few months from the Western Front. He knew that after their quick punch into Russia, the Germans were stalled.

Pete right clicked his mouse and bought up an aerial photograph. "This is a farm near Kalinin, occupied by soldiers from Group Army Center." It was a photo taken from the height of about thirty thousand feet. There was a small farm house twenty meters from a fairly large barn. The ground was white and there was a group of seven tanks positioned around the perimeter of the farm, all facing east. There were several hundred soldiers about, mostly huddled in groups of five to ten.

"The picture was taken at 11:07 yesterday morning. The temperature was approximately minus thirty degrees. Judging by the fact that the tank tracks haven't churned up any discernible dirt, we estimate the snow depth to be close to three feet. I'm going to zoom down to about five thousand feet. Take a look here," Pete pointed his laser to what looked like a row of about fifty soldiers lying on the ground, shoulder to shoulder. "These are dead bodies. As this battalion hasn't seen any action in close to two weeks it can be assumed that those men died from exposure. The ground is too frozen to bury them so they just pile up, a demoralizing reminder of how cold it is. Now look at this." He zoomed in so closely that the condensed breath of individual soldiers could be seen.

"Take a look at this guy," Pete pointed to a lone soldier walking towards a group of men huddled around a fire. "He's still wearing his summer uniform. Hitler moved so quickly during the summer and fall, his supply lines couldn't keep up. This guy is are wearing less than you gentlemen are right now. I suspect there isn't a man down there who isn't suffering from frostbite. At these temperatures, everything freezes. Try and throw open the bolt of a rifle, it's likely to break off in your hand. They probably don't have any antifreeze for the fuel or oil, making it impossible to start up any of their mechanized units without first warming them up, which is often impossible to do. Not only are they suffering from the cold, but food is also a precious commodity. Hungry, freezing and severely under supplied, these troops are demoralized in a big way. Can they repel the attack that is forming a few kilometers away? I doubt it."

"I suspect that this change of events will disrupt our timetable," Eisenhower had been involved with strategic planning for the incredibly complicated invasion of France, made somewhat easier with the files turned over to him by Captain Yoder. He was not relishing the additional pressure that was sure to follow with a shortened calendar.

"Yes Sir, it certainly will. We did not expect to do anything but fly overs for the next thirty days or so. Now, without our help, the Wehrmacht will be facing absolute defeat. As pointed out, the troops they have now in Russia are under equipped, poorly fed and demoralized. The fresh troops freed up from duty in Europe after the capitulation of Great Britain will take another three weeks, minimum, to get to the front, and that supposes a change in the weather. At these temperatures, armies do not travel well." Butter Bean had intelligence on every army in both Europe and Russia. He knew where they were, where they were going, the condition of their equipment and could extrapolate the moral of the troops. The German Army, in its current state, was not nearly formidable enough to defend itself against, much less defeat, the Red Army.

"Do we know anything about the disposition of their V1 missile program?" Harsh was hoping the fine revisions in history may turn in the Reich's, and ultimately, the Allies favor.

"We have a recent shot of Peenemunde, but there isn't any indication that they have anything near operational going on down there. The only way the Germans are going to survive the impending attack from Russia is with our intervention."

"How much time do we have to put something together?" Harsh was feeling a little panicked. If Hitler failed in his conquest of Russia, his ultimate goal would become dramatically more difficult.

"Forty eight hours on the short side, as many as seventy two hours on the long side. Although Stalin has the ground forces in place to begin an attack, his artillery is still not in effective range yet. While the weather is not as much a detrimental factor for Russia as it is for Germany, it still is slowing them down. Another concern is a storm front that is moving in from Siberia. If it keeps its present course, there will be a serious cloud cover right over the entire front within twenty four hours and may hang there for two or three days."

"That's just what we need." Eisenhower slapped the table for emphasis. "Weather is always the unpredictable element that can dash the best laid plans." Harsh was tempted to tell Ike about how untoward weather delayed D day '44.

"A cloud cover should not interfere with our air sortie's," Harsh attempted to console Dwight. "With infrared imaging systems on most of our planes we should be able to target what we need and deliver ordinance with unheard of accuracy, at least for 1942."

"All right, gentlemen, we need to develop a plan of attack." Harsh picked up the phone in front of him and called Captain O'Brien to tell her to eat without him, he was going to be late and to please get the *Stennis* ready for a big trip.

"**What do you** know Chief?" Kelly O'Brien had taken the arduous trip to the Jet Engine Testing room. It was located in the Hanger Bay, a huge three level high area where the planes were stored and maintained. There was a dedicated area for each type of craft. The engine testing room was located aft of the eight hundred and fifty foot long bay.

"Plenty, Captain, most of which would make your hair curl." Crusty White was just that, crusty. A lifer, he'd grown up in the Navy. His passion for tinkering with all things mechanical lead him to his current position running the engine testing facility.

"You forget, I've spent a few years at sea myself, I doubt you could even make me blush." Kelly had gotten to know Crusty while doing duty on the *Carl Vinson*. Crusty had been brought up on charges of insubordination and Kelly was the only senior officer to back him. He still did ninety days the hard way, but he never forgot her misplaced loyalty.

"We'll see about that on our next shore leave, Captain," Crusty wheezed.

Thank God there are fraternization rules, thought Kelly. Crusty was one of the foulest looking men she had ever met. His oral hygiene had to have been an afterthought. His breath actually smelled like shit. One eyebrow had its own agenda, wildly reaching for his scalp. The condition of his uniform was just on the edge of acceptable as was his disposition. As a matter of fact, had he not been such a brilliant mechanic, he'd have been asked to leave this mans Navy some time ago. He blew a cloud of foul smelling cigar smoke from the corner of his mouth.

"What do you know about this," Kelly slapped her open palm on the Pratt and Whitney J52-P-8B turbojet engine resting on a cradle, resulting in a hollow echo. The engine was off an A-6E Intruder that limped home a week ago. Fortunately for the pilots, there are two engines buried in its plump fuselage.

"Engines fine, Captain, electronics are fucked, I mean fried," he quickly corrected himself. "Look here," Crusty took a black box the size of a football off his desk. He pried open the cover. "See that circuit board, look closely at the copper connections and the silicon chips."

"They're all yellow, I've never seen anything like that before."

"Neither have I." If Crusty White hadn't seen anything like that before, then it was truly unusual.

"What do you supposed caused it, corrosion?"

"No way, Cap, these Intruders were designed from the canopy down to be carrier based jets, there's very little in these things that corrodes. And look at this wire, ripped it out of the cockpit, belonged to the radar system, take a close look at the cross section."

Captain O'Brien bent down to get a good look and caught another whiff of Crusty's stunning breath. "Jesus, White, see if you can dig some of that shit out of your mouth, hand that thing here."

The sheathing to the wire looked fine, the wire itself had that same yellow tinge to it that the circuit board did. "Have you checked the other Intruder's?"

"Of course," Crusty was insulted that O'Brien even asked that. His breath may be a tad overpowering, but he was a professional when it came to his birds. "This is the oldest Intruder we have, matter of fact, it's the oldest plane in our fleet by some ten years. Don't even know why we bought her along, piece of shit like this belongs on the *Vinson*."

"Good to see you got over that. If you recall, however, we made a fairly hasty departure, didn't really have time to cherry pick the fleet for the best equipment. You're lucky we ended up with any of those stanky cigars you're so fond of. Damn things smell like burned rubber. Let me know what you find out."

"Will do Captain."

This is truly distasteful. Lieutenant Ben-Gurion was leading a group of four F-18's on their way to England. There, they were to refuel and fly off to Russia to help Hitler stave off what could be a terminal attack against the Wehrmacht.

These bastards are murdering my people and I'm suppose to offer them air support? How could this be? With one bombing run we could annihilate the German front line troops, open up a hole large enough to allow the entire Red Army in. The Russians had liberated any number of concentration camps, why are we not helping them? God forgive me.

"Tower one, this is Warrior, requesting permission to land."

"Warrior, this is Tower," he had a clipped English accent and sounded sharp and awake even at three ten AM local time, "take runway one, landing north, welcome to England." Grafton Underwood air field was located approximately fifty miles northeast of London. The first time around, the 8th Army Air Force parked it's 384th Bomb Group there. Runway one, sixteen hundred meters long, could easily accommodate the heavy B17's that wreaked havoc on the engine plants at Stuttgart, the Lufwaffe in Kassel and the ball bearing plants in Bremheaven.

It had been a long flight. Between the four of them there wasn't an unused piddle pack. There would be a four hour lay over, just enough time to get enough sleep to remind you that you needed more.

Two ancient English lorries pulled up to the jets as they taxied off the runway. Makeshift ladders had been crafted in advance with specifications supplied by the *Stennis*. The soldiers assigned to ferry the arriving aviators back to headquarters were thunderstruck by these curious looking war machines. They had not been briefed as to what they were seeing, being told instead to keep their mouths shut and to forget anything that transpired.

"You look troubled." Lieutenant Savage had hooked up with Ben-Gurion as they both strolled towards one of the trucks.

"I used my last piddle pack two hours ago, I have a pressing personal situation that needs to be addressed." Kaitlyn was quite insightful, Allen appreciated her concern. She was the only one he felt comfortable talking to about personal issues.

"We all have some pressing personal issues, as soon as we get to the base, I've got dibs on the first crapper available, however, you know that's not what I'm talking about. Thinking about Rachel and the boys?"

"Certainly, they are never far from my conscious thoughts, but, no, there is something else." After the trouble he'd gotten into voicing his concerns to no less than President Roosevelt and Prime Minister Churchill, he was reticent to open this very private bag of worms with Savage.

"You can't be comfortable with this mission."

She is insightful, thought Ben-Gurion. "What makes you say that?"

"You must think I'm a dumb jet jock bimbo not to be able to recognize the fact that you, a devoted Jew, is happy aiding Hitler! Maybe he didn't say anything, but we all know Greenspan slewed those missiles a few degrees off because he couldn't deal with attacking his own people. This is a considerably more complicated enigma. Have you talked to Yoder about this?"

"I talked to Yoder and to a certain extent Roosevelt and Churchill."

"What'd they have to say?"

"Remember when I was in the brig for two days, that's what they said. I don't think Churchill or Roosevelt realize the true scope of what's going on in Poland and elsewhere, but Yoder sure as hell does." Kaitlyn was surprised at Ben-Gurion's use of vulgarity, as mild as it was. "He says there's a bigger picture here that I'm not privy to. Shit, I'm not stupid, I know we're using Hitler to crush Stalin," he was pounding the back of his flight helmet with his open palm, "but does that relieve us of any responsibility towards millions of my people who are being executed even as we speak?" Allen was eloquently passionate.

"I understand your pain," Kaitlyn had stopped walking and was facing Ben-Gurion, "but what do you think we could do? We rule the skies, liberating those camps will require ground troops. We can't just throw a couple of Mavericks in the area and expect the Nazi's to open the gates." They stood there, his face grimaced with hate, hers, with empathy.

He looked off in the distance, "I'll figure something."

Morning bought the fog England was renowned for.

"Warrior, you are cleared for take off, God speed."

"Thank-you tower." Lieutenant Ben-Gurion pushed his throttle to the stops and quietly enjoyed the sense of power he felt during take off. At one hundred and twenty knots, he pulled gently on the stick and mocked gravity. He took the four plane formation to twenty thousand feet and four hundred and seventy knots, the most economical speed and altitude for the Hornets.

They were heading for Kalinin, a city of a hundred thousand very hungry comrades and currently host to a fairly well equipped division of Russian soldiers. Commander Yeremenko controlled the bulk of the artillery and troops that would be used during the up coming campaign. His orders, directly from Stalin, were to drive a wedge between Group Army Center and Group Army North. He did not have to be told that failure was unacceptable. He knew that the weather was his ally now. His reconnaissance confirmed that which he suspected, the Germans were over extended. General von Kuechler of Group Army North and General von Kluge of Army Center were busy just trying to keep their troops alive. Breaking through the front shouldn't be terribly difficult. Once achieved, he would take each army out in detail, encircling one small pocket of troops at a time until the whole was nothing but a smattering of broken parts.

Lieutenant Ben-Gurion toggled the guard frequency transmit button on his stick, "Final update coming from the

MILSTAR link." Their target was located four kilometers east of Kalinin. Earlier recon photos showed that all of the Red Army artillery for this campaign was staged there, waiting for deployment. Butter Bean Peters estimated that they would be there for twelve to sixteen hours before being positioned closer to the front. It was a unique opportunity to destroy a large number of pieces quickly and economically. There would be six more sorties planned over the next ten hours that would address the ground troops, who were staged together, waiting final orders.

"Two minutes to target, your steering que is up." It was go time.

There was a large cloud cover over most of the Ukraine, but it was starting to break up as they approached the target sight. Captain Yoder was hoping the clouds would stay intact. The infrared target imaging systems couldn't care less what stood between them and the ground, it was almost impossible to hide a large heat signature. Yoder would much prefer for the Russians to have no idea what and who was hitting them. Each of the F-18's had all distinguishing marks removed from the planes, no American flags or squadron insignia's. The bombing runs were planned to be a low as possible for improved accuracy. Any soldier not killed in the attack would surly wonder what sort of machine was screaming down at him.

"Target in sight, master arm on." With those words, the most concentrated destructive power ever unleashed on a battlefield in corrected history was a squeeze of a trigger away.

"Roger that," Dancer was flying wing man for Warrior, "Pickle is hot."

The cloud cover broke 15 kilometers from the target. Before them lay hundreds of large artillery pieces glinting bits of sun that blanketed the area for the first time in days. With the sudden change in weather, Lieutenant

Ben-Gurion decided to use the more easily placed rockets for the attack over the Mavericks.

"Switch to rockets. Hold... fire on my mark." Ben-Gurion was going to ride it in to three klicks before releasing the CRV-7 rockets, armed with High Explosives tips, on his target.

"Let go multiple rockets." Each of the four pilots held down the fire button unleashing tens of rockets within seconds. Using the same fairly simple sight as is used for the cannon, the attack was much more personal than lighting up a few Mavericks from five miles out. From less than a thousand feet, the ensuing carnage was close up and spectacular.

On the first run, a good twenty percent of the tightly packed cannons disappeared in a catastrophic belching of fire. As they over flew the destruction, the secondary explosions could be heard from the erupting artillery shells.

It took two more unencumbered runs to decimate every piece of artillery Stalin had sent to Kalinin. Ben-Gurion had enough rockets left over for a forth run. He turned his sights on the large mass of troops he had passed over about five kilometers from the primary target.

"Form up on me, heading two four niner." He bought the four planes about and headed back from which they had come. The sky above the troops had also cleared, exposing a few thousand square kilometer area. The troops, also tightly condensed, were visible despite the white outer garments that helped them blend into the snow.

"Pick the densest concentration of soldiers you can and light up everything you have left on my mark."

At three klicks out, Ben-Gurion announced, "Fire."

The rockets sprang out from under the F-18's, doubling the jets speed in seconds. This time, the explosions were less dramatic, but the destruction was considerably more so. Now there were bodies being flung high into the sky, plumes of red permeating the air. Ben-Gurion banked hard to port, Savage followed.

Kaitlyn looked to her left as the planes pulled a four G turn, grunting as she did so to prevent blackout. What she saw, in that moment, horrified her. Like a snap shot she didn't want to take, riveted to her retinas, was a scene so ghastly that it took seconds to register. As her plane leveled off, the images of parts of bodies flooded her mind. The white snow was a magnifying backdrop to the blood that drenched the ground.

"We'll make one more pass with the cannons, from up on me."

Oh God no, not again. Dancer was traumatized by what was going on down there. Now she was expected to go back in with the cannons. That meant a very low level attack to get best results from the 27 mm gun stuck in the starboard wing root of her aircraft.

The four horsemen had banked again and were driving towards the mass of hysterical soldiers running for their lives. Flying on the deck, Warrior gave the order. Kaitlyn squeezed her trigger and unleashed seventeen hundred and sixty rounds of high explosive ammunition in less than a minute. It was like running a chain saw through a cub scout jamboree. Human beings evaporated within the funnel of death spewing from her F-18.

"We've done our work, let's take it back to England."

We certainly have, thought Dancer.

"Motherfucker, what's this shit?" Parnes Williams had just opened the door to the stores locker where huge slabs of meat hung. On the floor were rats, the uninvited sailing companion of every sea going vessel of size since ancient times. Parnes hated rats, especially dead ones. At least the live ones scurried away. Now he was going to have to pick up and dispose of these horrid creatures. "Irwin, get your ass over here."

"What's the matter?" Tim had bolted from the kitchen. From the intensity of his plea, it sounded like Parnes was being attacked by one of the Mountian of Shit brothers.

"Fucking rats, man, that's what's the matter. Look at them, all dead and squishy."

"Wow," Tim scanned the room, "looks like there was a rat war in here." He paused and counted the bodies. "Seventeen. More dead rats than I've ever seen in one place. You put some poison down?"

"Shit no, I didn't even know we had a problem here." Parnes' voice was getting squeaky. "Help me get rid of them."

"Better call the Chief. Rats just don't die, something killed them. Might have a bunch of bad meat. Let's quarantine this locker till we know what's going on."

Dr. Saul Cohen made a longitudinal incision down the belly of rat 01. He hadn't dissected a rodent since his undergraduate days at UCLA. Rigor had set in, giving the rats body the consistency of an overdone baked potato.

As the scalpel penetrated the skin, blood oozed quickly into the dish on which rat 01 rested. Dr. Cohen completed the cut and spread back the pelt. There was an excessive amount of blood present in the chest cavity.

"Yes Pattie, I know, I can't tell you how sorry I am for hurting your feelings." Father Anthony Salvatore had spent the past forty minutes apologizing to Seamen First Class Pattie Boyle for his unfortunate outburst a few weeks back. He expected this to take a few embarrassing minutes, but Pattie was going to make him pay. Anthony dug in his heels and decided he was going to ride this out. Weeks ago, he wouldn't have had the patience for this. But as of recent, nothing was getting under his skin, all the demons he had been dealing with just vanished, chased away by a fighter pilot code named Dancer.

This is what it feels like, he thought. He was flying. Being in love had transformed his life, given purpose to his existence and allowed him a clarity of vision that he never before imagined. His thoughts were consumed by her. They had taken to leaving messages to each other on the ships voice mail system. Anthony had saved every message Kaitlyn had left him and often played one back just to feel closer to her.

"It was wrong for a man of the cloth to have exploded like that," whined Pattie. Jesus, thought Anthony, who calls a priest a man of the cloth any more. *This guy is killing me*, he moaned to himself. They were going over the same ground. Pattie had Tony on the ropes and he wasn't going to let him go. He had been berated by authority figures all his life and was now going to make Father Anthony pay for the sins of every one of them. This was all becoming intolerable.

"Look, Pattie, I think..." Lieutenant Kaitlyn Savage appeared at the open door of his office. She had her flight suit on. Her face still held the red impression left by her oxygen mask, her hair was matted and oily. Despite the physical mess she presented, what made Anthony stop in mid sentence was the look in her eyes. Her stare was blank, she was looking at him but didn't seem to be registering that fact.

"Kaitlyn." He stood up from behind his desk and for a moment didn't know what to say.

"Excuse me, Lieutenant," Boyle swiveled his chair about to face the door, "but the Father and I are having a discussion."

"Get out of here." Anthony didn't take his eyes off Kaitlyn.

"But Father, I was here first," Boyle pouted.

"*Get the fuck out of here,*" Anthony screamed, still looking towards the door.

"But Father..." Boyle was on the edge of tears.

"NOW," Anthony expounded on his initial request.

Pattie Boyle jumped to his feet and brushed past Kaitlyn on his way out the door. Anthony heard a whimpering sound gradually fade away as Pattie bounded down the hall and realized that he was going to pay large for this.

He rushed over to Lieutenant Savage and gently put his arms around her. They stood there for an eternity. She was stiff and vacant.

"What happened?" he whispered into her ear. She said nothing, but he suddenly felt tears on his own neck. Tony pulled away from Kaitlyn, took her hand and guided her to the chair recently vacated by Pattie Boyle.

He sat across from her, knees touching. Anthony took her hands in his and looked into the face that drove him to such ecstasy and waited for her to speak. One tear tracked down her right cheek.

"It was horrible," she was looking straight ahead, still not seeming to see what she was looking at. "I killed today, I killed many men today..."

Oh my god, he thought. Anthony Salvatore knew exactly what she was thinking. He'd been through this in a modified form before and didn't have the words then. He didn't have the words now. What do you say to anyone who has taken a human life, taken multiple human lives, and bring them any kind of peace?

He squeezed her hands again. His mind raced for the words, the words he was supposed to have, the words God was supposed to give him. *I need them now*, he silently pleaded, *please, give them to me*. He felt absurd even as he asked the Boss for this new favor, please help me help this woman with whom I've been sinning.

"You were following orders." Shit, he hated those words as he spoke them.

There was no response. Kaitlyn was a bright woman, she knew that she was only following orders, that she had no choice in the matter, that they were the bad guys and needed to be killed. What she really needed was someone to validate her humanity.

"I love you." It was all he was thinking and it was all he could say. Kaitlyn leaned forward, put her arms around his neck and wept.

"Yes Captain," Butter Bean Peters was speaking to Yoder via the ship to shore communications system set up by the tech guys. The *Stennis* was traveling east, "I'd rate all eight missions successful. We're going over the recon photos right now. The artillery Uncle Joe sent to Kalinin is pretty much useless now, there seem to be a few pieces left in tact, but according to these pictures, there doesn't appear to be anybody left to fire them." Pete had seen pictures of destroyed equipment before. While he was learning his craft, he had reviewed a goodly portion of the pictures taken during the Gulf War. The pictures of the ground troops, however, were difficult to view. There were pockets of red, areas that were ten meters wide and ran for seventy to eighty meters that had no bodies in them. It took him minutes to figure out that he was looking at the path cut by the cannons on the F-18's. The soldiers caught in the corridor of the high explosive rounds spewed out from the jets wing literally disintegrated, leaving behind nothing more than a red stain to mark their passing.

"Is there any way they can mount any kind of an attack?"

"Absolutely not, Sir, the 1st Shock, the 20th and the 16th Armies are decimated, so are the 3rd and 4th shock Armies over in Rzhev. I wouldn't want to be General Yeremenko right now."

February 15th, 1942, 4:17 AM
The Kremlin, Moscow

"What happened?"

It was a reasonable question. General Yeremenko had just lost five armies in an eight hour period and comrade Stalin wanted to know what had happened.

"We were attacked from the air, Sir"

"It was my understanding that the Lufwaffe was ineffective in this theater."

Josef Vissarionovich Stalin was speaking with the unnatural calm of a man who just heard that one of the eight automobiles he owned had just been in an accident. Concerned, but not overly so. This controlled calm he was displaying was most discomforting.

"Yes, that was my understanding. They have not been a threat recently..."

"THEN WHAT THE HELL HAPPENED?"

The forced calm was gone. Josef Stalin's small, cold eyes were in rage.

"The Germans have some sort of new aircraft," Yeremenko was shaking, "they are like nothing that have been seen in the skies. They come in and leave at fantastic speeds and their destructive power is unprecedented." It didn't really matter what he said at this point. Stalin had a propensity for executing Commanders for retreating. No General, living or dead, had ever overseen such a monstrous loss as this. He had been escorted to the Kremlin by armed guards. Yeremenko knew that this was to be his last meeting with anyone. He found himself hoping that the state was wrong concerning its atheistic position.

"You have dishonored Russia." Stalin waved Yeremenko away with the back of his hand. Immediately, two of Stalin's body guards took him by the arms and escorted him out of the office. Yeremenko didn't protest. The die was cast and he began making peace with a God he had known from his childhood.

Josef Stalin sat back in his leather chair and took a hit on his pipe. He had just lost the best opportunity to push the Wehrmacht out of his beloved country since they had the gall to cross his boarders. He had given up territory for time, leading Hitler into a trap that he was prepared to close. Now, he needed to rethink his position. There were new weapons to learn how to deal with. There were concerns about the sudden lack of support from America and the demise of Great Britain and Japan. It was beginning to look like he was in this war with Hitler alone. Then so be it. There wouldn't be a Russian soldier standing before Germany entered Moscow.

"What happened?"

Field Marshal Kesselring was in Berlin trying to get scrounge fuel for his Lufwaffe. Just about all available gas and oil was being directed to the mechanized units. He wasn't able to get a plane in the sky for two weeks. He also did not have a clue as to what had happened in Kalinin.

"It was my understanding that you had no units in the air." Adolph Hitler did not like not knowing what happened. Without reliable intelligence, he was unable to fight a war.

"No, between the weather and the lack of fuel, I have not been able to sustain any kind of an air presence. The attack was not generated by us."

"Did your forward observers see anything?"

"Yes," Kesselring reluctantly answered. The information he had received from the front was startling. He knew enough about Adolph Hitler to know that he was not fond of startling news. "It was an air attack. From what we have been able to observe, it was quite a devastating attack. It appears that the Red Army was massing near Kalinin in preparation for an attack." Hitler's blood ran cold. He knew that his front line troops were in no condition to repel a large scale attack. "The air craft, however, were most remarkable, like nothing seen in the skies before. There were no visible propellers, my guess is that which ever country sent these planes has jet engine technology. We are a good two years away from a successful prototype. The ordinance they delivered was equally remarkable. They were firing rockets to great affect. The damage to the 1st Shock, 16th and 20th Armies appears to be total. I have advanced units checking the area right now. Early word is that there are hundreds of destroyed artillery pieces and to many dead to count."

"Were there any markings on the planes?"

"No, not that my people could see."

This is a most perplexing problem, thought Hitler, someone had gone to great effort to help the Wehrmacht. Who would do such a thing and more importantly, why? The United States and Great Britain are the only countries that could possibly have had succeeded with jet engine and rocket technology. England, however, was licking its wounds in disgrace and America seems to have decided to stay out of a war that had very little to do with them. Both countries were allied with Russia. None of this makes sense. He would exploit the situation nevertheless. Within two weeks he'd have a large and well supplied reserve force, recently freed up by the treaty with England, at the front. If his worthless Generals could hold out until the weather broke, he'd be in a good position to see Operation Barbarossa through to victory.

February 16th, 1942, 12:43 AM
USS *John C. Stennis*, Atlantic Ocean

They were all around him.   Their cries were
tortured, *"Help us, won't you please help us?"* They all
looked ghost like, their faces sunken and hollow, heads
shaved. Their cloths hung on bodies ravaged by starvation.
He was unable to move. He yelled back to them, "There is
nothing I can do, I am only one man, you must
understand."
        A little boy walked up to him. It was Dov. "They
killed mommy and Yehuda, do something Daddy, they will
kill us all."
        Allen Ben-Gurion woke up hard, his heart racing,
sweat enveloping his body. *I must do something.*

        "You're up late."
        "This is the only time I get any privacy to take care
of paperwork. I still run this ship ya know." It was past
one in the morning and Harsh Yoder couldn't sleep. He
didn't want to tell his physician that for fear of the blizzard
of calls he would be sure to get demanding that he take his
long overdue physical. "Have a seat." Harsh grabbed the
pot of coffee sitting beside his desk and poured Dr. Saul
Cohen a cup.
        "Did you hear about the rats?"
        "You telling me we have rats?" Harsh responded in
mock horror. He hadn't been on a ship that didn't have
more rats than sailors.
        Saul smiled. "Apparently. But as of yesterday, we
have seventeen less rats."
        "Love that killer instinct Doc. Aren't we proud of
ourselves," Yoder laughed.

"Didn't say I killed them myself. They were found in the kitchen, in a refrigerated locker where meat is stored. My first reaction was that we had a load of bad meat. Checked it all, of course, stuff is fine."

"So what killed our hairy little sailing companions?" Harsh questioned.

"Don't know. There are disturbing similarities to the death of Ensign Shaw, however."

"What do you mean?"

"Remember Shaw's circulatory system just seemed to self-destruct? Well, the same thing happened to the rats, every one of them. The walls of the major arteries had disintegrated to the point that blood was leaching out into the body cavity."

This was indeed disturbing. "Are you aware of anything like this happening in the animal kingdom?"

"No. I've never seen anything like this, not in humans, nor am I aware of anything like this happening in animals, although I'm not a veterinarian. This is really bizarre. There is no reason that I can discern for this to have occurred. God damn Harsh, I observed an autopsy on a ninety seven year old woman. Her circulatory system didn't look great, but it sure as hell wasn't leaching blood!"

"What about any diseases that affect both rats and humans?" Harsh was struggling to make some sense of this.

"None that I'm aware of. Something like the Black Plague, for example, that killed hundreds of thousands in Europe during the Dark Ages, didn't affect the rats at all, they were just carriers. Same is true of the monkeys in Africa and the AIDS virus. There is nothing I know of that can cause this disintegration of the arteries. The damage is occurring on the cellular level. The mitochondria are imploding."

"Help me out here, Saul, it's been a while since I studied cellular biology, what does the mitochondria do?"

"The mitochondria is basically the electrical power generator. It provides energy to the other parts of the cell."

"So," Harsh formulated, "this may be some sort of an electrical problem?"

"That's a little simple, but, yes. At this point, I don't have any idea as to what is causing this phenomena and am therefore at a loss as to develop a protocol to prevent it from happening again."

"Well, I'm not real worried about our rat population, but we need to figure out a way to keep our people safe from whatever this is. You sure it's not a virus or some sort of a bacteria?"

"I haven't ruled those out, but, at this point, it looks doubtful." Saul Cohen was absolutely baffled as to what took the life of Shaw and now, the rats. He was not a clinical scientist and hence, somewhat out of his element. But he had done an exhaustive amount of research on the ships newly expanded computers and had come up with nothing that could come close to helping him out. He sat back and took a sip of coffee.

"What are you going to do about Roosevelt?" Saul felt a need to change the subject.

"In what context are you referring?"

"He is scheduled to have a stroke in a few years, I can prevent it. A couple of tests to determine where the blockage is and them a simple angeoplasty and we could squeeze another decade out of him. Before we left, the NSA guys added all manor of cardio equipment to the ships hospital, some pretty impressive stuff." Saul's specialty was cardiology.

"You know, I've been wrestling with that question since my first meeting with the man. On the one hand, I'd like to save his life. On the other, I'm worried how it will affect history. Kinda like messing with the Prime Directive."

Saul fought back a laugh. "You must really miss *Star Trek*. You don't work for the Federation, Harsh."

Yoder looked down at his coffee. It had been a long day. "Yeah, I do miss *Star Trek*." Harsh never owned an *Enterprise* uniform and never went to a convention, but he did actually catch him self saying "Engage" one day when what he really wanted to say was all ahead full. He also found a number of parallels to where he was now and his favorite of the movie series, *Star Trek IV*.

MJ 12 addressed the question of saving Roosevelt, but were undecided as to what to recommend, so they left it up to his discretion. "Let me give it some more thought, Saul. Why don't we revisit this next week."

"Good, we'll discuss it during your physical."

"Great," Harsh responded sarcastically.

Tim stood on Vulture's row, he had finished lunch duty and had some time before setting up for the hectic job of feeding six thousand people dinner. The *Stennis* was four days out of Newport News. Just as well, he thought. Although he still much preferred being on dry land, he wasn't at all comfortable with the time he'd spent on the base. Or was he uncomfortable with the time he was in? Either way, it felt curiously good being at sea. They must have been making twenty plus knots. The wind felt sharp, a pleasant relief from the occasionally stifling kitchen area where half a dozen ovens ran almost continually. He pulled his coat tight against his chest, sucked in a lung full of sea air and enjoyed the view.

There had to have been fifteen ships from the battle group escorting the *Stennis* across the Atlantic within view from his perch six stories above the deck. It was a dramatic sight. Tim lifted the binoculars he had borrowed from Parnes, who seems to have liberated them from some guy named J. Gunzallas, and trained them on a battle ship fifteen hundred yards off the port side. It was the *Texas,*

AKA 61. Shit, Timmy thought to himself, she was one of the first eight of the American Dreadnoughts. Built before World War One he estimated. His father, Charlie Irwin, fought the war in the Pacific theater with the Navy. Tim grew up hearing about the great Naval battles of the War. His old man could name just about every ship in the fleet and has a story to tell about each. Yeah, he remembered, the *USS Texas*, a New York Class Battleship, the first battleship to launch an aircraft from its deck. Spent most of her time during the War cruising the Atlantic, bombarding shore positions in North Africa and Southern France. Probably had helped out during D Day too.

"Holy cow," Timmy uttered to no one, "the *North Carolina*." She was a quater mile aft of the *Leo*. First of the North Carolina Class battleships. She couldn't be more than a year or two old. What a majestic sight. He ran his binoculars up and down her proud flanks. She was the first of what became known as fast battleships. Had a kick ass record in the Pacific, if he recalled correctly. The excellent performance of the fast battleships led to the establishment of the fast carrier task force, striking Japanese forces with devastating results. Christ, Tim thought, it's a friggin living museum.

Steaming port side of the *North Carolina* was the light cruiser *Phoenix*. What a history she has, Tim remembered. A distinguished career in the Pacific, she was one of three ships to leave the base during the surprise attack on Pearl. Sold to Argentina half a decade after the war, she took part in the South Atlantic War with Britain in '82 and had the unfortunate distinction of being the first large warship to be sunk since the end of World War 11 and the further ignominy to also be the first ship in history to be sunk by a nuclear submarine, the hunter-killer sub *Conqueror*. Tim was surprised that he was able to recall these obscure facts his Dad had so casually tossed him when he was a boy.

He ran to the starboard side, field glasses in hand, anxious to see what other Naval treasures were steaming East. Tim tucked the binoculars into his eye sockets and focused on the bow of a ship not a thousand yards away, running a perfectly parallel course. *Oh my God.* He pulled the glasses away from his face and rubbed his eyes, wondering if he saw correctly. Tim pushed the binoculars back into his face and looked again. It was the *USS Leo*, his father's ship.

February 18th, 1942, 9:03 AM
Pentagon

Harsh had made his first trip back to Washington since setting sail five days ago. The WSO seat of a Super Hornet was not very comfortable, but the flight was mercifully short thanks to the generous use of the afterburners. On the agenda today was MacArthur's accelerated plan for Japan's initial thrust into Russia via the Port of Vladivostok. Harsh decided to also address the now known leaks in the Manhattan Project while he was in town.

Yoder was escorted into a small office in the Pentagon. There was a pervasive smell of new paint, leaded paint no doubt, Harsh thought to himself. There are so many issues that need to be addressed once this war is concluded, he realized. The Pentagon was still months away from being finished, construction was proceeding at a frantic pace.

"General Groves." Harsh extended a hand.

"Nice to meet you Captain." General Leslie Groves had the wacky look in his eyes that betrayed the fact that he knew he was meeting a man from the future. Harsh was growing weary of telling his story again and again. He delegated that chore to Junior Officer on Eisenhower's staff.

They were alone. "What I am going to tell you is, of course, top secret."

"I understand that Captain. Obviously you know I can keep my mouth shut." General Groves headed the Manhattan Project, the most highly classified operation in US history to date. He, like so many others who had been aware of Captain Yoder's unique time reference, had many questions that burned in his mind.

"General, I am here to discuss with you a number of leaks that are emanating from your project." As well as being in charge of the scientific, technical and process development, the construction and production of the first atomic weapon, he also bore the weight of security and military intelligence of enemy activities. He was sorely interested in leaks.

"We are in very virgin territory here," Yoder began, "I will be accusing people of treasonous acts that they will be committing, not that they have committed. We couldn't go into any court in the land and bring these charges. However, as they will be classified as being of national interest, we should be able to skirt the constitutional issues." Harsh was a big fan of the Bill of Rights, but was comfortable tossing them when it came to treason. The men and women who were listed in the file he bought with him were indeed guilty of that most hated crime.

"The people in this file were greatly responsible for Russia's success in splitting the atom." General Groves still couldn't get over the fact that this Captain Yoder was talking about efforts that had just begun in atomic research as factual, not theoretical. "They must be stopped by whatever means you deem appropriate. Let me highlight some of the more egregious offenders." Harsh opened the wax seal on the folder he had before him and removed a binder. He thumbed through the first dozen pages. Much of what he was about to turn over to Groves was still classified in the year 2002."

"Ah, the Rosenberg's, Julius and Ethel. Convicted of passing nuclear weapons secrets to her brother, David Greenglass, who in turn, passed them on to the Soviets. David is currently working for you out at Los Alamos. The Rosenberg's were tried, convicted and executed in 1953, but not before causing an immense amount of damage." He flipped through a few more pages. "Here's Klaus Fuchs..."

"Jesus Christ, Klaus Fuchs? I had lunch with him two weeks ago. He works in the theoretical division at Alamos, he's English for Christ sakes." Leslie Groves had been around a while, but he was still shocked that there would be such high level espionage going on right under his nose.

"Well, your pal Klaus had, or has, access to a tremendous amount of top secret material and has every intention to pass all he can over to the Russians. He'll be tried and convicted in the British courts in the '50's. He'll do a decade stretch on the government."

"Don't count on that, Captain." Groves' eyes were tight, he spoke very softly.

"Here's another one. This will be tricky. Right now, he's only seventeen years old. He probably won't be of issue at this point, but he was responsible for turning over to the Soviets the Implosion Principal in '44. That was the last piece they needed to go ahead with their first bomb. Name's Thedore Hall." Harsh closed the file and handed it to Groves. "It's all in there, the bad guys on our side, the bad guys on their side. Let's see if we can tighten up your project, General."

"You can count on it, Captain."

"General, will you bring us up to speed on our friends from the East?" Yoder noticed Halsey bristle as he said the words. He had to remind himself that for Yoder's entire life, Japan had been a strong ally and trading partner of the United States. These men were still raw from the cowardly attack on Pearl not three months previous.

"Captain, we are going to have a difficulty with this accelerated time table you've requested." General MacArthur had found dealings with the Japanese painfully taxing. There was an unreasonable amount of protocol and face saving involved, not to mention resentment from much of the military staff he was working with.

"You need to be in position to attack Vladivostok by 31 March, the latest."

"I'm looking at these recon photos and I don't see how Mac can deliver a full strength army to Vladivostok in less than a month." Eisenhower was sitting next to Yoder, he had a half a dozen maps spread out on the table before him.

"Here's what we are up against. Hell, Peters, you have a better handle on this than I do, show the General what you showed me yesterday." Yoder turned the meeting over to Butter Bean Peters.

"Yes, Sir." Pete turned on the large screen display hanging on the wall behind him. "As you all know, Stalin was prepared to begin his counter attack against Germany a few days ago. We successfully derailed that by terminating five of his armies and a large amount of artillery pieces. The bad news is that he has an almost inexhaustible supply of troops and his factories are working surprisingly efficiently at turning out big guns and tanks. He is planning his next offensive. Take a look at the map on the screen." Pete fired up his laser pointer and directed it to the Northern Def Region, the northern most area of the Eastern Front. "We have the 13th and the 48th Soviet Armies, all well supplied and rested. Down here in Karelion we have the 65th, the 21st, the 70th and the 2nd Tank Army, also very much ready for a counter offensive. There are over eight million troops and over fifty thousand mechanized units in the north alone, all operational and fully adapted to conditions. They are all on the move, heading towards the center of the front. The same thing is happening up and down the line, from the Archangel Mil District in the north to the Velea Mil District in the South. Until his reserves arrive, Hitler is in a very compromised position."

"This is exactly why we need Japan in this war," Yoder interrupted. "We need to freeze his armies in the south by having Japan attack Vladivostok."

"If you all remember, the Japanese occupied Vladivostok from 1918 thorough 1922 during the Sino-Russo War." Yoder paused and looked at Butter Bean. Pete realized that maybe nobody was really interested in his vast, if not somewhat obscure knowledge of Eastern History.

"Captain, I understand the objectives. I'll see if I can light a fire under the top brass in Tokyo and get some movement out of them." MacArthur was finding this new assignment much more of a challenge than he was expecting.

"In the interim, we will start planning some more sorties from the *Stennis* to try and disrupt their initial movements."

The rest of the day was spent in strategic meetings, planning for the fall of the Soviet Union.

Butter Bean dismissed his driver with a big good-bye. He wasn't used to being ferried around and treated like he was something special. He felt the need to let everyone who waited on him to know that he truly appreciated their help. All the attention made him somewhat self conscience. The fact that he was instrumental in helping plan the most important offensive in history seemed to have allude him.

Pete looked up at the elegant apartment he had been billeted in and smiled. Sixty years from now he lived not ten blocks from here, in a decidedly less grand building.

Although, by 2002, this luxury apartment will have lost quite a bit of its luster. The five block area surrounding this building will have suffered from both urban decay and two terms under Mayor Marion Barry. Pete had never done much more than drive though this part of town way back in the future for fear of becoming a police statistic.

It was only six thirty. He had already eaten what he considered quite an acceptable dinner at the Pentagon commissary. Artificial coloring and preservatives had not really taken off yet and food, especially institutional food, tasted decidedly better. He decided to go visit the bar, no, the saloon, on the corner across the street.

Everything seemed so much more formal here in the forties. Every man he saw was attired in a suite and a hat, a fedora they called them, or a military uniform. The woman were equally well dressed in sharp suites or dresses, usually with the broad shoulder look that appeared to be so popular now. And hats, the woman seemed to love hats as much as the men did. Sometimes they had a band of what appeared to be fishnet draped over the front of the hat, obscuring their eyes. That had to be annoying, he figured. He could do without the hats, but Pete was growing quite fond of the silk stockings with the seam that ran down the back. He found himself following a woman down the street more than once just to ogle their, what are they calling them now, gams.

As far as he knew, he and Captain Yoder were the only ones from the *Stennis* to spend any appreciable time on dry land and he alone had a somewhat permanent address. It was an incredible thrill for him to be stationed in 1940's Washington. The month he spent aboard the *Stennis* was hardly his most memorable one. Pete Peters was not a sailor. The handful of times that the weather was rough enough to rock that monstrous boat, no, he got a proper ass chewing from a sailor for calling it that, the ship, he was green for two days. Pete was a landlubber and he was just fine with that.

Pete dodged a Hudson as he crossed the street and strolled into O'Gradys Saloon. He couldn't help thinking that this sumptuous wood paneled interior was destined to become a bodaga. Maybe not, he thought, history has already changed, it is bound to change some more. At the very least, he needed to put a note in a corner stone that would be opened in the late 1980's warning the citizens of Washington about electing Marion Barry to the top city spot.

"Good evening lad, what can I get ya?" the bartenders brogue was so Irish thick Pete needed a moment to process the words.

"How about an Amstel Light?"

"I suppose you'll tell me what that is? I've never heard of it, but I'm sure I can whip up a fine Amstel Light if that's your pleasure."

Oh Jesus, this time shift is going to require some rethink on quite a few levels if I'm going to have any kind of social interaction. "Why don't you get me a Pabst Blue Ribbon," Pete was unfamiliar with the offerings from Pabst but decided he would be safe ordering something that was advertised behind the bar. How bad could it be if it had been awarded a blue ribbon?

He crawled up on a red leather stool and looked around the room. It was fairly crowded, understandable considering the hour. Easily half the men in the bar wore a uniform. There was something missing, however. Pete looked around and realized that there was no TV over the bar entertaining the patrons with a Lakers game and beer commercials. There also wasn't any background music seeping from a DVD juke box. He loosed his tie, balanced himself on the stool and eyeballed the room. This is quintessential 1940's, the atmosphere, the clothes, even the beer tasted different than the imported stuff he had grown accustomed to.

There was a crowd off in the back corner of the bar. Half a dozen men and women were huddled around a chest high wooden cabinet. "What are they doing back there?" he asked Shamus, the bartender.

"We just installed a Soundie, folks seem to be drawn to it."

"And a Soundie is?"

"It's like a miniature moving picture show, son," he replied, sounding like he should have been handing out adult beverages in county Cork.

"Think I'll take a look." Pete jumped off his chair, grabbed his Pabst Blue Ribbon beer and headed towards the back of the bar. There was a small screen on the top of the unit and a metal manufacturers tag on the front of it that read Panoram. The image was black and white and the quality was lousy. Probably an old 16mm projector in there, he speculated judging by both the flickering movie and the sprocket sound emanating from the cabinet. No, he rethought, it's probably a new 16mm projector. He was suddenly disturbed by the fact that it would be years before he's see anything half as sharp as the DVD images he enjoyed in his old apartment.

Pete pushed his way into the small crowd to sneak a better look. There was a new film starting, they didn't seem to last but two or three minutes. The title of the next presentation was "The King's Men performing The Chool Song." It started with a group of power wigged chamber musicians playing a piece from Bach while two people danced a minuet. The sound was atrocious. Suddenly, the guy steps on the woman's skirt, which falls to the floor. Now the band breaks into a high energy boogie while the couple begins to swing dance. While the music left him unmoved, the dancers were outrageous. There had been a resurgence of swing dancing in the late nineties, he'd even taken a few classes at Princeton. Collins and Collette was the dance team, according to the short list of credits at the end of the film. Everyone seemed greatly entertained. The gentleman nearest the machine shoved another coin in to the slot to the delight of the crowd. According to the title of the next vignette, Dorthy Dandridge was about to perform the 'Cow-Cow Boogie. Pete decided he needed to go and directed his feet back towards the bar.

Things were really hopping now. The pre dinner crowd was in full swing. There were two nice restaurants on the same block as O'Gradys, most of this crowd would probably be heading over there shortly. He enjoyed being out in public. It was nice to be around people in the evening. Pete hadn't been told directly not to go out, but there had been some covert suggestions thrown his way not to venture far from either the Pentagon or his apartment. It was getting a little difficult sitting home alone by himself each night. There wasn't a television to be found and listening to the radio just depressed him. Hell, it was Friday night, he was sure no one would care if he were to get a little R & R after a tough week of locating the bad guys.

Pete's seat was taken, so he walked to the end of the bar, near the door, to the only vacant seat left. He nursed his ten cent beer and continued observing the living history around him. Though the decibel level had peaked, he thought he heard a woman crying. Pete scanned the bar and saw nothing untoward. Suddenly, the front door swung open and as a handsomely dressed couple entered the bar, the location of the muffled cry became evident. Yes, across the street was a man and a woman in a heated discussion.

Pete put his beer on the counter and walked out the door. The street was empty save for a handful of people heading towards the restaurant at the end of the block. He took a closer look at the arguing couple. The man was talking in a low, threatening growl. She appeared apprehensive and frightened. He had her by the wrist and was pulling her aggressively down toward the other end of the street.

Pete took off, walking forcefully toward the developing situation. The guy looked kinda big, he thought. As he drew closer, the man also appeared to be drunk. At a pudgy five foot three, Pete was not an imposing figure. He was not prone to feats of heroism, but nothing pissed him off more that a man roughing up a woman. Maybe he identified with the "Weaker sex," not being much more imposing than the average woman himself. But though small, he was still a man, and a woman's honor was to be upheld, despite the odds. Besides, he was a secret agent, sort of. The NSA had its share of 007 types. He wished one of them was around just about now.

"Unhand that woman, sir!" It being the forties, he figured he could get away with that kind of talk.

"Scram, it's none of your business." The guys voice was slurred, he was unsteady.

"You touch a woman, it becomes my business." His voice was meaningful, sounding like it belonged to a man a good six inches taller than he.

"Please," she pleaded, "just let me go." Her face was covered with tears.

"Fat chance of that," he responded, and then raised his right arm and backhanded her in the face.

Pete exploded over the ten feet of distance that separated him from the transpiring nightmare. He moved quicker than he had ever moved in his life. Instinctively, his left leg came up, just like he had been trained in hand to hand combat, a course he nearly failed, and he planted his foot squarely in the cowards stomach. The man dropped to his knees and began to puke.

"You bastard," he croaked between heaves. Pointing towards the woman, he threatened, "I'll get you for this."

Pete took her hand and helped her off the pavement. Her cheek was red where he had struck her. Fortunately her attacker was loaded, otherwise his strike could have caused her terrible damage.

"Come with me." He wasn't going to leave her on the street in the dazed condition she was in. She offered no protest. He dragged her half a block up to his building. Within moments they were in his second floor apartment.

Her long dark hair was disheveled. Her makeup was streaked from the tears. She sat quietly on his couch and tried to compose herself.

"My name is Pete, Pete Peters." She was such a mess he didn't even extend his hand.

Between muffled sobs, she responded "My name is Karen Slater."

The adrenaline had subsided and Pete began to shake.

"Thank-you," she said quietly.

Pete looked at her as he sat there shaking and she sat there sniffling. He could see past the smudged makeup and the unkempt clothing and recognized that this damsel in distress was quite pretty. Her eyes were dark and gentle. Her face was long and perfectly proportioned. Though he had yet to see one, he suspected that she had a killer smile. And that hair, it was long, thick and wavy. The kind of hair a fella could really get his hands into.

"Do you have a match?" She pulled a cigarette out of her bag.

Pete was not a smoker, but he happened to have a pack of matches in his pocket. He found them at the bar this evening and was so amused by the message on the cover, he decided to keep them. There were simply two bold letters on the outside, VD. He wasn't sure if someone was suggesting that he go out and get himself a case of venereal disease or was suggesting he not run with dirty women. After not lighting three of the matches, Karen took the pack from him and lit her own cigarette. She inhaled deeply, clearly being calmed by the smoke.

"I'm sorry for all of this." Her voice was still quivering. My God she's beautiful, Pete thought. I'm having inappropriate thoughts here, he realized. This poor woman has just been beat up and I'm thinking of my own carnal needs. Shit, he looked down at her left hand, she's married!

"Please, don't apologize, I'm glad I could help."

"I guess it's lucky that you can fight better than you light matches." There, beneath the smeared makeup, the slightly bruised cheek and the ravaged ego, was the smile. He was right, it was like a beacon guiding him home.

"It's impressive that you can still have a sense of humor after what you've been through."

"I'm normally a very peppy person." She took another drag from her cigarette and looked wistfully out the window. She seemed sad that her first impression to him was that of a beaten woman.

They were quiet for a while. Pete was unsure what to say, he hadn't spent a lot of time alone around women, especially beautiful women. Finally his secret agent training kicked in and he asked, "Who was he and why was he hitting you?"

Karen looked at him, prepared to dodge the question, but then she took a look at his face for the first time. It was soft and smooth, making him appear probably considerably younger than he was. But his eyes held her attention. They were blue and full of emotion. They made her feel like she was in church, all safe and loved. Before she could make a conscience effort to deflect his query, she found herself talking. "He's my husband. He gets angry when he drinks."

Pete hated that. How could a grown man strike a woman? He had have been six foot plus, she didn't appear to be much more than an inch taller than his own five foot three. "Why do you put up with it?"

"He's my husband, there's not much I can do." Karen looked down at the floor. Her voice was small.

Pete was enraged at the absurd notion that apparently pervaded the psyche of woman of this time. He had read about it in an intro Psychology class his sophomore year at Princeton. It seems that some woman suffer from such low self-esteem that they measure themselves by their marital status. So afraid of what friends and family will think, they cover the bruises with makeup and lies and live in a duplicitous world of light and dark. This current society is partly to blame for looking the other way, for allowing men to hide behind alcohol and rage, not forcing them to face their inner selves.

Karen looked so lonely as she sat there, the occasional tear still tracking down her cheek, smoke obscuring one eye. "You don't have to take it, you know." Great, he thought, what was he going to do, send her to a battered wives center.

"He's my husband, *you don't understand.*" She began to cry again. Pete moved near her on the couch and put his arms around her.

"Yes I do understand. You do not have to put up with this. It's wrong." Her tears melted his heart.

Karen put her cigarette out in an ash tray Pete didn't even realize was on the coffee table. She sat back a took a deep, cleansing breath.

"Those things are bad for you," Pete said, pointing to the smoldering butt.

"I'm not an athlete," she was smiling again, "they're not a problem."

There's so much that needs to be changed back here, Pete thought. From wife abuse, to the myriad of health risks, smoking, asbestos, to the unfortunate lack of home entertainment. Could he, and his fellow time travelers, hasten some of these societal and technological changes, he wondered?

"How long have you been married?"

"About a year and a half," Karen replied.

"He looks older than you."

"He is. I'm twenty six, he's thirty four. His name is Jack, Jack Slater. His family owns a defense subcontracting business. They make barrels for guns, I think they call them 50 caliber something or others, I really don't pay much attention. His dad's very well politically connected, the war should make them all very rich."

"It should make you very rich. Isn't your marriage a partnership?"

"That's funny," there was that smile again, "a woman's place is in the home. That's his business, I have nothing to do with it."

"Your love and support make you an equal partner in everything he does."

She didn't tell him that there wasn't any love left.

"I think I have to go. You've been so kind... and courageous."

"I'd like to see you again." This is ridiculous, Pete thought. She's beautiful and married, I'm short and portly, OK, fat. What the hell am I thinking saying that.

"I do owe you something." What am I thinking, Karen thought. I'm married. I can't go out with a single man. "Meet me at O'Gradys at seven on Monday."

Pete got Karen a cab. As he was waiting for the elevator to return him to his apartment, he suddenly felt like his life was going to change.

February 20th, 1942, 12:56 AM
Oval Office, White House

Harsh had three items on the agenda for his trip back to Washington, this was going to be his most delicate task.

"Thank-you for seeing me, Mr. President," the stewards had left brandy. The White House was quiet, the President looked tired.

"Please, Captain, I think we know each other well enough by now, call me Franklin, will you?"

"Thank-you, Franklin." First name basis with President Franklin Delano Roosevelt, an icon in history, and all the people in his life who would be impressed by this honor don't exist yet. Ever?

"Henry tells me your strategic sessions went well. I wouldn't want to be a one of Stalin's Generals when he learns that the Japanese have designs on Russia. He is a much more ruthless man than I had any idea of before I read the papers you left me. The notion that he had been responsible for the deaths of twenty million of his own people is staggering." Roosevelt had been given and had read close to two thousand pages of "History."

"Yes, Josef Stalin is a maniacal, evil despot. The world will be better off without him... And the evils of Communism."

Franklin took a sip of his brandy, then stuck a cigarette in the long, black trademark holder of his and fired it up. Sitting behind the most powerful desk in the world, smoke wafting about his head, Franklin Roosevelt looked like a world leader. Despite similar secrets that almost ruined the man who sat in the same chair in the late nineties, he had an aura of greatness. If confronted with the truth of the two mistresses who were currently known to a very few, Harsh suspected Franklin would have had the courage to speak the truth and to handle the fallout with distinction.

Harsh sat for a moment, nursing his brandy. The subject he wanted to broach was delicate, he was of no mind to rush into it.

"Tell me, Harsh, is the future a better place. Did we leave a decent legacy?"

"You will be very kindly remembered by history, Franklin. The programs you instituted, the compassion you showed and the strength you demonstrated set the tone for America at the dawn of her ascendance to world dominance." Harsh didn't think he needed to discuss Roosevelt's unfortunate decision to allow the Soviets to enjoy in the spoils of a dissected Germany. Allowing Patton to take all of Berlin may have eased the transition of power and minimized the tension of the impending Cold War.

"I appreciate the material you had left for me, some of it was somewhat disconcerting to read. The opportunity to look into the future is filled with Pandora like complications."

"There is one future event I would like to discuss with you tonight."

"I suspect it is the one that has caused me the most introspection." Franklin gazed over Harsh's head, appearing to be studying the magnificent crown molding ringing the room.

"It had to have been difficult for you to learn the date of your death."

Franklin smiled. "Yes, Captain, it was. I was somewhat surprised by my reaction, however. I'm not a young man. I haven't had my health for some years now. When a man reaches a certain age he becomes acutely aware of his mortality. Perceptions change, so do priorities. Personal needs seem to become less important.

Desired goals take on urgent proportions. There is so much more I want to accomplish." He shifted his gaze to Captain Yoder. Franklin Delano Roosevelt looked him square in the eyes. "I'm not afraid to die though." He spoke with conviction, seeming to be talking to himself more than to Harsh.

"Well, Franklin, we have been fairly busy altering history. The reports of your death may have been greatly exaggerated, if I can paraphrase Mark Twain."

"How so, Harsh."

"The advances made in medicine through the turn of the century have kept pace with weapons development. Mr. President," it was going to take Harsh some time before he became comfortable using Roosevelt's first name, "with the technology in the hospital onboard the *Stennis*, it is possible to push off your departure date. There is no way of knowing how much additional time we can give you until Dr. Cohen, the ships surgeon, runs some tests on you, but we may afford you the opportunity of seeing your dream of a United Nations realized."

Roosevelt showed no outward emotion. Harsh was somewhat surprised. His offer of an extended life span had not been received with the exuberance Captain Yoder was expecting. They sat quietly for some minutes before Franklin spoke.

"This is a more Byzantine decision than I think you realize, Harsh." Roosevelt's voice was thin and tired. "Altering history as we have already done for the good of mankind was a difficult decision to make. Now you are suggesting that I alter history for personal gain. To what end?"

"You will be recognized as one of the best presidents the United States ever had. Your contributions to society are legend. I believe that your further contributions will be important to the stabilization of the country and of the world. If I didn't feel this way, I would not have made this proposal."

"There are many men as capable as I," Franklin argued, "from what I've read, Harry Truman did an excellent job of winding down the war and positioning America to grow to a position of power and dominance in the world."

"He certainly had, Franklin, however, mistakes were made. He allowed Stalin to carve up Western Europe and set the stage for a cold war that would result in the possible end of life on this planet. I don't mean to place the burden of all that on Vice President Truman, but a strong presence in the White House may have alleviated some of the conditions that lead to that most unfortunate outcome."

"Your argument lacks substance in light of the fact that, if all goes according to plan, Stalin will not be of issue by the end of this terrible war," Roosevelt countered.

"That's true," Harsh replied, "but we will be in an even greater need of a strong leader when both Russia and Germany are in defeat. There will be a dramatic shift in world power that will beg for a wise and strong man to ease the rest of the world through this transitional period."

"Your words are well spoken, Harsh. Please don't think that I am in any hurry to visit the other side. I must contemplate your proposal. I am just a pawn in this game and am reticent to make a decision of this magnitude before considering the larger implications. We will visit on this again, Captain."

February 21st, 1942, 7:23 PM
O'Gradys Saloon

Pete Peters was sitting at a table secluded in the back of the bar. He positioned himself to allow for a view of the front door. She was late. Karen Slater was supposed to have met him at seven. He kept checking his watch, a thirty five dollar Timex quartz watch that, he suspected, may be keeping time better than any other wrist watch in the world.

Butter Bean was anxious. He so wanted to see her again. For most of the day he found it difficult to concentrate. He looked at the recon pictures spread across his desk and could only see her face. He could still smell the perfume she wore. He found himself unconsciously rubbing the cheek that she had kissed when she left him less than seventy hours ago. His feelings stirred for this woman he barely knew.

Each time the front door opened, his heart raced. He would sit up in his chair and crane his neck to get a better look. Each person who entered the bar made his heart sink a little more. Why would she come back. She's married, I'm a physical wreck. It was not the first time he cursed the body he'd been dealt. Pete had tried any number of times to lose weight. He was a fixture at the NSA gym for close to six months. The twenty pounds he lost were so inconsequential to his overall look that he became disheartened and binged, replacing his hard lost weight within two weeks. Short sucked so badly that fat just wasn't really much of an issue, and there was nothing he could do about short.

"Oh my God," the words just burst out of him. He ran towards the front door.

"Karen, over here." He was waving his hands frantically, trying to catch her attention in the midst of all these annoying taller men congregated about the bar.

She looked beautiful. Now her eyes weren't puffy from tears, her makeup was fresh and she wore a smart looking violet dress. He stood before her and was lost for words.

"I'm so sorry I'm late, you must hate me."

"Oh my, hardly. I was afraid you weren't going to come," he looked down at the floor as he said the words.

What a cute man, this Pete Peters is, Karen thought. His face was like a cherub, all smooth and round. He wore an ill fitting navy blue suit. Must be difficult fitting a body like his, she thought. It was his boyish charm, his naive honesty, that made him attractive. He had haunted her mind the past weekend. He was such a sharp contrast to her husband. Jack was tall, six one, and a terribly handsome man. Women were talking to him all the time. They often said he looked like Gary Cooper.

It was there that their differences took an unfortunate turn. Jack was an unsympathetic man, full of spite and rage. It took very little to set him off, and when he drank, which was often, he could be horribly abusive. Pete was a gentleman, she could tell. His face bespoke compassion and understanding. The minutes she spent with him in his apartment three days ago were very comforting. He made her feel cared for, protected. Feelings she had not had for some time.

"I had every intention to be here, I wouldn't have suggested it if I hadn't. Jack left later than I had anticipated, he has meetings in New York through to Thursday evening."

Pete was leading her back to his table as she spoke. She seemed more at ease tonight. Her smile was quick and comfortable. He pulled out a chair and guided her into it. A waiter appeared, Pete ordered them both a Pabst Blue Ribbon beer. He was developing a taste for this fine domestic offering.

"How do you feel." He noticed her right cheek was still a little red. Jack must have hit her harder than he thought. But wait, he realized, he had struck her on the left cheek. Pete felt his blood grow angry. He decided not to bring it up just now.

"Oh, I'm fine. Karen Slater can take a punch," she said with a laugh.

Pete was appalled by her cavalier attitude towards the domestic violence in her own home. "You should never have to take a punch." His face grew serious, his voice was stern.

"I was just joking," Pete's sudden change in demeanor startled her.

"I am concerned about you," he shot back, "until you take this seriously, the beatings won't stop." His voice changed, he was full of emotion.

Karen was touched by Pete's concern. It had been to long since anyone had shown her any compassion. Jack had structured and controlled her life in such a way as to preclude much in the way of outside contact. He grew jealous when she would develop friendships even with other woman. Ultimately, it was just easier to be alone than to fight with him about it.

She looked down at the table. Her eyes welled up, a single tear rolled down her bruised right cheek. "I know." Karen sat quiet for a moment. "I just don't know how to make him stop," her voice was soft.

Pete sat quietly. Now that he had opened this terrible can of worms, he wasn't really sure what to do with them. The modern solution of seeing a marriage councilor was just a little to radical for these times and Jack didn't sound like he was the kind of guy who'd agree to take that course of action anyway. The obvious solution of leaving him was too aggressive a recommendation for him to make after having spent a total of thirty five minutes with her.

The waiter arrived with their beers, saving Pete from what had become a very awkward moment. "I toast your beauty," Pete held up his mug in a chivalrous effort to break the mood.

"You won't get an argument from me," she met his mug with hers causing a clunk. Karen was smiling again.

The beautiful smile that seemed to suggest everything was OK. Only Pete knew what it was masking, and despite that knowledge, he couldn't help but smile right along with her.

"You have a nice smile. I like to make people smile." Before she married Jack, she had been a very happy young woman. Karen had a big heart and a generous spirit. She grew up in Farmington, a small town in up state New York, not fifty miles from the Canadian boarder. One day when she was twelve, she found out that her friends father had lost his job. Karen collected all the food in her house and delivered five full shopping bags to Judy's door step. Karen's parents were initially angry, but were unable to stay that way for long. Even then, she had a way of making the most outlandish act seem sensible. It was a skill she had been using for the past year and a half to convince herself that her situation was not as bad as it seemed.

Karen pulled an unfiltered Lucky Strike from her purse. She held it to her lips, waiting for Pete to give her a light. It took a moment for him to catch on. He grabbed the matches on the table, the cover of which requested that he buy war bonds, and ignited the match on the first try. She took a drag and blew a cloud of smoke over Pete's head. Job two, Pete reflected, was to get her to stop smoking.

"Why did you marry Jack?"

Karen's smile disappeared. This was clearly a painful question. She took another hit from her smoke and began to speak. "He was, is, so good looking. When we were dating, he was so wonderful. He brought me flowers, took me to the theater. Remember, I grew up in a small town. I was really star struck. He came from a powerful family and I was just swept up."

She paused. Her expression became pensive. "He hit me for the first time on our honeymoon. We were in Bermuda, it was so beautiful. We stayed in a wonderful suite in the *Princess Hotel*, I remember everything was pink. On the third night, he got drunk on champagne. We argued about where to go for dinner, then he hit me." There were tears in her eyes. "He apologized profusely, he really seemed sorry. When we got back to the States, he seemed to have become a different person, controlling, easy to anger. I found it was easier just to agree with him and do what he said. The more I gave in, the more he demanded." Her voice quivered.

"Why do you stay with him?" It was a simple but powerful question, one that she probably had been afraid to ask herself.

"Where are you from, Pete?"

Well, that was a mistake, he realized. She is not ready to go there yet.

"Saddle River, New Jersey."

"That's not so far. Tell me more about yourself."

This could be tricky, he thought. Should I tell her I graduated from Princeton in 1999? Maybe tell her my hobbies include surfing the web and screwing with computers? They spent the next two hours talking about all manner of things, none of which occurred past February 21st, 1942.

March 3rd, 1942, 2:34 Am, local time
Kremlin, Moscow.

Iosif Vissarionovich Dzhugashvili sat cloistered in his birch paneled office deep within the bowels of the dark towered Kremlin. He had adopted the pseudonym Stalin, meaning "a man of steel," in 1910. He was born in Gori in 1879 to Georgian peasants, neither of whom spoke Russian. Stalin was forced to learn the language when he attended the Gori Church School near the turn of the century. Soso, his childhood nickname, was the best pupil in the school and earned a full scholarship to the Tbilisi Theological

Seminary. It was while studying for the priesthood that Iosif had the opportunity to read the forbidden literature of Karl Marx's *Das Kapital*. He was moved by this radical ideology and quickly converted to a new orthodoxy, Russian Marxism. Stalin began his career in the Social-Democratic party as a propagandist among the Tbilisi railroad workers. Between 1902 and 1913, he was arrested eight times and sent to Siberia. He escaped seven times. The government was successful in containing him only once, keeping him in exile from 1913 to 1917.

Stalin married Yekaterina Svanidze after returning from Siberia in 1904. It was a comfortable marriage until she died in 1910. Almost a decade later, he married his second wife, Nadezhda Alliluyeva, who committed suicide thirteen years later.

During the last years of czarist Russia, Stalin was more of an up and coming follower than a leader. His contributions to the Bolshevik faction were more theoretical than practical. After helping to organize a bank holdup in Tbilisi to "expropriate" funds, Lenin raised Stalin into the upper reaches of the party in 1912 by co-opting him into the Bolsheviks' Central Committee. The following year Stalin edited the new party paper, *Pravda*. While there, he wrote his first major work, *Marxism and the Nationality Question*.

Stalin returned to Petrograd after the revolution and together with Lev Kamenev, he dominated party decisions in the capital before Lenin arrived in April of 1917. Stalin and Kamenev advocated a policy of moderation and cooperation with the provisional government. While he played a somewhat significant role in the armed uprising that followed in November, he was not remembered as a revolutionary hero.

Stalin was Lenin's choice to head the Commissariat for Nationality Affairs. Together with Yakov Sverdlov and Leon Trotsky, he helped Lenin decide all the emergency issues during the difficult period of the first civil war. Stalin was appointed commander of several fronts. He strengthened his position with aggressive organizational work and an almost religious devotion to administrative details. By 1922, he became secretary general of the party. By the time Lenin died, the two were at odds. Lenin came to regard the flaws in Stalin's personality as political liabilities. Adroit maneuvering enabled Stalin to suppress Lenin's concerns.

Stalin joined in a troika with Grigory Zinovyev and Kamenev to lead the country after Lenin's death. Once his only true threat, Trotsky was neutralized, Stalin realigned himself with Bukharin and Rykov against his former partners. Through cunning and ruthlessness, Stalin cemented his position of power by his fiftieth birthday in 1929.

In the early hours of this new day, however, Josef Stalin recognized that he was the leader of a country that may not see the following year. He shifted his gaze to the huge globe on his desk showing the course of campaigns over territory he himself had defended in the civil wars of 1917-20. Now, he had to defend them again. There were new streaks of gray in his hair and his granite like face was etched with fatigue. He was known for putting in eighteen hour days and they were now devouring him. This fresh piece of correspondence sitting on his desk could prove to be the end of Russia. The Japanese had closed their embassy and recalled their ambassador. That could mean only one thing, a war on two fronts was inevitable.

March 12th, 1942, 11:16 AM
USS John C. Stennis

"Come on, dig it out, dig it out, push yourself." Nick Papus was sprinting a measured length on the flight deck of the *Stennis*. As always, he was looking for not just a personal best, but a squad best. Kyle Rogers had broken his previous record of 12.7 seconds two days ago and this did not sit well with Nick, not well at all. Standing mid course was Conrad Schmidt, barking words of encouragement.

Conrad was rousted from bed early on the morning of December 15th, 2002 and told to assemble his SEAL team and report to the *Stennis*. As a seven year veteran of the Navy SEAL's, this was not the first time he'd received cryptic orders like that. Within minutes, he'd been in contact with the seven other members of his squad and less than an hour later, they were all in line with the six thousand other crew members struggling to board the *Stennis*.

Ensign Schmidt had wanted to become a Navy SEAL since he was a child. His Dad had taken him to see Demi Moore in a movie called *GI Jane*. This movie was memorable for him on two levels, it was the first time the post pubescent Conrad had seen a naked breast, and it marked his life long fascination with the toughest sons of bitches in the service.

He learned to live by the SEAL creed, "The only easy day... was yesterday." Personal courage and determination drove him in everything he did. On morning of his eighteenth birthday, Conrad arrived two hours early at his local Naval Recruiting Office. By nine fifteen AM he had signed the papers that would allow him the opportunity to prove to himself that he had the stuff to be part of the most elite and highly trained fighting forces on the face of the earth, the US Navy SEA, AIR, LAND Team.

Throughout High School, he read all he could about the SEAL's. From their early work on the beaches of Normandy during World War II reconnoitering the beaches and clearing them for the impending invasion, to their unsung work in Korea, to their legendary exploits in

Vietnam, Conrad dreamed of measuring up to the highest of military standards.

Birthed from the Underwater Demolition's Teams created during the second World War, they were officially reorganized in 1962 by President Kennedy as a maritime counterpart to the US Army Special Forces. The SEAL's remarkable history of successes had become legendary. SEAL teams have operated in every hellhole known to modern warfare. Most SEAL missions had been classified and unreported, hence unknown to the public. Due to intense training, dedication and focus they have been hugely successful.

It was in Vietnam, however, that they were transformed into modern day Naval Commandos. The Viet Cong referred to them as "Devils with green faces." And now here Ensign Schmidt was, twenty years before the SEALS were even dreamed of, preparing to do battle with an already vanquished foe, at least in his mind. He had been told to prepare for an insertion. That meant some hairy behind enemy lines mission that had a serious chance of being his last. And Conrad Schmidt celebrated the challenge.

Now it was time to train hard, to push his men so that when pieces of shit were being flung by the fan, his team wouldn't even be around to see them. "Move your ass, Papus, see if you can get your record back from pansy boy Rogers." Nick didn't look well today. Had this been an office job, Conrad would have sent him home. But it wasn't. In this line of work, the luxury of bailing out because you didn't feel well was not an option. You fight or die.

Nick was pushing himself, he always did. He had blown through the First Phase of SEAL training. Even Hell Week didn't push him to his considerable limits. On the last day he had been issued the moniker Iron Nick. With about two hours of sleep over a five day period, he still had enough stuff left to drag a drowning Ed Smalls three miles along the San Diego coast line to safety. Today, however, Nick wondered if he was going to be able to finish this short sprint. Maybe he was coming down with the flu.

"What's this shit, Iron Nick, fourteen flat? Shit, my dead Grandmother could do better than that." Conrad was not above riding his men even when they were down... Especially when they were down. Now was the time to reach inside yourself to find what you were made of, not when things became real.

Nick was doubled over, a position no one could remember ever seeing him in. He took great pride in never showing physical distress. But now, here he was, after a hundred meter sprint, unable to straighten up.

"Look at me you fucking tadpole," Conrad was standing over Nick, staring down at the back of his head. Nick summoned up all the strength he had and willed himself to an upright posture.

"Holy shit!" Ensign Schmidt couldn't believe what he was seeing. Nick's face was blue, as blue as the Caribbean Ocean. Before Conrad could react to this ghastly sight, Nick dropped to his knees and hurled. Torrents of blood gushed from his mouth and all over Con's boots.

"Let's get this man to sick bay."

Even as he was speaking, Nick's teammates were already rushing to his aid. Conrad and Kyle Rogers each grabbed an arm and lifted him back to his feet. But Nick had nothing left, he was dead weight. Olsen and Vega each took hold of a leg and the four of them charged to the tower while the three last team members ran ahead, clearing the way and opening bulk heads. All the while, Nick Papus disgorged massive amounts of blood.

Dr. Saul Cohen had his finger up Crusty White's ass when SEAL Team Three burst through the door. "Your prostate's fine, Crusty, pull up your pants." Saul quickly removed the thin latex glove that separated him form all manor of evil in Crusty's colon and bolted towards this fast moving group. He knew there was trouble. Nobody comes through a door with that kind of urgency unless there's a most immediate problem.

Saul mentally prepared himself for ugly. The sight of real physical trauma still unsettled him. Even his internship at Bellevue Hospital in New York City didn't anesthetize him from the sight of blood gushing and missing body parts.

"Put him on this table," he guided the fast moving group to a white sheeted bed in the middle of the OR. Dr. Cohen saw his patient for the first time. There was blood everywhere, had to have been an open artery somewhere, he speculated.

"What's his name?"

"Nick Papus," Schmidt volunteered.

"Nancy, pull his file." Nancy Prudente was heading for the computer before Dr. Cohen even opened his mouth. Lieutenant Prudente was the head nurse with seventeen years of experience behind her, not much of which was necessary for her to know this man was going to need a massive transfusion.

The blood was deep red, indicating internal bleeding. "What happened?" He turned to Ensign Schmidt for an answer.

"He was running, then turned blue, dropped to his knees and began puking blood." Conrad's economy of words was appreciated.

"He has no open wounds?"

"No sir."

Saul grabbed a towel and wiped the blood from Nick's face.

"Oh my God!" The last time he'd seen a face that color was on the very dead Ensign Shaw.

By now, the patient's clothes had been cut off and Saul could see the same blue tinge all over Nick's body.

"He's type A positive, let's get him started," Nancy directed the OR nurse to start an IV.

"You guys get out of here, I'm going to open him up."

The remnants of SEAL Team Three vacated the room.

"The pulse is weak, blood pressure is 45 over 60, we're loosing him." Nancy's voice was flat.

Saul made an eight inch incision over the breast plate and peeled back the skin. The chest cavity was full of blood. He knew what was going on, he also knew that there was nothing he was going to be able to do to save this man.

Dr. Cohen suctioned the blood from the area around the heart. Blood was leaching from the arteries. Blood was probably leaching from every artery and vein in his body. The circulatory system was terminally compromised.

"No pulse."

Saul reached in and began a heart message. He knew it was a futile effort. Even if he got the heart pumping again the blood was not going to get to where it needed to go. After a few false starts, Nick Papus's wonderfully conditioned heart betrayed him, seeming to know further effort was pointless.

"Time of death, 11:52 AM." Dr. Saul Cohen turned disgustedly from the remains of Ensign Nicholas Zorba Papus and walked into the adjacent room, completely baffled as to what had killed two well conditioned men and a dozen plus rats.

Crusty White was standing near a window which overlooked the OR. He had his pants in his hands. He was in the process of donning them when all hell broke loose next door and he was compelled to watch. Despite his two decades in the service, he had never seen a man die before.

The one time he'd seen real blood was when some greenhorn swabbie got his hand stuck in an engine turbine. The hand evaporated and there was a crimson haze cast about the engine room. Crusty recalled that scene as being quite disturbing. This was dramatically more so. He was shocked at the amount of blood a human body held. He was also surprised at the emotions he felt watching this young man die mere feet from him. Crusty hadn't heard Dr. Cohen come into the room.

"I said get your fucking pants on and get the hell out of here!"

Crusty was not known for his compassion and typically would have had a handful of his own expletives ready in reply to such an aggressive comment, but he'd known Saul for the better part of a decade and he never heard him speak that way before.

"What happened Saul?"

"Shit, Crusty, I don't have a fucking clue." His words were heavy with emotion. "This is the second guy to die on me like that and I can't tell you why. It seems that their circulatory system has just," Saul looked up at the ceiling, searching for an explanation, "worn out. Blood is leaching from the arteries, and to a lesser extent, the veins, almost like a garden hose that had been left on for twenty years and finally wore out. It doesn't make sense. Both of these guys were in excellent shape. I may expect this to happen to an overweight slob like you, but not from conditioned athletes."

Crusty let it slide. He really wasn't exactly off the mark, and right now, Saul was the one in need of what ever support Crusty could muster.

"Don't beat yourself up over it, Doc, there doesn't seem to have been much you coulda done."

"You're right Crusty. That's the problem."

March 24th, 1942, 1:22 PM
Pentagon, War Room

Pete Peters was scanning the latest recon photos of the Eastern Front. As was promised by MacArthur, the Japanese were staged and ready to attack Vladivostok. German reserves were less than four days away from the front lines and Russian troops were being redirected north to prepare for the expected entry of Japan into the war.

Pete reflected on how one fairly small air campaign had such a dramatic effect on the complexion of the war. Less than a month ago, Hitler was poised for defeat. Now, he was tasting victory while Stalin was trying to deny that the taste in his mouth was defeat. Things were going to get very busy in a couple of days.   He decided to take advantage of this short respite as these two giants prepared for the intense battle that was inevitable and do a little research.

Over in the corner of the War Room, as it was now being called, was a photon computer. Pete was aware of the research being done at *Stanford University* but had no idea that it was beyond the theoretical.

The challenge to develop faster computers was a given since the IBM Univac's were built in the late fifties. Electronics were approaching physical limits as hard drives maxed out a few terra bites. CPU speeds had run into a wall at three gig and new technologies were needed to keep Moore's Law a reality. Researchers at Ludwig-Maximilian University in Munich turned to quantum physics for the answer. Store digital bits with a light pulse. It proved to be a difficult task. Light, by its nature, is always moving at the speed of light. Trying to keep a photon in one spot meant bouncing it back and forth between mirrors or pumping it through coils of optical fiber, neither method was practical outside the lab because of the large amount of space needed in comparison to a silicon memory chip.

The scientists in Munich developed a semiconductor structure that transformed photons into electron hole pairs. Electrons have a negative charge and holes carry a positive charge. When they meet, they annihilate each other and give off a flash of light. The hard part was to control the timing of annihilation and temporarily delay the recombination and thus retrieve the photon at a predetermined instant.

It was the researchers at *Stanford* who developed a chip that uses electron hole annihilation to create photons in vast numbers. Their chip was studded with thousands of posts, each of which emit millions of photons a second. The posts act as turnstiles, ensuring that only a single photon pops out on schedule. This computer sitting next to Pete's desk, not much bigger than the PC Pete had left sitting on his desk back at his apartment, was a hundred times faster than the Cray Super Computer that had been housed in this very building some sixty years from now.

The amount of information this tiny unit held was staggering. And the speed at which it processed information was astonishingly fast. As fast as the speed of light. The information Pete needed now could have been easily been harvested from the Internet, with its hundreds of millions of pages of information available at the tip of his fingers. But the Internet wasn't even a dream yet. He suspected that this photon computer probably contained everything that was available on the net, and probably much more. Had he the time to check, he would have found that he was correct.

In the search box, Pete typed "Karen Slater." It seemed as if his finger had just released the enter button and there was a message saying that there were three hundred and fourteen pages that may hold interest to him. Pete refined his search by adding "Washington, DC" to his query. A more workable twenty two suggestions were placed on his screen. He perused the entries in order. Most of them seemed to have come from the pages of the *Washington Post*. The first entry was the announcement of Karen's impending nuptials to Jack. She was beautiful in the picture that accompanied the details. He lingered over it for a while before saving it to his personal file.

Next was a short article in the society pages of the wedding day. It sounded like quite the affair. This Slater family must be loaded, Pete surmised. For some reason Pete didn't take the time to find out, Karen had been mentioned in an article about the plant where the gun barrels were being manufactured. He decided to start from the end of the list. The date was December 19th, 1943. Pete wasn't sure what he was looking for, but felt a desire to learn about Karen's future. Did she have children. Would she stay with Jack?

The article was on page sixteen of the business section. Pete scrolled to the headline. He recoiled in horror as he read the fifth word: "Business man charged with murdering his wife." Pete's eyes jumped to the text below the most horrific headline he had ever read.

"Jack Slater, Vice President of Development of Slater Industries, was formally charged with the beating death of his wife, Karen Slater, last evening. As he was being lead out of his brownstone, neighbors heard him repeating "She was going to leave me." According to these same neighbors, there were often loud arguments heard emanating from within the building, sometimes lasting into the early hours of the morning..."

Pete sat back in his chair, his face white. "Oh my God , what am I going to do." His words hang in the air before him. It's my fault, he thought. She was leaving him for me, and now it's my fault that she is going to die. Pete gripped the sides of the desk to keep himself from falling over as he felt his head get light.

Tears welled up in his eyes. Then he shook his head. It couldn't have been my fault. This article was written before I got here, before the *Stennis* arrived back in late '41. History has changed now. He was aware of any number of things that had not gone according to history since they had intruded upon the past.

This doesn't necessarily need to happen, he comforted himself. He could help her get away from this horrible man, save her life. He could marry her?

March 28th, 1942, 5:58 AM
The Sea of Japan

"**Arm your weapons**." Lieutenant Ben-Gurion was leading the first sortie on the Port of Vladivostok, flanked by Lieutenant's Savage and Clark. They were twenty miles out, cruising at three hundred and sixty knots. Allan glanced down at the armada heading north. The last time he'd seen any of the Japanese Navy, it was not doing so well. They seemed to have cobbled together quite a fleet. Not a good looking bunch of ships, many appeared ancient, he thought he saw oars protruding form the side of one! They only needed to transport troops to battle. Allan suspected there might have been a few British ships sprinkled amongst the fleet, properly disguised no doubt.

This morning's mission objective was to "soften up" the Port of Vladivostok. He found this an amusing euphemism. A single AGM-65 series Maverick had a fifty seven kilogram warhead stuck on the business end of it and was going to do a hell of a lot more than soften up whatever it fell on.

At three miles out, Allan Ben-Gurion issued a single command, "Fire." Six missiles departed from their host rides and within seconds were disrupting key defensive positions held by the Russian Army. The F22's continued a true course in order to deliver some additional pain in the form of a few dozen CRV-7 rockets.

The damage inflicted by the Mavericks was evident as the three jets made their first and only pass over their collective targets. Judging by the carnage caused by this initial sortie, Ben-Gurion figured that the Japanese Army would be able to stroll onto Russian soil with no more concern than vacationers debarking a cruise ship in Bermuda after the last mission of the day delivered their air born punch.

"Form up on me and let's take it home."

Kaitlyn Savage looked over her shoulder and shuddered at the death she had just delivered. This wasn't getting any easier.

March 28th, 1942, 7:44 AM
Oval Office, White House

"The last sortie just arrived back on the *Stennis*, it appears that their mission was a complete success." Henry Stimson had just placed the receiver back in its cradle. He was speaking to Captain Yoder, who was sitting one hundred and fifty miles north of Japan in the Pacific Ocean.

"I can only imagine the correspondence I'm going to be receiving from Stalin once the Japanese Army sets foot on Russian soil." It had been getting increasingly difficult for Roosevelt not to respond to his former ally's urgent requests for information and support. Stalin clearly knew that he was in trouble. Fortunately, he did not know how much trouble he was in. Yet.

"This two front attack is surly the beginning of the end for Russia as we have known it. I feel no sorrow for Stalin, especially after learning what a truly evil man is." Stimson disliked Stalin form their first dealings. That dislike had evolved into a white hot hatred.

The two statesmen sat quietly in the Oval Office for a few moments. The Cherry Blossom trees outside the window were just beginning to wake after a long winters nap, the small outer branches swelling with life. "Won't be long before the trees will be in bloom, Henry. If our Captain Yoder is correct, I'll only be around to see this metamorphosis three times more."

Henry was a little taken aback by his friends comment. They hadn't spoken of Roosevelt's impending death since that black date had first been uttered. He wasn't sure what to say.

Feeling Stimson's uneasiness, Franklin spoke. "Let's not have such a long face, Henry, we all will be making the journey to Valhalla at some point."

"I don't want to know when that trip will be, Franklin, and I'm uncomfortable knowing when yours is."

"April twelfth, three years and," Roosevelt looked up at the ceiling as he did some calculations in his head, "thirty days have September, April, May and December. March has thirty one. Fifteen days Henry, three years and fifteen days I have to live. You know, that knowledge shook me at first. I tried to not allow myself to calculate the exact number of days. But then a claming came over me. I looked back at my life. I've accomplished much. History, if what has been shown to us from the future is correct, has looked kindly on my life's work. I had accepted my fate, became comfortable with it."

"You're using the past tense, Franklin, I suspect you are now not exactly comfortable with this most complicated bit of knowledge."

"You are an intuitive man, Henry. That is one of the reasons I choose you to be part of my Cabinet. Yes, there has been an additional complication. It seems that the Doctor aboard the *Stennis* has the medical wizardry to correct my condition, to add a number of years to my life."

Henry smiled broadly. He felt deep affection for Franklin Roosevelt. "Well this is a wonderful bit of news. When will they perform this bit of black magic?"

"I'm not sure that I am going to let them, Henry. I don't know if the country will be better served with my life being prolonged."

"Are you daft, Franklin? You are the most important man in the world right now. You and Churchill are the only men in power who can be trusted with the legacy of man kind." Henry Stimson was a passionate supporter of FDR and had been troubled when he too learned that come April twelfth, 1945, his friend would no longer be of this world.

"Henry, I'm an elitist. I was raised in a fine family, never wanted for anything. I was educated in the best schools. I've been wealthy all my life. Now, do to my position, I can cheat the reaper. Is that the ultimate insult to the common man. How many police officers, teachers, tradesmen or soldiers will be offered this opportunity? Why should I be the one? What value will I offer this country on April thirteenth that would require this extraordinary technology? From what Captain Yoder showed us, this country got on just fine after my demise."

"That's foolish talk, Franklin. Look at the wonderful things you have accomplished. This country is demonstrably better for your efforts and will be better served with your continued guidance. You mustn't think only of your self, think of the country."

"You know the words to move me, Henry. I am, after all, just a public servant. It may be my philanthropic bent that sways me to your position." Franklin Delano Roosevelt gazed off at a very unsure future. "This will not be a decision that I will make lightly, I assure you of that, my friend."

April 21st, 1942, 10:26
War Room, Pentagon

Pete Peters was draped over the latest recon photos of the new front. Still a wavy line running north and south, it was on average ten to as many as twenty kilometers further east than it had been three weeks earlier. Army Group Center now occupied Smolensk, Briansk and Yartsevo. Army Group South had crossed the River Don and was now, for the second time of the war, threatening Stalingrad. Von Kuechler's Group Army North had made the largest gains thanks to the surprise, if not still disturbing entry of Japan into the fray.

Hitler had been particularly effective in moving reserves up to the front while Stalin was forced to move his armies about to counter new threats in the north. Added into Stalin's already overly complicated life had been thirty seven sorties flown by F-22's and F-18's placing more explosive tonnage in a three week period on Russian positions than had been cumulatively dropped to this date in the war. As of close of business today, baring a truly unexpected event, Russia's life expectancy was now months.

It was close to nine PM before Pete was able to cut loose and head to O'Grady's. By the time he'd arrived, Karen had been sitting in a booth for nearly an hour and was on her third beer. She perked up as she saw him making his way towards her. She stubbed out her cigarette, jumped from her seat and threw her arms around the newly arrived Pete.

"Sorry I'm late, Angel, but no one cared when I told them that I had a beautiful woman waiting for me." Pete had conjured up this sickly cute nickname for Karen one day when she had worn a baby blue sweater covered with small white angels to lunch one day. "I love angels," she shared with him.

Pete waved a hand to the waiter, who needed nothing more to know that Mr. Peters would like a Pabst delivered to his table. Pete was now a regular at O'Gradys and was enjoying the advantages that accompanied such a position.

During the past month, Pete and Karen had gotten close, very close. He was the first person in her short life that had ever treated her so specially. She could do no wrong in Pete's eyes. He told her she was perfect. At first, that caused her some discomfort. Finally, he made her appreciate what a fine woman she was and that he celebrated all that she had done, all that she was and all that she would ever do.

It was an overwhelming experience for her. No matter what she did, Pete was there with a smile and a soft word telling her that everything was all right. It was always all right. Even when she treated him poorly, it was always all right. Eventually, she found it impossible to treat him poorly. His sensitivity was staggering, not at all like any man she had ever met. He wasn't afraid to cry. She had never seen a man cry before and she found it endearing. What a contrast, she thought, to the monster she had married. She wondered if Jack had ever felt passionate about anything enough to weep over.

Two days before, while walking her to her car, Pete told her that he had been having some very strong feelings but didn't think that he had the courage to address them. What a sweet man, thought Karen. "I love you too!" was her reply.

She thought he was going to crush her he hugged her so hard. With tears in his eyes, he echoed her words. They stood on Fourth Street for an eternity, holding each other and luxuriating in the magic that is new love.

Since that day, Pete had been flying. There was nothing that bothered him. For the first time in his life, he felt good about himself. He laughed at long lines in the commissary. Lockups on his state of the art computer that had him using the Lords name in vain three days previously were responded to with a simple shake of the head. Pete Butter Bean Peters wondered if life could get any better.

Karen had been flying too. While her marriage to Jack Slater was still fairly new, the constant abuse made it seem like a lengthy prison sentence. Then, along comes this little, round man and her life changes. She suddenly was excited by the new day. She lived for their next contact. Phone calls were a treasure, physical meetings were an adventure. Each new beating from Jack was just a little more endurable.

Two hearts had joined and the world celebrated.

May 1st, 1942, 4:52 AM
Ready Room, Grafton Underwood Air Field, England

"This sortie will require two midair fuelings." The Air Wing Commander, Captain Van Pelt, was giving a mission briefing. "Our target is Stalingrad. We'll fly thirteen sortie's. The 22's will lead..."

"This should end quite differently this time around." Kaitlyn Savage had taken a keen interest in history since her unexpected arrival in the past. High School history was a blur. She started to develop an interest in the past during the handful of college courses she had taken, but living in the past made it all just that much more immediate. Now, she was going to be involved in what had been the historic attack of Stalingrad.

May 1st. 1942, 6:22 AM
USS John C. Stennis

Yoder and O'Brien were on the bridge, watching the first launch of F-22's on their way to Stalingrad.

"You have to give it to Hitler for his organizational skills. He got reinforcements to Russia with incredible speed." Yoder was not above giving credit where it was due.

"Certainly didn't hurt him to have had a mysterious guardian angel dumping high explosive war heads on his enemy while he regrouped," Kelly countered. She would give Hitler no quarter.

"Well, this time around, the results should be dramatically different. In November, '42, the German Army was dreadfully overextended. Every available soldier was throw into that mess. The Soviets had a force of half a million men in defense and plenty of hardware to back them up. They formed a north pincer movement and within days routed the German Sixth Army. There were over three hundred thousand German soldiers trapped in Stalingrad. The Soviets did what the Germans had done in the beginning of the war, they divided them up and destroyed them in detail." Yoder was a student of World War 11 and was particularly fascinated with the war in the East. The loss of life was appalling. The fighting conditions inhuman.

"Hitler hauled Field Marshal Erich von Manstein to Army Group A headquarters and ordered him to relieve the troops at Stalingrad. Manstein had no troops and had to beg other commanders for men and machines to from Army Group Don. Hitler then ordered General Paulus to hold out based on the boasts of General Goering who claimed that he could keep the troops supplied with his

Luftwaffe. But he had too few planes and airfields. This guy loses half of his units in the first few weeks, and Paulus is left with his thumb up his ass and no supplies.

"By late December, Group Army Don is slam dunked at the Myshkova River. A month later, it's all over but for the crying. Almost a hundred thousand German prisoners are taken, only of which, I think, about five thousand return to the Mother Land. Another hundred and fifty thousand are killed and this is the end of Operation Barbarossa. Next stop for the Soviets, Berlin."

Harsh watched as the catapult hurled his airplanes into the sky with a huge mechanical whoosh and the ear splitting noise of the 22's engines going to afterburner. "It certainly is fun rewriting history."

May 1st, 1942 1:13 PM
Eighteen kilometers North East of Soesterberg, Holland, 15,900 feet above sea level

Ben-Gurion activated his ILS system. He switched to his refueling HUD, which now began tracking the KC135 flying tanker. Within moments he could discern the anti collision lights at the tip of the planes fin and under the center fuselage. His was fifteen miles away and ten thousand above the tanker as he switched to Victor 4 radio frequency and requested refuel permission.

"Affirmative Warrior, weapons and nose cold?"

Allan responded "Yes."

He reduced his radar output to EMCON 2. At a quarter of a mile out, Ben-Gurion was given the command "Cleared, pre contact.

"Approach now to tanker altitude, request permission to refuel." Allen was a thousand feet astern of the tanker.

At fifty feet behind the KC135, Allen heard "Cleared contact."

The fighter was now in position. He bought the plane forward slowly while watching the Recover Director Lights under the fuselage. There were markings to indicate whether he was coming in to high, hence a letter designation of D, to low, U, to fast, F or to slow, A.

Once in the proper position, Allen heard the operator on the tanker say "Stabilize, hold position while boom is flown to you." He then guided to boom to the fuel filler door on the top of the fighters fuselage. Allen couldn't see what was going on and relied on the operator in the tanker to place the boom. This was not nearly as difficult as putting down on the deck of a moving air craft carrier, but it still required intense concentration

"Contact made, fuel flowing." The tanker turned off the lower strobe. The upper and lower beacons now began to flash red.

"Affirm." Allen had felt the boom lock onto his plane.

Several minutes later the fighter had taken on a full load of fuel.

"Disconnect."

Allen throttled back the engines as the boom cleared his plane and slowly backed his F22 away from the tanker. He reduced altitude and banked right, keeping five thousand feet below the tanker so as to avoid collision.

Twenty minutes later, the three other fighters were fully fueled and on their way to alter history.

Lieutenant Ben-Gurion looked at his center MFD where there was a map displayed. Before takeoff, he had reprogrammed the way points in his navigational computer to take him to a new objective. As the flight flew over Thuringia, Germany, Allen keyed his mike.

"Dancer, I seem to be having a problem with my port engine." Kaitlyn Savage was flying wing man to Ben-Gurion.

"Sit tight, I'll do a fly around." Kaitlyn dropped fifty feet and eased her plane to the aft and right of Warrior. She took a hard look at both engines.

"I'm seeing nothing, what's your MFD saying."

"Port engine is running hot. I'm losing pressure."

"Let's take it home, Warrior." Protocol required the two planes to fly back together, the healthy one watching over the sick bird.

"No," answered Allen, "this is to important a mission. If our objectives are not met, the next sortie could be in real jeopardy. I can get home myself, this things got two engines."

"Roger that, but that's not by the book, I'm going home with you."

"No," Allen told his friend, "that's an order." Savage had no option now.

"Safe trip, Warrior."

Ben-Gurion banked his fighter north. He took it slow until his fellow pilots were out of visual range, then kicked in his afterburners. A few minutes later, he was not surprised to hear from Dancer.

"Warrior, what are you doing in afterburner with a hot engine, and why are you heading north?"

"Thanks for the concern, Dancer." Allen reached out and turned his radio off.

He was now to far away from anything in the air to interfere with his plans. His mind was on his mission, and on his people. Images of Jews being herded into gas chambers filled his thoughts. News reels showing babies being ripped out of the arms of their mothers brought him to despair. He could see huge trenches filled with the naked bodies of those persecuted because of their heritage. Tears charged down his face as he felt the pain of a not yet born nation. I will not allow this to continue, he vowed as his plane charged through the German skies at mach three.

Lieutenant Ben-Gurion turned on his target MFD, also reprogrammed before takeoff. The city of Berlin was now displayed. There was a red box marking the Chancellery Building.

At fifteen miles out, he lite off both of his AGM-65 Mavericks. Moments later, he unleashed all of his CRV-7 Rockets. Seconds later, there was a monstrous explosion directly in front of him. He recognized the Chancellery Building and smiled as he watched two thirds of it collapse.

Warrior now dropped the nose of his F22 and aimed it squarely at the still standing portion of the building. Audible warnings of low altitude filled the cockpit. Allen didn't hear them. It seemed to be taking a very long time for him to reach his final destination.

Finally, he was at roof height of the surrounding buildings. He held his stick true, touched the picture of Yehuda, Dov and Rachel that was tapped to the control panel and screamed "For my people!"

May 1st, 1942 3:42 PM
Bridge, USS. John C. Stennis

"Just got a visual confirmation from his wing man. What had been the Chancellery Building two hours ago is a big smoking hole now. He must have unleashed everything he had before sticking his fully fueled jet through what remained of the roof." Captain O'Brien was reporting to Captain Yoder.

"Think there could have been any survivors?"

"Doubt it, from what Dancer was saying. We'll have recon photos within the hour." There are times, Kelly O'Brien realized, when being the guy in charge was not good. He was going to get his ass kicked for the incredibly irresponsible act of one of his pilots.

"Maybe he wasn't in the building at the time," Yoder thought out loud.

"Don't you sort of hope he was?"

May 2nd, 1942 4:18 AM
Kremlin, Moscow

"Are you sure?"

"Yes, this has been confirmed." Viachislav Molotov, Commissar for Foreign Affairs, had just been given this most startling news.

Joseph Stalin sat back in his chair, put his hands across his belly and stared out the large window across from his desk. This was curious news indeed. His nemesis, Adolph Hitler, was dead.

"Is there any word as to how this happened?" He was not full of elation at the death of this miserable dictator, there were to many questions flooding his mind. So many strange things happening of late, most of them bad for Russia.

"The Chancellery was attacked from the air. The building was leveled."

Stalin knew the answer to his next question before asking it, "Do you know who was responsible for the attack?"

"No, sir, we don't. There was a series of rockets that struck the building. Apparently, the air craft responsible for the attack then crashed into the part of the building that was still standing. This was where Hitler's office was."

"You're dismissed." Stalin needed to ponder this new development in a war that was getting stranger by the minute. These phantom planes that had been screaming out of the sky from nowhere had decimated his artillery hours before in Stalingrad. The German Army was massed at its gates and without that artillery support, the probability of keeping them at bay was seriously diminished.

It was time to focus. Something he was finding it increasingly difficult to do. Sleep alluded him. His empire was being systematically wrenched from his formerly iron grasp. Russia seemed to have an unknown enemy who had strategic knowledge of his every move and possessed a mystical air power that destroyed his might almost at will.

Hitler was dead. How could he exploit this?

May 2nd, 1943, 6:13 AM
Captains Wardroom, USS *John C. Stennis*

"It's confirmed, Harsh, Hitler's dead." Captain O'Brien braced herself for the hurricane that was to come.

"God damn that son of a bitch, I knew I should've keel hauled him." The "angry" vein on Yoder's fore head was dancing like a worm on a hot sidewalk. Not only had this renegade pilot killed a temporarily important alley, but he lost a particularly valuable asset in the process. F22's are a finite commodity and not a reasonable use for kamikaze missions.

"Do we know who else was with him, for all we know, his entire staff could have been wiped out. This certainly is going to give an edge to Stalin, maybe just the edge he needs to turn this war around. Christ," Harsh slapped the table in front of him hard enough to make Kelly's coffee cup prance about, "what a stupid move."

"No, this isn't the days of CNN. There are no neutral reporters on the scene giving a blow by blow of the rescue efforts or the body counts. Don't count on the Wehrmacht to be sending out a press release telling us who was killed, either."

"Does Roosevelt know yet?"

"Yes," Kelly responded, " he was informed a few minutes ago. I expect you'll want to speak with him."

"I need to think for a few minutes. I don't think there's anything in the MJ 12 files that addresses this, shit, why would there be?" Yoder sat and stared at the brass clock hanging on the wall. It had been fashioned out of a steam gauge salvaged from the *USS Saratoga*. Interesting, he thought, what would happen if he bought it over to the *Saratoga*, would the two items still exist side by side in time? Would that act cause a rip in the time continuum? Had he watched to many *Star Trek* episodes back in the future?

"This Ben-Gurion wanted me to stop the Holocaust, like I could do that from the air. Shit, with Hitler gone the war will probably be prolonged at best. How many more Jews will die thanks to his absurd act. What a cluster fuck." Harsh went back to staring at the brass clock.

"We have Roosevelt on the line," Kelly was just informed.

"Put him on speaker." Harsh sat back and tried to collect his thoughts.

"Is that you Captain?" Even with this latest technology, speaker phones still sounded poorly.

"Yes, Mr. President, and I have Captain O'Brien with me."

"Good evening, Captain, though I suspect that it is still morning for you two. I have Henry with me. Harsh, what happened?" The Presidents voice was dripping with anxiety. He was very disturbed that one rogue pilot could cause such havoc.

"The pilot in question, one Lieutenant Allen Ben-Gurion, was passionate about ending the holocaust. He created a disturbance the afternoon you were first aboard the *Stennis*."

"Yes," answered Roosevelt, "I recall."

"Well, the short story is that he hijacked a full loaded F22 and stuffed it into Hitler's office. Adolph's dead and I'm concerned about the effect this is going to have on the will of the German people and the added resolve it will afford the Russians."

"We just heard about this less than an hour ago and haven't had much time to reflect on the consequences, but Henry has some thoughts."

"Yes, Captain Yoder, I do." Henry Stimson was to far away from the speaker and his voice was barely perceptible. The Navy tech always in attendance during these calls could be overheard directing Henry to lean forward. "Who fills Hitler's roll will determine, to a great extent, whether there is a lag in Germany's offensive strategy currently. We know Hitler had appointed Admiral Karl Von Donitz, the head of the Kreigs Marina, as his immediate successor. He is not a particularly adept political player and that could work very much against him, but he is a good military man.

"Next up is Herman Goering. He is a blow hard, full of bravado. He runs the Lufwaffe, but isn't much of a Field Marshall. His political muscle may be enough to bully his way into the position. Under him, however, is a fellow named Adolph Galland. Despite the rank of General, he will still jump into a plane and fly missions with his troops. He's enormously popular in military circles.

"Lastly, we have Field Marshal Irwin Rommel. Rommel is probably a military genius. He is also a reasonable man and beloved by those he commands. I think that any of these men, aside from Goering, will be a sound replacement for the departed Furor."

"This just in, Gentlemen," Harsh was just handed a slip of paper, "the attack on Stalingrad is underway. It doesn't look like Hitler's death is going to have an immediate effect on this war."

"**You two were** quite close. I'm so sorry about this." Father Anthony was sitting beside Kaitlyn Savage on the small couch in his office.

"It's bad enough to loose a friend in combat. Shit, that happens. I lost a fairly close friend in a training accident. But Allen killed himself! What the fuck did he do that for?"

It wasn't the time to address Valerie's aggressive vocabulary just now. "From what you've told me, he was quite torn up over the holocaust. Didn't he spend some time in jail because of his strong beliefs?"

"They call it the brig." She left it at that, not being in the mood to give him her customary hard time about his unfortunate knowledge of naval vocabulary.

"Clearly he thought that killing Hitler was going to end it," Anthony said, "though I don't know how. Hatred of the Jews ran deep in Nazi Germany."

This was a painful blow to Kaitlyn. Next to Anthony, Allen was her closest friend. She admired him as a professional and as a person. She felt the need to write a letter to his wife, Rachel, to let her know what a hero her husband was. She wondered if his insane but selfless act would even be recognized by the country he so loved, a country that had yet to be born?

May 3rd, 1942, 1:07 AM
War Room, Pentagon

Pete Peters was pouring over the most recent recon photos of the battle at Stalingrad. The sheer number of troops was astounding, more than three quarters of a million men with murder in their hearts. Stalingrad had taken a terrible beating from the German artillery for the better part of twenty hours without the wherewithal to answer back, thanks to air attacks delivered by the *Stennis* the previous day. The Russians had a clear advantage in the number of soldiers, but not, as was the case the first time around, in the number of big guns and tanks.

Stalin was using the same strategy he had been using all along, throw men into the machine and grind the enemy down. This time, however, Group Army South had far superior mechanized equipment and was inflicting serious damage on the soldiers of Russia with minimal loss on its part.

Pete thought he had become immune to the horrible human cost of war after the thousands of pictures he had viewed thus far, but this spectacle was truly devastating. The snow was crimson on the Russian side of the city. There were already thousands of dead Cossacks obscuring the ground and the battle was not even a day old. This was going to be a slaughter of epic proportions. Pete Peters was going to be an armchair witness to the whole sale destruction of hundreds of thousands of human lives. He felt queasy.

Within the hour, the pictures from the First Far Eastern Front would be in, promising to be equally disturbing from a human perspective. Japan had close to one million men on Russian soil and would be moving as a steam roller behind a path cut by the high tech war planes from the *Stennis*. Stalin was in a true two front war against hungry advisories who sensed that victory was predetermined. And then there were the phantom attacks from the air, making it impossible for him to move troops or set defensives without terminal harassment. Pete found himself feeling a moment of professional empathy for this horrible dictator.

There was constant activity on board the *Stennis*. Germany's war with Russia was at a critical mass. War planes were being directed to crucial areas to soften the road to Moscow and ultimate victory. Russia's ability to re-supply itself with mechanized equipment had been seriously hampered by air attacks. They were turning out less that twenty percent of what they had been able to historically manufacture based on figures in the *Stennis* data base. This loss of hardware, combined with the horrible destruction being administered from the air put Russia in a terminal position.

And then there was Japan.

"MacArthur will be following the opposite route the Russians took in '45 when they attacked Japan, he's charging right up through Manchuria." It was the end of a very active day. Harsh and Captain O'Brien were sitting in the Captain's mess, winding down. It was just after midnight.

"Do you expect Stalin to set up the same three fronts he did in '45?" Kelly was fascinated with military tactics, sometimes thinking that maybe she should have accepted the Governments offer to attend West Point instead of the Naval Academy, a thought she kept very much to herself.

"The First Far Eastern Front has already been established. He's been sending troops East for a few weeks, according to the intelligence Pete has given us. I don't think that he was shocked to find Japan at his back door. There is evidence that he's got more troops moving through the Gobi Desert and the Greater Khingan Range to form the Trans-Baikal Front. I would expect the Second Far Eastern Front to be formed after Japan kicks Stalin's ass at Iman and Khabarovsk."

Kelly's intense fatigue of a few minutes ago seemed to lift as she tried to crawl into Stalin's mind to imagine how he was going to combat this latest threat to his sovereignty. "What do we have planned in the way of sorties to Manchuria?"

"We are not going to be quite as aggressive in the East. We need to be a little conservative with our material. You know as well as I that we can't replace those Mavericks we've been air mailing to Stalin. At some point, we'll be using the Sidewinders and the ASRAAM's on ground targets. And, quite frankly, there is no real need to keep the Japanese army strong. When this is all over, if we play it right, America will be exactly where it was, influence wise, when we left. I firmly believe that we are the only country on earth that can be trusted to maintain a balance of power amongst all nations."

"Gosh, Harsh, you're going to make me cry." O'Brien had been on the boring end of Captain Yoder's patriotic posturing before, she wanted to stay on subject. "Pete estimates that Russia will send upwards of a million and a half men East."

"He has no choice. The first time around, Stalin was able to direct almost thirty thousand guns, five thousand plus tanks and close to that many aircraft to the three fronts. With what we've done to his factories, he'll be lucky to put ten percent of that on the ground. He's got nothing but man power now, and that ain't gonna stop a motivated, well equipped Japanese Army, even with our participation being somewhat truncated."

"Do you think the Chinese will sit by and allow Manchuria to be ceded to Japan without a big stinking fuss when this is all over?" Kelly had been concerned about China. They certainly had the ability to unbalance the new world order at some point.'

"China is going to be something of an issue. However, without support from Russia, both from a military perspective and financially, MJ 12 does not believe that China will develop into the military threat they were towards the latter part of the century. Russia will not possess a nuclear capability and therefore can't pass it along to them. Our nuclear weapons will give the United States a stick big enough to keep all the lesser nations in line. Fuck with us, and we'll give your country a half life of two thousand years."

"That's almost poetic Harsh. I think you need some sleep."

May 5th, 1942, 12:58 AM
USS John C. Stennis

Statistically, the odds of it happening were less than one in a hundred.

"You're what?" Father Anthony's face had been drained of blood. He looked painfully whiter than his normal pasty self.

"You heard me." Kaitlyn Savage was sitting on the couch in Anthony's office. She had been flying sorties for the past thirty hours and was buzzed. She couldn't sleep and decided now was as good a time as any to break the news to her lover Priest.

Anthony had stood up, then sat down. He didn't know what to do.

"How did it happen?"

"You might want to talk to the Little Pope about that."

He hated it when she called "it" that.

"I still don't understand, I..." He was at a loss.

"Were you paying attention during high school biology class. Remember that whole happy little sperm swimming to the egg thing?"

She was being a little to playful about this, he decided. Dear God, he'd been called upon to council a young couple three years ago who had gotten themselves into this predicament, he would have never wagered that he'd be on the ugly side of that talk one day.

"I thought you were on the pill?" he was almost pleading now, hoping that she'd say yes and therefore this could never have happened.

"I was. But even the pill isn't one hundred percent effective. The failure rate is dramatically low, but this does happen."

Anthony sat down and stared at his shoes. "This whole thing was wrong. God is surely punishing me now, punishing us now. This is horrible."

Kaitlyn moved closer to him and put her arm around his shoulder. "I think that you are looking at this from the wrong perspective. This is not a punishment, it's a gift. A gift of life. This child was conceived in love." Her voice was soft and gentle, he had never heard her speak this way. She took his face in her hands and turned it towards hers. "I love you and I want to marry you and I want to have this child with you."

Father Anthony felt tears erupting from his eyes. They had never spoken of any kind of a commitment. He had harbored such thoughts deep in his mind but never had the courage to give them the light of day. He was overwhelmed.

"With me?" he choked out.

"Yes, of course with you." Kaitlyn was touched by this gentle mans humble nature. She fell in love with him all over again.

It had been close to two days since Pete had seen the inside of his apartment. The Battle of Stalingrad was ostensibly over. It would take another week before Russia would agree to that, but from the unique perspective Butter Bean had, there was no possible chance for Stalin to turn the fight around. He had no troops within a few days march to aid the terribly beleaguered men currently trapped in Germany's killing machine, and if there were, Yoder would most likely destroy them with a few air sorties. Stalin was pulling troops, but they were on their way to Moscow where he was obviously engineering his last stand. That, worried Pete, was going to be an epic World War 11 battle. Men were going to die the hard way, as if there was any other way in war. He estimated over a million casualties for Russia in that engagement on top of the quater of a million plus that have lost or will be losing their lives in Stalingrad.

His head was spinning with both the staggering amount of death he had been privy to for the past two days and the loss of sleep he'd been dealing with during that time. Pete was looking forward to a few hours of snooze time before the next batch of recon photos arrived. He pushed open the door to his place, threw the keys on a desk in the foyer and headed to the bedroom.

As he passed the living room, something caught the corner of his eye. Pete stopped and looked at the couch. He was so painfully tired he suspected that his eyes were deceiving him. Stepping a few feet closer he recognized that there was indeed a body on his laying there and that it was indeed Karen. Pete smiled broadly even before his cognitive powers caused him to wonder just what the hell she was doing there.

Karen stirred as she heard Pete come into the room. She opened her eyes and returned his smile. It took a moment for her to clear her sleep soaked mind.

"The Super let me in." She answered the question she knew was coming.

In his current mental state, it took him a moment to realize that the question he was formulating had been addressed and that it was time for a new one.

"How long have you been here?" He really wanted to just tell her how pleased he was that she was there but was unable to think very quickly just now.

She looked at her watch. "Oh my, it's almost two in the morning, I guess I've been here since nine."

Karen sat up. She was rumpled and had that dopey look that is unique to those newly arrived from the land of nod. He hair was pointing in several directions and the make up that was not on the pillow she had been sleeping on was smudged all over her face. What a beautiful sight, Pete thought. He walked over to the couch and sat down besides her and noticed that the blob of mascara under her left eye was not mascara at all. He pulled her close to him and hugged her hard. He didn't ask. She tucked her head into his shoulder and cried.

"I'm glad you came to me." Pete so wanted to be supportive to her. He had never been in this role before and it felt good.

"There was no where else I could turn," Karen sobbed. "There was no one else I wanted to turn to."

He pulled her closer to him. He felt stirrings that he immediately deemed inappropriate. They had kissed and fondled a few times, but now he wanted more. Pete just couldn't understand why he'd feel like this while she was in such a vulnerable position. When she tilted her head up and kissed him, he was in no condition to counter her move.

Their lips locked, tongues darted. They both knew that their passion would not be ebbed tonight. For an eternity they exchanged touches. Hands migrated to places of intense intimacy. Clothes were discarded.

Pete had shared love, no, had sex, exactly once in his life. It was more of a mercy fuck by a particularly pretty woman his senior year at *Princeton*. She found out that he was a virgin and decided that he shouldn't graduate that way. It was memorable for its newness but he decided that he'd not do that again unless there were some fairly strong feelings involved. Tonight the feelings were strong enough to move a warship.

Holding Karen's naked body close to his filled him with feelings he'd not known before. He wanted to take this moment and preserve it forever so that he could retrieve it whenever he wanted. He kissed every part of her body that he could get his lips near. Pete was sure he was not dazzling her with his technique, he felt clumsy. But he did feel passionate and that was exactly what she was sensing.

Jack was a talented lover, but he was without feelings. It was all very mechanical with him. Karen hadn't known such passion. This short, heavy little man was making her feel more like a woman than she had ever felt in her short life.

"I need you inside me."

Pete was not about to make that move without a clear invitation. Her request, he figured, was pretty clear. Pete did as was requested.

And then it was over.

"It's all right," Karen purred in his ear. She could feel his tears on her face. She knew that he must be terribly embarrassed. What she did not know was that he was not embarrassed at all. Pete was so full of emotion at sharing this most intimate of acts with someone he loved so dearly that he could do nothing but cry.

May 23rd, 1942, 9:07 AM
Oval Office, The White House

"Stalin will not roll over and take it in the shorts." It was a phrase that had seen enough usage on either side of the desk that Yoder was not at all uncomfortable using it anymore. He had returned to the States just last evening to have an important strategy session with all the major players.

"I'd not expect him to, Captain, but what you are proposing seems somewhat drastic." FDR was indeed a humanitarian, he abhorred the horrific loss of life that he had been privy to thus far and the use of another nuclear weapon made his stomach turn.

"Mr. President, I appreciate your discomfort with this new technology, but people are going to die. They're going to do it slow or fast, it is to our benefit, and probably theirs, to do it fast." The weapon stores onboard the *Stennis* were dwindling and there was still another enemy to fight.

"Captain," Roosevelt's voice was pitched. He paused to give himself a moment to gather himself. "Harsh, I still have nightmares about the women and children we obliterated in Sapporo, I don't want to add the women and children of Moscow to those awful reveries."

Those sitting about this most powerful office in the world were fairly well divided as to how to proceed with the covert war they were fighting.

"While Rommel was brilliant with his tactics at Stalingrad, I think we were all greatly surprised by the appalling losses Group Army South suffered on their way to Moscow." Eisenhower had been pouring over recon photos at the Pentagon for the past three days. It was certainly an antiseptic way to watch a war, but it didn't make death any easier to view.

Stalin had taken a page from America's Revolutionary War strategy guide and pretty much abandoned Stalingrad. He played a hit and run war with Germany. He knew where they were going. It was easy enough to place platoons all over the place to harass the invading Hun at every step. Group Army Center couldn't set up camp for the night due to the lightening fast attacks by poorly equipped but highly motivated Russian soldiers. By the time the Germans were able to muster a counter attack, the Russians were gone and there were fifteen to thirty dead Germans lying in the mud. These attacks were occurring all up and down the snake path of men and machines marching toward the final showdown.

The early rains were not a friend of the Germans heavy Panzer tanks or half track trucks pulling artillery. There were days when forward movement was measured in yards. A dozen tanks were lost to suicide attacks by lone soldiers carrying satchel charges.

The Russian resistance was so splintered that the incredible air superiority of the *Stennis* was all but impotent. Yoder was not about to trash a Maverick on a platoon of vodka soaked Russians hiding in a barn.

"Yes, I concur, General, but do we really have a problem with that." Henry Stimson was again acting the role of the devil's advocate.

"We do," interjected Captain Yoder. "Without our help, the attack on Moscow may not be successful. To have come this far and wind up with an intact Russia would be tragic. We need to take every precaution to make certain that the Soviet Union does not attain world power status and a nuclear capability. The future of man kind depends on this."

"Rommel has already shown himself to be a dramatically more competent commander than Hitler, don't you think he has the skills to take Moscow." Roosevelt was looking for any reason not to authorize the use another nuclear weapon.

"He'll take Moscow, but the cost will be overwhelming. Remember, we need Germany to not only defeat Russia, but to dismantle it. Without the ground troops, that is going to be impossible." Yoder realized, after looking at the recon photos of the defensive position Stalin had taken in Moscow that the only way to assure victory of Nazi Germany was the use of nukes.

"We need to act quickly. Rommel already has troops within five klicks of the city, they will probably be killed in the blast. We want to minimize his losses at this point." Harsh Yoder sat back to let the inevitable debate rage until the politicians and the military men both came to terms. He needed to get a Seahawk in the air soon.

May 27th, 1942, 7:31 AM
Berlin, Germany

"Would you repeat that."

General Alfried Jodl repeated what he had just told Commander-in-Chief Rommel moments ago, "Moscow has been destroyed."

Irwin Johannes Eugen Rommel sat back and digested this bit of information.

"How?" The frontal attack by Group Army South was not scheduled to begin for another forty eight hours. Reserves were being diverted in preparation for what was to be expected to be the most difficult battle of the campaign.

"Eye witness reports say that the city just blew up sometime after two in the morning. The blast was so large we lost close to three thousand men who were encamped a few kilometers for the city. There are reports of large number of injuries to troops considerably further out."

This was the oddest military occurrence he had encountered since he joined the 124th Infantry Regiment as an officer cadet in 1910. Rommel served as a second lieutenant during World War 1, fighting on the Romanian and Italian fronts. His excellent service earned him a regimental command after the war. His textbook on tactics, *Infanterie greift*, was published in 1937, affording him strong exposure. Shortly thereafter, he was appointed commandant of the War Academy at Wiener Neustadt. During the marches into the Sudetenland and Prague, Rommel was responsible for Hitler's safety.

His career really took off in June of 1942 when he was made the youngest Field Marshal in the German Army in recognition of his success in forcing the British back from Cyrenaica to El Alamein. Now, after Hitler's death, he found himself in charge of the best fighting force in the world. The war in the east was going fairly well and Rommel was confident of a final victory at Moscow.

Now, Moscow has mysteriously disappeared. Miraculously disappeared? He was aware of the phantom rocket planes that had been appearing out of no where and aiding Germany's efforts. More than likely, the super bomb that eliminated Sapporo was used against Moscow. At what point would it be used against Berlin?

Stalin was probably dead. More that half the Russian Army had been disintegrated in an evening. Now it was time to move his forces west to destroy what was left of Stalin's army and to keep the Japanese from occupying any more territory.

Then, it would be time to resurrect Operation Sealion.

"Hey, they just nuckleated Russia." Parnes Williams was freshly arrived from serving duty.

Tim continued squeezing his pastry bag, intent on creating yet another perfect pastry puff. It was beginning to frighten him that he so enjoyed creating elegant deserts for the officers. If those fucks on his high school soccer team could see him now, they would have no questions concerning his sexuality.

"Wait a minute," Tim smiled. He was beginning to wonder if Parnes was just putting him on with his malicious use of the Queens English. Could anybody be that stupid? "There's no such word as nuckleated."

"Shit man, you know, we dropped the big one on Russia."

Tim put his pastry bag down and wiped powered sugar from his cheek. "Where'd you hear this?"

"Heard it from the man his self."

"Yoder, you heard this from Captain Yoder. You his father confessor now?"

Parnes laughed, "He don't confess nothin to me. Heard him talkin about it while I was serving him some of those fine pastries you made." He reached over and popped some raw dough into his mouth.

"Russia is an awfully large place, we couldn't possible have nuked the whole thing. Could you be more specific?" Tim was real interested in what was going on outside the kitchen of the *USS John C. Stennis*. There was plenty of scuttlebutt as to exactly why they had been catapulted back sixty years in time. Tim thought he had it figured and this latest bit of news was giving credence to his hypothesis.

"Jesus Irwin, how much payin attention do you think I can do when serving the man? Think I want to end up in the brig for pouring wine on the Captain's lap?" Parnes knew it was important to Tim and put on his "thinkin" face to let him know. To add emphasize his mental exertions, he placed his giant left hand under his chin. Had he not been eating raw dough with that very hand, he would not have gotten white flour all over his ebony chin. "I'm thinkin Moscow. I might have overheard them say Moscow."

"Holy shit! If they whacked Moscow, then Stalin must be dead. History suggests that he'd never leave the city. If he's gone, then Germany's war with Russia must be about over." Tim was smiling now. "That was the objective, don't you get it?" He knew Parnes didn't get it, it was really just a figure of speech. "We needed to destroy Russia in order to keep them from developing into a world power and gaining their own nuclear capability that ultimately wound up in the wrong hands." He was all but dancing with excitement. His first thought was to go share this news with his friend and frequent cell mate, Lieutenant Ben-Gurion. What a sad personal loss that was, he thought.

"Well, if that's the case, our work is done here, let's go home."

"We're home, partner, get used to that," Tim slammed him with some needed reality.

"Shit, I know some big redneck white boy in a sheet is gonna lynch my ass. I gotta get home." Parnes was still suffering from nightmares generated by the "Mountain of Shit" incident.

"Yoder already told us that they can't back engineer this time travel technology. Don't worry, I'll watch over that big black ass of yours." Tim was sincere about that. "Now, however, what do you think they are going to do with Nazi Germany?"

"They can't be much better than those assholes in the white sheets."

"They are considerably worse than those assholes in the sheets. There is no way the Wehrmacht is going to be aloud to stand whole. I suspect that now that they've done our bidding by destroying Russia, the US is going to pull a modified D Day and get troops over to Europe but quick to kick some Nazi ass. Might be a little tougher with Rommel in the big chair. He can command rings around the dearly departed Furor."

Tim looked down at the rows of pastry puffs he had so lovingly created. "I've got to figure a way to get my ass into this war."

June 13th, 1942, 9:32 PM
Oval Office, White House

"**Doug, can you** hear me?" A rig unit had been set up in Tokyo to enable instant communications between the Roosevelt and MacArthur. This was it inaugural use.

"Yes Sir, I can hear you fairly well." Mac was alone in his office, except for a tech from the *Stennis*. He did not want his Japanese counter parts privy to this conversation.

"From the photographs we are getting, your yellow hoard is experiencing some success on their march through Manchuria." Roosevelt and Stimson were also alone with their *Stennis* tech man.

"As of twenty one hundred hours, they have secured the Trans-Baikal Front. Iman is unprotected and what's left of the Russian Army is holed up in Khabarovsk."

"General, have your armies attack Khabarovsk." Roosevelt was reading from orders drawn up by MJ 12.

"To what end, Mr. President?" An odd question coming from the man who wanted to chase the Chinese Army across the 38th parallel during the Korean Conflict, Roosevelt thought. Having the hind sight of history certainly added keen interest to many proceedings.

"We are not interested in a particularly strong Japanese Army at the end of all of this. If they even tangle with the Germans, so much the better, don't you agree Henry?"

"Yes, Franklin. General, I'd rather like telling the Japanese that they can have as much territory as they can grab, give them some incentive to mop up the Russians and give the Germans a bit of a go of it. It will all serve our purpose."

"So be it, Mr. President." Douglas MacArthur had orders he could sink his teeth into.

June 13th, 1942, 7:32 AM
Briefing Room, *USS John C. Stennis*

"Here it is, Gentlemen, Pennenmunde." Conrad Schmidt had just placed a large map on the table the six other SEAL team members were surrounding. "The good Captain has booked us on a one day, all expense paid trip to the island of Wolgast, where the Nazi's have been developing and manufacturing their dastardly V-1 rockets."

"Did he get us round trip tickets?" Hector Vega asked.

"Sure, check your vacation packets and you'll find first class tickets on Delta," reported George Olsen.

"All right, fellas, let's get focused here. We'll have two objectives. Our primary mission is to assassinate three Nazi scientists. Apparently, they were doing advanced work in nuclear fission and somebody wants to make real sure they don't ever complete their research."

"Who are they." George Olsen was nicknamed Einstein. He had a Masters from Columbia and a vast knowledge of just about everything.

"Let's see." Conrad leafed through the binder before him. "Fritz Strassmann is first up."

"Jesus, he and Otto Hahn won a Nobel Prize in chemistry for discovering that barium could be produced by bombarding uranium with neutrons, which brought about the process of fission."

Schmidt looked up for the binder with a clear look of surprise on his face. "Where the hell do you store all this information, Einstein?" He went back to the papers before him. "His pal Otto is also on the list. Last up is the unfortunately named Weiner Heisenberg."

"That should be Werner. He's known for the uncertainty principal. If memory serves", Olsen looked up at the ceiling, causing Hector to glance up to be sure there weren't answers taped to a light fixture, "he led the German efforts at the Max Planck Institute to construct an atomic bomb."

"Thank-you for the background, George. Our secondary goal is to destroy the research center, right over here," Conrad pointed to a square building in the north east corner of the base.

"Why don't they just drop a few Paveway 11's on the place and be done with it?" Kyle Rogers was a thinking man. He wasn't shy about putting himself in harms way,

Time Shift/340

but not before making damn well sure there wasn't an easier way to do things.

"They want to be certain that these three scientist are terminated with extreme prejudice. An aerial campaign couldn't guarantee that. Intelligence has determined that there is going to be a big meeting held on the island in five days. Typically these three guys don't get together. We have a great opportunity to whack them all at once. It is also extremely imperative that we destroy the records that are stored on the base."

"Someone is going to great deal of trouble to staunch the flow of nuclear weapon information." Dempsey was the junior member of the team. He had turned twenty four three days ago.

"Do you remember," Olsen asked him, "why we traveled back in time?"

Lieutenant Savage glanced down at her center MFD to confirm what she had suspected, she was at the correct coordinates, there wasn't a landmark in sight. "Break right and go out a hundred yards, start the camera on my mark." She and Lieutenant Jim Clark were flying their F22's on a photo recon mission. They were on the outskirts of what had been, six hours earlier, Moscow.

Kaitlyn had flown over the city three times during the past few weeks on her way to deliver ordinance and had visited Moscow back in 1999 while on a joint operation with the Russian Air Force. It had been a fairly depressing city back then. The economy had been ruinous for two years and there was a pall over the city that was palpable. The place, however, looked much worse now. Hell, there wasn't anything left. There was a huge crater at ground zero and nothing for miles around.

"Start cameras."

June 16th, 1942, 9:54 AM
War Room, Pentagon

"**As you can** see from the latest pictures, Moscow is a vacant lot now." For twenty kilometers from ground zero there wasn't a building standing. Past that, any structure still standing was heavily damaged. There were no bodies visible until close to fifty klicks out.

"What is your estimate as to the number of people killed?" Roosevelt wondered if he really wanted to know the answer.

It was another heavy weight audience Pete was speaking with. Roosevelt, Stimson, Eisenhower, MacArthur, Knox, Bradley, Hawlsey and half a dozen other men he couldn't immediately recognize. It was still heady stuff giving a briefing to such a historically august group. "That is difficult to say, Mr. President. A nuclear blast doesn't leave much in the way of physical evidence, as you can see, there aren't any visible bodies for miles from ground zero, however, looking at the recon photos taken twelve hours earlier, there was an estimated three quarter to one million people in the city. Now, there are none."

"When will it be safe for the German troops to enter the ruins?" Captain Yoder, also present at the meeting, found it odd that he was concerned for the safety of the Nazi's.

"My estimate is that no one should enter the restricted area unprotected for at least a week. This is information I pulled from my data base, there could be two days plus or minus depending on the condition of the soil. The rains they've been getting have softened up the ground and that will probably mean the fallout will stick around a little longer. The latest pictures we have do show soldiers on the move into the city. These guys will probably be dead within two weeks. Unfortunately, they will die slowly so there won't be any immediate warning to additional troops to stay away. Unless we can warn them, they are poised to loose upwards of thirty thousand men to radiation poisoning."

"Would we want to warn them if we could?" asked Ike. "Now that Russia has been defeated, Germany will now be fighting us. I'd love to eliminate thirty thousand soldiers without firing a shot."

"I tend to agree with you General," returned Yoder. "as long as they have enough troops left to mop up the remnants of the Russian Army, I don't have a whole lot of concern for Rommel's boys."

"Doug, what's going on with your Japanese Army?"

"Well, Mr. President, we, they, were stalemated at Khabarovsk for two days. When Moscow went up in flames, the Russians retreated. I don't know that they really know where they are going, they are just moving north. I suspect that without the Central Committee to tell them what to do, they are acting with self-preservation in mind. They certainly don't want to tangle with the German Army and I suspect that they don't feel there is any reason to stand at Khabarovsk. I would like to pursue and destroy them."

"Do you have the capability to do that?" asked Yoder. "I'd like to not have a Russian Army roaming about as the country is being partitioned."

"I believe we do. I still have half a million troops, a quarter of them are fresh. The rains have not been a problem in Manchuria and my mechanized units are healthy. I have an army that can move quickly. These Japanese are surprisingly good soldiers. I'm glad we didn't have to fight them in the Pacific."

"General Eisenhower, how are you set for the invasion of Europe?" Once the US entered the war, realized FDR, it all became real. It would be American boys dying.

"Very well, Sir. We have two million men in place and the ships necessary to get them to England. Once we declare war on Germany, our friend from the future should be able to secure the English Channel and allow for an unfettered landing."

"That's correct, General," added Yoder. "We will be able to eliminate all resistance at Calais to allow for a safe and orderly transfer of troops onto French soil. At the same time, my fighter planes will be reeking havoc on Germany's horribly extended supply lines. By the time our troops engage the Wehrmacht, they will be tired and poorly equipped."

"Splendid, gentlemen, then I shall expect a short war." No reason not to put a little early pressure on his Generals.

CHAPTER 10
The Covert War with Germany

June 18th, 1942, 3:13 AM
35,000 feet over Wolgast Island

"Ten minutes to drop zone," the Jump Master announced to SEAL Team 3.

"Gentlemen, final check." Ensign Conrad Schmidt turned around so George Olsen could check his gear, in a moment, he'd do the same for George.

Halo jumps were always inherently dangerous. Any time you jump high and open your shoot low, small problems can become real big problems in nanoseconds. Their altimeters were set to open at five hundred feet. The good news was that the time in the air hanging like big, living targets was greatly minimized. The bad news was that if there was a problem, it would likely be a terminal one. They weren't even rigged with reserve shoots, there just wouldn't be time enough to deploy them.

They were all dressed in black. Each wore kevlar body protection, capable of stopping rounds from any of the small arms they were likely to encounter once on the ground. Each man carried a varied assortment of weapons and accessories. Due to the parameters of the mission, they were all issued a HK MP5-A2. The A2 was a short range but highly accurate, fully automatic weapon. It was also silenced, as was their secondary weapon, the Beretta 9mm 92FS hand gun. Their primary objective was to terminate three scientists. There was no reason to make a big ruckus while doing so and attract the attention of close to three hundred Nazi soldiers. Their secondary objective, destroying the research facility, would make a big noise and attract all manner of attention, all the better to aid their extraction. The plan was to spend no more than sixty minutes on the base. The team members carried little else other than extra ammo, PVS-5 night vision goggles, door charges, communication gear and C4 explosives.

"Go to oxygen." The Jump Master ordered as he opened the rear doors of the C130 transport plane they were flying. The Hercules was borrowed from the Air Force hours before the *Stennis* departed the future and was hoisted onto her deck. As it was not Air Craft capable, it had to be hoisted back off the deck and trucked, in pieces, to the nearest air base.

The plane slowed to one hundred and twenty five knots. They were thirty five thousand feet above the island of Wolgast. There were few lights on down below at this hour but there was a full moon. The moon cast a beautiful blue light over the sleeping towns they were flying over. It was, however, a potentially deadly light. The advantage the night vision goggles afforded these warriors from the future was going to be negated by the moons light. In many of the situations they were going to be in, the German soldiers were going to be playing on a pretty much equal visual playing field.

The Jump Master watched the release lights draw closer together. There were a series of red lights on a console near the door to indicate exactly how close they were to the drop zone. When the lights went green, it was go time.

"Sixty seconds."

Despite the number of jumps he'd made, this was when Conrad started to feel the tension. He had nothing to do now, his mind was free to catalog all the things that could go wrong. The drop zone was ten seconds long. That gave the Jump Master plenty of time to get all seven of them out of the plane, especially as they were jumping from the huge rear door. They would essentially step out into the darkness together. That was the easy part. Landing together would be critical to a successful mission. There just wasn't going to be enough time to wait for stragglers to catch up to the main group.

"Five, four, three, two, GO, GO, GO."

They took more of a leap than a step. Almost in unison, SEAL Team 3 departed the C130 and began a trip that would take them thirty five thousand feet straight down at a terminal velocity of one hundred and twenty five miles an hour.

Conrad fell easily into the classic sky diving position, face down, back arched, arms and legs splayed. He had approximately three minutes of free fall before having to deploy his chute. He made a quick check to be sure the others were with him, then looked down and enjoyed the ride. It was an even more exhilarating jump than usual as he was falling into hostile territory.

Peenemunde was barely three km wide by nine long. Their landing zone was on the west coast of the base, equidistant between Docks 1 and 2. There was a small POW compound less than fifty meters from the barracks that they would be passing and there was talk of liberating the prisoners. That noble plan was abandoned when Conrad figured that the prisoners would just be shot down as they attempted to make the coast.

"Shit," Conrad barked to himself. At about fifteen thousand feet, he saw a lone guard strolling along the beach almost directly underneath them. There was no way he wasn't going to hear the sharp report of seven MC1-1 shoots popping almost as one. Conrad calculated that by the time the sentry figured out where the sound had come from, he'd have his MP5 liberated from his leg holster and have been able to draw a bead on the soldier. This was going to be tight.

Conrad looked to each of his fellow flyers and realized that they all had formulated the same plan. He indicated, with a series of finger points, that he and Vega would attempt the shot. No sense in all seven of them lighting off rounds in the dark while in such close proximity to each other.

Conrad looked hard at his altimeter. He decided to open early to give himself a few additional seconds to line up his shot. Maybe the sound of one shoot opening would not alert the guard to the falling assassins.

At seven hundred and fifty feet, he pulled his rip cord. Within four seconds he heard the reassuring whack of silk slowing his decent. From one hundred and twenty five miles and hour to almost zero in moments was tough on the body. It took him another second to orient himself, then another two seconds to get hold of his weapon.

It took a moment more locate his prey. The moonlight certainly was beneficial here. The guard had heard the shoot open but was unable to discern where the noise had come from. Conrad was about to unleash a pair of rounds when suddenly Rogers shoot deployed right between he and the guard. Within a second, all six shoots opened with enough noise to aide the Nazi guard in locating where the strange sound had originated from.

He looked up and saw the amazing sight of men drifting down from space. Rogers was still in the way, obscuring Con's shot. As Hector pulled his gun, the guard hoisted his rifle to his shoulder and fired three rounds. Before he could get a fourth released, he caught two bullets in the chest. Rogers shoot glided by just in time for Conrad to see the guard fall.

The chest shot delivered by Vega, unfortunately, was not an instant kill. They all heard the soldier crying out in pain. Conrad let go a three round burst, two of which struck the solder in the head. He would make no more noise in this world.

As they hit the beach, each man rolled to absorb the impact of the landing. The plan was to gather up the shoots and cache them in a stand of trees near the beach so as not to announce their arrival to a wandering guard. There would be no time now. They could hear the sound of soldiers heading their way. There would be just enough time to jettison their shoots and harnesses and move out.

"On me," Conrad whispered. The six other men fell in behind him. Conrad had to make a quick decision, move forward and head toward their first objective or stay and eliminate the pursuers. There seemed to be only one path leading to the beach. He suspected that their charge would not be particularly orderly and decided that it may be fairly easy to take them out as they ran in a nice neat line like a row of ducks. He quickly divided his men into two groups, each flanking the path.

They waited less than ten seconds before seeing the first soldier. The silenced MP5's made a puffing sound as rounds were dislodged from their stubby barrels. The fastest man in the group caught close to thirty rounds in his head and chest. He dropped quickly, opening up an opportunity to do the same to the second fastest man. All five guards died before anyone of them could react.

Conrad pointed his finger in the sky and revolved it about an imaginary ball. The rest of the squad fell in behind him as he began what would now be a treacherous trip to the building that billeted the scientists.

The base was waking up. Sirens were blaring, soldiers were running about. Without a living eyewitness to let the Commander know what the threat was there appeared to be a tremendous amount of confusion amongst the guards.

As they approached an open area that had to be traversed, the first bit of good luck since they had arrived occurred, a large cloud passed in front of the moon. What had, moments before, been a magnificent killing field, was now a dark and somewhat safe twenty meter stretch. Without a prompt, each man put on his night vision goggles.   The world turned bright green as the optical system took minute amounts of ambient light and magnified it many times to make the darkest recess of the camp eminently viewable.

"Keep to the shadows." Conrad took point and led his team towards the "Kill house," the sobriquet assigned to the barracks housing the marked scientists. They had a good two klicks to go and lots of ways to die before they hit their primary objective.

A compromise had to be made between moving safely and quickly. Had their infiltration been clean, they would have chosen the former, but with the current activity on the base, speed was of the essence.   It was this unfortunate conundrum that had Conrad facing a German soldier with his weapon leveled at Con's chest as he came running around the corner of a building. The soldier fired from a distance of less than five meters.

The bullet struck Conrad in the left shoulder. The impact lifted him off his feet and spun him around. He hit the brick wall near him and then dropped to the ground. Before the soldier could fire again, there was the distinctive puff of Olsen's MP5 dispatching the soldier.

"You OK?" Rogers was the first to reach Con. He knelt near him, pulled off his goggles and began a visual check for a sign of blood that would suggest an entrance wound.

"Christ," Conrad rasped, "I feel like I've been hit by a truck."

Kyle found where the round had hit Con's kevlar vest. There was a black ring surrounding a deep indention. "Doesn't look like it went through."

The remaining five formed a perimeter around their fallen leader, each looking outward, preparing to intercept any new incoming threats.

"Can you move your shoulder?"

Conrad attempted the request and then vibrated in pain.

"I think it's dislocated."

Conrad took a breath. "This isn't the first time. Help me sit up, get behind me and put your knee on my shoulder blade. Try to pop it back in."

This is gonna hurt, Kyle knew as he helped Conrad up.

The first two attempts were horribly painful and unsuccessful. Conrad didn't make a noise, but Kyle could feel him shake with each failed attempt. The third effort resulted in a satisfying pop as the shoulder snapped into place. The pain that was torturous seconds ago was greatly minimized.

Conrad jumped to his feet and shook his head. Though the pain was lessened his head was still not clear. "Olsen, take point. Let's get the hell going."

Most of the activity seemed to be centered at the beach. Good news for now as most of the soldiers were heading in that direction. The bad news was that their exfiltration point was exactly where all the action was.

Olsen stopped the squad behind a small brick building. "There it is." The Killing House was ten meters away. There were no guards around the building. They still had the security of that large cloud obscuring the moon. "Once we get inside, Vega comes with me upstairs, Con stay down and watch the door." There was no reason for Conrad to sweep the second floor as was originally planned in his current condition. "Let's move."

The front door was surprisingly unlocked. The seven men entered quietly but quickly, three headed up the stairs directly in front of the door. Two stayed on the first floor, one black clad figure went left, the other right. Conrad moved to the left of the door, keeping watch for anyone unfortunate enough to enter the building. Each had memorized the faces of the three targets from photos in the files.

The scientist behaved as expected, they kept their lights off and cowered under the covers. Two had gotten out of bed and had their noses pressed against a window at the back of the building. Vega cut them down with two three round bursts, neither a designated target. Conrad heard the muffled reports from Vegas MP5 and the thud of two bodies. He hoped he'd gotten lucky and caught two of the intended together.

They had not planned on executing everyone in the building, but it turned out to be easier to shoot first and then ID the body later. It took less than two minutes to sweep both floors. Twelve men lay dead.

"Report," Conrad ordered as the team assembled near the front door.

"Heisenberg is a confirmed kill," reported Olsen.

"Strassmann is toast," added Vega.

"What about Hahn?"

There was a group head shake.

"Have all the bodies been ID'd?" A thirty percent failure rate here was not acceptable to Ensign Schmidt.

"We checked them all, he's not here. There's a bed on the second floor that hasn't been slept in," volunteered Vega.

"Fuck, they were all suppose to be here." Conrad's shoulder began to hurt again, so did his pride. Only two of three primary targets were eliminated and there was a zero probability of destroying the secondary objective.

"Let's get out of here, Rogers, take point."

Each man stepped out of the door and turned left, hugging the side of the building, trying to make himself as visually innocuous as possible. By now, the base was alive with soldiers. Most of them were heading for the V-1 launch pads and the rocket storage area. Clearly, protecting those assets was of prime importance to the Nazi's. This meant the south eastern end of the base was fairly quiet.

SEAL Team 3 made their way towards the shore. They moved quickly, but deliberately. Kyle stopping to peer around the corners of obstructions before charging across open areas. The cloud that had been of such a help minutes ago was now beginning to break up, causing moments when the moon light was so strong, the night vision goggles shut down. This presented a possibly deadly situation as there was close to a second when the wearer had no vision at all.

"Lose the goggles, except Vega." Kyle figured that at least one of them should keep his activated, there were still pockets of dark that could prove problematic.

Kyle led the team, as was the operations plan, around the back of the army barracks, which had been vacated, and past the POW camp. It was difficult not to pop the handful of guards and blow open the gate. They were making good time on their way to Dock 3 where the exfiltration helicopter would be waiting five miles off shore.

Because the secondary objective was dropped, the full sixty minutes that had been allocated to the mission was not needed. It had been less than thirty five minutes since they had landed on the island. There was little between the squad and Dock 3 now but a field of sea grass. The dock, however, was another story.

A stand of scrub trees seventy meters out provided protection as Olsen scanned the dock area with a pair of binoculars. There were thirteen soldiers scattered about the area, five on shore, eight positioned on the dock itself, a wooden affair that was about one hundred meters long. There was an empty barge moored port side.

"Let's break into two groups, Vega, Olsen and I will approach from the left, the rest of you from the right. We'll take out the land based guards, then Vega and I will slip into the water and see if we can eliminate the rest of them one at a time. When the shit hits, Schmidt and Dempsey will sweep right up the dock. Let's go." Kyle crouched and stepped out from the cover of the trees, Vega and Olsen followed.

The shore based guards were walking anxiously back and forth, eyes scanning both inland and out. There was little cover, other than the fortuitous return of darkness. "Give us eight minutes," Rogers quietly requested of the clouds. They all donned their night vision goggles.

It took three and a half minutes to position themselves twenty meters down from the closest guard. Kyle and his group waited for the signal from Schmidt that his group was in place, protected only by the dark. Conrad would flash an infrared strobe twice to indicate they were ready to start the killing. The strobe could only be seen by someone wearing the PVS-5 goggles.

"There it is," he needn't have told the others. The firing would take place in ten seconds. Kyle got up on a knee and drew a bead on the head of the nearest guard, who was facing his direction. "Seven, six, five..."

Suddenly, the cloud betrayed them. The burst of blue light shut down their goggles in order to protect them from the blinding flash of light that could cause damage to the retinas. The Nazi soldier was shocked to see a kneeling figure so close to him. The second Kyle lost to the goggles shutting down was fully taken advantage of by the guard, who had enough time to fire off one round before Vega dropped him.

There were approximately eight square vulnerable inches exposed to any real danger on Kyle Rogers. The body armor he was wearing protected just about all his vital parts, all except his eyes. The lone bullet tore through the lens of his goggles and entered his head just above his left eye. Kyle dropped straight down.

Hector knew from how the body collapsed that Kyle was dead. The sound of the guards shot alerted the seven other guards and a fur ball was underway. There was no time or need to look after Kyle Rogers, there were more pressing concerns now.

Within seconds, the four remaining shore base guards were terminated. The eight guards on the dock were running towards the commotion. It was a turkey shoot, the guards had no cover and all eight went down within moments of each other.

"Dragon, this is Crane, we'd like to come home now." Schmidt was talking into his PRC68 radio. It broadcast on an FM band and would have been secure in 2002, there was no worry now, however, of the signal being intercepted.

"Copy that Crane, please fire up your IR strobe, we'll be down in forty seconds." Lieutenant Smolinsky had been monitoring the fire fight and had started moving the chopper closer. He was flying the Sea King, which had been painted black for this mission. "Is the LZ still hot?"

"That's a negative, Dragon, but that will be changing shortly. There's six of us, no wounded," Conrad reported.

One killed, realized Smolinsky, "I'll put down on the barge, I have a visual on you, turn off the strobe."

The comforting sound of the Sea King's rotors could be heard. Moments later the darkened shape to the chopper appeared hovering above the barge. Smolinsky expertly held the ship a foot above the deck as what was left of SEAL Team 3 clamored aboard. As the door slid shut Conrad realized he had fucked up. Kyle Rogers was lying on the beach, his body covered in twenty first century body armor, a terribly advanced pair of night vision goggles on his head and a MP5 clutched in his hand. He should have retrieved the equipment.

"Dancer, this is Dragon, pick up complete, you are cleared to make your delivery."

"Roger that."

Lieutenants Savage and Greenspan armed their missiles and prepared for the first of three runs that, when complete, would leave Peenemunde strategically insignificant.

July 1st, 1942, 12:15 PM
USS John C. Stennis, Mess Hall

So what the fuck do you say to your father who is ten years younger than you are now?" Sean Cooney couldn't understand why Timmy wanted to jump ship and meet his Dad.

Sean and Tim had, as often happens after two adversaries finally do battle, become fast friends. "I certainly have given that much thought, but right now, I don't have an answer." Tim was becoming obsessed with the idea of meeting the young Charlie Irwin.

"If I could get my hands on my old man I'd probably beat the shit out of him."

"You have some unresolved issues there," Tim responded sarcastically. He was not terribly surprised at Sean's sentiment. From what he had learned of his childhood, it seems that his Dad communicated as much with the back of his hand as with his mouth.

"I don't know what I'd say to my Dad."

"Shit Walter, let's not even go there." Sean was sorry the Professor had felt the need to bring him into that sordid loop. "Man," he continued, "what if you killed him, just stuck one of those big kitchen knives in his chest? How could you be born?" Sean asked the question like he was the first one to have ever voiced that enigma.

Tim was so weary of this pseudo philosophical question that had been running through the crew like a virus almost since they left New Port News the first time. He wasn't about to engage in that discussion with a power thinker like Sean. "I'll kill him and let you know."

Parnes laughed hard and slapped those two huge hands of his together. "Hey, if you suddenly disappear, can I have your shit?" Tim owned a fine Brietling watch he had purchased another life time ago. Parnes had his eye on it.

"Yeah, you guys can divvy up my stuff." Tim sat quietly for a moment. "I've got to figure a way to get aboard the *Leo*."

July 22nd, 1942, 1:53 PM
War Room, The Pentagon

Pete Peters had given enough briefings in front of these historical figures that he was fairly comfortable now. He still found himself clearing his throat more often than was probably necessary, however. All of the major players were present this time, from Churchill to Roosevelt and everyone down the line. They were twenty days away from D Day 2. Everyone wanted to know where the German Armies were and what they were doing.

Pete aimed his laser pointer at the electronic map of Russia. "Let's start in the east. It appears that Rommel is going to leave the better part of Group Army Center in place to maintain control of the new territories that he has recently won and to neutralize the Japanese threat, who are still parked in Manchuria."

"I suspect that that will help our goal," interrupted Yoder, "these occupied territories are terribly destabilized. They have been under three different governments in the past twenty five years, the Czar, Stalin and now Germany. There must be a portion of the population that has to be glad to see Stalin gone. Germany will be in position just long enough to add a certain amount of stability to the region. When they're defeated the place is really going to become a mess. That should make it easier to break the Soviet Union into seven or eight small and separate countries, none of whom will ever come close to developing into a world power."

"That was your sole purpose for joining out little war, was it not Captain Yoder?" asked Churchill.

"That was the game plan, Sir. But we have plenty of war left before we achieve that objective," Yoder responded.

Pete took back control of the meeting, "Let me finish with my overview, gentlemen."

Ballsy little bastard, thought Yoder.

"At the other end of his new empire, Rommel has been sending troops and material west in preparation for, I suspect, the resurrection of Operation Sealion. Take a look at the coast of Calais. They have been throwing troops there for the past eight days. Their navy has been mobilizing over here, clearly preparing their transport ships for duty. They seem to be planning on using Calais as their jumping off point to England."

The electronic map had small swastika's spread across Europe and Russia, representing each of Germany's armies. "Rommel is fortifying Western Europe with armies that have been doing duty in the Balkans. The first Panzer Group, under General Ewald von Kleist, is on the move, as are the Second Army, the XL Panzer Corps, the XXX Infantry Corps..."

For forty minutes, Pete pinpointed the placement of close to two million troops. For another hour, Major Albert Wedemeyer, of the US War Department General Staff, updated the specifics on the formerly named Wedemeyer's Victory Program. Now, Operation Overlord, christened as such by Winston Churchill, was just about complete. Wedemeyer had spent the past two and a half years devising the plan. Many modifications had been made during the past seven months. It was decided, for example, to bypass England and deposit the troops directly on French soil after observing the things that could be accomplished with the fire power provided by the *Stennis*. It is also decided to hit the shore of France before putting American and English troops into North Africa, Sicily and Italy.

Yoder was next up to address the role MJ 12 had plotted for his war ship from the future. "The sea lanes will be cleared of any interference by Doenitz's U-boats. Calais will be completely neutralized, allowing for a safe and relatively orderly disembarkation of American and English troops and supplies." Any time one and a half million men are moved enmass, orchestrated by the military, havoc was likely to reign. As many men would be added to the ground troops later and put under control of Eisenhower, already having been appointed Supreme Allied Commander.

"We have already given Rommel a taste of what he can expect when we destroyed Peenemunde." Harsh didn't feel the need to address the whereabouts of Otto Hahn. His disappearance troubled Yoder. "On D Day minus four, we will be running sorties over Calais, of course, and deeper into France and Germany to disrupt supply lines as well as destroy troops and tanks. There should be little keeping us from establishing a beach head quickly and a proper base of operations shortly thereafter. Gentlemen, any questions?"

"Captain," General Bernard Montgomery asked, "are there plans for the additional use of your nuclear weapons?"

"Not if we can help it," Roosevelt interjected quickly. He was still terribly uncomfortable unleashing such concentrated and devastating amounts of destruction.

It was now time to hear from Montgomery. English troops had been quietly preparing for the invasion of France. The conditional treaty with Germany was surprisingly vague as to the disposition of English troops.

Those who were abroad were to stay where they were, being of no real threat to Germany. Hitler had figured it would be better to keep the English Armies apart, hence making it easier to dispatch them in detail when it came time to break the treaty.

This was going to be a vastly different war this time around, thought Yoder.

July 30th, 1942, 1:14 PM
USS. John C. Stennis, Captains Mess

Do we have a pastry chef?" asked Dr. Saul Cohen as he wiped whipped cream off his chin. "This is the flakiest crust I can remember tasting this side of Paris."

"That's why I joined the Navy, Saul, for the food." Harsh had noticed the rising quality of deserts being offered during the past few months. "The guy responsible for these fine confectioneries is Seamen First Class Timothy Irwin."

"Looking at your gut, I'm not surprised that you know the name of the sailor who makes the deserts," responded Captain O'Brien.

"Fact is, I've slapped him into the brig no less than twice during this tour!"

"What the hell for, and please don't do it again," asked and pleaded Saul.

"He seems to have a proclivity for pouring wine on dignitaries." O'Brien laughed as she conjured up the face of Churchill as his glass of port tumbled into his lap.

"Christ, I hate that." Yoder was looking past Saul's shoulder. "That clock from the *Saratoga*, it's stopped."

Saul turned around and looked at the brass steam gauge that had been converted into a clock. Harsh had already gotten up and was heading for the wall where it hung. He retrieved it and sat back down across from Dr. Cohen. He shoved his plate in front of Kelly, put down the clock and reached into his pocket for his Swiss Army Knife.

"Don't we have maintenance people to do that?"

"I used to love messing with clocks, Doc. Don't think I've seen the inside of one since I became a Captain. I feel the need for a little diversion." He had gotten the back off the stilled time piece and was peering inside.

"Shit, it's got a quartz movement, I can't fix this. Look at all those little circuit boards. That's no way to tell time. Give me springs and gears any day." Harsh was plenty disappointed that somebody would take the time to custom build a clock from this bit of history and plop a modern day quartz movement into it. He examined it a little more closely. "Isn't that odd, all of the silicon chips seem to have a yellowish tarnish to them. I've never seen anything like that before, almost like something is leaching out of the chips."

That was one word that Dr. Cohen had implanted in his short term memory. Leaching is not a word that comes up often. He had been consumed with the reason blood was leaching out of the circulatory system of two of his now dead patients. He suddenly had an interest in this wall clock.

"Let me see that." Harsh pushed the defunct clock across the table to Kelly. She studied the inner workings for a moment. "I saw something just like this a few weeks ago. Remember the Intruder that lost an engine? Well, it turns out that the problem was not mechanical but electrical. I visited Crusty down in maintenance and he showed me the black box. All of the chips had turned this color, he'd never seen anything like it either."

Saul Cohen sat back quietly and began to consider the similarities between silicon chips and the human circulatory system.

The moon was a curved sliver hanging low over the ocean. From his perch in the Vulture's Row, Father Anthony was almost eye level with it. He found this a good place to stay in touch with himself, to browse his heart. There certainly have been some heavy issues he'd addressed while standing high above the sea over the past few months. It was nearly one in the morning and he was alone with his thoughts. And what thoughts they were.

He was going to be a father. A real father. Anthony never had any ambitions of having a child of his own. He had two nieces and four nephews, ranging in age from one to five, and while he enjoyed playing with them, it was nice to leave them after a few hours. There was always something going on, laughing and giggling, crying and pouting. One of them was constantly getting into something that he/she shouldn't when they were all together at a family outing. He quickly grew weary of the unending tumult and secretly allowed himself a private thanks to the Boss for not burdening him with a small human who could not control his bowels.

But now, his perspective was changing. It helped that he was very much in love with the intended mother. The whole concept made him feel closer to Kaitlyn. They were going to share something that was indeed a blessed event, despite an embarrassing lack of planning, the creation of a life.

He was going to have a little boy. A little boy who'd be just like Dad. Hopefully he'd look just like Mom, but he'd have Anthony's sensitivities, his love of people, his moral strength, although there was some question lately about that. Dear God, please don't give him my nose! Little Anthony, was that hubris to name a child after yourself? Who cares, he thought, I'm Italian, I can get away with it.

I'll teach him to play football, and basketball, and baseball he thought, as soon as I learn myself. Anthony suddenly wished that he'd spent a little more time in the gym learning skills he never expected to need. I'll teach him to catch, Anthony cheered himself up with, an expertise that his child will need to be proficient in to excel at all of those athletic endeavors. How hard could it be to teach a kid to catch? Funny, he thought, how he gave so little import to athletics when he was young and now he wanted his kid to be the star quarterback. Maybe excelling at sports will keep him out of the priesthood!

HIM. Oh my word, thought Anthony, there's a fifty percent chance that it will be a her! This thought gave Anthony some pause. "You can have fun with a son, but you gotta be a father to a girl." He suddenly recalled a line sung by Billy Bigalow in the Broadway Revival of *Carousel* he had seen a when he was in High School. Billy had reconciled himself to the probability of having a daughter by the end of the song. Anthony thought it might take him a little longer. He knew what he had done to Mr. Clarks little girl and he sure as shit didn't want some fancy fly boy doing the same to his daughter! There was a double standard floating real close to the surface of that thought, he realized. Well, there's not much I can do about it now, he knew. It's time to figure out how to marry Lieutenant Savage so his child isn't born a bastard.

"Oh, how am I going to work that out," he asked the moon? Protocol suggests the purchase of a diamond ring, first of all. Not likely the commissary carries them and even if they did, what kind of a stone could he purchase for six hundred and eighty five dollars, the total amount of cash he had accumulated over the past few months. He had close to ten large in Citi Bank back in the future, but that was probably a dead issue, what with the bank not having been founded yet.

There was also the issue of quitting his Priest gig and then getting permission from the Captain to get married. He and Kaitlyn were still in the service of the

United States Navy, there surely was some arcane regulation forbidding the marriage of a pilot to the Chaplain. It was time to do a little research and make some plans.

CHAPTER 11
D Day 2

August 7th, 1942, 5:56 AM
USS John C. Stennis, Atlantic Ocean, 110 miles east
of Calais, France

Captain Yoder was on the Primary Bridge
watching his fighter jets being catapulted off the bow of his
ship. This was where he needed to be when there was an
operation underway. This was where he wanted to be
during flight ops. He was ultimately responsible for what
ever happened on board the *Stennis*.

"How many do we have in the air," he was in
communications with the Air Boss.

"Thirteen, with seven more to go. We'll have 'em
all out of here in another twelve minutes."

The F18 Super Hornets were on there way to
"Soften up" Calais. The largest flotilla in history was three
days behind the *Stennis* and her carrier group. It was
important that there be no opposition when the combined
forces hit the beach. That meant taking out hundreds of
cement bunkers, an equal number of big guns and
thousands of troops. The next twelve hours were not going
to be the best in the history of either Calais or the Nazi
Army.

"**Sean said to** get your ass top side and grab any
shit you think you'll need." The Professor was out of
breath, having run almost the full length of the ship to reach
Tim, who was trying to catch a nap before starting his
dinner shift.

"What's this all about," he wasn't sleeping, but had
gotten into that wonderfully relaxed twilight state.

"Don't know," responded Walter, "but we're pulling along side the *Leo*."

Tim was out of his bunk in a shot. He pushed up his mattress to reveal a storage area under it. Out of that, he pulled his jacket, a spare set of skivvies and his Brietling watch. "Give this to Parnes," he handed the watch to Walter. Parnes was pulling KP duty, cleaning up after the lunch shift. Tim suspected that he may never see him again.

The two sailors raced up to the main deck. The deck was fairly empty without the twenty jets that normally were parked there. Walter led Tim to the middle of the port side where a large door was open.

"Holy shit, there she is." Less than thirty meters away was the *Leo*, driving parallel with the *Stennis* and matching her speed perfectly. There was an un-rep underway. Tim had been part of a dozen underway replenishment exercises before, taking on food and fuel from supply ships.

They required enormous amounts of skill by both of the Captains and their crews. A line is literally shot over to the supply ship where it is anchored. Pulleys are erected and the material in need is hoisted over to the ship being re-supplied. If the ships are to close together, there is danger of the smaller ship being pulled into the larger ship by the venturi affect. If they drift, the lines could snap, resulting in a loss of supplies and the possible injury to the crews.

"Hey Jerk Off Boy, get your ass over here." Sean Cooney was surrounded by fire fighting equipment. "Here, put this on." He handed Tim one of the blouses distinctive to the fire suppression team. Tim stripped his shirt off and slipped it on.

"Seems that there have been three fires in the galley of the *Leo*. The Captain wants me to go over there and set up a fire suppression system. I told him I needed a helper.

You're him." Tim would have hugged Sean had they been in private. "Come on, we're next.

The equipment was transported first, next went Sean. Tim was finally lashed into a basket like chair and shoved out over the open waters of the Atlantic. Had the line broken, he'd be pulled under which ever ship he was closest to and run through the propellers, being turned into chum. After taking a close look at the cables responsible for his safety and deciding that they were sound, he allowed himself to enjoy his forty second ride.

"Welcome to Timmy's big adventure." Sean greeted him on the other side.

"Sirs," Seamen First Class Billy Bob Tater delivered a sharp salute just like he had been taught two months ago in basic training. His parents signed waivers allowing him to join the service at seventeen. Sean looked at him and figured that the uniform he was wearing was probably the smallest size available and he still looked like he was swimming in it.

Both Sean and Tim returned less than energetic salutes. "I assume you are our guide for the day?" Sean offered. Billy Bob hailed from Arkansas. He joined the Navy to find out what the rest of the world had to offer. So far, it hadn't been very much, but today, he was meeting men from the future. Billy Bob Tater was spooked. He still had his right hand tucked up tight against his forehead.

"At ease, Sport," Sean laughed, "Grab that duffel bag and take us to the galley, we got stuff to do." With that, he and Tim gathered up the boxes containing the equipment they needed and followed a very uncomfortable Billy Bob.

"Hey Tater," Sean read the name stenciled on Billy Bob's blouse, "you can take you hand off your forehead." Billy Bob was still in salute mode. "Calm down, son, we aren't gonna eat ya." He turned to Tim, "This guys a rip."

During the ten minute walk to the galley, Billy Bob hadn't uttered a word. He dropped the bag he was carrying and took off the minute they arrived. Tim took a visual tour of the galley. It was tiny compared to what he was used to on the *Stennis*. The ship was old, even in 1942. It had probably been in commission for close to thirty years. Tim was overwhelmed with a sense of history.

A sailor stepped out of a food locker at the back of the galley. "Thought I heard something. You must be the guys from the future," he was walking towards them with his hand out. "Nice to meet you," he stood in front of Tim, "I'm Charlie Irwin, the fellas call me Cookie."

Tim stared at the extended hand. "I don't have any diseases, go ahead," Charlie pumped the hand up and down a few times to assure Tim that it worked. Tim reached out and took the hand of his father. "You're a quiet one. What's your name?"

This was mind blowing. Tim felt the blood draining from his face, his mind was unfocused. He willed himself to respond to the voice that sounded so familiar. "Tim Irwin," he finally responded. That put a big smile on Charlie's face.

"Where you from? I wonder if we're related, you certainly have that rakish Irwin look."

Shit, what the hell did I tell him my real name for, he wondered? Tim needed to pull himself together real quickly. This man looked like a very smooth version of his Dad. His skin was taut, he had a full head of hair and a cocky way about him that Tim had never recalled his father having. "Brooklyn, Brooklyn New York," he finally replied. He didn't want to say that he was from Babylon, Long Island. Babylon was a relatively small town and Charlie was sure to bombard him with questions about his lineage, something Tim was simply not prepared to address just now.

"Holy cow, I'm from Brooklyn!"

Christ, Tim remembered, his Dad grew up in Brooklyn and didn't move to Long Island until after the war. "Where do you live?"

Charlie lived in Park Slope, "East New York," Tim lied.

"Say, that's a nice section, near the beaches."

Jesus, if Dad could see what a hole East New York had turned into. "Yeah, real close to the beaches." Tim was beginning to feel extremely strange. There were emotions clashing all over his heart. He missed his father. Although it had only been a few months since he'd seen him last, he had already said good bye to him as if he was dead. The entire crew had gone through similar emotions during the past few months. Loved ones who were technically not dead were still never going to be seen again, and each in his or her own way mourned their loss. But now, he was back. Certainly in a modified form, but there he was, in the flesh.

But this wasn't the father Tim knew. This was not the man he had complicated issues with. How could he talk to this man about the pain he had caused when Tim was a child. How could he take him to task for the unnecessary beatings he had received, all the times he wasn't there for him, the verbal abuse that made him feel to this day that he would never be anything but a failure? This man before him was ten years younger than Tim was right now and decades away from committing the sins he was being accused of in Tim's heart.

"We'll have some chow later, after you guys are through," a couple of guys made their way into the galley. "It's time for us to get dinner going." Charlie grabbed an apron hanging on a hook and slipped it on as he walked back into the storage locker from which he had emerged. "See you guys later."

"Swell meeting ya," Sean yelled after him. "Your old man didn't even acknowledge me, nice guy."

"He was looking at me funny," Tim said quietly, "do you think he suspected that I am his son?"

"Well, it was pretty clever of you to tell him your name was Irwin, then let him know your from his home town! Shit, if he isn't thinking something now then I'll know where you got your brains from," Sean sensitively answered.

Yamamoto Greenspan had just jammed his Super Hornet onto the heaving deck of the *Stennis*. He caught up with Lieutenant Savage at the Island.

"Another big day for the *Pukin Dogs*, eh Savage." He slapped her on the back.

"Can't tell you I was real comfortable putting down on this deck." There were ten foot swells on the ocean making landing particularly difficult. They were heading for the ritual debriefing down below decks.

"The PAVEWAY's made quick work of those bunkers." The *Dogs* were responsible for relieving the world, and Calais in particular, of the concrete bunkers that housed both big guns and automatic weapons. Had they been allowed to stand, their strategic positions would have made placing troops on the beach a very costly exercise.

Kaitlyn much preferred structural targets to those that bled. She had been waken every night with visions of desiccated bodies in the snowy plains of Russia. "They had no idea what we'd be throwing at them when they built those things. Hell, even the concrete bunkers in Iraq were no match for what we're packing."

"The scuttlebutt is we've got another day of sorties before the area is clean." Yamamoto stepped through the door into the briefing room and threw his flight pack on the floor. Kaitlyn took a seat next to him.

It would be another half an hour before all the *Pukin Dogs* would be assembled, Kaitlyn put her head back and closed her eyes. Is this what a pregnant woman should be doing, she wondered, pulling eight g turns and dropping bombs on the bad guys?

"I'm going to be a mother," she whispered softly to herself. Kaitlyn Clark/Savage never had any aspirations toward motherhood. The whole family thing eluded her, several times. She was born into a family she had little recollection of and spent time with six different families she wished she had no recollection of. She wouldn't wish her childhood on anybody. Her experiences conspired to repress any maternal instincts that she may have at one time possessed.

Kaitlyn never really expected to be married either. There had never been a man who was capable of corralling her heart. Oh how life can change, she mused. She placed a hand on her womb. Kait was already beginning to get protective feelings toward her unborn daughter.

Yes, she decided, it was going to be a girl. A little girl she could hug and touch and love. A little girl that she could play dolls with, have tea parties with. A young woman she could talk with into the wee hours of the night about fashion, about boys. About putting value on her most special gift. Lieutenant Savage's daughter was not going to grow up like her, she vowed.

"We've done one hell of a job clearing Calais. Rommel must be shitting in those goofy pants he wears."

"Jodhpurs, I think they're called, riding pants," Yoder educated his second in command. "Guess they made sense when he was crawling in and out of tanks, I hope he's still not wearing them now." Over one hundred sorties had been flown over the past thirty six hours with nothing more than a broken front strut on one of the Intruders. "This is how wars should go, O'Brien. Send them up, break some stuff and bring them all back alive." He poured both of them another coup of coffee. They sat huddled in the back of the Captain's mess. It was after two in the morning.

"That is some sight out there." It was hours before D Day 2 and there were ships for as far as the eye could see bobbing up and down in the Atlantic Ocean, preparing to disgorge a million and a half men.

"Thanks to what we've accomplished, most of these men will arrive on shore alive," Yoder beamed. Unfortunately, there were going to be some foul ups. Moving this vast army of men was going to result in a few deaths by drowning, or maybe a soldier being crushed to death. Some idiot was bound to accidentally fire off a round into the guy in front of him. It was inevitable and Yoder hated sending letters to the next of kin that their loved one was killed in some stupid way.

"It's going to be a big day tomorrow," he looked at his watch, "I mean today. I don't think I've seen my bunk for two days. Well, our responsibilities under Operation Overlord are done, now it's up to Eisenhower to get his troops on the ground and into position. That's an operational nightmare I can do without. I need to sleep."

"OK, I've dragged this job out as long as I could. I'm gonna get plenty of shit when I get back." Cooney was hanging in a hammock above Tim's, both had been strung up in the hallway leading to the engine room. "It'll be nice to sleep in a bunk, too, my back's been killing me."

"I appreciate your help here. They'll be sending equipment over to one of the transport ships this morning and I'm gonna follow it over." Tim had discovered an opportunity to possibly get into the ground war and he wasn't going to miss it.

"You got it all worked out?"

"Yeah," Tim answered, "I bribed the guy in charge with my Seiko watch. Wait until the battery dies. He's getting me an army uniform and will send me over to the transport ship. Apparently, he knows the guy in charge on the other side. Once I get there, it shouldn't be to difficult to attach myself to a squadron and stroll onto the beach with them."

"You sure you want to do this, you're giving up some pretty cushy living."

"You know, I actually started to enjoy being the Pastry King," a moniker anointed him by none other than Captain Yoder himself, "but I want to go to war. I want to see what I'm made of. I want to find out if I've got the stuff. This is an incredible opportunity to crawl into the biggest war in history. Shit," Tim had passion in his voice, "I've been fascinated by this war since I was a kid. I know every battle, all the armies, who won and who lost. I can't pass this up."

"I'm gonna miss you." For the second time in his adult life, Sean fought back a tear.

"Shit, Father, I mean gosh, Father, this ring cost me close to two grand." Ensign Bittle had bought the ring in New York City just days before leaving New Port News. He made the purchase in the Diamond District on 47th Street after haggling with a Hasidic Jews for close to an hour. He got a hell of a buy on the one karat ring with a platinum setting. It had excellent color and cut, but was of a somewhat lower grade, none of which meant a thing to Father Anthony. Anthony needed a ring and Ensign Bittle's was the only game in town. Bittle was planning on asking his girl to marry him when he returned at the end of the tour. "A little late now," Anthony chided him after hearing his sad tale.

Bittle had come to Anthony, as if he was sent by God, to see if the Chaplain could help him out with his depression. Anthony's councilor work was taking most of his time these days as men and women were finally coming to terms with their losses. Bittle was horribly depressed about losing the only girl he'd ever loved. When he mentioned that he'd purchased the ring Anthony had to fight with himself to keep from smiling.

"Did you bring it with you?" He wasn't proud that he had asked that question of the sobbing Ensign Bittle.

It took some balls to ask Bittle if he'd consider selling his engagement ring. So as not to sound too mercenary, he quickly concocted a lie about a couple on the ship who had come to him looking to get married. They needed a ring, he told them. Maybe it wasn't such a lie after all, he realized. The names were omitted to protect the innocent, or the guilty depending on one's perspective.

"OK, Father, but six hundred and eighty five bucks is a little light for a ring like this."

It was time to pull out the big guns. "Look, Ensign, that's almost seven hundred 2003 dollars. Factoring in backwards inflation, that's close to three grand in 1942 dollars." He was making that amount up, but he didn't suspect that he was all that far off. "You could buy a house for that." He recalled that Mr. Levitt would be selling his tiny houses in the as yet to be developed Levittown for about two thousand dollars in a few years.

Bittle put his pain behind him and traded his ring to Father Anthony for what was pro ported to be a small 1942 fortune.

August 10th, 8:32 PM, 1942
USS. Leo, Atlantic Ocean, 16 miles off Calais

"**How do expect** me to wear these?" Tim was fuming. The Army uniform he had in his hands would have been to big on him if he was six feet tall and two hundred pounds.

"Look, this is a fucking Navy Ship, you're lucky I could scrounge this stuff." Ensign Fine already had Tim's Seiko watch in his hands and was scrutinizing it as he spoke. "Have your ass down below at 0600, that's when

I'll be making the delivery to the *Hudson*. You're not there, she sails without you. I don't know why you want to get on that ship, everybody on it is going to war. You can get killed doing that," Fine laughed.

"What about a belt, how the hell am I going to keep these pants up without a belt?"

"Use the one you got on, seems to work pretty well," he shot back.

"Right, my white belt will look real inconspicuous with this olive green piece of shit you got me," Tim caustically replied.

"I thought I'd find you here." Tim had headed right to the galley, hoping to find Charlie. They'd spent a good deal of time together during the past couple of days as he and Sean were installing the fire suppression system.

Tim had the chance to interact with his father on a man to man level, rather than the son to father level that precluded him from ever really getting to know Charlie. He was surprised to find that he liked his father. The older, now younger, Irwin, had a wicked sense of humor. He had a joke for pretty much any situation that arose. Having been in the Navy for a year already, he had any number of salty stories he was more than willing to share with his name sake. One evening, they sat on the weather deck of the *Leo* and talked about dreams and ambitions. Tim was surprised to find that the man who berated him most of his life had real depth and poetry to him. He wondered what happened to it by the time Tim came into his life. The two Irwin's bonded tightly.

"I thought you took off with Sean," Charlie was glad to see Tim's face, "what can I do you for?"

"You think I would have left without saying good-bye?" Tim slapped his Dad on the back. Look, I need to turn this green." He held up his white Navy issue belt. "Got any dye or something."

Charlie looked at the hanging belt and wondered why Tim would need to turn a perfectly white belt green. He also spied what appeared to be an Army uniform tucked under his arm and started to put things together in his head. He decided not to say anything just yet.

"I don't have any dye, but I do have food coloring," Charlie disappeared into a locker as he spoke. He returned moments later with a silver can. "Fill that pot with water."

For half an hour, Tim and Charlie fooled with the belt. Charlie figured he could always make it darker so he began with a conservative amount of coloring and worked his way up. The final product was an excellent match.

"I guess you're wondering why I needed the belt dyed green. I was expecting you to ask," Tim said as he shook the belt to dry it.

"I figured you'd tell me when you were ready."

"Charlie, I'm going ashore tomorrow."

"No shit. Why?"

For the second time in twenty four hours, Tim explained his need to prove himself on the field of battle, to find out if he had the stuff... To see if he was a man.

"I'll tell you this, if the shit hit the fan down here, I'd want you watching out for my ass."

Tim was touched at Charlie's crude sentiment. He couldn't remember his Dad ever giving him a compliment since he had reached the age of consent. The two men stood there, seeming to want to hug, neither wanting to make the first move.

"I'm going to miss you, Charlie."

"I need to ask you one question before you go." Charlie Irwin was looking down at his shoes.

"Sure, go ahead," Tim responded.

"Are you my son?"

Tim's eyes filled with tears. They came on him so fast he didn't have a chance to fight them back. He reached out and hugged his father.

"I must have done something right," Charlie whispered, "to have a son like you."

"Yeah Dad, you were a hell of a father."

August 11th, 6:23 AM, 1942
USS. Hudson, Atlantic Ocean, 1 mile off Calais

Tim hadn't been on board the *Hudson* for more than ten minutes when he was met by Sergeant Bill Brock. "Hey soldier, where the hell did you get that uniform." His Southern accent was so thick Tim needed a moment to process the information.

"I...," shit, he hadn't thought this through. This wasn't like him. Tim was a master of detail, he was rarely caught with his metaphorical pants down. The way he figured it right this moment was he had to either come up with a fantastic story, maybe something about a poker game, or he could feign stupid.

"What do you mean, Sir." He went with stupid.

"That is the worst fitting uniform I've ever seen, you steal it off a giant?" Brock barked.

"No Sir, I ain't seen no giants on this here boat," the words were distasteful in his mouth.

How does a moron like this even get into the Army, wondered Brock. I hope he knows which end of the gun the bullet comes out of. "Follow me."

Irwin Rommel sat alone in the newly created bunker complex some sixty feet below the streets of Berlin. It was closer to morning than night. This was the hour that he found that he could think his clearest. There were few distractions and he could focus on problems. And he had some problems.

Goering called the new headquarters the Tomb. While he appreciated the protection from the phantom jet plane attacks that took from him his beloved Hitler,

Goering was terribly uncomfortable with the fact that there were no windows. He identified himself with his Lufwaffe, soaring high, nothing overhead but clouds, despite the fact that he couldn't fit his fat ass into the cockpit of a Stuka anymore. Rommel felt very snug in the new complex. Coming from a tank background, he found comfort in close quarters.

The glory of defeating Russia was short lived. The fact that the war on the Eastern Front ended far more quickly due to external intervention troubled him. It was finally clear to him who his "Angel" had been. The Americans. But why? Why would they help the Axis against their ally and then turn on Germany?

The attack on Peenemunde answered the question he feared, when will the attacks turn on Germany? Rommel was not a naive man, he knew that the aid he was given would have a heavy price. What did America have to gain by the destruction of Russia?

"Power." The word exploded from his mouth. With Russia a smoldering ruin, where did the power shift to. Germany? For the moment. But if the Wehrmacht were to be defeated, the United States would be the most powerful country in the world. FDR is a brilliant man, realized Rommel. He used Germany to defeat Russia without getting his hands dirty. Now, while Germany was bloody, a fresh America could enter the fight. He allowed himself a moment to admire the genius of his adversary.

Even as he deciphered Roosevelt's diabolical plan, he was reading reports on the troop build up at Calais. For days, his fortifications had been dismantled from the air. His troops and mechanized units were squashed with little apparent effort. And now there were hundreds of thousands enemy soldiers preparing to sweep through France and right into Berlin. They had to be stopped.

But how? The Armies he had in Europe were not going to be enough to fight off an invading force of this size. If he pulled too many troops out of Russia, the Japanese would fill the void and usurp his hard won prize. It was obvious that Japan was Roosevelt's lap dog, doing his bidding for the promise of Manchuria, at the very least. There must be the threat of yet another super bomb being dangled over the Japanese Islands to keep them in such a subordinate position.

The super bomb, he contemplated. The Americans must have learned how to split the atom, there was no other explanation concerning the destruction of Sapporo and Moscow. How could the Americans have gotten so far ahead in that area. German scientists at the Max Planck Institute were years away from achieving nuclear fission. They must be made to work harder. And faster. Otto Hahn, spared death thanks to a stomach virus that delayed his trip to the conference at Peenemunde, would need to redouble his efforts. Germany must have an atomic bomb.

Surrender was not an option, Rommel realized. Germany's allies were either defeated or useless. Japan went under in days and Italy, under that pompous jackass Mussolini, was impotent. He should be hung by his thumbs, thought Rommel.

Once the world finds out what the Nazi's have been doing to the Jews, there will be little sentiment for leniency. The Treaty of Versailles will look like a slap on the wrist. Rommel was appalled when he learned of the concentration camps. He had heard rumors, but the reality was so much worse. The killing had to stop, but he lacked the political muscle to put an end to the atrocities just yet. He also had more pressing issues to confront. Without victory, Germany will be dismantled. The Fatherland will be no more.

Father Anthony looked at himself in the reflection from the glass door leading into the Chapel. He liked what he saw. The dress whites he had borrowed from the effects of Allen Ben-Gurion looked well on him. The pants were a little tight, but the jacket hid that short coming nicely.

Anthony took another look at the bouquet he held in his hand. It was his best work. He had taken up origami when he was in High School. As he admired the roses he had created with his own hands, the tauntings he had received from his classmates for his less than manly pursuits receded from his heart. Unfortunately, he couldn't get his hands on red paper, so he made due with gray. In his other hand were the vows he had written for this occasion. He patted his left pants pocket for the tenth time to make sure the ring was still there.

There was only one light switch to control all nine overhead lights in the Chapel, so he got a ladder and loosened the bulbs of all but the center light fixture. He wanted to add a little visual flare to his proposal. He stood off in the back corner, just out of the glow. Father Anthony was ready. Now he only needed Kaitlyn.

She had been summoned ten minutes ago. Anthony shuffled around while he waited. He was horribly excited. All the preparations he had poured himself into during the past few days were coalescing. As he had heard the aviators say, it was go time.

And indeed it was as Kaitlyn walked into the Chapel.

"Anthony?" she looked around. "What happened to the lights?"

He took a breath and stepped out from the cover of the shadows. Kaitlyn Savage stopped and stared at him. Her mouth hung open.

"Where did you get that..." she couldn't finish her sentence. Laughter poured out of her mouth. He looked so absurd in that ill fitting uniform. And what was that he was holding, paper flowers? Gray paper flowers? She couldn't control herself.

Anthony did not have a protocol for this situation. In the hundreds of times he played this moment out in his head, it never started with his beloved laughing at him. Stick with the script, he decided. Just do what you have planned.

He walked towards Lieutenant Savage. She was standing directly under the light. Kaitlyn was struggling to compose herself. Anthony waited until she was silent, then bent down on his right knee.

He felt the seam of his pants give way before the noise was audible. Things were not working out as he had hoped and he really hadn't started yet. Kaitlyn erupted into giggles. Undeterred, he handed her the paper bouquet. Three of the flowers dropped off their wire stems.

He unfurled the vows he held in his hand. They were held closed by a pink ribbon. The ribbon was borrowed from one of his flock whose daughter had used it to decorate a tin of cookies she had given him just before the *Stennis* left the future. "Please give it back, Father, it's all I have to remember her," he pleaded.

Anthony looked at the vows for a moment, then began to read them.

"Will you be my best friend?
Will you hold my heart?
Will you let me hold yours?
Will you take care of my emotions?
Will you give me unencumbered access to your heart?"

He felt a lump welling in his throat, tears started to run down his cheeks. He took a moment, then continued. "Will you heal my pain?
Will you let me heal yours?
Will you follow my dreams?
Will you tell me yours that I may follow too?"

It was to much. He was so full of emotion and embarrassment, he couldn't continue. The tears poured from his eyes. He opened his mouth, but he couldn't get any words out.

Kaitlyn took the vows from his trembling hand. She began to read them.

"Will you venerate my vision?
Will you celebrate life with me?
Will you help me not to fear?
Will you laugh with me?
Will you cry with me?"

Valerie's voice began to quiver. She reached into that place where she kept her emotional strength and continued.

"Will you help to give me the strength to be who I am?
Will you find me when I'm lost?
Will you call to me when you loose your way?
Will you take my love and put it in a special place?
Will you find joy in every "I love you" that I send your way?
Will you understand that we are us forever?
Will you let me try to give you the moon and still love me if I fail?
Will you grow old with me?"

She stopped before the last line. Anthony looked up at her, his face was streaked with tears. He offered her a small box, and then repeated the last line of his vows, a line he didn't need to read.

"Kaitlyn, will you marry me?"

CHAPTER 12
The Ground War

August 13th, 6:13 AM, 1942
Calais, France

Tim woke up with a start. "Hey, what the fuck you..." someone had just kicked him awake. He sat up and looked around. I'm not in Kansas anymore, he realized. It took him a few moments to place himself. Oh yeah, I'm in the Army now, he realized as his head cleared. The past forty hours had been spent marching inland. His marching muscles were a very much out of shape and he was accustom to a more palatable cuisine. His dogs were barking, new boots and tender feet were not a match made in heaven. He started to wonder if he could get himself a launch back to the *Stennis* in time for breakfast. Tim's back was either sore from sleeping on the ground or from hauling a forty pound pack who knows how many miles.

Sergeant Brock had taken pity on this simpleton he had stumbled upon and had him outfitted before hitting the beach. Tim was now a proud member of the Blue and Gray, the famous 29th Infantry Division. If he was reading the patches correctly, he was also part of the 3rd of the 116 Infantry, whose roots hearkened back to the middle of the 1700's. Their objective had been to protect settlers from the Indians.

The 3rd Battalion furnished several regiments in 1861 to form the First Virginia Brigade, Army of the Shenandoha, Confederate States Army, commanded by Brigadier General Thomas Jackson. It was at the Battle of First Bull Run that the brigade won the nickname "Stonewall Brigade."

This was somewhat of a home coming for the 116th. The last time they visited France in 1917 they saw heavy action against the Hun and earned the motto "Forever forward" due to their reputation of never having given up ground in battle.

Their efforts during World War 11 were equally impressive. They spearheaded the invasion of Normandy, fought their way through Northern France, up through Central Europe and right into the Rhineland. Tim was ensconced in a fighting unit and that suited him just fine.

As he walked off the LST two days ago, up right, he celebrated, he couldn't help thinking about those poor bastards who took the beach the first time around. Their plight was made vivid for him in the Spielberg film, *Saving Private Ryan*, one of his favorite movies. As he strolled up the beach, he quietly thanked the aviators from the *Stennis* for their splendid work softening up the area. From where he stood, he could see five concrete bunkers positioned perfectly to murder any soldier who would have tried to take the beach a few days before. It would have been a blood bath. It was easy to see why Eisenhower had not chosen Calais the first time around. The city of Calais had been fortified by the Count of Boulogne in 1224 and again by Hitler in 1940. It took twenty first century technology to neutralize it.

After leaving the immediate beach area, France hardly looked like a country that was involved in a war. Of course, the French hardly posted an epic defense of their home land. The country had been bisected, Germany overtly in charge of half and the German controlled Vishy Government running the other half. Tim despised the French for their cowardly attempts at defending their own country.

As the 29th marched down a pretty country lane, the artists eye in him was touched by the bucolic scenes presented at each turn. The thatched roof cottages were separated from the road by low stone walls. The fields were rich with amber grain. There were cows meandering around meadows. He ached to set up an easel and capture this beauty on canvas. Unfortunately, that would have to wait, he had some killing to do.

They spent the night in the town of Frethun. From the direction they were heading this morning, Tim suspected that they would be going to Bourbourg to request that the Nazi's in attendance kindly vacate the town. His blood ran hot at the thought of his first engagement, assuming, of course, that the Germans did not heed the 29th's request.

A second pair of socks helped his feet some, though he knew that it was going to take time for the blisters to heal. He wasn't the only one having foot problems. Seems everybody got a little soft during the two week cruise to Europe. Some of the guys he had spoken with had gone most of the way aboard the *Queen Elizabeth*. Word is that not everybody got off!

It was difficult to feel like he was actually in a war right this moment. The sun painted a smile on his world, the dew still clinging to his uniform, the birds were chirping. It felt more like a Boy Scout Jamboree. The weight of the Springfield '03 rifle hanging on his shoulder pulled him back into the deadly reality of why he was vacationing in France.

Tim was the only soldier he could see sporting a Springfield. By 1936, the Springfield was phased out in favor of the M1 Garand, but by the time Sargent Brock got him outfitted on the *Hudson*, there wasn't much left to choose. Tim's request for a M1 Carbine was met with a big laugh by the supply Sargent.

The Springfield was a manual, bolt action gun. Tim had owned a fine collection of guns, all of which he eventually sold in an effort to keep his failing Karate School a float. One of the pieces he particularly appreciated was an '03. With a muzzle velocity of twenty eight hundred feet per second, it made for a fine target rifle. He owned the M1903 that was designated as a sniper model with a range of six hundred yards. It was an excellent gun except for two factors, it weighed close to ten pounds and it was bolt action. Tim was going to have to chamber a round after every shot while the Nazi shooting at him would merely have to squeeze the trigger of his Gewehr 43 Semiautomatic to deliver five rounds into his soft tissue. It wouldn't take long, Tim knew, for him to rectify this inequity. It would unfortunately come at the extreme misfortune of one of his comrades.

By noon, there was a palpable tension running down the line. Way off in the distance Tim heard the first sounds of war, the rumble of heavy guns, probably 88's.

Dr. Saul Cohen was tired. He'd had his right eye stuck to his microscope for almost nine hours. He had been staring at blood samples, cross sections of arteries and pieces of computer chips. It was the relationship between silicon and the mitochondria in the cells of the arteries that was the main thrust of his laborious investigation.

Saul had spent some time with Crusty White. Despite his painfully uncouth manner, Crusty was quite helpful. He showed him the fried electronics from the Intruders bum engine and pointed out similarities between those and the chips in the clock that had failed in the Captains Mess. Under magnification, there was no question that the chips in each device suffered from the same problem. It was the silicon that had deteriorated. It was unable to do what it was designed to do, carry the electrical charges across its surface.

The mitochondria in the cells had also deteriorated. Without the engine, as the mitochondria in essence was, all other activity within the cell ceased. Over time, because the cells were not dividing, there were no new cells to replace the ones that normally would die. The result was a thinning of the artery walls to the point that the blood within began to leach out.

Both the cells and the silicon were organic material. Both suffered premature breakdown. Both were made up of differing amounts of carbon, hydrogen and oxygen.

"It's time for a few chemical tests."

The first shell landed about eighty yards from Tim. He was in mid stride when the concussion slammed him to the ground. There was an acute pain in his left ear and his unsecured helmet was still rolling down the road as he tried to pull himself together.

Now he heard the high pitched scream of another incoming round. With his good ear, he could discern that the pitch of the shell went from high to low. It exploded way behind him. Despite the distance, it was the second loudest sound he had ever heard. The ground he clung to vibrated as the shock wave created from the detonation raced through the dirt. The next round was only seconds behind, but this time the scream of the shell kept rising.

This round landed way to close. It was the loudest sound he had ever heard in this quickly escalating cascade of tremendous noises! The ground bucked under him, tossing his body two feet away from the blast. The concussion felt like he had been slammed by a foam covered bat. The violently misplaced earth came crashing down about him giving Tim the sensation of being buried alive.

The next round followed the last within seconds, each shell landing closer. There was a spotter, Tim figured, somewhere high up, walking the shells in. The following round detonated yards from the stone wall that he was curled up against. The blast blew the wall down like it was a paper mashie prop in a high school play. Small boulders covered his body, protecting him from the next round that landed on his side of the wall. Had it not been for the rock blanket he was under, he would have been obliterated.

Tim tried to make himself as small as he could. He stuck his unprotected head between two rocks. The ground rumbled as each new round tore up the earth. The sound of the exploding shells was unimaginable. The hearing was gone in his left ear, but his right ear was painfully registering every decibel.

There was a new sound added to this horrible cacophony, the screams of men in pain. With his head still securely tucked away, he couldn't see anything, but Tim knew there were soldiers near him who were probably missing body parts. The thought disturbed him. Taking a direct hit would most likely be painless, but having a leg ripped off your still living body was just unacceptable. For the first time since the shelling started, he became frightened.

There was nothing he could do but lie there like a bag of potatoes and shake. The warm sensation he suddenly felt in his pants was about as proactive as he could get. There was no way anyone could have prepared him for the visceral horror of being on the ugly side of an aerial attack.

Tim began to feel panicked. His inclination was to get up and run. His head told him that would most likely be a fatal mistake, but his gut begged him to go, just get up and remove himself from this unpleasantness. Had he not been trapped by the remnants of the rock wall, he would have done the senseless. This was torturous. Time slowed. Life or death was a random event in this Danteisque world. Certainly God was not directing each 88mm shell, deciding that Jones would live today and Smith would die. All the good works of a life time meant nothing here. Where you lay was more important than a brace of angels hovering over you. Death was near, Timmy could smell it.

It took minutes before his mind would accept that the barrage was over. The quiet was almost painful, it lay as a blanket of fog over the area. Soon, the cries of the wounded and the terminally wounded grew louder. Tim struggled to get up, but the rocks pinned him down. He tried to yell for help, but his mouth was so dry he couldn't get a sound out. Dirt had invaded every orifice of his body. He could feel it grind between his teeth, it was in his eyes. Something was dripping out of his left ear, mixing with the dirt as the fluid traveled down towards his neck.

"Tim, you down there?" He had just met Shane Kehoe, who was marching behind him when the shelling began. Shane was blown into an irrigation ditch by the same shell that put Tim on the ground. Tim still couldn't speak, but he let out a loud enough grunt to let Shane know that he needed to be extracted from his stone tomb.

"Dev, get your ass over here and help me." Devin Kehoe hustled over to his older brother and began grabbing rocks even before Shane explained what he was doing. Once the larger rocks were pushed away, they each grabbed an exposed arm and pulled Tim from the rubble.

He was too dazed to stand on his own. One of the rocks that both protected and entombed him now provided him a place to sit. Tim held his head. It hurt. It hurt badly.

"Thanks," he croaked to his liberators. He blinked the dirt from his eyes and took a look around. It was a ghastly sight. The pretty little farm house he had been in front of had taken a direct hit. The walls were still standing, but the interior was gutted. He had waved to a little girl who was hanging out of a second floor window just moments before the attack began. He hoped that she didn't have any siblings.

There were men meandering about, aimless and unsure as to what to do. Others were charging around, trying to aid those who were injured. There were soldiers still sitting, realizing now that they were really in a war.

Some of the men still on the ground were moaning, some were thrashing about in terrible pain. Some were bloody lumps on the road, impossible to distinguish as formerly human.

There was no romanticism in this scene. Death came from above, there was no opportunity to distinguish oneself. The bravest could do no more than cower on the ground, praying to a God who may not have been listening to end the attack quickly. This was not what Tim left the *Stennis* for, to be killed without honor.

"We better do something about that ear," Shane was pulling a wad of gauze out of his pack. The medics were busy with guys who were short limbs and wouldn't have time for the walking wounded for quite a while.

"What?" asked Tim? Shane was standing to Tim's left, he couldn't hear what was being said.

"Your ears is all messed up," Devin clarified, "Shane's gonna clean it up."

"Shit," Tim said dejectedly, "my eardrum's blown."

August 17th, 1942, 9:43 PM
Baethesda Naval Hospital

"Mrs. Slater?" the head nurse asked as Karen entered the emergency room.

She had been away with Pete for two days. They stayed at the *Inn at Star Light Lake*, a terribly romantic bed and breakfast three hours out of Washington. She'd told Jack that she was visiting her sister in Maryland.

It was a most wonderful forty eight hours. Every second they were together was music. Pete was romance novel romantic. He held her hands across the table during dinner, gazing into her eyes. He bought fudge for them to eat in bed. Karen couldn't lift a finger without Pete jumping over to see if he could help. He painted her toe nails! His touch was soft, his kisses were gentle. She had never felt so loved.

They stood before the moon streaked lake on their first night together and pledged to love each other until eternity was just a memory. It was a poetic love that neither thought could ever end despite her current situation. "I'll always be with you," she promised. Pete felt emotionally secure for the first time in his life.

Leaving him was painful, tears were shed. When she walked into her home there was a message lying on the foyer floor asking her to get to the hospital, Jack had an accident. Feelings of guilt invaded her as she sped along the empty streets of Washington. While she was with her lover, her husband may lay dying.

"Yes, I'm Mrs. Slater, where is my husband, is he alright?" Karen's voice trembled.

"Follow me." Nurse Brenda Heart turned and walked down the hall towards Jacks room. "I don't mean to be brash, Mrs. Slater, but your husband has a drinking problem."

That was hardly news to Karen.

"He apparently was drunk when he stumbled into the street and was hit by a car. When he arrived, he was in a coma. We treated him for three broken ribs, a broken wrist and a number of contusions. He came out of the coma about five hours ago. We have been trying to contact you for two days, where were you?"

"I...," Karen was too shaken by the question to respond that it was none of her business, "was visiting with my sister," she lied.

"He'll be OK, but he needs to stop drinking. We also had to treat him for DT's." They entered Jacks room, "I'll leave you two alone."

Jack sat up in his bed. He looked awful. His head was bandaged, the right side of his face was puffy and purple. His eyes were glazed. He forced a smile as Karen walked to his bed. Jack tried to speak, but couldn't, he just grabbed her hand and pulled it to her lips.

"I'm sorry I wasn't there," Karen cried. The months of abuse drained from her heart and she was filled with emotions for her husband.

Jack took a breath. He was sober for the first time in months. His head hurt, but he could think clearly. He had been thinking clearly for the past few hours and he wasn't pleased with himself.

"I'm so sorry," he began to weep, "I'm so sorry for the way I've been treating you. I don't know why, I just don't. I am so ashamed, can you ever forgive me?"

Karen Slater's life suddenly became extremely complicated.

It was the end of another twenty hour day. Harsh and Captain O'Brien were sucking down their last gallon of coffee of the day.

"Our part in this war is winding down." Harsh was staring at the spot where the clock from the *Saratoga* had hung. "We're almost out of air to ground ordinance. Crusty just informed me that there are twelve planes grounded. Apparently we are very short on spare parts and there is no way to get most of them manufactured in 1942."

"It would be nice to continue supporting our troops the way we did the Nazi's."

Harsh gave Kelly a nasty look. "I didn't feel any better than you about making it easier for Germany, but shit, O'Brien, you know we had to look at the big picture." He was feeling quite edgy, but he did appreciate an XO that could speak her mind.

"I know, but to have to cut back support for our own troops, that makes me real uncomfortable."

"Well," Harsh said after a moments thought, "the up side is that our boys should have quite the upper hand. We pretty well fucked up their Armies in Russia. Christ, it was like shooting ducks in a barrel, the Russian tundra offered those poor bastards no place to hide, did you see any of the recon photos? Man, Group Army North, Center and South didn't fare any better than Hussain's weenies in Desert Storm. The 22's, 18's and especially the Intruders butchered those guys. Rommel isn't going to have any reserves when the shit gets hot. Ike will have over three million troops in Europe by next Monday, fresh troops I might add. Rommel can't be terribly comfortable just about now."

"Where will our next engagement be?" Kelly asked.

"The Siegfried Line." Harsh suddenly felt a surge of energy, he loved giving the younger Captain O'Brien history lessons.

Captain O'Brien slumped in her chair and poured another cup of coffee. She hated Harsh's impromptu history lessons.

"South of Luxembourg is Lorraine, the virtual doorway into Western Europe. This place has been a battlefield for about two thousand years. The Germanic tribes used it as an invasion route coming from Central Europe into France. It's really a plateau, elevations range from two to four hundred meters. Over the centuries, the locals grew weary of invading armies, what with the pillaging and raping invading armies are so fond of, and started to fortify the place. The area is bound on the east by the Saar River, on the north by Luxembourg, the south by the Vosges Mountains and the Mosselle River on the west.

"The city of Metz in on the Mosselle River. Nancy, the historic ruling city of Lorraine, is about fifty klicks north." Kelly was fighting to stay conscience.

"As opposed to Nancy, Metz is probably the most heavily fortified city in Europe. Hell, this is the most heavily fortified area in Europe. During the early part of the seventh century, a French military engineer named Vauban built the first set of modern fortifications. There were fifteen of these citadels sprinkled about the city. None the less, the Prussians took the city in 1870 or so. Bismarck lost no time annexing the city when he incorporated Lorraine into his new nation. The German army then constructed a second outer belt of twenty eight forts north and west of the city. By 1918, Lorraine was returned to France, who then build the Maginot Line twenty klicks east and north of Metz."

Harsh caught Kelly nodding off. "Wake up O'Brien, there's going to be a quiz on this." He continued, knowing full well that his second in command couldn't care less at this point in her day. It's good being in charge, he thought.

"The Germans built the Siegfried Line twenty kilometers to the east along the linc of the Saar river. Hitler, thanks to his World War 1 experiences and subsequent love of concrete, dumps thousands of cubic yards of the stuff into the area. By 1940, the strongest part of the Siegfried Line faces the strongest part of the Maginot Line. After France bends over and takes it in the shorts, Hitler brings Lorraine back into the Reich.

"Eisenhower must cross this mess in order to get into Germany. Last I heard, he has three army groups, the Twenty First, with Montgomery in charge, over my and MJ 12's objection, I might add, the Twelfth, under Bradley and the Sixth, under Devers. There are close to sixty divisions, mostly infantry. I think there are half a dozen armored and a couple airborne divisions mixed in. This was one hell of a fight the first time around. We'll be dropping everything we have left in the area. The Lorraine will be Rommel's Waterloo. Once we break through, his war will be ostensibly over."

"When do you suppose they'll be ready for our help?"

Harsh pondered for a moment. "They expect to be in Lorraine in three weeks."

August 18th, 1942, 5:39 AM
Bourbourg, France

Tim hadn't slept all night. It might have been the unfortunate sleeping arrangements, but more than likely, it was pre-battle jitters. The Germans had not responded well when they were requested to vacate the picture perfect town of Bourbourg. Now, they were going to have to be forcibly ejected. Bravo Company was sequestered behind one of those stone walls Tim had credited with saving his life. The sky had turned from black to midnight blue to indigo in minutes as the sun chased the dark from the land. The moment the sun broke the horizon, he and his new friends were going to run across the open meadow in front of them and chase the Nazi's away.

During the past two days, Tim had gotten to know his fellow soldiers in Bravo Company. His first introduction was to the Fighting Kehoe Boys, from Monterey, California. Their moniker was derived not from any heroics on the battle field but from the fact that they fought each other as aggressively and as often as a pair of lion cubs. Devin turned eighteen days before war was declared, Shane was a year and a half his senior. Shane couldn't open his mouth without giving Dev some shit, Dev would respond in kind, and the fight would begin. Equipment would be discarded, fists would fly, blood would spill. It happened so frequently that the rest of the squad eventually just let them fight. Sargent Brock hoped all that pent-up energy would translate well when the enemy was confronted.

Clarence Thorn walked into the recruiter's office in bare feet. He was born in the hallows of western Kentucky somewhere along the Appalachian Trail, the oldest of thirteen. "That's a fucking litter in the civilized world," Tim let him know. Clarence didn't need Tim to remind him that he hailed from the back woods. The entire family lived in a two room shack that didn't have indoor plumbing. They only had electricity for the past two years. The War was the best thing that could have happened to him, Clarence figured, keeping him from a slow death mining coal.

The middle of the country was nicely represented by Rob Passerino, a mild man from Ohio who looked considerably older than the twenty five years he claimed. He was drafted right out of a cushy job running his fathers printing shop. Rob was soft and pasty, even after months of basic training. No small accomplishment, Tim credited him.

Every unit had a smart mouth punk from Brooklyn, at least according to just about every war movie Tim had ever seen. As it turned out, in Bravo Company, it was Tim himself. His acerbic wit dazzled the less sophisticated, affording Tim all manor of pleasure introducing humorisims from the great comedians of the late twentieth century and taking the sole writing credit.

Now, however, he and his comrades waited for the sun to wash the land. By the time the moon reclaimed the countryside, any number of men who breathed now would be dead. As the sun rose above the azmuth, Tim could feel the fear around him. He was not the only one who realized that running headlong into machine guns was not a recipe for longevity. As the minutes to zero hour ran out, he began to shake. It was a warm, misty morning, yet he felt cold to his core. He could hear his equipment rattling as he fought to gain control of his shivering body. His mouth was cotton dry and he tightened the grip on his Springfield to keep his hands from trembling. This was it, he thought, this was exactly what he had wanted, the opportunity to find out what he was made of, to measure his courage. As the sun traced the curve of the earth, he wondered just why the hell he felt the need to prove himself.

A shrill whistle sounded somewhere down the line, a call to death. The men of Bravo Company climbed over the stone wall that had afforded them comfort and protection and started to run. They screamed and shouted as they raced towards Armageddon. The sounds they made were strange and otherworldly, unlike any Tim had ever heard before. It was the sound of fear and anger joined in one voice and unleashed before them almost as if the noise they made would shield their bodies from the wall of lead that was forming to meet them.

Tim had cleared the wall, but he couldn't move. Fright had wrapped his body like a Christmas gift nobody wanted to open. His mind started to wander in a heroic effort to extract himself from the impending horror. He was shocked back to reality by the feel of a cold steel barrel. Sargent Brock was holding a pistol against the back of Tim's neck.

"You've a better chance against the Hun," he growled as he cocked the hammer back.

Tim moved out. The grass was slick with dew and a cloud of morning mist hung just feet off the ground, affording him a false sense of obscurity. He watched as muted figures ran away from him. As his feet finally obeyed commands from his head, he noticed pinpoints of light, shinning for a moment, then disappearing, only to reappear moments later. The deadly lights danced for him through the mist.

Then the muted figures began to drop. Their protective cries were supplanted by the staccato cadence of MG42 Machine Guns. Had he gone through basic infantry training, he would have been somewhat more prepared for this. He would have been taught to follow orders and not to think. But he was thinking now. He was thinking what a foolish idea it was to run towards men shooting guns at him with fatal intent.

Every step Tim took was counter to his inbred desire for self preservation. As he forced his legs to propel himself forward, the stupidity of war consumed him. The men on this field, the men in the picturesque town of Bourbourg, all would rather be somewhere else right now. The statesmen who sent them all here were somewhere else right now, divorced from the immediate prospect of meeting God this very morning.

The air was heavy with the taste of war and death. Each breath Tim took was a celebration that he wasn't yet dead. The feel of his wool pants against his legs, the way the sun was sending rays of light through holes in the mist, the smooth wood of the rifle he gripped tightly in his hand all brought him unexpected pleasure. His life could be done in an instant and he found himself enjoying the most pedestrian of sensation afforded him.

His mind was processing information faster than he could have ever imagined. Between each step memories raced through his head even as he was developing a strategy for how to stay alive. Pleasant thoughts of long ago were mixed with the ugly realities of war and he fought with himself to focus on getting to the next wall, the rock sanctuary where he could hide.

Five feet from cover he heard a bullet. Tim had grown up around guns and had spent a good deal of time hunting, but he had never been on the loosing side of a weapon before. The five ounce wad of lead screamed like a banshee, announcing its arrival before the expected sonic boom. Amidst the classic sounds of war, this bullets wail stood out as clearly as the Statue of Liberty in New York Harbor. Tim dropped to the ground and crawled to the wall.

"Christ, that wasn't much fun," Private Thorn squatted down besides Tim. They were the first words Tim had heard since his baptism of small arms fire began and they sounded sweet, if not somewhat difficult to understand under the haze of Thorn's thick Kentucky accent. "What the hell do we do now?"

Tim peaked over the wall. A two story farm house was thirty yards east of his position and there was a barn directly in front of him. Each window had a weapon sticking out of it which was laying down fire into the pasture he and Clarence had just run though. "I'm thinking we need to clear that house."

"You Brooklyn boys sure are tough. Suppose, though, we might get us some help?"

Nice fella, thought Tim, but a little obtuse. "Sure," he yelled, "Get those guys and drag them over here." There were only eight soldiers at the wall, the rest were either dead or pinned down.

While waiting for Clarence to gather help, Tim poked his head over the wall. Bravo Company was going to have to get through this farm before they could enter the town of Bourbourg, where, Tim suspected, it was going to get shit hot.

As he was reconnoitering the layout, one of the barn doors blew opened and a German soldier charged out of it, heading towards the house. Instincts sharpened by his deer hunting days on Eastern Long Island took over. Tim pulled his weapon to his shoulder and drew a bead on the soldier just as if he was a ten point buck.

Though he hadn't fired a gun in quite some time, he went through the ritual; clear your mind, take a deep breath, track the target, slowly let the breath out and gently pull the trigger.

But his mind wouldn't clear. This was not a ten point buck, it was a man. A human being. Tim was moments away from committing murder. Where the hell were these thoughts coming from, he wondered. Maybe they are valid philosophical concerns for a Sunday night debate, but this is Goddamn war, shit, killing people is the whole point.

He kept tracking his target as this battle raged in his head. Another quarter pound of pressure from his index finger and this man will be dead, Tim realized. Somewhere, his mother, maybe his wife, maybe even his children, were busy doing things, living life, with no way of knowing that their son, husband, father, was going to die in moments. Just ounces more of pressure on the trigger and Tim was going to change a bunch of lives, none of whom harbored any responsibility for starting this war. Why were *they* being made to pay such a terrible price?

The report of his '03 startled him. The last ounce of pressure came so gradually as to be imperceptible, exactly as he was taught so many years ago. His shot was lower than planned, the head shot disintegrated into a neck shot. The bullet knocked the German soldier on his back instantly. His hands grabbed for his neck, his back arched. Tim was just close enough to hear a horrific sucking sound. This was not like in the movies, the soldier was not going to die quickly. Had he been able to, Tim would have dispatched another round into his head to end it quickly, but the body had fallen in such a way as to preclude a mercy kill.

Tim couldn't take his eyes off the writhing body. The son, husband, father was trying to scream but the hole in his neck siphoned off any air before it could reach his vocal cords. He began to kick his legs in an effort to relieve the pain, or maybe to relieve the anger as he realized that within moments he'd be dead.

Tim shut his eyes and prayed for him.

"OK, what'd you want us to do?" Clarence had gathered six soldiers, a third of whom consisted of the Kehoe boys. Tim slumped down and sat with his back against the wall. This was not at all what he expected war to be like.

Now he had to continue killing. The Germans in the house had most of his platoon pinned down in the field.

Those with minimal cover were dead. The rest had no place to go. It was up to he and seven other men to take the house and silence the guns.

Tim cleared his head and focused. If he failed, he was not the only one who was going to suffer. He would not fail. "We're going to have to flank the house," he screamed between gun blasts. "There's no way we can penetrate with a frontal attack. First, we need to clear the barn. I suspect there may be more soldiers in there, I just saw one run out of it," he couldn't bring himself to say that he had killed the man. "We'll be out of the field of fire. Me and Clarence will go first, I'll pull the door open, you lob in a grenade. Once the barn is neutralized, you six guys jump over the wall and meet up with us."

As Tim drew the second phase of his plan in the dirt with a stick, Sargent Brock watched from thirty feet away, sequestered behind an over turned wagon. Although he couldn't hear what was being said, it was clear that Tim Irwin was developing a plan of attack and taking charge. Could this be the simpleton who lost all of his gear hours before hitting the beach at Calais?

Three seconds after having broached the wall, Tim pulled the door of the barn open and Clarence tossed in a grenade. Both men hit the dirt and waited for the explosion. The old barn was none to pleased and shook in protest as its main support beam shattered. The roof collapsed, pulling down the south wall. If there were any German soldiers in there, they would no longer be a threat. The noise, however, drew attention from the house. Just as the six other men cleared the wall, a door opened and out stepped a German holding a Schmeisser. Tim, still prone on the ground, caught him in the chest with one round. The only thought on his mind now was the need to retrieve the dead Germans gun. There was no way he was going to get involved in an indoor fire fight with a bold action rifle.

Tim scrambled to his feet, chambered another round and charged forty feet to the fallen soldier. As he was grabbing for the deceased mans weapon, another German came charging out of the door. He tried to stop when he saw the American, but he had time to do nothing but cringe as Tim lite off another round squarely in his face. In a move that confounded Tim's limited knowledge of physics, the man fell forward!

Tim took the Schmeisser and pressed himself against the wall near the door, his chest was heaving, adrenaline charging through his body. He tossed the Springfield to the ground. Seconds later, a third soldier ran out of the door. He took half a dozen rounds in the back from his friends gun before he even knew that he was in peril. Tim waited a full minute to be sure there were no more soldiers anxious to die, he then waved the rest of his makeshift squad over.

"After I heave in a grenade, wait for the explosion. I'm going in first, you guys follow. Remember, go the opposite direction I go, spread out quickly, keep a sharp eye and kill anything that moves." Tim pulled the pin on a grenade and hurled it though the open door.

He followed it up so quickly that he was immediately confronted with a wall of dirt and debris that completely obscured his vision. Tim dropped to the floor and rolled to his right. Despite the poor visibility, he recognized that he was in the kitchen. Shane was the second in. His visibility was zero, he had no idea where Tim was, so he dropped to the floor and rolled right. "Get the fuck off me." This had the potential of turning into a deadly Three Stooges skit. "Go left, go left," he yelled at the next man in, "and keep down."

Tim heard voices, they were speaking German, and for a reason he would never be able to give, this surprised him. Within seconds, one of the Germans had turned his MG42 on the side door and was spraying it with bullets at the rate of twelve hundred rounds a minute. Two of the soldiers who had made it to the wall with him were cut down in a torrent of bullets. Tim watched in terror as their chests exploded in a film of crimson, which hung in the air as the bodies dropped to the floor.

It was Devin who silenced that gun with a five well placed rounds. Tim, Shane and Clarence quickly worked their way through the kitchen and then through a door to the back of the house. The remaining three went straight, stumbling over the body of the newest dead who was blocking the doorway leading into the dinning room at the front of the house.

The noise of half a dozen MG42's was blaring. Those firing from the other side of the building were unaware of the grenade blast, nor of the exchange of fire in the kitchen. Private Thorn emptied all eight shots in the clip of his Garand into two of the German soldiers making trouble for his brothers in arms who were pinned down in the pasture. He quickly replaced the vacant clip. Devin dashed through the foyer and into the sitting room while spitting bullets from his rifle. One German was killed instantly, the other was wounded badly enough so as to become a non threatening combatant in this deadly scenario.

Tim had swiftly climbed the back stair case. He unleashed a short burst into a soldier at the top of the stairs. Close on his tail was Clarence. At the landing, Tim turned left, Clarence right. Both began to shoot, Tim wondering how many of the thirty two rounds in his clip were still available as he sprayed one of the bedrooms. Clarence was taking single shots because he knew exactly how many rounds were available to him in his eight shot Garand.

Four seconds later, neither had a round left. Fortunately, they didn't need any. Five Germans lay dead, their terrible weapons stilled. Tim and Clarence turned and looked at each other. Tim felt a surge of adrenaline like he had never felt before. He clenched his fist, flung it in the air and purged every emotion imaginable with a series of screams. Out went the fear of death, with it, the anger of being forced to kill. He felt a perverse sense of power. "What a fucking rush," he whispered to the men he had just killed.

Clarence was already hanging out of the second floor window yelling to the soldiers in the pasture that the house had been cleared, "Come on, nothin to be feared of, these guys is dead, probably standin at the gates of somewhere a fer piece from here." Was there a school in this country that taught kids to speak that way, Tim wondered as he began to settle down? Even Clarence's attack on the Queens English couldn't ruin the elation Tim was beginning to feel as endorphins cascaded though his body.

"Yeah," Tim proclaimed proudly, "it's a German Schmeisser." He was holding court beside the partially collapsed barn. He was regaling half a dozen of his comrades with his vast knowledge of firearms. He held the Schmeisser up for all to see. "It's correct name is the MP40 Machine Pistol. It was based on the prewar MP38. The Krauts modified it for ease of mass production. Please observe the folding metal stock," Tim pointed a finger to the rear of the gun. "It fires 9 mm rounds at a rate of five hundred per minute. Muzzle velocity, figure about twelve hundred feet per second. Has range of over a hundred yards. All in all, it is one fine weapon." Sure beats the hell out of the Springfield he wouldn't be toting around any longer.

"An interesting paradox, gentlemen. Although this piece is often referred to as a Schmeisser, homage paid, of course, to the brilliant firearms engineer Hugo Schmeisser, he actually had no hand in it its design. And now," Tim mocked a yet to be known Paul Harvey, "you know the rest of the story."

Bill Brock, sitting behind a stump, took in Tim's little dissertation on the MP40. Before recommending this guy for a medal, Bill thought, I need to find out just what the hell is going on. This guy's no simpleton.

August 24th, 1942, 10:53 AM
USS John C. Stennis

"**What the fuck** is happening to my sailors?" Harsh was enraged. He hated not having answers.

Saul Cohen looked up from his microscope. He was exhausted. Four crewmen had died of this mysterious circulatory disease within the past thirty six hours, one of whom was the first woman to go. Crusty had reported to him that electrical failures were abnormally high, all related to malfunctioning computer chips.

"The question is not what the fuck is happening to your sailors, but *why* the fuck is it happening? They all died from advanced degeneration of their circulatory system. More specifically, from the failure of the mitochondria in the cells of their circulatory system to regenerate new cells." Saul had spent every waking minute, which was twenty plus hours a day, on this conundrum and was no where near an explanation as to why these apparently healthy people were dying.

"Could it be environmental?" Harsh queried.

"I've checked everything, air samples from all over the ship, water samples, the food stuffs. I've checked for radiation leakage from almost every computer on the ship. I even tested the jet fuel, thinking that the stuff we're having manufactured now might be somewhat different from what we were using in the future. I've found *nothing*."

"Is it contagious?"

"We've been over that before, Harsh. There is no indication that this is being passed around. None of the crew who contracted this horror had anything to do with the any of the others who died other than living on this floating monstrosity." For observational purposes, it was probably better that they all are confined to a relatively small area, though Saul. "One thing they all had in common though, they were all in exceptional shape. Two of them were marathon runners, one was a SEAL, the others worked out aggressively. There is no logical reason that they should have circulatory problems. It would make more sense if they were more like..."

"Me?" Harsh was feeling momentary justification for his unfortunate conditioning.

"Sorry, but yes. It would certainly make a little more sense. Is there something within the bodies of the more corpulent that protects them from the degeneration? That's what I'm working on now." Saul pointed to the outer office at the ideally corpulent Pattie O'Boyle, who was having blood drawn by Nurse Prudente.

"Shit, Saul, we need to get a handle on this, the crew is starting to get a little panicked." Don't need a panicked crew, Yoder thought, cuts way down on productivity. "One more thing, you said the dead sailors all had one thing in common. They, and everybody else on this ship, has one more thing in common, we all time shifted."

August 25th, 1942, 1:33 AM
The Bunker, Berlin

We must shut down the Concentration Camps." Irwin Rommel had been fighting with this decision for weeks. The ethical implications were unquestionable. There was no possible justification for genocide. And now, the tide of the war was turning. For the first time since

Hitler's death, complete victory was seemingly out of reach. If the Allies breached the Siegfried Line, he'd have no option but to sue for peace.

Heindrich Himmler was not pleased. He was very much in favor of the final solution. "I don't know that we can do that. What do you suggest we do with the four plus million Jews we have in detention now, apologize to them for the inconvenience and issue them a travel visas back to their homes, which, by the way, are currently occupied by your officers?"

What an ugly little man, thought Rommel. As head of the SS and Gestapo, control of the camps fell into his purview. Himmler was an extremely powerful and influential man in the Third Reich and Rommel knew that without his support, the death would continue.

"All of our troops on the Eastern Front have been neutralized. That means we have no reserves for our war in Europe. The Allies have an estimated two and a half million men on the continent with more on the way. They have far superior numbers of mechanized units and they own the air." Rommel's voice was rising with his anger. He hated the SS. While they did have fighting troops, some to the best in the army, they also spent much of their time doing the filthy and unscrupulous work that was going to make keeping Germany in tact very difficult if total victory was eluded. "You may have also noticed that they have some remarkably advanced aircraft that can destroy targets at will. *The Reich is in extreme peril*," he pounded his fist on the desk for emphasis. "What do you think our chances of negotiating an acceptable peace treaty with the Allies are after they find out that we have been exterminating the Jews?" Rommel was furious.

"I want the camps shut down and all records of this abominable crime eradicated! We'll blame this horror on Hitler. Germany's very survival may hinge on this issue."

Heindrich Himmler nodded curtly and left the office. We must accelerate the final solution, he thought. There was going to have to be a more aggressive use of Zyclon-B. By the time Rommel has the political muscle to do his will, the Jewish problem will be mute. If not, Himmler thought, the SS had the means to deal with him. Europe will be rid of the stench the Jews have placed on everything they have touched!

Pete put his ocular down and stretched his arms. He'd been tracking armies around the world since seven in the morning, it was closing in on noon. He sat back and stared at the phone. Karen had called him everyday for the past two months at twelve sharp. Except for yesterday. His watch now read 12:03. And today.

His heart sank. She was in town, he knew that. Jack was out of town, he knew that too. Why wouldn't she call? She had been somewhat aloof the past few days, her conversations were fairly pedestrian. During the last call, she didn't even return his "I love you," she just hung up quickly.

Pete hated the feelings he was having. He had no right to expect anything from her, she was married. But, Christ, the love they shared was epic, he had never experienced anything like it, nor had she. At least that's what she said. He fought urge to call her, it was difficult.

Pete was confused and hurt.

September 14th, 1942, 8:13 AM
14,000 feet over Lorraine

"Did you get a look at the place during the last run?" Dancer was driving an Intruder, quite a departure from her F22.

The A-6E Intruder was phased out of active duty in 1997. MJ 12, however, recognized the planes exceptional air to ground capability and had twelve of the thirty four A-6E's built by Grumman placed in storage for use in the event of a time shift.

The Intruder entered service in 1963 and had gone through over four hundred improvements and modifications during its thirty four year tenure as the "Workhorse of Naval Aviation." Its mission capabilities were continuously updated to include state of the art avionics and sensors. The A-6 wasn't the fastest or prettiest aircraft on the deck, but it was an exceptionally durable and capable air to ground weapons platform. With a range of over a thousand miles and a cruise speed of four hundred and seventy four miles an hour, it could go far and fast.

"That's affirmative, Dancer, I dropped enough shit right on top of that place to make Detroit a parking lot, didn't seem to have made a dent." Jim Clark was flying wing for Kait Savage. Their mission was to level Fort Driant.

To breach the Siegfried Line, Eisenhower needed to take the city of Metz. In order to take Metz, he needed to take Fort Driant. The Fort, built in 1902, loomed over the Moselle River, surrounded by clear fields of fire. With Driant occupied by the Germans, it was not possible for the Allies to forge the river.

Reports left by MJ 12 confirmed what any green Lieutenant could have figured out, it was going to take some extraordinary efforts to capture Fort Driant. The three hundred and fifty five acres containing the fort was surrounded, in good medieval fashion, by sixty foot wide, thirty foot deep moats, which were then surrounded by a sixty foot thick wall of barbed wire. Virtually all of the fortifications were underground. There were living garrisons for two thousand troops and enough supplies to keep a fight going for a month.

The only way in or out was over a causeway, which was carefully avoided during the bombing runs. Four casement batteries surrounded the area, each with a 100 mm gun. Deadly concealed machine gun pill boxes were sprinkled strategically about.

"It's going to take a tactical nuke to shake the Nazi's out of that place," Clark surmised.

"Nothing we can do about that now, let's take it home." Lieutenant Savage banked port and bought her plane to cruising speed.

Yoder and O'Brien were on the bridge waiting for the A-6's to come home.

"Doesn't sound like we were able to help out much this time," Kelly was going over the early reports from the flight wing.

"I'm not surprised," Harsh replied, "the place has concrete walls up to forty feet thick. I'm afraid Ike's going to have to take Driant the old fashion way. It's gonna be expensive."

There were several handsets sitting on a console in front of the elevated leather chair Yoder was sitting in. Each one connected him instantly to a vital cell that aided in recovery operations. Harsh grabbed the one nearest him, the one that was ringing. When that one rang during ops, it was never good news.

"We have a problem with one of the Intruders. Savage has lost hydraulics, she's trying to finesse the bird in." It was Viga Hall, the acting LSO of the day.

"Let's get ready for a bad recovery, alert the fire suppression team, tell Saul he may have some business." Harsh thought for a moment. The clock from the *Saratoga* came to mind, could there be a connection here? "Better erect the crash barrier." The crash barrier looked like a giant tennis net, the purpose of which was to catch errant planes.

"How you doing Dancer?" Clark was flying fifty feet aft and twenty feet port of Savages crippled bird.

"It's like driving a truck on ice, control is slow, gotta plan ahead." Kait was facing another challenge. She loved this. The thought of punching out was never rejected from her palate of options because it was never there in the first place. Kait Savage was going to bring this plane in. It was going to be ugly, but within the next sixty seconds, her A-6E Intruder was going to be sitting on the slightly heaving flight deck of the USS John C. Stennis.

"Bring up your nose, Dancer." Lieutenant Hall knew that was going to be a tricky task. He had the misfortune of parking an F-16 with hydraulic problems two years ago. He, however, had the luxury of landing on a nonmoving landing strip.

"Watch the meatball, your lined up well, you need to bring that nose up. Bleed off some speed," there were a thousand things to think about during a normal carrier landing, with a bad plane, there were a million things to consider.

The stick was fighting every input she made. Sometimes the plane would respond, sometimes it would over respond and sometimes, it wouldn't respond at all. Dancer was so focused she didn't notice the sheets of sweat encasing her body.

"Fifteen hundred feet, bring up the nose, Dancer."

She was seconds from the deck.

"Eject, eject, eject." Jim Clark's blood went cold as he saw hydraulic fluid blow out the back of Savage's jet. She just lost any control she had over the plane.

Viga Hall jumped into the safety net hanging just over the side of the ship. There was nothing he could do for her now, he was thinking of his own survival. This was going to be bad.

Valerie's feet were hard on the rudders, she was working the stick aggressively. She could have churned butter with less effort. Dancer was getting no satisfaction.

There was no time to eject. Lieutenant Kait Savage was going to ride this beast in.

Captain Kelly O'Brien thanked God that the jet did not explode as it slammed hard onto the deck. She wondered if now she should be cursing that same God as the Intruder erupted into flames after a second bounce. The fire ball slid into the crash barrier and stopped abruptly.

Sean Cooney ran into the inferno, ensconced in his silver flame resistant suit. His prime objective was to save the pilot. Even with his state of the art protection and the torrents of foam being heaped upon the jet, he knew that he had less than thirty seconds to locate the cockpit, open the canopy and extract the pilot.

The Intruder had broken in half on impact. That made it easier for him to get up to the cockpit. The canopy opened easily. Savage's body was slumped forward in her harness. He deftly unbuckled her and with the stunning strength he forged in the gym, he lifted her out and onto his shoulder.

Sean took two steps back and fell.

The four foot trip to the deck was without incident. It was the landing that sealed his fate. Sean landed on his back, Lieutenant Savage landed on her back, on his face. The lexan face plate sewn into his hood broke open. They lay prone in a pool of fire.

Walter Swenson had followed Sean in but was knocked on his stomach when he was slammed in the back by a blast from the hose shooting foam. He recovered and arrived below the cockpit as Sean and Kait hit the deck. He immediately followed the primary mission objective and scooped up the unconscious pilot. After gently placing her safely on the deck, he raced back into the inferno to help his friend.

Sean was still on his back. Walter grabbed his right arm and dragged him twelve feet to safety. The medical team already had Savage on a gurney and was racing her to the ships hospital. Her body was still smoldering.

"Sean," Walter hollered. Cooney didn't move. The inside of his mask was black, his face was obscured. Two medical personnel arrived and pushed Walter out of the way.

"Oh, shit," one of them cried, "get his hood off."

Sean's face was black. His eyelids were burned off and his eyeballs were yellow pools of pus. Sean's regulation crew cut was burned back to the middle of his head. One of the medics placed a mask over his Sean's nose and mouth, hoping to pump enough oxygen into his lungs to force them to work again. Another placed his hands over Sean's heart and began to pump his chest. They both knew that if his lungs looked as bad as his face, they were wasting their time.

He was writing Sunday's sermon when he was called to the ships hospital. Immediately. The fact that there was a recovery going on added urgency to the request. Somebody was facing death.

"Father, please give him Last Rites," Nurse Prudente requested of him as he ran through the door, her voice was flat. This woman had been around death way to often. She pointed to a naked body on a table and walked quickly towards the operating room where there was much activity. "We may need you in here soon," she added as she passed by him.

Anthony walked over to the deceased sailor. The body was fine, the face was a horror. He quickly looked away. The smell of burned flesh suddenly assaulted his olfactory senses. He gagged. It was an effort to keep his lunch where it belonged.

Father Anthony Salvatore opened his prayer book and began preparing the dead man's soul to meet the Heavenly Father. As he was reciting the words, an orderly pushed through the door to the OR. He heard the voice of Dr. Cohen, "I don't think she's going to make it."

Anthony abandoned his task and grabbed the orderly, "Who's in there?"

"Don't know her name, one of the jet jocks. She's burned real bad." He seized a bottle of oxygen and charged back into the operating room.

"Oh God, don't do this to me, please don't do this to me." He stood before the OR door trying to gather the courage to walk in. "Please don't let it be her."

Anthony cautiously pushed the door open. It was a hectic scene. There were half a dozen green clad figures bent over the patient, each doing something different, something heroic, to save her life.

She was nude. Her feet and legs were pink. Large blisters had already formed on them. Her torso was black. He moved to his left to get a look at the face, it too was black. It was covered with an oxygen mask making it indistinguishable to him. Just as he was about to ask her name, he noticed a ring on her blackened finger.

"**Father, if you're** going to stay the night, here's a blanket and pillow, I'll have an orderly bring in a cot for you." Nancy Prudente ended one of the worst shifts she'd had in years.

Kait Savage had second degree burns over two thirds of her body. She had been in a coma for the past four hours. Anthony stared at her through the plastic sheet that kept her body surrounded by pure oxygen. There were tubes stuffed into every orifice on her body and half a dozen needles were jammed into her arms. Dr. Cohen told him that he did not expect her to survive the night.

Anthony pulled up the plastic sheet just slightly and slipped his arm under it. He took Valerie's hand in his. While she was being wheeled into her room, one of the orderlies had tried to remove her diamond ring. Tony asked that they leave it on. The request was honored. He could feel the ring under a layer of gauze that covered her hand.

He began to weep again. He knew that there were going to be questions asked when this was over. There was a young man in a freezer nearby that didn't garner any emotions at all from him. He was going to have to explain, at some point, to someone, why he was so distraught at the probable death of this woman. Anthony didn't care now.

"Why," he looked up at the Boss, "why take her from me. I was just learning to be happy, I was beginning to understand what your world was all about." The tears poured from his eyes. "Why would your plan for me include this pain, this loss?"

The unspoken answer he heard in his head was that he was being punished. Punished for the sin of hubris; thinking that he could have something that he shouldn't have. Punished for the sins of the flesh; sharing himself in a way that disgusted God. Punished for breaking his vows; what were his words worth?

Punished for falling in love.

Isn't that what life is all about, he silently asked? Isn't that why you sent your Son, to teach us about love? I would have loved her in a way that would have pleased you. And my child, I would have loved him in a special way. But you're taking him too? Will you leave me nothing?

"Will you leave me nothing?" Tony screamed out loud.

He felt the hand in his move. "Kait."

Her eyes were opened. They were the only parts of her face not covered in gauze. She struggled to speak.

"Tony." He could hardly hear her.

"Don't leave me," he cried, "please don't leave me."

"I love you." She pushed the words out with all the strength she had. She needed him to hear them.

"And I love you. I will love you through this." They were desperate words.

Kait Savage knew that she was not going to live. There was peace in her eyes, a peace Tony had never seen before in anyone.

"I will always be with you. You can find me in your heart." Her voice was stronger now. "Please don't loose your faith. God is near, I can feel Him. When the time comes, you must speak His words." It was almost as if she was prophesying. "He will call on you soon."

Anthony felt her hand go limp. One of the machines she was hooked up to announced her parting with a high pitched scream. Saul Cohen raced into the room moments later. He put no effort into reviving her.

September 23rd, 1942, 7:56 AM
32,000 feet over Eastern Russia

Yamamoto Greenspan took Kait Savage's death hard. They had joined the Pukin Dogs together. She taught him the finer points of how to finesse an F22 into a seven G turn to out maneuver a surface to air missile. She stole the LSO's book and changed the grade of one of his worst carrier landings. She got him laid in Vegas! She was a good friend.

He was of the opinion that she should have bailed out of her damaged Intruder. A debate had raged amongst the pilots on board the *Stennis* as to what she should have done, most coming down on her side, fly the damn thing in. Her courage was much admired. Yamamoto thought, however, that her death was profligate. That aged plane was not worth her life.

Another debate was raging amongst the entire crew. What was killing sailors and was there a link to the sudden rash of equipment malfunctions? The deaths of twelve men and two women had the crew spooked. Rumors flew as to what was behind it all. Viruses, botulism, bad karma, nothing was overlooked in the tight community of six thousand.

These thoughts ran rampant through Lieutenant Greenspan's head as he flew his 22 north towards eastern Russia. Rommel had decided to pull most of his troops from the Eastern Front to strengthen the Siegfried Line. Doing so pretty much ceded the area to Japan, but he had decided if the Siegfried Line was breached, Germany's control of Russia would not be of issue. Ike decided that those troops would be destroyed before they got anywhere near the Lorraine.

His plane was acting hinky. At least he thought it was. Maybe it was the air currents, maybe his hydraulics were failing. Yamamoto was not inclined to take a chance. Punching out over Russia would probably be as deadly as trying to land a sick plane on the tundra down below. Better to cut and run and come back to fight another day.

"Lead, I've got hydraulics problems." That was enough to get some attention these days.

"Are you getting any warning lights?"

"Yes," he lied.

"Let's get that bird on the ground in a hurry, wait one."

Viga Hall scanned his MFD for the nearest airfield. There were several, all in the hands of the Japanese.

"Head zero one niner, there's a field where you can put down about fifteen minutes from here. Don't know what kind of facilities they have, but the runway should be in reasonable shape. I'll escort you."

Twenty minutes later, Captain Kuniaki Suzuki watched the oddest air craft he had ever seen touch down on his airfield.

Dr. Saul Cohen sat behind his desk, his head back, his arms dangling. He hadn't slept for close to sixty hours. His body finally decided it was time to rest, so it just shut down. There was a growing pool of spittle on his shoulder. Harsh stood in the door way of the office wishing he didn't need to wake his friend.

"You look like shit," he bellowed. Saul's arms shook, like they had heard something and were trying to wake the rest of the body. He opened his eyes, it took a moment to focus.

"Harsh," his mouth was slow to form the word. "I must have fallen asleep."

"Gauging by the size of the puddle of spit on your shirt, I'd say you've been down for the better part of an hour. I'm sorry I had to wake you, but I need to know what the hell is going on Saul, what do you know?"

Saul took sat quietly for a few moments. While he still needed to do a little more research, he was quite confident that his hypothesis was valid. He took a breath and began.

"This is all somewhat preliminary, I haven't received all the results from the lab yet, but I think I have an idea as to what is going on, if not why it is going on. As you know, the circulatory system of the deceased sailors had disintegrated to the point that blood was leaching out of their veins and arteries. All of these men and women were in exceptional shape, their cholesterol was low, their body fat was below fifteen percent, all parameters of good health were indicated, yet they died." Saul stood up and pushed his chair away, he needed to wake up. He poured himself and Harsh a cup of coffee.

"Here," he handed the cup to Harsh, "you don't exactly look rested yourself."

"It's been a tough couple of weeks."

"Yes it has. Well, getting back to the point at hand, I decided to take a look at the living to see of I could get an idea as to whether this was a bizarre isolated illness or something that is incubating in all of us. I took a look at Seaman First Class Pattie Boyle. He was that overweight kid you saw in my office last week. I took a small section of vein from him. It showed a sixty percent reduction in thickness. I extrapolate that he has about five months to live. The autopsy I did on Lieutenant Savage showed the walls of her veins were close to ninety percent deteriorated. She would have been dead within the week. By the way, she was pregnant."

"What?"

"She was in her first trimester. She's the first woman on this cruise who found herself in a family way. Doubt she did it for the usual reason."

Harsh detested woman who got pregnant on purpose to get out of the Navy. "Have any idea who the father was?"

"As a matter of fact, I suspect it was Father Salvatore."

"Holy shit, you pretty sure about that." That would be a first under his watch.

"I could prove it if it was important."

"No," countered Harsh, a wayward priest was way down on his list of concerns. "Tell me more about your research.

"After reviewing this anecdotal evidence, I dragged in fifty crewmen of dispirit physiology's and yanked bits of veins out of each them. Every individual demonstrated moderate to near terminal deterioration of the circulatory system. I expect that within the next ten days, we are going to loose upwards of one hundred crew."

Harsh's face was drained of blood. "What is the difference between the near dead and the not as near dead?"

"Conditioning. Harsh, the individuals who are in the most immediate danger are those in the best shape. What I am suspecting, and should be able to quantify within the next few hours, is that the men and women who were in less good shape had, as you'd expect, higher cholesterol levels. There is much more to it, but, to put it simply, the plak that has been deposited on the walls of the veins and arteries seems to have slowed the degeneration of the walls."

"You said slowed, not stopped?"

"Correct."

"What's caused this?" The immensity of what was going on was beginning to hammer him.

"Again, I can only speculate at this point. I believe that the time shift altered us on a cellular level, right down to our DNA. Remember right after the shift how your bones felt like they had liquefied and were hardening again. Things happened to our bodies that I'll never be able to identify in the time I have here. The telomeres, those are the DNA stretches at the tips of chromosomes, are just not working. Their job is to dictate the number of times a cell divides during its life span. With malfunctioning telomeres, the cells are not reproducing. Once the walls of the veins and arteries are worn down by the normal mechanical processes of the body, they simply cannot contain the blood anymore. We will all bleed to death internally."

"We all?"

"Yes, Harsh, all of us. Within two to four months, there will be no one alive from the next millennium." Saul Cohen just pronounced a death sentence on six thousand human beings. Both men sat silently. Both men were very much aware that they were part of the damned.

"Is there a cure?"

"Don't know. I have one or two avenues I will begin pursuing immediately."

"Christ Doc." Harsh was faced with the most complicated command problem of his career. "Let's try to keep this under wraps as long as we can."

"That's going to be tough to do by late next week when people start dropping like flies."

Father Anthony Salvatore stood at the fan tail of the ship preparing to commit the most mortal of sins. Father Anthony Salvatore had nothing to live for. The past forty eight hours went by in a blur. The days had no beginning, the nights had no end. His pain was as epic as his love for Lieutenant Kait Savage. He held a pervasive sadness that was to weighty for him to carry, it drove him to his knees.

How could he live in this empty world now. Life mocked him. The laughter of others mocked him, as did the sun, and the moon, and the stars. Anthony felt vacant. Hours ago his life was full of possibilities and excitement. There was nothing behind him now but the mediocrity of an unfulfilling past. Before him lay the haunting memories of a joy he would never experience again, a path that was devoid of purpose and passion. There was no reason to continue.

Anthony missed Kait. Her essence was like a coating of powered sugar that had been sprinkled about his world. She was everywhere he looked. He saw her in his office sitting knee to knee with him discussing everything from the folly of Vatican Two to the thrills of the flesh. He felt her arms around his shoulders as he wrote his Sunday sermon. He felt her hand in his as they walked in the dark corners of New Port News Naval Base. He tasted her last kiss. Father Salvatore began to weep again. There were no more tears now, his life time allotment had been exceeded. He was left with only sobs of anguish, of pain, of anger. In one moment he lost his best friend and the love of his life. How do you rebound from that, he asked himself? You don't, was the answer. He stood before the vast, black ocean. Shortly, he'd feel no more pain. He closed his eyes and allowed himself one more indulgence. He allowed himself to see her the moment before she was taken from him. Her eyes were so full of emotion, even as near to death as she was. Her eyes had always been portals to her soul. He began to loosen his grip on the rail that kept him from the next world. Then he heard her words "Please don't loose your faith."

Tony gripped the rail tightly. I have lost my faith, he realized. He heard her voice again, "When the time comes, you must speak His words. He will call on you soon."

October 6th, 1942, 1:43 PM
Khabarovsk, Russia

It had been a long and arduous journey. Sergei Korolev had left Moscow just days before it had been destroyed. His driver had abandoned him two weeks ago and it was becoming difficult to procure petrol for his car. Sergei's position as head of the Soviet Rocket Program was beginning to be of less help to him the further east he traveled.

His country was in chaos. Once word had gotten out that Stalin was dead, all central authority had dissolved. Areas not occupied by the Germans had been divided by the Russian Generals into personal fiefdoms. Law was Marshall, soldiers were committing atrocities against their own people with the passion of conquering armies. It was time to get out.

Sergei Korolev held little allegiance towards his home land. His only allegiance was to science. Science was pure, with no obscure doctrines that changed with the frequency of death in the Gulag, a place with which he was intimately familiar. During the peak of Stalin's purges in 1937, Sergei Korolev and most of Russia's other aerospace engineers were exiled to the Kolyma gold mines, the most dreaded part of the Gulag. There, he toiled with his body, but kept his mind active working on the RP-318, Russia's first rocket propelled aircraft.

In 1939, Stalin finally realized the importance of his aerospace engineers while preparing for the impending war with Hitler. He collected Korolev and his colleagues into a system of sharashkas. The newly created sharashkas were prison design bureaus that exploited prisoners whose specific areas of expertise could be harnessed by the war machine. Two weeks ago, Sergei left the TsKB-39 sharashka to meet with Stalin to give him an update on the progress of the rocket propulsion system currently under development. On his way back to the camp, Moscow had been destroyed and Sergei realized that his dreams and plans would never be realized as long as he stayed in Russia.

Kololev had plans beyond just a simple airplane. His goal was to place a man on the moon. He knew that is was possible. The most difficult hurdle was to create a rocket powerful enough to lift a payload out of the earth's grip. Sergei had been working on those concepts since his early days at the Gruppa Isutcheniya Reaktivnovo Dvisheniya in Moscow. His preliminary work on manned space flight caught the eye of the military and they recognized the potential of utilizing a rocket with the power to deliver ordinance across the ocean. Plans for an intercontinental ballistic missile were being hatched even as Russia was disintegrating.

But now his only hope for continuing his lifelong passion was in America where, if rumor was to be believed, they had made fantastic gains in propulsion systems. The super bomb that had devastated Moscow was most likely an atomic weapon. Yes, America was the place for any scientist with dreams and ambitions.

Sergei P. Korolev stopped his car on the outskirts of Khabarovsk. He walked over to a barricade obstructing the road, waved over a lone soldier and spoke to him the only Japanese he knew, "Take me to the Americans."

"It's the same problem I've found with all the other electronic units, the Goddamn chips have failed." Crusty White held a scorched metal casing from Savage's Intruder in his hand. He was pointing to the yellow green silicon chips inside it. "This box controlled the hydraulics. When it shut down there was an overload in the system eventually causing a coupling to bust. Happened seconds before she touched down, there was no way she was going to land that plane in one piece."

Kelly O'Brien took the box from Crusty and peered inside it, poking a finger in, pushing loose wires out of the way. "Looks like the same corrosion as on the chips in that clock from the *Saratoga*."

"It is, Captain. And this is just the tip of the iceberg. So far, this problem has just affected the Intruders. They are the oldest birds on the ship. I've been checking the electronics on everything I can get my hands on and the older the unit, the more evidence there is of deterioration."

"Are you suggesting that every jet in on the ship will be disabled at some point?"

"No, Captain, I'm suggesting that every piece of electronic equipment on this ship that has a silicon chip in it is going to fail at some point in the near future."

"He was the first person in my life that treated me well, Father." Walter Swenson wept quietly. The only person he could think of turning to at this moment in his life was a priest.

"I understand the depth of your loss, Walter." Father Anthony could very well understand the depth of his loss. He felt tears forming in his eyes. He needed to be strong for this apparently simple young man. But it was becoming increasingly difficult as he felt the emotions that mirrored his own.

"Why would God take my friend away from me?" Walter was inconsolable, tears flowed freely.

"How are we to know God's plan? He works in mysterious ways. Don't you believe that Sean is now in a better place?" Crap. These words were crap and Anthony knew it. The answer to all the unanswerable quandaries was always 'we, mere mortals, could never understand His ways.' Sean is floating somewhere in the Atlantic Ocean, his face burned off him. That doesn't sound like a better place. God's on holiday.

"Yes, Father, I'm sure he is, but I feel so lonely. We hung around all the time, we ate together, we worked together, we ran together, we slept together."

I'm sure he meant the latter in the figurative sense, Anthony surmised. "He touched every part of your world." Anthony understood that. How can I help him through this when I haven't any idea of how to heal myself?

"Kneel with me, Walter, and let's pray for the courage to get through this." Maybe He'll start listening.

October 16th, 1942, 12:23 PM
Oval Office, White House

"Has it been confirmed yet?" Captain Yoder had spent the better part of the past day in transit from the Atlantic where the *Stennis* was cruising. He was scheduled to attend a conference on the seventeenth to discuss the recent cease fire overtures from Rommel. This current piece of intelligence caused all of the major players to head back to Washington immediately.

Roosevelt and Stimson were huddled together passing a piece of paper back and forth between them. "This is not definitive just yet, Captain, but there is no reason to disbelieve the intelligence we have received from the British." Henry was holding the cable he had been showing the President in his hand.

"Great," Harsh said with exasperation, "Himmler may not be as good a General, but the man is ruthless. Do we know what happened?"

"From what we can gather, SS soldiers stormed into the bunker Rommel had himself ensconced in and shot him at his desk. Himmler strolled in and appointed himself Commander- in-Chief of the German armed forces. I believe he has the muscle to make it stick." Stimson had been in touch with M1 during the past fifteen hours trying to piece it all together.

"We are assuming that he has no ambitions of peace at this point. Possibly after Eisenhower breaches the Siegfried Line he may have a change of heart." Roosevelt had been hoping for an early end to the war. Crossing the Siegfried Line was going to be a costly fight.

How long will it take?" Heinrich Himmler sat in his new office in the Tomb. He'd had the desk and chair replaced. Rommel's blood had tainted them even as he had tainted the goals and ideals of Nazi Germany. Too many men had sacrificed their lives to walk away from the mission of the German people. "The struggle for the extermination of any sub-humans, hydrocephalics, squinters, deformed individuals, semi-Jews and all inferior peoples." Germans were the custodians of human culture.

Born at the turn of the century, Heinrich Himmler grew up the son of a pious, authoritarian Roman Catholic school master who had once been tutor to the Bavarian Crown Prince, Heinrich von Wittelsbach. When the First World War erupted, he dreamt of doing battle against the enemies of the Father Land. He turned eighteen in 1917 and immediately enrolled in officer's college. His plans were dashed when the war ended before he completed his training.

His father convinced the young Heindrich to quite the army and pursue his passion for agriculture. In 1920, his life changed when he met Adolph Hitler. After taking part in a failed putsch in Munich, he became secretary to Gregor Strasser, one of Hitler's close aids. By 1929, Himmler had been placed in command of the SS, a small division of the SA, whose primary objective was to be the body guard for Hitler. Through cunning and ruthlessness, he fabricated an internal uprising allegedly planned by Captain Ernst Rohm, commander of the SA. During the Night of the Long Knives, the SA was purged of traitors, Captain Rohm was executed, and the SS became one of the most powerful and feared departments in the Reich. Heindrich Himmler was suddenly one of the most potent men in the Wehrmacht.

Himmler was a fanatical follower of the Fuhrer. He backed and helped develop the policy of National Socialism to cleanse the continent of "non-Aryan impurities" and restock the land with carefully selected blonde, blue eyed Edelgerman. He developed a number of bizarre schemes to realize his goal, the most peculiar was Lesbensborn.

Beginning with his procreation order in October, 1939, which, in part, suggested that "...it will be the sublime task of German women and girls of good blood, acting not frivolously but from a profound moral seriousness, to become mothers to children of soldiers setting off to battle." Himmler created a state regulated human stud farm. Lesbensborn was populated with young girls who met his criteria based on physiognomy, mental and physical tests, character and spirit. They were mated with SS soldiers who too demonstrated the perfect Nordic traits. He further decreed that war heroes would be allowed a second wife.

Himmler's new super race would now undertake a messianic mission to colonize the east. Though creative action and achievement, this synthetic aristocracy would demonstrate the value of its blood.

Lesbensborn was an almost comical aside when paired with his unfortunately successful series of concentration camps, beginning with Dachau. Himmler's interest in the occult, which he shared with Hitler, his fascination with herbal remedies and homeopathy and his philosophical mysticism danced in macabre unison with his fanatical anti-Semitism and commitment to the Aryan ideal.

"I believe we could be ready for our first live test in ten days." Otto Hahn was very uncomfortable sitting alone with Himmler. He had not met him before this meeting but was very much aware of his reputation.

"There will be no tests, there is no time."

This is crazy, thought Hahn. Work at the Max Plank Institute on the atomic bomb had proceeded at a stratospheric pace. Knowing that splitting the atom was beyond theoretically possible and knowing that the direction the Americans had taken was correct eliminated time consuming side trips, but Otto was not at all confident he could produce a working atomic bomb without tests. "That would be highly unusual and equally risky. We have enough heavy water for one test, or one bomb. It will take weeks to produce enough for another attempt if the first one fails."

"If the first one fails, Dr. Hahn, there will be little reason for a second attempt." It was only a matter of two to three weeks before the Siegfried Line fell, then the Allies would have unencumbered access to Berlin. Germany would fall along with his dream of Aryan supremacy.

"Have it ready in ten days."

It had been raining for two days. Tim was as wet as it was possible to get. Although the temperature never dropped below sixty, he was chilled to the bone. Right this moment, he'd give all he owned for a hot shower.

Time Shift/428

"I think it's time you came clean with me," Sargent Bill Brock handed Tim the cigarette he was smoking. Tim accepted it and took a heavy drag. The warm smoke felt good in his lungs. He never thought he'd take up such a vile habit, but when the only definitive constant in combat is that life is evanescent, perceptions are redefined, conventions are reborn.

The rain had turned to a misty drizzle, Tim pulled the poncho off his head. He and Brock were sitting in a small muddy puddle under the branches of a tree that should have been covered with leaves. War was not good for God's little green things, thought Tim. "What do you mean?"

"Drop the goofy accent, first of all. I want to know why you are pretending to be a Goddamn retard?" Back home, Bill was celebrated, and on occasion lambasted, for his bluntness.

Tim looked off at the horizon. Everything was brown. It was almost as if the primary colors were in hiding. There doesn't seem to be any reason for obfuscation at this point, Tim decided. He had accomplished what he needed to, for better or for worse, Seaman First Class Timothy Irwin was a participant in World War 11. There wasn't much chance that he'd be sent back to his ship at this point. "OK," he responded sans affectation, "I jumped ship."

"What the hell did you do that for?"

"Probably for the same reason you joined the Army." Tim answered.

The allure of war was strong. Bill had become bored with his life and yearned for adventure. It was a calling for young men throughout history that was as strong as a salmons need to spawn up river or an eagles need to soar. Without this perverse desire, there would be no one to play when the politicians called a war.

"You crawled off that big damn boat, the *Stimson*."

"We prefer to call her a ship, and she is the *Stennis*."

"Shit," Brock replied enthusiastically, "there were all kinds of fucking rumors flying around about that boat, ship. The day before we hit the beach, I guess we were taking on supplies or something, I got a close look at the planes she was carrying. That fucker has to be from the future!"

And why not offer up full disclosure, "It is."

The words hung there. Sounds of men's boots squishing though the mud provided a back drop to the show that was going on in Bill's mind. Tim silently followed the mental gymnastics Bill was performing; The *Stennis* is from the future, Tim is from the *Stennis*, therefore, Tim is also from the future.

"Holy shit!"

Here it comes, thought Tim. He had gone through this with his dad.

"You're from the fucking future!"

There were going to be more questions, lots of them, but it was going to take just a few more minutes for this reality to settle into the brain of one Bill Brock. Tim amusedly watched Bill do the mental calculations again.

"You're from the fucking future!"

"Sixty years in the future, Bill." It was the first time Tim had addressed his superior in the familiar. He took another hit off Bill's smoke and returned it to his bewildered comrade in arms.

"Two thousand, no, two thousand two, he corrected himself. That's the next, what the hell is that called, the next millennium. You must know some stuff." Tim braced himself for the torrent of questions that were only now formulating in Bill's head. His opening volley would be about the outcome of the war. He'd then show some interest in the health of the country. Then he'd want to know about cars, homes, entertainment. Sports would be addressed with an idea towards maybe making a few bucks on this years World Series. Inevitably, he'd quietly ask if Tim knew how long he'd live, as if Tim carried mortality tables of every American born in his head.

It was past one in the morning before Tim passed out from both physical and mental exhaustion. Bill couldn't seem to fall asleep.

"I told you that I'd be busy and may not be able to call you as often as you'd like."

This was the first call from Karen he'd received in three days. Pete was unsettled and finally addressed his discomfort.

"I know," he sadly rejoined, "but if even you could call for ten seconds just to say hello?" It was more of a plead.

"Look, Pete, Jack is still not doing well, I need to be there for him."

Like he hasn't been for you, Pete thought.

Karen was having a difficult time. Pete was the love of her life, she knew that. And that was the source of her greatest conflict. Jack would never love her or treat her like Pete did, no one ever would. But she was married to Jack. Divorce was out of the question, especially now, since Jack had seemly turned a corner. While he had hardly become a sensitive man, he had stopped hitting her and was treating her quite civilly. Karen wanted to marry Pete, more than anything, but she knew it wasn't going to happen.

She thought that she could live in this fantasy world, loving two men; loving one more than the other. But it was getting very complicated. It all came to a head a few weeks ago when she found herself on the side of the road, having pulled her car over just in time, throwing up lunch. She realized that she was consumed with Pete. Karen was overwhelmingly in love with him. It was a remarkable love, a love she thought only existed in dime store novels. But it was hers now and it was real.

Karen had given herself to Pete completely. She recalled phoning him late one afternoon in tears to tell him she realized that she needed him. It was a stunning revelation she'd made to herself, Karen Slater had never needed anyone in her life. She had insulated herself from everyone. If she did not let them in, they could not hurt her. But she let Pete in, way in, and now she was frightened. As the last of her lunch splattered onto the pavement, she knew at that moment that she had to begin the difficult process of pushing him out of her heart. Karen was going to do what she did so well, repress her feelings. She was going to send the love that had redefined her life to the place where all her pain was, where she could lock it tight; where it could not confuse her. It was time to start listening to her head, not her heart. Karen felt exposed for the first time in her life and she just couldn't handle it.

"Things are changing, change is good."

"Sure," Pete replied, "change is good." He hoped she could not hear him crying.

Pete was losing Karen in degrees.

Captains Yoder and O'Brien sat in the officers mess, finishing the last of the coffee. Kelly had learned to drink hers black over the past few weeks. The days were starting earlier and ending later, it was currently close to two in the morning.

"You'll get the official report tomorrow, but the condition of our air fleet is deteriorating rapidly. All the Intruders are grounded, nine of the twelve showing terminal corrosion of their electronic systems. A few of the 18's are too compromised to take a chance on putting them in the air. Both helicopters are grounded. The list grows every few hours. Crusty is working twenty four hours a day trying to stay on top of this." Kelly had been spending most of the past two days tracking down problems. "There are a number of systems on the ship that will not be operational within six weeks, specifically, the radar system, which will be the first to go."

"It appears that the older chips are the first ones to go." Harsh massaged his temples, he'd had a headache for two days. "Goddamn, we're in a race to see if we can win this war before the *Stennis* self-destructs."

"How do you handle knowing that you're going to die?" It was time now for personal reflection.

Harsh thought for a minute. "Were you under the impression that you weren't going to die?" He smiled at his XO.

"Not quite so soon." She laughed for the first time in days.

"Shit, Kelly, I haven't allowed myself to think about it much. Can't say that I'm thrilled at the prospect of an early check out time." Harsh poured the last of the coffee into O'Brien's mug. "I spoke with Roosevelt a few weeks ago. I don't believe I told you that he has declined Saul's invitation to extend his life through some medical procedure."

"No, I was aware that there was that option though."

"He's a very interesting man, very philosophical. He's decided that he's done what he was sent here to do and now, when the good Lord decides it's time for him to go, he will be ready. There was some talk of not wanting to use his privileged position to circumvent fate either."

"That's all very noble, but I'm not done. There's plenty more I'd like to accomplish." Kelly suddenly felt previously unearthed maternal feelings wash though her head. While she did not expect to ever have children, she took comfort in the prospect that she could. That option had just been squashed.

"Ever since Jeb died, I haven't felt any real joy. There have been times when I've wished for it all to just end. Now, as it seems that wish is on the verge of being granted, I'm feeling ambivalent, I'm just to tired to care anymore." They sat quietly for some time.

"Think Saul can figure a way to beat this?"

"He's in the lab as we speak, he isn't ready to quit just yet." There was a part of Harsh that didn't want him to succeed.

Dr. Saul Cohen popped another amphetamine, his third of the day. He had successfully avoided a drug habit during his medical career, but if he didn't come up with a protocol fairly soon, the downside of a drug habit would be inconsequential.

His research had borne out what he had suspected. He was dealing with a variation of the Hayflick limit. In 1961, a biologist named Leonard Hayflick figured out that normal human cells divided about fifty times during a human life. Each time a cell divides, the chromosomes and their DNA need to be replicated. With each division, the telomeres, which are the DNA sequences found at the ends of the eukaryotic chromosomes and are responsible for maintaining the fidelity of genetic information during replication, are slightly shortened. Ultimately, they become so short that the cells can no longer make accurate copies of themselves.

Post time shift, the telomerase enzyme, a ribonucleic protein that synthesizes telomeric DNA on the chromosome ends, ceased functioning. The cells stopped dividing and, for reasons Saul was unable currently to ascertain, the aging process of the cells had accelerated.

The telomerase enzyme had been isolated and sequenced by the turn of the century. It was isolated from Euplotes, a pond dwelling organism. It was the Euplotes enzyme sequence that was responsible for the creation of the first AIDS vaccine in 2001. It had been discovered that telomerase uses an RNA template to add DNA to the ends of chromosomes. Reverse transcriptase and telomerase were found to be closely related and similar strategies were found successful in inhibiting either of them.

Similar research was promising a cure for cancer by early 2003. Telomerase is active in a majority of cancer cells. The telomerase activation was discovered to be a necessary step for all tumors due to the fact that cancer cells are immortal. They are capable of dividing indefinitely. Research was focusing on inhibiting the telomerase in the cancer cells, therefore acting as a brake on the cell growth.

Saul needed to go where next century researchers hadn't yet gone. He needed to produce a telomerase enzyme, transport it to where was needed, the circulatory system, and then get it to repair the cells damaged telomeres. Success would not only save almost six thousand men and women, but would dramatically increase the age span of those treated to somewhere around one hundred and fifty years!

October 27th, 1942, 9:13 AM
War Room, Pentagon

"Has it been retrieved yet?" Yoder had heard the shocking news only hours ago.

"What's left of it, Captain? M1 has taken the pieces to their laboratory and is endeavoring to reconstruct it right now." Eisenhower had been in close contact with Churchill during the past day.

"Do they know it contains radio active material?"

"Of course, they're taking all precautions."

At twelve ten PM, Nazi Germany had dropped an atom bomb on the outskirts of London. It did not detonate.

The bomb crashed through a flat on Kingston Street, killing a little girl and her mother.

"Does anybody know how the hell Germany has developed this technology?" Harsh was feeling stress, lots of stress. This wasn't suppose to happen. This scenario hadn't been predicted by MJ 12, this was completely out of left field.

"We suspect," volunteered Pete Peters, "that the work was done at the Max Plank Institute in Berlin. Historically, that is the only place where it could have been done after we neutralized Peenemuende."

"What a tactical mistake it was not to level that place too," added Harsh.

"The bigger problem, I suspect," countered Pete, "was our failure to terminate Dr. Otto Hahn. He's the only scientist in Germany with the skill to even attempt building an atomic weapon."

"Speaking of dangerous scientists," Yoder turned to General MacArthur, "I understand the Japanese have picked up one Sergei Korolev."

"Yes Captain, I believe I mentioned that in my last report."

"WE NEED TO RETRIEVE HIM, GENERAL." Harsh struggled to keep from raising his voice much past where it was. The worm vein on his forehead was making an appearance. There was an awkward silence. It was clear to everyone in the room that General Douglas MacArthur had just been dressed down. Harsh tried to minimize the damage with an explanation.

"Sergei Korolev was the father of the Soviet space program. He developed the first long range intercontinental ballistic missile, it was called the R-7. It was the R-7 that was used to launch Sputnik, the first man made object to enter space. It was his work on missiles that enabled the Soviets to threaten the West with nuclear destruction once he devised a delivery system. It wouldn't be terribly hard to put blame on him for much of the Cold War. General, where is he?"

"The Japanese have an estimated four hundred thousand prisoners, Captain Yoder," MacArthur did not like being dressed down, his tone was indignant. "It will take some time to locate him."

"Make it a priority." Harsh was surprised by his own onerous temper. The war was going to be won and won soon, but the *Stennis* was not going to make the victory as clean as it could have been. Most of its weapon stores had either been expended or had been affected by deteriorated silicon chips. His air fleet had been seriously compromised and he and the crew were going to be dead within months. Every time he hiccuped he thought the grim reaper was reaching for his throat.

"One more thing, General," might as well just get it all out of the way. "When can I expect to get my pilot and plane back?"

MacArthur looked down at the desk. He was embarrassed. General Kuniaki Kosio had been acting dangerously independently of late. Mac did not have the control he expected and wanted. He had been pressuring Japan for the return of the F22 for some time now, but they had been obfuscating the issue.

"It was taken back to Japan and it now, apparently, is in the possession of a military contractor called," he looked through a black binder before him, "Tokai Seiki Heavy Industries."

Harsh put his head in his hands. Great, he thought to himself, Soichiro Honda will be making knockoff F22's in months. Cheaply.

Harsh took a moment to compose himself. He recognized that he was dealing with important men with monster egos. He was not going to push his next point through without a goodly amount of support from those around him.

"Mr. President, as you know, we are having serious problems with the hardware on the *Stennis*." That was general knowledge. What the rest had not been made privy to was the medical complications facing the crew. "We have done all we can do to soften up the Siegfried Line and I'm afraid we weren't much help. Our conventional weapons have been depleted. Himmler is bringing everything he has down to counter our offensive efforts. Without extraordinary measures, this fight is going to be horribly expensive in terms of both men and machines."

"Would you qualify what you mean by 'extraordinary efforts,' Captain." Franklin Roosevelt knew what he meant but desperately did not want to face that decision for a third time. By putting it on the table in this quasi public forum, he hoped he could distance himself from the reality of another man induced Armageddon.

Harsh steeled himself for the debate that he was about to unleash. "I believe we should use a nuclear weapon on Berlin." It would be the second to last one in his arsenal.

Roosevelt looked outwardly pained despite the forewarning of Harsh's suggestion. "Why, Captain?" It was the shortest sentence Yoder had ever heard Roosevelt utter.

"First of all, I can't tell you how long the *Stennis* and her compliment of weapons, what's left of them, will be operational. There is a real danger of Germany fighting to a stand off. With what they have just demonstrated with their failed nuclear attack on England, we cannot leave the current government in place. A nuclear attack will destroy their research facility as well as end the war swiftly. It will also save the lives of hundreds of thousands of soldiers. Taking the Siegfried Line is going to result in a blood bath for both sides."

The debate lasted into the late evening without resolution.

He found himself standing on a precipice, high above the ground. The view was spectacular. He felt strong, invincible, whole. Loved. She was floating near him, the most beautiful angel. She had taken him here. It was she who had brought him high above human emotions. It was she who had made him feel, for the first time in his life, worthwhile. He celebrated the view. He celebrated the emotions. He reached out to touch her, to draw her near.

She moved away from him. Without words being exchanged, he knew that there was something wrong. Something had changed.

"It's time for me to go." She looked sad. Her voice was small.

"How do I get down," he felt afraid and alone, confused.

"You must jump."

He had known, deep in his heart, that it was going to end painfully. She was an angel, he, merely a mortal. He spread his arms and prepared himself.

"Why did you bring me here?" He had one last question.

She cast her eyes down. "To teach me how to love!"

"Then it was worth it." He gave her his last smile and then leaped.

Pete woke up in a puddle of tears.

Parnes Williams sat on his bunk. Walter Swenson had his chair tilted at a precarious angle across from him. Both were dazed. Walter was still fighting to come to terms with the loss of his best and only friend. Parnes just missed Tim. Now, however, the ache in their hearts had been replaced with some painfully reliable scuttlebutt that the entire crew was doomed.

"I seen him, man, he's face was blue as the sky. He neuroed out, you know, legs going all crazy, arms flapping around. Then he just kicked." Parnes had never seen a man die before. He was shook.

"Two of our guys did the same thing, I didn't see it happen, but I saw one of the bodies. I had to puke." The probability of this horror happening to him was starting to caress his simple mind. "I heard over fifty guys have been killed by the Blue Death."

"I heard it was closer to a hundred. If we was just a little closer to shore, I'd jump ship."

They were in the middle of the Atlantic Ocean. "You most be a real good swimmer," responded an impressed Walter. Without their mentors, these two mental giants were stuck in a web of stupid that neither would ever extricate himself from. Throughout the ship similar, if not more cogent discussions, were raging.

October 31, 1942, 5:15 AM
Lorraine

"I could've used another couple of hours of snooze." Tim shook his head in an effort to get the neurons and synapses going. "Could you get me a cappachino and an Egg McMuffin? "Happy Halloween, Private." Sargent Brock stood over Tim, his left foot still kicking at his ass. "What the fuck is an Egg McMuffin? Sounds good, shit, even my mothers meat loaf would taste good right now."

Tim crawled out from under his government issued blanket. He grabbed his left boot and shoved his foot in it. "Sounds like it's show time. Where we going?"

"I need your help, Tim." He and Tim had been spending quite a bit of time together. Tim was a bright man with a furiously wicked sense of humor. That, coupled with his knowledge of the future, made him an excellent companion. Bill no longer thought of Tim as

Private Irwin. His knowledge of war and military tactics was stunning. He felt no shame coming to Tim for advice. "We're slated to attack Fort Driant this afternoon. I'd hoped you'd know something about the place."

Not a month ago, Tim had procured, from the ships library, a copy of Stephen Ambrose's *Citizen Soldiers*. An outstanding treatise on World War 11, it was written with the voice of the common foot soldier. Ambrose gave the war a very personal face. More importantly, he wrote extensively about the Allies efforts to cross the Siegfried Line and, very specifically, the difficult attack on Driant.

"I believe I can help you out on that subject, Sarge."

For the next two hours, Tim filled Bill in on what he knew about Fort Driant and then discussed strategy on how to enter the fort to engage the bad guys.

November 4th, 1942, 9:00 AM
USS John C. Stennis

Harsh was addressing the entire crew for the first time since announcing the capitulation of Japan. His face was drawn, his eyes red. What was left of his hair was definably grayer than it had been only a few months ago. He was about to impart the most difficult news he had delivered since informing his family that little Jeb had died. This was the kind of information that should have been addressed on a one to one basis. The magnitude of his message and the number of people involved precluded that courtesy.

The red light on top of the camera burned. "All of you, I'm sure, have been aware of the recent deaths of our fellow crewmen. To date, two hundred and ninety eight men and women have died from a mysterious aliment that has been dubbed The Blue Death." Harsh had spent hours deciding how to address this information. He considered trying to sugar coat his initial approach, hoping to make it easier on the crew, but ultimately concluded that a direct approach was mandated. The message was that they were all going to die. How do you make that sound good?

"The time shift we all experienced has made some fundamental alterations on the cellular level in our bodies. I'm not going to address the mechanics of those changes now, that information can be obtained on line after I am finished, but the resultant complication is that our circulatory systems have been severely compromised." And now the sentence he so did not want to deliver, "This is a terminal condition. Dr. Cohen has exhausted all efforts in finding a cure, I'd like to thank him for his Herculean struggles. The question on your collective minds is how long do each of you have to live."

This was no sensitive way to tell the crew that they were going to die shortly. "Some of you will die today, some will last for as many as three months." He and Saul decided that there would be no reason to explain that the more fat one had, the slower the breakdown of the circulatory system would be.

Harsh paused, giving time for his horrible prediction to settle in on his horrified audience. He had struggled for the words to say that would make this news easier, but he failed. What do you say to mostly young men and women after telling them that they had days or weeks to live. He was just too overwhelmingly tired to attempt to deal with the immense personnel complications that were now arising amongst the crew.

"We are still United States Navy. I ask each of you to look within yourselves and find the strength to persevere. Let us leave a legacy of courage in the face of dramatic adversity. Our final efforts will assure that freedom reigns, that dictators will never succeed and that tyranny is never tolerated. Let us rise above this set back. We have a war to win, an enemy to vanquish. Each of us has a job to do, let us do it to the last."

There was only one more job for the crew of the *Stennis* to perform. That would be completed within forty eight hours.

Father Anthony prepared himself for an expected deluge of distraught souls to come to him looking for the words to make it all better. Always the words. Where was he going to get them?

Timmy and the Kehoe boys shared a crater. It had been raining since the 29th had set up shop forty eight hours ago. Tim recalled Patton had a wicked dislike for the Lorraine the first time around. He had written Stimson suggesting that in the final settlement of the war, Germany should retain Lorraine because "I can imagine no greater burden than to be the owner of this nasty country where it rains every day and where the whole wealth of the people consists of assorted manure piles."

Earlier in the day, he watched from a distance as P-51 Mustangs ineffectually attacked Fort Driant. He knew their bombs would have no impact on the Fort and was surprised that Captain Yoder hadn't made it clear to Ike that the only way to take the place was with ground troops.

It had been an easy stroll to this point, less than a thousand yards from the front door. Tim knew that the Germans were letting them get close only to spring up from one of the hundreds of underground machine gun nests scattered around and cut the attackers into small bits with their highly effective MG 42's. He had given the word to his squad, move slowly and be ready for lightening quick attacks.

The sound of the falling rain was thunderous. It cut the noise of the invaders and reduced visibility, all helpful to the good guys. They were getting too close now, however. It was time for the Germans to announce their displeasure at this massive trespass. Tim studied the landscape looking for signs of man's unnatural touch, hoping to discover the pillbox that was no doubt hidden mere yards before him.

"They're close, I can assure you of that." He had to almost yell, the rain had begun to fall in sheets. "Let's move one at a time to the next crater, pick one no more than twenty yards away. I'll go fir..."

Devin was already out of the hole he had been sharing with his brother and Tim and was on his way to victory. Shane had been particularly brutal to him this morning, stealing his K-ration, tying his boots together with a vicious double knot that required a knife to disentangle and just giving him the business in his annoyingly inimitable way. The inevitable fight was choked with that special anger only two men who had shared the same womb could have for one another. Devin hadn't spoken to Shane since the two were ripped apart.

Within five yards Devin was out of sight. Seconds later the sound of a light machine gun cut through the bespattering sound of rain.

"God Damn, the bastards shot me." It was shouted more in surprise than in pain. Tim guessed from his dislocated voice that Devin was about fifteen yards directly in front of where he and Shane laid.

"Oh shit," Dev yelled, "I'm gonna need this stuff." He held most of his lower intestines in his hands. He lay in the open, covered only by the torrents of water cascading from the sky.

"Shut up, just shut up before they shoot your ass again." Shane was panicked. He'd promised his parents that he'd look after his little brother, make sure nothing happened to the kid. The guilt had set in within seconds. Had he not given Dev so much shit this morning he probably would have let Tim take off first. He'd still be here, safely laying in the mud with him.

Shane loved Devin. He never really understood why he gave his younger brother so much trouble. Maybe he never really got over having to share mom and dad with the new kid. Maybe the baby sibling got more attention. Maybe he just didn't know how to tell his brother that he loved him. Now, for all the undeserved shit he had taken from his older brother, it was time to say thanks. It was time to save his life.

Shane jumped out of the muddy hole, took two steps and was blown back into the muddy hole by four 7.92 mm rounds. There was a gap in his chest big enough to stuff a fist into. Tim looked at the wound and didn't bother to try and close it up, Shane had seconds to live. His eyes were wild, his face was deadly white. He reached up with a very unsteady left hand and grabbed Tim by the collar of his jacket. "Save him."

Tim had to pry Shane's dead hand off his coat. He sat back in his hole. The sound of Devin's cries began to invade his head. It wasn't supposed to be like this. Tim always thought when it was time to perform the heroic act that would define his life, he wouldn't have to think about it. He figured it would be an instinctual act that would happen without forethought. Now Tim knew he was wrong. He was thinking. He was thinking hard.

Probabilities. He had studied them in a College Logic course. Do *this* and the probability is *that* will happen. Go rescue Devin and the probability is Tim dies. There is a machine gun nest somewhere real nearby. The only thing he had going for him was this relentless curtain of water. Not much protection against a MG 42. Logical reason not to go? An overt desire to live.

Logical reason *to* go? Fear. The fear of living life knowing that when the moment came, he blew it. Now was his chance. Tim had faced some challenges so far. He'd left the relative security of the *Stennis* and put himself in harms way. He survived an artillery barrage without shitting himself, if barely. He killed a man. He killed men.

But this act, this is was what separated the sung from the unsung.

Tim looked deeply into his soul. Hiding there he found the frightened little boy who had been hiding there all his life; the kid who was humiliated in the lunch room by Pat Collins in front of half the class; the teenager who couldn't get a date for his own High School Prom. The man whose wife left him. Tim found the fear that had infected his life, that had compromised every decision he had ever made, the fear that made him less of a man than he knew he could have become.

"No fucking more," he screamed to the sky, "no more fear."

Tim slipped out of his pack and bolted out of his hole. The rain was constant and thick. He ran upright, deciding that speed was more of an asset in these conditions than stealth. Devin's low moans acted like a beacon. It took seconds to locate his prostrate friend. Tim looked at Dev's wound and immediately realized that his efforts were wasted. Devin was incoherent. Tim bent down anyway and grabbed him behind his left shoulder and pulled Dev onto his back. As quickly as he could, Tim headed back to the hole.

It was the distinct lack of sound that first alerted Tim that something had changed. Instantly a line of light overtook him from behind. Flashes glinted from the many puddles around. It had been a week since he'd seen the sun and Tim was momentarily mesmerized. His next thought was, 'I'm exposed!'

He heard the report of the gun before he felt the first round enter his body just above his left buttock. He dropped Devin. The shock caused him to skip involuntarily like a school girl. The next round tore into his lower back. The rest of the rounds stitched a diagonal line up his back and over his right shoulder. Tim dropped to his knees, then flopped to the ground, face up.

He had no feeling below his waste. His legs were awkwardly splayed to either side of his torso. Tim raised his head up and looked at his prone body. Blood was spurting through three small holes in his chest, each in concert with his heart beat. Each spurt traced an arch almost a foot high through the air leaving a trail in the mud. His sensory system was finally sending his brain a damage report and it wasn't good.

The pain was overwhelming. It felt as if half a dozen hot pokers were being slowly pushed into his back. His body convulsed and he tried to unburden his pain though a series of screams. The screams were guttural and animal like. They did nothing to alleviate the agony.

Tim suddenly felt cold. He felt the warmth of his own blood as it pooled below him. He experienced an instinctual need to move, to get to a safer place, to lick his wounds. With a great deal of effort, Tim pulled himself a few inches to his left. Each small movement extracted a terrible price in pain. He realized that there was no place to hide. He laid his head back down in the mud and prepared to die.

It began to rain again. Just a few drops at first. They seemed to be very large drops. He watched one fall. It drifted a little to his left as it hurled through the sky, probably in response to a slight breeze. Then it landed inches from his face. It exploded into a thousand tiny droplets that washed his bad ear. Time was slowing, maybe an effort by his dying brain to ease him into the nothingness that was now so close.

"You're gonna be alright." It was the medic, Tim only knew his first name, Bart. He wanted to laugh. Wait till you find out what's going on inside me, he thought.

The medic began to stuff gauze into the three holes in Tim's chest. Tim felt nothing but pressure, the acute pain was gone. Suddenly, the top of Bart's head disappeared. Tim hadn't even heard the single shot. A fine spray of blood crowned him like a halo. His expressionless eyes opened wide and his jaw clenched tight. He appeared as if he had just been given some unfortunate news. The medic paused for a moment, looking as if he was trying to decide what to do next, then he dropped straight down.

What was left of the Bart's head lay on Tim's chest. The cranium was gone, exposing internal parts that should never have seen the light of day. The ashen gray of his brain caused Tim to gag. There was surprisingly little blood. The jagged edge of the skull was milky white. With all the available energy he had, Tim pushed Bart's defunct body off him.

Tim laid back and waited for his life to flash before his eyes. It wasn't happening. This whole fucked up war thing has just been one huge disappointment. War is best experienced from the pages of a book, he decided.

Death was near. Tim felt a calm overtake him. He was ready to go now. It was still raining, but the sun shone. It was overwhelmingly bright, it was hanging right before him. He felt himself drifting towards the light.

Karen gently probed her left cheek. She could feel the swelling and fought the urge to look in the rearview mirror, she knew it wasn't going to be pretty. This had been the worst beating she had ever been administered by Jack. Karen hadn't been especially clever hiding the letters and poems Pete had written her and Jack stumbled upon them in the late afternoon. By the time she returned home after an evening with a friend, he'd been drinking for hours. His fist was the first thing she saw after opening the front door.

Her left eye was beginning to close on its own. She probably should have driven herself to the hospital, but all she could think of was being with Pete. She had to see him now.

What a mess she'd made of this whole thing. Karen thought of how she'd been treating him for the past few weeks and shivered. How could she have run from a love like Pete's? How could she not have celebrated the epic love he'd offered her? Now, in the early hours of a new day, as she piloted her car through the empty streets of Washington, she hoped he would forgive her, she prayed he would accept the love that had never left her heart. Karen was going to marry this man.

By the time she got off the elevator in his apartment building, her left eye was officially closed. She slowed her pace, fearing she'd trip on an unseen door mat. Karen pushed Pet's bell even before coming to a stop in front of his door. After a moment, she rang it again. Then again.

It was after one in the morning, he was usually home at this hour, unless he was kept late at the Pentagon. Or he had a date! Karen decided to just let herself in, she still had his key.

The foyer was dark, but off in the living room, his reading light was on. Karen could see Pete's head sticking up from behind his favorite wing back chair. His right arm was hanging loose, a book was splayed open on the floor. He must have fallen asleep reading, Karen decided.

She quietly walked up behind him and picked up the book.

"Pete," she gently called out. Karen reached out and stroked his hair. She came around in front of the chair.

Pete's face was blue.

November 6th, 1942, 1:32 AM
Berlin, Germany

Faith in anything with a computer chip in it was minimal. Lieutenant Clark was ordered to drop his ordinance conventionally, which necessitated a direct run over the target as opposed to a shoot and forget scenario.

Jim had not been certified in the F117 Seahawk, but he was now the most experienced pilot left. The transition from his more familiar F22 was fairly simple, all these planes were fly by wire, a number of computers did the flying, interpreting the pilots suggestions, deciding what he really meant, then performing the needed actions. The 117 is an inherently unstable craft and would be unflyable without the nanosecond decision making capabilities of its computer systems.

Lieutenant Clark dropped the third nuclear warhead of the war from fifty five thousand feet. Pinpoint accuracy wasn't an issue, "Park this baby somewhere in Berlin," Captain O'Brien advised him, "close is good enough in horse shoes, hand grenades and nuclear weapons."

He was twenty seconds out when the weapon detonated. He saw the ground below him light up with an intensity he could have never imagined. Then he felt the shock wave rock his craft. How many millions of people have just died, he thought? Jim focused on keeping his plane in the air.

Father Anthony was haggard. Between saying mass, hearing confessions, consoling friends of the recently departed and attending funerals, he was emotionally wrecked. This was not necessarily a bad thing, he told himself. It was increasingly difficult to find the time to mourn his own devastating loss.

Time Shift/450

He found himself immersed in the Book, looking for answers, searching for the words that would bring peace to those facing death. But the words still alluded him. Anthony feared that he'd spend what was left of his life with nothing but trite answers to the most difficult and important questions these men and women would ever have.

As for his own impending appointment with the reaper, Anthony welcomed it. He had nothing to live for, he felt nothing but pain. Valerie's death sapped his will to go on. Let's end it, he prayed to the Boss, bring me to her, please bring us back together.

November 27th, 1942, 10:36 AM
Oval Office, White House

Four days after the destruction of Berlin and eleven days after the Allies broke though the Siegfried Line, a cobbled together German government sued for peace.

Harsh Yoder was having a terribly difficult time concentrating. On the helicopter flight to the White House, his friend, Kelly O'Brien, died. She died in his arms. It was a violent passing, unlike Jeb's gentle escape. Harsh returned her immediately to the *Stennis*, it was Kelly's wish to be buried at sea.

Harsh had overseen four thousand plus funerals, most over the past three weeks. Each day, at sunset, the bodies, placed in plywood coffins draped with American flags, were delivered to the sea. It was an impersonal way to honor these fine heroes, often burying as many as eighty in a ceremony. They deserved more.

He listened dispassionately at the passionate debate raging between Roosevelt and Stimson. "We need to bring all of the world governments together to oversee the rebuilding of Europe and Asia. Now is the time for the birth of the United Nations." Franklin was tired of war. He was still haunted by the specter of the hundreds of thousands of men, women and children he had sentenced to death each time he permitted the use of future technology. His time on earth was short, he wanted his final legacy to be that of peace.

"The United States is the only country in the world with the vision and the might to deliver democracy to all the peoples," Henry stood before Roosevelt, hands clenched, face red. "We have control, we need to keep a tight reign. Despite the problems with the equipment on the *Stennis*, we will still be in a position to harvest the technology and remain decades ahead of every other nation on earth. Our sole possession of nuclear weapons gives the United States the biggest stick ever wielded, there will never be a world power that will equal ours."

Roosevelt had been thinking about the technology long and hard over the past few weeks. He was determined to take the original plan of MJ 12 further by eliminating the horror of nuclear weapons completely. This was the first time he'd voiced his thoughts to anyone on the subject. "I am quite concerned that the knowledge the *Stennis* represents is a Pandora's box, Henry. Is mankind prepared to deal with technology that is half a century advanced from ours? Can even our government be trusted to be responsible with the power this technology represents? Absolute power, Henry, corrupts. Few men can dare resist it."

Stimson was shocked. You don't give up an advantage in a fight, he'd learned that simple lesson as a boy on the school yard. "You must be daft, Franklin. Are you suggesting that we mothball the *Stennis* without gleaning all we can of her inner workings? And what about the planes and these new weapons systems, surely you are not suggesting that we walk away from these gifts, Franklin. Think of the security of this country, for once stop trying to be the President to the world and be the President of the United States."

"God damn it, Henry," Roosevelt slapped the desk with his open hand. Harsh was now focused on the tempestuous discussion before him. "We need to concern ourselves with larger issues than our own. The United States is better served by a world living in harmony, a world where war is not tolerated, where each nation is treated with dignity and allowed to grow and flourish. A world where young men are not called upon to sacrifice their lives for obscure political goals and innocent women and children will not loose their lives because they live in a place coveted by one Government or another." Franklin vowed that the world would never again face the unforgiving and total destruction delivered by nuclear weapons. All research in that arena would cease.

Stimson was still reeling from Franklin's position. As he was conjuring up a response, he looked to Captain Yoder for support. Roosevelt was expecting Yoder to join legion with Henry and decided to invite the so far silent Captain into the fray. "What say you, Harsh?"

The speed with which he delivered his response did not surprise Roosevelt, the content of his response did. "I don't believe that this country or the world is prepared to handle the advances represented by twenty first century technology. There are moral and ethical quandaries that accompany such advances."

There were so many areas of concern Harsh barely knew where to begin. "The computers we bought with us can perform two trillion calculations a second. This hardware is a quantum step in evolutionary progress that will be traumatic and, I believe, dangerous. Society will not be able to react quickly enough to adjust to these changes. Just the number of jobs lost due to the vast improvements in efficiency and productivity computers will bring to manufacturing will devastate the economy.

Time Shift/453

While manufacturing costs will plummet, unemployment will sky rocket. This country is just out of the depression, introducing next millennium technology at this point in history would be catastrophic.

"Birth control pills! I know they have nothing to do with technology per say, but they certainly do have something to do with society. When a simple pill was introduced in the sixties that enabled women to engage in sexual relations without fear of becoming pregnant, the country changed in a big way. Is 1940's America ready for that. How about abortion? We have a pill for that too. It's not uncommon for a woman to have two or three abortions due to the ease of administering them. Do you want such a fast and radical change in the sexuality of this country?"

"That is foolish, Captain, there is no reason to disseminate that kind of information to the public. I'm talking here about military applications, not social." Stimson was, for the second time in minutes, taken by surprise by a colleague's position.

"If you think that you will be able to bury some of the knowledge contained on the *Stennis* and protect the rest, you are unfortunately naive. This information is like a row of domino's, one goes down, there all going down. The government, especially during times of peace, is notoriously bad at keeping secrets. Information has a tendency of leaking out at what would probably be the worst time. When people find out that their government is hiding information from them they begin to distrust those very individuals they thought they had sent to Washington to represent their interests. Now you have internal trouble. You are then open to external trouble. Take a look a the Roman Empire. Aside form over expansion, they rotted from within. This Country was founded on the principals of a fair and open government. This technology will change the very fabric of society. The most dangerous time for the United States in the latter half of the century was during the 1960's. The danger was not external, but internal. We had a population that lost trust in their leaders. A country in turmoil is truly exposed in the world arena. Unleashing this technology on 1940's America will be a tragic mistake."

It took four days of impassioned discussion to come to a decision as to what to do with the ailing *Stennis* and her future technology.

December 17th, 1942, 11:45 AM
USS John C. Stennis, Atlantic Ocean

Father Anthony was sequestered in the chapel. He needed some help and he needed it now. There were nine hundred and eighty seven sailors on the deck waiting for him to say Mass. They were preparing to make peace with their God. It was his terrible responsibility to help them do that. He needed the words now. "My God Almighty," his fists were in the air, his head thrust back, "I need to know that you are there." He was weeping as he spoke to the Boss for the last time, "I need my faith back. I need a sign." His eyes were tightly shut, tears flowed down his cheeks. He felt forsaken.

A flash of light with an intensity so strong it caused Anthony to drop to his knees suddenly enveloped the chapel. He struggled to open his eyes. The room shimmered with an iridescent green light that seemed to hang in the air, the crucifix on the small alter glowed and appeared to be moving. The hair on his arms danced wildly and his entire body was charged with a feeling he had never experienced before.

Prostrated before God, Anthony held his open palms up to heaven and felt the rush of the Holy Spirit enter his body. A lifetime of fear and pain was washed away with every sin he had ever committed. The wonder of the Trinity became clear to him for the first time. The sacrifice of Jesus filled him with joy. Mysteries were no longer mysteries. Anthony now walked with the power of God, a power to heal hearts, a power to forgive souls. A power to invite nine hundred and eighty seven men and women into the Kingdom of God. For the first time in his life, Anthony Salvatore was filled with conviction. He knew now that he had made the right decision to serve God. He knew now that he was forgiven for all he had done and for all he had thought. Anthony recognized that he had never been alone.

Father Anthony Salvatore now had the words.

With his divinely granted serenity, he donned his vestments and went to meet his flock.

"What the hell was that?" Crusty White was standing next to Yoder on the deck. The ship shook violently for less than a second, almost as if it had been struck by a giant stick.

"A breach in the reactor core," Harsh knew immediately what had happened. The Island was glowing, there was a green haze covering everything and everyone on the deck. Yoder couldn't help smiling. Both he and the crew had just received a lethal dose of radiation poisoning.

Captain Yoder scanned the sea and took simple pleasure in its rhythmic pulsing and deep blue color. The sky was cloudless, holding nothing more than a gaseous orb of hydrogen that was hurling light rays to the sea at a velocity of one hundred and eighty six thousands miles a second. "It is a good day to die," he said aloud.

The final nuclear weapon had been armed. It was rigged with a remote control device that would allow its detonation from a distance. Harsh held the device in his hand. He stood on the deck with the remainder of his crew, save sixty two who opted to leave the ship and take the days or weeks they were owed by fate.

Earlier that morning, a flotilla of ships paid homage to the *Stennis* and her crew. Each ship passed the port side, decks laden with sailors, all in dress whites, all holding salutes. Roosevelt had boarded earlier in the day and issued citations to the entire crew. He thanked them on behalf of the country for their ultimate sacrifice. He thanked them for himself for the courage they showed, for the inspiration they will have provided to future generations. Franklin Delano Roosevelt saluted the men and women of the *USS John C. Stennis* before departing.

After Father Salvatore's particularly moving and passionate service, Captain Yoder requested one last radio check to make sure all ships were out of range of the impending nuclear eruption. While waiting on deck with the crew, he looked into the faces of those around him. Some had tears tracking down their cheeks. Some seemed almost cocky, staring into the face of death without fear. Some stared blankly at the horizon.

All displayed a sense of acquiescence. They seemed to be at peace, as he was. He hoped that he would be reunited with little Jeb, this thought brought him joy and purpose.

"All clear, Captain." The message was whispered to him by an Ensign.

Harsh stepped up on the make shift alter near him. The persistent mechanical heartbeat of the ship had gone dormant; the only sound was that of the sea slapping the sides of the ship.

"It has been my honor to have served with each of you. It will be my profound honor to die with you as well."

Harsh Yoder executed his last executive order as Captain of the *USS John C. Stennis*.

EPILOGUE

December 17th, 2008, 8:32 AM
Shaolin Province, formally the state of Utah

"Do you know why we are celebrating Liberation Day?" Jeb Stocktin was driving his son to kindergarten school. Little Harsh was looking at the mountains off in the distance and wasn't really interested in any holiday that didn't involve presents for him.

"No."

"We are honoring the men and woman of the *USS John C. Stennis* who gave their lives so that we could live free of repression, so that we could have liberty." The bored look on his son's face suggested that these words were flying high over his head. Someday he'd begin to understand.

Jeb was rearing his son in the isolation of Utah so he could educate him to be part of a new generation that would grow up learning about liberty, freedom and self government. It would be incumbent upon these children to develop the conviction and the courage that would be necessary to reclaim the United States.

"We were the greatest nation in the world," Jeb said with pride.

Harsh turned his attention back to his dad. "Then why did we surrender to Japan?"

THE END

DEDICATION

This book is dedicated to a single value;
Courage.

Courage, a virtue we all claim as our own, few getting the privilege to demonstrate fewer still succeeding. Courage, in its most public form, is validated in a most dramatic way.

War is where courage is most often witnessed. American history is stained with the blood of hero's who looked into their very souls and found where their courage lay:

There was only one thing between the wool tunics of the Minute Men at a bridge in Lexington, Massachusetts and the musket balls of the mightiest army in the world, courage.

Shiloh, Antietam, Chancellorsville, Vicksburg, Gettysburg... all haunted by the souls of men to whom courage was merely a commodity.

When the young men from Alabama, New York and Texas crawled out of the safety of their trenches and charged the deadly volley of the Kaisers machines guns, there was only one thing that kept their path steady, courage.

As the landing crafts dropped their doors on the shores of Iwo Jima, there was only one thing that could have motivated sane young men to step into chest deep waters and face a wall of steel delivered by Japanese guns, courage.

When the temperature slipped below zero during the Battle of Chipyong-ni and they were outnumbered four to one by the Reds, what kept our boys feet planted and guns poised? Courage.

What is there that would enable a helicopter pilot to hold his craft steady while hovering over a jungle in Southeast Asia in an effort to rescue a wounded comrade while being shot at? One thing, courage.

What was the glue that bound our soldiers to their duty in Kuwait, Iraq, Mogadushu, Bosnia... Yes, courage.

Without intense pride and courage so evident in the fighting forces of the United States of America, Iraq would still be burdened by a tyrant... and without the national courage proudly demonstrated by the citizens of the most powerful country in the world, terror would reign.

I salute those who have faced death and lost.
I celebrate those who have faced death and persevered.
I hail all who have shown courage.

Thank you... To my Dad for infusing me with a love of history and especially a fascination with World War II. Thank you Ed Weinum for helping me understand how words and emotions resonate and interact. A very special thank you to Tim Irwin for his prescient insight, his staggering knowledge of *everything*, particularly his knowledge of history. I am especially thankful for his unflagging friendship, his astounding ability to predict future events and for his deep support during a most complicated and difficult period of my life. He is missed. Lastly, I would like to thank my beloved brother, Billy, for his wisdom and spirituality.